P9-CFQ-302

Praise for the novels of Martha Grimes

The Grave Maurice

"Grimes's writing has rarely been more lovely, especially when describing horses racing over fences at night or mares running for sheer joy." —*Chicago Tribune*

"Beguiling characters . . . [a] blissful setting."
—*The New York Times*

"This satisfyingly old-fashioned detective tale pays homage to Josephine Tey's famous historical mystery *The Daughter of Time* . . . vintage Grimes." —*Booklist*

"[Grimes is] a reigning queen in the realm of mysteries. . . . Delightful details and complex characterizations."
—*Hartford Courant*

"Another 'veddy British' effort from Grimes's wickedly clever pen. And fans will rejoice that Jury is eventually once more back in action."
—*Chattanooga Times–Free Press*

"Grimes's considerable narrative skills are evident in this compelling story. . . . Beneath the charming innocence are deeper psychological undercurrents. Obsession, greed, revenge, and loneliness are recurring themes and Grimes always manages to present believable villains."
—*The Tennessean*

"A satisfying tale that should delight mystery fans."
—*Publishers Weekly*

"Quintessential Grimes, with a rich canvas and suspicion bouncing from one quirky character to another like a pumped-up pinball." —*Kirkus Reviews*

continued . . .

The Blue Last

"[Grimes] excels at creating a haunting atmosphere and characters both poignant and preposterous."
—*USA Today*

"A diverting, chilling mystery of the past. . . . [Grimes] is at the top of her form. . . . Profoundly affecting and hauntingly sad . . . [an] explosive cliffhanger ending."
—*Richmond Times-Dispatch*

"[Grimes's] gift for evoking mood and emotion is as keen as her talent for inventing a demanding puzzle and solving it."
—*The Wall Street Journal*

The Lamorna Wink

"Atmospheric . . . an elegantly styled series."
—*The New York Times Book Review*

"Swift and satisfying . . . grafts the old-fashioned 'Golden Age' amateur detective story to the contemporary police procedural . . . real charm."
—*The Wall Street Journal*

"Charming, delightful. . . . Grimes fleshes out her characters with witty dialogue. Long may she write Richard Jury mysteries."
—*Chicago Tribune*

The Stargazey

"Wondrously eccentric characters. . . . The details are divine."
—*The New York Times Book Review*

"The literary equivalent of a box of Godiva truffles . . . wonderful."
—*Los Angeles Times*

The Case Has Altered

"Richly textured."—*The New York Times Book Review*

"Grimes is dazzling in this deftly plotted Richard Jury mystery."   —*Publishers Weekly*

I Am the Only Running Footman

"Grimes at her best . . . more than mere suspense."
                              —*The New Yorker*

"Literate, witty, and stylishly crafted."
                              —*The Washington Post*

The Five Bells and Bladebone

"[Grimes's] best . . . as moving as it is entertaining."
                              —*USA Today*

The Old Fox Deceiv'd

"A good puzzle . . . unusually well written."
                              —*The Boston Globe*

The Man with a Load of Mischief
The first Richard Jury novel

"For readers who value wit, atmosphere, and charm in their mysteries."   —*The Washington Post Book World*

Martha Grimes

The Grave Maurice

A RICHARD JURY MYSTERY

AN ONYX BOOK

ONYX
Published by New American Library, a division of
Penguin Group (USA) Inc., 375 Hudson Street,
New York, New York 10014, U.S.A.
Penguin Books Ltd, 80 Strand,
London WC2R 0RL, England
Penguin Books Australia Ltd, 250 Camberwell Road,
Camberwell, Victoria 3124, Australia
Penguin Books Canada Ltd, 10 Alcorn Avenue,
Toronto, Ontario, Canada M4V 3B2
Penguin Books (N.Z.) Ltd, Cnr Rosedale and Airborne Roads,
Albany, Auckland 1310, New Zealand

Penguin Books Ltd, Registered Offices:
80 Strand, London WC2R 0RL, England

Published by Onyx, an imprint of New American Library, a division of Penguin
Group (USA) Inc. Previously published in a Viking edition.

First Onyx Printing, September 2003
10 9 8 7 6 5 4 3 2 1

Copyright © Martha Grimes, 2002
All rights reserved

"At Grass" by Philip Larkin is reprinted from *The Less Deceived* by permission
of The Marvell Press, England and Australia.

REGISTERED TRADEMARK—MARCA REGISTRADA

Printed in the United States of America

Without limiting the rights under copyright reserved above, no part of this publi-
cation may be reproduced, stored in or introduced into a retrieval system, or
transmitted, in any form, or by any means (electronic, mechanical, photocopying,
recording, or otherwise), without the prior written permission of both the copyright owner and the above publisher of this book.

PUBLISHER'S NOTE
This is a work of fiction. Names, characters, places, and incidents either are the
product of the author's imagination or are used fictitiously, and any resemblance
to actual persons, living or dead, business establishments, events, or locales is
entirely coincidental.

BOOKS ARE AVAILABLE AT QUANTITY DISCOUNTS WHEN USED TO PROMOTE PROD-
UCTS OR SERVICES. FOR INFORMATION PLEASE WRITE TO PREMIUM MARKETING DIVI-
SION, PENGUIN GROUP (USA) INC., 375 HUDSON STREET, NEW YORK, NEW YORK 10014.

If you purchased this book without a cover you should be aware that this book
is stolen property. It was reported as "unsold and destroyed" to the publisher
and neither the author nor the publisher has received any payment for this
"stripped book."

The scanning, uploading and distribution of this book via the Internet or via any
other means without the permission of the publisher is illegal and punishable by
law. Please purchase only authorized electronic editions, and do not participate
in or encourage electronic piracy of copyrighted materials. Your support of the
author's rights is appreciated.

To little Will Holland,
nearly a year,
and his grandparents,
Virginia and Scott

He told where all the running water goes,
And dressed me gently in my little clothes.
—Robert Pack, "The Boat"

Do memories plague their ears like flies?
They shake their heads. Dusk brims the shadows.
Summer by summer all stole away,
The starting gates, the crowds and cries—
All but the unmolesting meadows,
Almanacked, their names live; they

Have slipped their names, and stand at ease,
Or gallop for what must be joy,
And not a fieldglass sees them home,
Or curious stop-watch prophesies:
Only the groom, and the groom's boy,
With bridles in the evening come.

—PHILIP LARKIN, "AT GRASS"

PROLOGUE

In the distance, the horse looked white, but nearer, one could see the white was muted, more the color of a winter dawn, a shadowy white, like blue snow. It was barely dawn, the boy's favorite time of day. He loved all of the horses in the stable but this horse in particular.

The pale horse watched the boy coming toward him, bridle and saddle over his arm, walking through the mist. *Not him. What had happened to that jockey who could really ride him? Where were the ribbons, the roses, the shouts and the cheers? Or that girl, for that matter, who handled him better than the boy, her fingers curled on the reins like chrysanthemum petals. If there was one thing the horse knew it was hands—the boy's the trainer's the jockey's the girl's. She must be a filly in disguise; she couldn't be a human girl. For some reason.*

The boy came up to him, patted and smoothed his neck, and handed over a couple of lumps of sugar. Then he threw the plaid blanket over him and they both walked off on the path through the trees, across the pasture, toward the track. The boy still carried the saddle, not wanting to mount until they'd reached the track, which lay at the bottom of a low-rising hill. This early-morning gallop around the stud farm's training track was the high point of their day.

Your day.

The boy and the horse were only a couple of years apart—fourteen and sixteen—but the horse (the boy knew) was infinitely more talented, even though its racing days were past. Though he knew it wouldn't happen, the boy hoped the horse would outlive him. The horse had outlived his father, who had been killed during a race, thrown from another horse. When he thought about his father, the boy found it hard to picture him in anything except his blue and gold silks. His father had been famous. But this horse, Samarkand, was fabled.

The boy, whose name was Maurice, often wondered if Samarkand missed the race, the hectic thrash of hooves, the cries and cheers of a summer afternoon, the excitement of the winner's circle.

He remembered vividly a day when he was small, his dad up on Samarkand, winning the Gold Cup at Ascot. He saw himself and his little cousin Nell jumping up and down for joy like two corks popped from champagne bottles. The year before it had been Newmarket and the first time that Samarkand had astonished them all. In the back stretch the horse had opened up. Already running hard, Samarkand ran harder, leaving the entire field seven furlongs behind in his smoke.

His father's surprise at this totally unexpected show had wiped his face clean of expression, even when they all got into the winner's circle. The stud farm's owner—Maurice's grandfather—could find nothing to say. The trainer was the only one who seemed to take it in stride, as if he expected nothing less of Samarkand, but took no credit for himself when people slapped him on the back and said Brilliant, brilliant. People reached up to grab the jockey's hand as wreaths of flowers descended on horse and jockey as if they'd fallen from the sky.

The one in the circle who was least vainglorious and most dignified was Samarkand himself.

Samarkand wasn't just a horse; he was one of the greatest horses in horse history, was mentioned in the same breath as Red Rum or that American horse known for being a weight carrier, for winning no matter how much they piled it on—Forego.

Forget it.

Samarkand had run every high-stakes race there was, won nearly every significant purse. Not just in his own country, but in America, Churchill Downs, New York, the Derby, the Belmont and the beautiful Hialeah Park.

Maurice often wondered about Thoroughbreds. Did things get imprinted on their minds? Events, races, the winner's circle? This was not to wonder if Samarkand simply remembered the day-to-day rounds, but were important things printed, branded on his mind? Images of happiness, images of hay? Memories of Newcastle or New York, Doncaster, Cheltenham, Hialeah, the colors, the silks, the roses?

. . . the pink wading birds, the brilliant suns and colors rushing toward him, partly hidden from his blinkered eye, a whole vista of colors and faces, cheers and shouting. Forced to the rail (he hated that), he waited for an opening and when it came, he blew straight through it.

Freedom. Nothing ahead nothing beside. Even the cheers faded before they reached his ears.

Right now, they were doing a five-furlong breeze and Maurice knew Samarkand could do it in little over a minute; he'd done it before.

When they were coming out of the back stretch, Maurice noticed a figure with binoculars standing on the hill. It wouldn't be their trainer; he didn't come this early. It must be Roger. His uncle, Roger, sometimes came here to watch before he left for the hospital in London.

Not Roger. Wrong hands.

Samarkand did not appear to feel the loss of his old agility, his old gait, nor the loss of the nimble orchestration of his jockey's hands and legs. The horse seemed as willing, if he'd been given rein, to pull out all the stops for this sixteen-year-old, too-tall lad as for the boy's father. They galloped round the track at no record-breaking speed. It didn't matter.

In memory, they flew.

Day Trader

ONE

Twenty months later

Melrose Plant looked around the rather grim environs of the Grave Maurice and wondered if it was patronized by the staff of the Royal London Hospital across the street. Apparently it did serve as some sort of stopping-off point for them, for Melrose recognized one of the doctors standing at the farther end of the long bar.

As Melrose stood there inside the door, the doctor emptied his half-pint, gathered up his coat and turned to leave. He passed Melrose on his way out of the pub and gave him a distracted nod and a vague smile, as if he were trying to place him.

Melrose stepped up to the place the doctor had left, filling the vacuum. He was looking at the woman close by, one of surpassing beauty—glossy, dark hair, high cheekbones, eyes whose color he couldn't see without staring but which were large and widely spaced. She was talking to another woman, hair a darkish blond, whose back was turned to Melrose and who drank a pale drink, probably a Chardonnay, whose ubiquity, together with the wine bars that loved to serve it up, Melrose couldn't understand. The dark-haired one was drinking stout. Good for her. The bartender, a bearded Indian, posed an indecipherable query that Melrose could only suppose was a variant of "What will it be, mate?" The operative term was either "grog" or "dog," as in "Want a bit o' grog?" or "Walkin' yer dog?" Having no dog, Melrose ordered an Old Peculier.

The Grave Maurice had its foot in the door of "hovel-like." Melrose looked all around and made his assessment, pleased. For some reason, he could always appreciate a hovel; he felt quite at home. The incomprehensible barman, the patched window, the broken table leg, the streaked mirror, the clientele. The two women near him were a cut above the other customers. They were well dressed, the dark-haired one quite fashionably, in a well-cut black suit and understated jewelry. The blond one, whose profile Melrose glimpsed, appeared to know the barman (even to understand the barman) with his raffishly wound turban. After he returned, smilingly, with the refills and Melrose's fresh drink and then took himself off, the dark-haired woman picked up their conversation again. The blonde was doing the listening.

They were talking about someone named Ryder, which immediately made Melrose prick up his ears, as this was the name of the doctor who had just departed and whom, he supposed, the one woman must have recognized. But he was rather surprised to hear him further referred to as "poor sod." The second woman, whose voice was distinct while at the same time being low and unobtrusive, asked the dark-haired one what she meant.

Melrose waited for the answer.

Unfortunately, the details were getting lost in the woman's lowered voice, but he did catch the word "disappeared." The dark-haired woman dipped her head to her glass and said something else that Melrose couldn't catch.

But then he heard, "His daughter. It was in the papers."

The blonde seemed appalled. "When was that?"

"Nearly two years ago, but it doesn't get any—"

Melrose lost the rest of the comment.

The one who had made it shrugged slightly, not a dismissive shrug, but a weary one. Weary, perhaps, of misfortune. If she was a doctor too, Melrose could understand the weariness.

Then she said, ". . . brother was my . . . killed . . ."

The blonde made a sound of sympathy and said, "How awful. Did—"

If only they'd stop talking clearly on the one hand and whispering on the other! Melrose, who kept telling himself he couldn't help overhearing this conversation, could, of course, have taken his beer to a table, and he supposed he would if his presence so close beside them got to be a little too noticeable. But he wanted to hear whatever he could about this doctor's daughter; it sounded fascinating. He thought the phrase "poor sod" suggested some unhappy tale and he was always up for one of those. Sort of thing that makes you glad you're you and not them. How morbid.

He then heard something about insurance and the dark-haired woman was going on about South America and a warmer climate.

She appeared to be planning a trip. He didn't care about this; he wanted to hear more about the person who had disappeared. The blonde occasionally turned to retrieve her cigarette, and then Melrose could pick up the drift.

"—this doctor's daughter?"

The woman facing Melrose nodded. "So it never ends for him . . . closure."

"I hate that word," said the blonde, with a little laugh.

(Melrose was ready to marry her on the spot. Inwardly, he applauded. He hated the word, too.)

"All it means is that something's unended, unfinished. Why not just say that?"

The blonde was not in the mood for a semantic argument. "There never is, anyway," she said, slipping from the stool.

"What?" The dark-haired woman was puzzled.

"Closure. Everything remains unfinished."

The dark-haired woman sighed. "Perhaps. Poor Roger."

Roger Ryder, thought Melrose. When the blonde caught Melrose looking and listening, she gave him a rueful half smile. He pretended not to notice, though it would be difficult not to notice that mouth, that hair. Melrose paid for his beer and slid off the stool.

His daughter. Two years ago something had happened to her, and it hadn't been death. Death would have closed it. The girl had disappeared. Had something happened in South America? No, he thought that must be another story altogether. On the other hand, Ryder's daughter's disappearance—*that* had been in the papers. But Melrose wouldn't have to search the *Times.*

Roger Ryder was Richard Jury's surgeon.

TWO

Melrose had spent more time in Jury's hospital room than out of it in the past week. For thirty-six hours, Jury had lain in a coma, which he dropped into just after Melrose had found him lying on that dock, as if able to relax his own efforts to hold on to life, now that someone else could do it for him. Melrose and Benny had found him. Melrose and Benny *and* the dog Sparky. Most definitely Sparky. For it was Sparky (one could say) who had found him and had saved Jury's life. Sparky was the dog of the hour, a dog's dog, a hero's hero. Had Benny not been searching for Sparky along the Victoria Embankment, Richard Jury would be dead.

"No question of that," Dr. Ryder had said. *"Another twenty minutes—?"* The doctor had shrugged away the outcome.

Jury's nurse, Nurse Bell, had said (more than once), "Lucky, you are, my lad," as she'd strong-armed Jury away from the pillows behind him so that she could plump them.

Which was, as far as Melrose was concerned, all she was good for. Melrose couldn't abide that "lucky" response to disaster. Had his limbs been blown to smithereens and only one arm left—no, no, make that one *stump* of arm left, Nurse Bell would say, "Lucky you, at least you've got your stump. Could've been worse."

As soon as she'd whisked herself off in a crackle of starched uniform, Melrose went over to the bed and messed the pillows about.

Crossly, Jury said, "What in hell are you doing? Isn't it enough to have that simpering nurse about?"

"I'm just unplumping them. There."

A sanguine Sergeant Wiggins said from his chair, "She'll just be back and plump them again."

"Rats," said Melrose, returning to his folding chair. Wiggins had the only chair with armrests, and he was making the most of this find as he raked through a basket of fruit sent by some well-wishers in Victoria Street.

"What," asked Jury, "are you in such bad humor about? *You* didn't get shot."

Melrose was looking out of the window. "Your nurse puts me in mind of one of my nannies."

"So you're reverting to nanny behavior. Well, that's grown-up, that is."

Wiggins's rather condescending air was prompted by his having been in hospital himself not long ago (although certainly not from stopping a fusillade of bullets). Right now he was handing over a paperback book to Jury. "It was Mr. Plant himself who brought me this when I was in the Royal Chelsea." He made it sound like an heirloom. "I think you might like it; it more or less deals with our predicament."

Our? wondered Jury, who thanked Wiggins. *"The Daughter of Time,"* Jury said. "Josephine Tey." He studied the cover. He wondered how this dealt with "our" predicament. "You know, you two are getting more mileage out of my hospital stay than I am." He fixed first on Melrose. "You get to work out your childhood aggressions, and you"—he turned to Wiggins—"get to relive your hospital adventure in South Ken."

"Now, now—" Nurse Bell was back already. "We mustn't get excited and upset." She handed Jury a plastic cup with a straw. "This will make you feel ever-so-much-better."

"I already feel ever-so-much-better." He made a face at the cup.

"I had a cup just like that," said Melrose, "when I was three. Only I could drink without a straw."

"And here your friends have come to see you—"

Swiftly, Jury looked around the room. "Where, where?"

Nurse Bell had another go at the pillows. "You do mess your pillows about, don't you?" She left.

For Wiggins, his head lost—but unbeheaded—in the Tower of London, the last five minutes might not have happened at all. He was back there with Josephine Tey and *The Daughter of Time*. "You'll be wanting something to chew on while you're in here; you'll want to keep your mind busy—"

"Why would I want to do that? It never was busy before."

Ignoring this, Wiggins went on. "What it is, is the detective inspector in this book is laid up in hospital and a friend brings him some books, one of them about Richard the Third and the princes in the Tower. You remember all of them?"

"As a matter of fact, I do. It's quite a popular tale."

"*This* detective"—he pointed to the book—"reads about it and at some point decides the whole tale of Richard's killing the princes is codswallop. So he does more and more research, getting his girlfriend to bring him books and finally comes up with a totally different solution. Clever idea, I think."

"If I had a girlfriend, maybe I would, too." He riffled the last pages. "How does it end?" Jury did not like detective stories, especially those starring royalty, so he cut to the chase.

Wiggins, however, wouldn't follow. "You'll just have to read it, won't you?" Wiggins laughed as one might at an intractable, bedridden child. "What I thought was, I could bring you information about one of our cases and you could chew on that."

"Ah," said Melrose, tilting his chair back against the wall and crossing his arms over his chest. "Why don't you chew on *this*?"

THREE

Maurice was always up early, up at first light, when the world was waking. Cold as it was, rime on the panes, old snow still crusted at the roots of trees, stiff grass more like ice shards than pasture—still he loved it. Although he had to admit one of the reasons for this early hour was that he wouldn't have to see or talk to, or be seen or talked to by, anyone. It was even too early for his uncle, Roger, who occasionally stayed over. When he did, he liked to come down to the track and watch Maurice exercise the horses.

A couple of nights ago, at dinner, Roger had said, *"I've an interesting patient, a police superintendent. Scotland Yard, no less. Well . . . I was just thinking"*—his laugh was artificial—*"I might tell him the story. Of course he might already have heard . . . and it's been almost two years—"*

"Tell him," Maurice interrupted, *"the story."*

You can't give up, Maurice thought now. You can't give up trying. "Right, Sam?" He tossed the blanket over the horse, then the bridal and saddle. Samarkand nudged his shoulder as if to say *Let's go* and Maurice led him out of the stall. This walk from stable to track was just about the best part of Maurice's day—except, of course, for the ride itself.

No school because it was still the Christmas holiday, but that would end soon. He didn't really mind school; he had

always had a capacity for discipline. He thought it came
from caring for the horses, from watching George Davison,
the trainer, from watching exercise lads and jockeys, from
watching his father, his father up on Samarkand years ago.
That horse and Dan Ryder—this was what the sportswriters
called the "racing dream team."

He thought about his father. In no other way was Danny
Ryder a "dream." *Too bad he ain't a horse—it's the only
thing he's good with,* he'd heard the exercise boys say. *No
wonder she left.* Maurice spent a fair amount of time trying
not to hate his mum. She had not been a weak woman; she
could stand up to his father when she wanted to. She had
been—Maurice searched for a word—vague. Vague, yes.
She had never seemed certain of what she wanted. It was,
he thought, a peculiar flaw in character, maybe even a dangerous one. His mother had been small, pretty and American. She had been as indecisive about having a child as she
had been about leaving New York or choosing a restaurant
or a dress. Marybeth was definitely a wait-and-see person,
lazy rather than careful. Certainly not reckless. No, recklessness was his father's style.

It would appear she had left without a qualm. It was as
if he were no more than a bad climate she wanted to get
away from. He had heard a good bit of this from conversa-
tions between his granddad and his uncle. Maurice could
sympathize with Roger. He was nice. Distant, but nice. And
God knows the distance of these last twenty months was
understandable. Maurice himself felt at a distance from everyone. And because guilt weighed so heavily on him, too,
there had been no one to go to for consolation when
Nell disappeared.

*"Kind of queer, Dr. Ryder. Why was your girl sleeping
out here?"*

*The skin around Roger's mouth was very white, papery
and pinched, and his indrawn breath sounded more like a
gasp, as if he'd lost his source of oxygen.*

*Maurice had followed his uncle Roger and the detectives
out to the stables. He had stood back by the door, in the
shadows, listening, wanting to hear her name, as if its mention were hortatory and would call her back.*

In the night his grandfather sat with Roger, an arm draped over his son's shoulder.

Maurice hung back, sitting on the stairs and looking through the rails, listening for her name.

FOUR

"You're looking remarkably well this morning, Superintendent." Dr. Roger Ryder looked at Jury's chart again and smiled. "You've got real stamina."

"Good," said Jury, "but now aren't you going to tell me I'm lucky to be alive? Nurse Bell reminds me of that a dozen times a day."

Ryder laughed. "No, somehow I don't equate three bullet wounds with good luck. You're feeling okay, are you? I mean emotionally as well as physically?"

"Absolutely. When will you throw me back into the cesspool of police work?"

"Ah. As far as releasing you is concerned, I think another two or three days ought to do it. But as far as police work goes, uh-uh." Dr. Ryder held up an admonitory finger. "Have to wait several weeks for that. Are you bored?"

Jury held up *The Daughter of Time.* "I've this to entertain me; it's a policeman in hospital working on the historical case of Richard the Third. Unfortunately, as he solves it, it doesn't leave me anything to do." Dr. Ryder, Jury thought, was hesitating over something. He kept looking at the door and not leaving. "Something wrong?"

"I just wondered," Ryder smiled, trying to contain his anxiety, "if you'd like a real case to think about. Fact, not fiction." Ryder moved over to the one good chair and placed his chart on the floor.

"Of course I would. Tell me."

"It's about my daughter. You might have read or heard

about some of this. It happened nearly two years ago. She vanished."

For a second, Jury shut his eyes. Even though Melrose Plant had told him the story overheard in the pub, he was still unprepared. *Vanished*. Was there a word in any tongue, any language that was more affecting than that one? It chilled him. "My God. How old is she?" He would try to keep the girl in the present.

"Now she'd be seventeen. Then she was fifteen. And Nell didn't run away." Ryder, in a voice that Jury imagined would be forever tremulous when he talked about her, gave Jury an accounting of what had happened. "It was bad enough before, but it got to be worse when there was no demand for ransom. That threw us completely."

"I can understand why. What about . . . Could you hand me some water? My mouth keeps drying up."

"A reaction to the medication. It'll soon go away."

"What about her mother? Where was she?"

"Her mother's dead."

"I'm sorry." Jury hesitated. "You're quite sure your daughter didn't leave voluntarily?"

"She didn't run off, no." Roger rubbed his hand over his cheek, a nervous gesture. "I know any parent would say that, but Nell was a very contented child. Unlike Maurice— that's Danny's son—who never got over his mother's walking out. But why shouldn't Nell be happy, given the life she led? For kids a stud farm would be, well, idyllic."

Idylls, thought Jury, have a bad way of banging up against reality, if, indeed, they were idylls in the first place. Roger Ryder struck Jury as a doctor who took nothing at face value, but as a parent, probably everything. Such parents, well meaning and loving, weren't unusual. And actually could hardly be blamed for not knowing what was in their kids' minds and hearts.

Roger got up and walked over to the window, where he leaned his arm against the frame and bent his head toward the glass as if he hoped to extract some bit of knowledge from his reflection, but he said nothing.

"How did Nell react to her mother's death?"

"She was quite accepting of it, quite cool."

No she wasn't. She only appeared to be.

"Your brother's wife walked out."

Roger nodded. "Marybeth's leaving didn't really surprise me. I don't think it surprised Danny, either, to tell the truth. I think she was a token wife—you know, one more beautiful thing that sticks around for the winner's circle, accepts some flowers, takes a bow and then departs. Danny always had plenty of women around. He had some sort of charisma that attracted women. He was flamboyant, probably trying to fill the emptiness most of us fill with food, booze, cigarettes. A jockey has to give all of that up, every habit in the book. Danny was always trying to lose that extra pound. It's a hell of a life, so I guess you make up for it in other ways. Marybeth seemed totally indifferent to Maurice, who was and still is a very sweet boy. Just awfully sad. So much so it can be irritating."

Jury thought he heard an undertone of something alien to sweetness and much more aligned to "irritating." It could be jealousy or envy or even a well-tamped-down rage. His own child, Nell, was gone while his flamboyant, quixotic brother's child was here. All of these feelings were darkly cloaked in shame or guilt. "Your daughter lived with her grandfather?"

"At his prompting. He could think of nothing better than having the grandchildren around. Danny lived in Chiswick, but Maurice spent nearly all of his time at the farm. The thing was that both of us had the kind of careers that just didn't allow us to be home enough and the farm is such a wonderful environment."

"What about you?"

Roger shook his head. "I have to live in London because of my work. But I go to the farm nearly every weekend." Roger smiled. " 'Lucky you,' as Vernon says."

"Vernon?"

"Stepbrother."

"What did he mean by that?"

"That Dad was taking over his sons' responsibilities. Not that he really meant it." Unoffended, Roger smiled and looked out the window again. "Vernon came as part of the package when Dad married again. Felicity Rice, an extremely nice but oddly colorless woman. Our mother had been quite beautiful. I never understood Felicity and Dad. Except I can say for Dad, it was no midlife crisis. Felicity wasn't exactly one of your blond bombshells. She's dead now, too."

"You're smiling, though. Why?" Jury saw the adolescent kid peering out from behind the doctor's mask.

"Not about Felicity. About Vernon. He can say things without cutting you down, if you know what I mean. Vernon's very smart, very ambitious and very rich. He lives in a classy penthouse in Docklands. And he's generous. Dad got a loan from him a while back. We were—well, Dad was—assuming he had a buyer for one of the yearlings, a colt he was supposed to get one and a half million for and the buyer backed out. He knew he'd find another buyer, but he needed some money to tide him over—"

Jury interrupted. "One and a half million for a horse that hasn't proved himself yet?"

Roger laughed. "Oh, hell, that's nothing. Thoroughbred racing is a lucrative business. And the colt was one of Beautiful Dreamer's. Ever heard of him? You would if you knew anything about racing. There was never much doubt this colt would perform."

"It sounds like one hell of a gamble."

"It always is. It's a risky business. But one with huge rewards."

"Your brother Vernon. What does he do, then?"

Roger smiled broadly. "Money."

FIVE

"A taped interview with Dr. Ryder," said Jury, sliding the file Wiggins had brought him onto his tray table. "Interview conducted by DCI Gerard, Cambridgeshire constabulary. Gist of it is that Nell Ryder, fifteen years old, was abducted from Ryder Stud Farm on the night of May 12, 1994. Twenty months ago, that would be. The girl was sleeping in the same horse stall as a horse named Aqueduct. He was sick, feverish and Nell Ryder often spent the night in the stables to keep an eye on a sick horse.

DCI GERARD: You're a wealthy man are you, Dr. Ryder?

RYDER: No, I'm comfortable.

DCI GERARD: Ryder Stud then. Your father is quite wealthy.

RYDER: Intrinsically? Yes. Depends on how you look at it. In terms of liquidity, I mean money lying around, no. In terms of the stock—the Thoroughbreds—very.

DCI GERARD: Could money be raised fairly easily?

RYDER: I don't know. Probably. I know his stepson's got a lot of money, and he'd certainly help.

DCI GERARD: We can expect a ransom demand.

"Questions follow relative to the doctor's whereabouts; he was asleep, no witnesses. He's incensed, naturally, to be

taken as a suspect. Questions about Nell's mother. She's
dead. About his brother, Danny Ryder, also dead.

DCI GERARD: Your brother was the famous jockey,
   wasn't he?
RYDER: Yes. One of the best. He rode Ryder Thor-
   oughbreds in every important race in this country
   and in Europe and the States. He was a great jockey.
DCI GERARD: He died—
RYDER: In France, a racing course near Paris. Auteuil.
   Thrown from his horse.
DCI GERARD: Hell of a life, it is. It seems to explode
   all over the place or thinking about food food food.
   Lester Piggot lived on champagne and a lettuce leaf.
   [*Pause*] Well, pardon me, Dr. Ryder. I get carried
   away sometimes.

Jury looked up, smiling. " 'Carried away.' I like that. Apparently, Gerard has a cousin who's a jockey. I like the
description. Questions about the Ryders' wives. The doctor's is dead, her name being Charlotte. The jockey's—
Marybeth—is living somewhere in America. His first wife,
that is. He married again after he went to Paris. Woman
who lives in Paris but as none of the Ryders have met
her, Ryder doesn't know if she's a Parisian or possibly an
Englishwoman." Jury closed the file and sat back against
his pillows.
   Melrose asked, "What about ransom? What happened
there?" He had captured the one decent chair, leaving Wiggins to arrange himself on the unforgiving wooden one.
   "Never was one, it seems."
   "What?"
   "They just took her. End of story. I mean, insofar as
Cambridgeshire police knew. Oh, they didn't stint in looking for her; it's just that nothing else turned up. And, of
course, in the absence of any ransom demand, it would be
treated as an abduction rather than a kidnapping."
   "Then maybe," said Melrose, "it was the horse. What's
the name?"
   "Aqueduct. Quite valuable, especially for breeding pur-
poses. I wondered about that, too. I expect when you find

an animal missing along with a human, you assume the target was the human."

"They didn't expect to find a girl along with the horse. Do you suppose they had to take her to keep her quiet?"

"Very possibly." Jury looked again at the report from Cambridgeshire police. "A number of valuable Thoroughbreds: Beautiful Dreamer, Criminal Type—"

"Criminal Type, I like that name. Odd for a horse."

"So is Seabiscuit," Wiggins said. "Do you know how that name came about? Seabiscuit, I mean?"

Trust Wiggins to know the derivation of anything with *biscuit* in it. He was sitting there eating one right now.

"There was a horse named Hard Tack, which is what sailors are often left with to eat. See? Hard Tack/sailor."

Both Jury and Melrose looked at him. Neither spoke.

"*Sea* relating to sailor; *biscuit* meaning a lesser version of hard tack. It's rather clever."

Jury and Melrose still looked at him, neither commenting.

Wiggins was leafing up pages in his notebook. "Ryder Stud Farm has diminished somewhat since Nell Ryder disappeared. It's almost as if she were the heart of the place. Perhaps she really was, to her grandfather. Then there was also Danny Ryder. Not only was that a personal loss, but a real financial hit. When he was up on this Samarkand, they were virtually unbeatable."

"What's the chief source of income? The purses?"

"No. Breeding. Ryder has a stable full of Thoroughbreds retired from racing, but worth a lot in breeding."

"Owners take their mares to Ryder Stud and pay for the pleasure?"

"Pay a lot for the pleasure for a stud such as Samarkand. It's the practice, I heard, to sell shares. An owner pays, say, anywhere from a hundred thousand to a quarter million for the privilege of bringing one of his mares one time a year."

Melrose sat up. "A quarter million? For that price I'd do it myself."

"Who'd pay that much for you?" asked Jury. "So a return on the stallions set to stud in a given year could be how much?"

Wiggins again thumbed the pages of his notebook, said, "In '92, for instance, over five million."

Jury sat up. "What? And that's just the breeding part of it?"

Wiggins nodded. "Just from breeding, yes."

"How much from the purses?"

"From Samarkand alone—this would be a decade ago—1.8 million."

"No wonder they call it the sport of kings," said Melrose.

"Of course, looking at the other side of the ledger," said Wiggins, "it's an exceptionally pricey operation. The people you need working for you, many of whom are highly trained—jockeys, vets, trainers, grooms—do not come cheap. Arthur Ryder wanted the best of them. His trainer alone got a quarter million a year, and that's low for a trainer. It's expensive and it's very dicey, as much as farming is, and farmers don't have to carry insurance on each cow and plot of swede. Insurance on Samarkand alone was two million. But Arthur Ryder hasn't been in tip-top shape since first his son Danny and then his granddaughter Nell went. Financial reverses, accidents with the horses, troubles seemed to heap themselves on Arthur Ryder's head."

Jury lay back, closed his eyes. " 'Not single spies but in battalions.' "

"Sir?"

"Trouble coming. Claudius."

As if to bear out Claudius, Nurse Bell entered the room. But only single spies, Jury thought. A blessing.

"I'd say you two"—here she crossed her arms and glared at Melrose and Wiggins—"have visited quite enough for one day. And I warned you he"—she smiled ungraciously at Jury, it was more of a sneer—"shouldn't be listening to police business. He's supposed to be resting, not listening to you two. You don't seem to appreciate he was at death's door, and though we snatched him back once, we mightn't be so lucky again."

If she once more told him how close he'd come to death, Jury swore he'd hit her. Having been saved by so slight a margin, the unfortunate patient would feel that margin vanish in a moment. "Not out of the woods yet, my lad. So you'd better say an extra prayer tonight."

Melrose said, "That's ridiculous. He's never looked healthier. It looks as if he'd hardly got shot at all. It's your brilliant care of him."

That put Nurse Bell on the horns of a dilemma. She certainly did not want her role diminished. "Even the best of care can't guarantee a patient will make it."

Jury, Melrose and Wiggins sighed.

SIX

Vernon Rice "did" money all right. He had his own investment firm in the City and moved a lot of money around, both for himself and his clients. He liked start-ups; however, he would warn his clients away from volatile-looking ones, but they didn't always take his advice. It astonished him how reckless people were with their money, how eager to part with it at first sniff of something that looked promising (but probably wasn't), like hounds on the trail of a fox.

Vernon's days (and a lot of his nights) revolved around money. His primary moneymaker was his small investment firm in the City, a "boutique" firm, he supposed it would be called, consisting of himself, his receptionist, Samantha, and his two young assistants, Daphne and Bobby. They watched the daily financials for him, let him know how the market was operating and did some day trading on their own. He had hired both of them more or less off the streets and had never regretted it.

Daphne had appeared to be disoriented when Vernon came across her one day, standing on the corner of Threadneedle and Old Broad Street, just by the Stock Exchange. What he noticed about her was that she just stood there, not joining the foot traffic that crossed one street or crossed the other. She had dark hair, ringlets poking out from underneath a gray wool cap, which fit her head tightly and had two little gray ears sticking up in front. Her curls, her smooth oval face, wide brown eyes and—of course—the ears, put her, in Vernon's estimation, at anywhere between twelve and thirty-two.

Probably she would think he was putting moves on her, but he took the chance, unable to resist both her apparent predicament and the ears on the wool cap. "Pardon me, don't think I'm trying to pick you up or anything, but you seem to be having, well, a difficult time moving. I mean, more than the usual 'which-street-is-it-I-want?' challenge, and more of a 'what-city-is-this-I'm-in?' quandary. I thought perhaps I could assist you." Vernon went on in this fashion, unable to stop explaining both her difficulty and his proffered role in it. Finally, he just wound down while she stood and stared and the foot soldiers coming from London Bridge flowed all over the place, too many of them, or at least T. S. Eliot thought so.

He even threw T. S. Eliot into the frying pan before he stopped.

She waited, squinting up at him. Then she said, "You're finished, are you? You're done? This is it for you? Through? Ended? Over? Fini? It's a wrap?"

He nodded, started to say something and stopped when she held up her hand. "No, it's the rest of the world's turn. Around ten miles back you asked me, or I think you asked me, why I didn't go one way or the other. The answer is: one way is *like* the other, and I don't see the point in choosing. So I can't cross over. It's some existential turning point. I can't go either way."

"Um." He wondered if he could say something now. Since she hadn't pushed him in the way of an oncoming double-decker when he'd made the *um* sound, he thought perhaps he could. "How about not crossing either street?"

"How about—?" Again she squinted at him, as if finding him harder to believe than a saint's vision. "Excuse me, but that's just what I've spent the lunch hour explaining."

"No, no. What I mean is, why not just go back?" Vernon looked over his shoulder. "Back along this pavement you're already on. There's a coffee bar a few doors back and I'd be happy to buy us an espresso or lattè."

She considered. "I hate those drinks. But I could do with some regular coffee."

"Let's go."

They sat at the counter drinking plain coffee, hers with (he counted) five sugars, and Vernon asked Daphne where she lived. "Disneyland?"

"Clapham. Same thing."

"Where do you work?"

"Nowhere. You know that 'resting between plays' that actors do? I'm resting between tending bar in the George and clerking at Debenham's."

"Do you know anything about the stock market at all?"

"Of course. My portfolio's split fifteen different ways."

"Is it the poor-little-matchstick-girl life you lead that makes you so sarcastic?"

Daphne appeared to like that image; she laughed the way some people sneeze, an *ah-ha-ah-ha-ah-ha* that segued into a brief explosion.

"The reason I ask is that I might be able to use you."

"I doubt it." She drank her coffee and stared at the phony turn-of-the-century signs.

Vernon ignored this reply. "If you have, say, a head for numbers?" Only, looking at the head with its two little ears, he doubted it.

She was holding her cup with both hands, frowning slightly. "Actually, I'm good with that. I took a first in maths at university."

"Which one?"

"Oxford."

Vernon's eyebrows shot nearly up to his hairline. "Oxford? You?"

She turned her head to give him her signature squint. "Do you think I'm dumb just because my cap has ears?"

Vernon offered her a job on the spot. On the spot, she declined.

Finally, he talked her around to coming to work for him, aware that she could be a disaster, and she would probably try to sell his shares of British Telecom if the market took a tiny dip. But he found her caustic sense of humor bracing. And he couldn't resist that damned cap.

Bobby, now, was a whole different thing.

Bobby (who might also be anywhere from twelve to thirty-two) ran into him on a skateboard. Bobby said he

was "messengering" a document to someone in Vernon's
building. (He held up a manila envelope as if it were proof
of legitimacy.) He'd knocked Vernon down in the lobby,
given him a hand up and rattled off a stream of apologies.
An apology dialectic, you could say, laying the groundwork
for future apologies, if need be.

"You belong to a messenger service that uses
skateboards?"

"No. But my bike got in an accident and I'll use this
until it's fixed. Don't tell them."

"Me? They could put hot pokers in my eyes and I'd
never tell."

Then Bobby asked him what firm he worked at. When
Vernon told him it was his own investment firm, Bobby
asked him to recommend a good hedge fund and what did
he think about this new company Sea 'n' Sand?

"How do you even know about Sea 'n' Sand?" This was
a brand-new travel business dealing exclusively in cruises
and coastal vacations. Why it was becoming so popular
Vernon put down to a masterly PR and ad department
because it offered nothing new by way of destinations or
service.

Bobby shrugged. "Same way as you do, I guess. I think
it'll tank, myself."

And Bobby went on. He pointed out to Vernon that the
Dow was really no barometer; it didn't call any shots. It
was too heavy with industrials. "I mean, where's Yahoo!?
Where's Macintosh? Where's any of the high techs?"
Bobby was a day trader who "always checked the financials. Always." He paid no attention to financial gurus such
as Hortense Stud (her name arming her competitors with
endless sobriquets), who, he said, was a Michelin tire with
a serious leak.

While the news in the manila envelope grew whiskers,
Bobby talked. He asked Vernon what he thought about
SayAgain, a purportedly hot new firm in the cellular war
that was marketing phones for the almost-deaf. It was supposed to merge with CallBack—"You know about that,
don't you? Even hush-hush as it is?" Not only did Vernon
not know about it, he wished to hell he'd thought of it.
Damn. Bobby said he was going to short the stock if the

merger took place because a little down the road Call-Back's image manipulators were going to have trouble with ads picturing old geezers plying these phones. "Remember," said Bobby, "Planet Hollywood?" And he set his hand on a downward spiral.

"Bummer," said Vernon.

Bobby, clutching his skateboard and envelope, just went on and on. He was every bit as bad as Vernon on the day Vernon had met Daphne. So Vernon offered him a job on the spot. Unlike Daphne, Bobby accepted on the spot.

Vernon could easily have supplied each of them with an office, but they insisted on staying together. He called her Daffy; she called him Booby. They argued about everything—penny stocks, IPOs, short selling. Actually, they brawled a lot of the time. So what? Vernon said to Samantha. Let them brawl; they're brilliant.

And they, in turn, thought Vernon walked on water. He had saved them from running people down on skateboards and standing indefinitely on street corners.

Vernon lived alone in a penthouse condo overlooking the Thames with white walls and three fireplaces, filled with angular, streamlined furniture by Le Corbusier, Mies van der Rohe and other seriously Swedish or German designers. He had never married. He was thirty-six years old. He did enjoy the company of women, two of them, one named Janet, a good-looking brunette who thought marriage for them was in the cards or the stars. Why she thought this he couldn't imagine as he had never suggested it and never would. The other woman was a high-class whore named Taffy, whom he actually preferred to Janet, certainly on the sexual front—as well he should, when he was paying five hundred quid for two hours of her time. Taffy looked like her name—smooth and golden—tasted like it, stretched like it. She was inventive (but then, again, for that price, she ought to be).

Vernon loved his life. He loved coming home to the white walls and slick furniture, the polished floors, the aquarium he had paid thirty thousand pounds to have installed in one wall, flanked by paintings by Pollock and Hockney. His cat oversaw this arrangement. He knew Bar-

ney's seemingly relaxed position—tail encircling torso, paws
curled into chest—masked a busy mind trying to work out
how he could get in there. He had found Barney wandering
along by the river near the Town of Ramsgate pub. Probably the cat remembered better times, when alleys were full
of dumps and jellied eels was the plate *du jour*. He admired
cats' self-sufficiency; they weren't always barking at him to
be let out. Barney's "out" was the patio, where he could
look at the Thames and the night. The patio was utterly
glamorous and exotic. There were palm trees and hibiscus
and fruit trees. He was not a gardener but he did take very
good care of everything and the plants and trees flourished.
He bet it was the London rain, which more often was thick
mist or drizzle, so that his plants were fanned with water,
not beaten with it.

Janet didn't like cats; she felt they were sneaky. "On
the contrary," Vernon said, "they're perfectly open about
flouting rules or stealing shrimp from your plate."

"You know what I mean."

Actually, he didn't. It irritated him to death that she
really thought "you-know-what-I-mean" was an answer.

At this point in his evening return he always made a
pitcher of Manhattans if he was feeling really Art Deco, or
martinis, if he was feeling like a drink. Now he was finishing
stirring their ten-to-oneness. He tapped the stirrer against
the pitcher and poured the drink into a stemmed glass to
which a paper-thin peel of lemon had been added. He
sipped. It was cold and quick, knife-edged.

In the last couple of weeks, when he drank this home-
coming martini he had thought up his new dotcom start-
up. He had been to a number of AA meetings, not for his
own sake, but to see what they were selling, and for God's
sake, were they ever selling! No wonder this organization
was so successful. What they had on offer was: one, salvation; two, friends for you everywhere—in every city, every
country on the globe; and three, childhood's return. At the
very least these three things and a whole lot of others.
Members probably stopped drinking because they couldn't
fit it in.

Now, would he give up his two-martini predinner evening
to have someone make his decisions? No, he wouldn't, but

a lot of people would. AA offered that, in addition to end-less evenings of acceptance, no one trying to punch your clock or do you one better or go for you. And you had Dad back again in the form of a sponsor, an absolutely blood-chilling prospect to Vernon, not because he didn't want his dad back, but because he didn't want a sponsor.

He found it interesting that any alcoholic, if asked What do you want most in the world? would gaily cry, "A drink!" But this was self-delusion, for they wanted something else even more: salvation, Dad, acceptance no matter what—one or all of these things, and Vernon supposed they blended together like Stoly and dry vermouth.

He was calling his start-up SayWhen.

Money gave Vernon the same rush he knew Arthur Ryder got out of watching Aqueduct win the Gold Cup at Cheltenham, not once, but twice, the second time carrying twenty-three pounds. Yet he could not get Art to see how the stud fees would quadruple if he incorporated Ryder Stud and made an initial public offering by selling seasons for, say, Beautiful Dreamer and Samarkand. "It would bring in millions, Art."

"Vernon, I don't want millions."

Vernon was much too kind to point out that his stepfa-ther had certainly wanted at least one near million two months before.

"But listen, Art. Look what they did in the U.S. with horses like Seattle Slew. Just for one breeding season they pulled in three quarters of a million. Multiply that by the number of stallion slots for one horse like Aqueduct. Then multiply again by the stallions you have at stud."

Arthur continued his round of evening stables, Vernon walking with him. He shook his head and said, "Vernon, this is what you do for a living? Why not just play poker?"

"Because this is more fun. And I'm trying to help you out, you know. How about foal sharing? That's getting popular."

"*Foal* sharing? Jesus." Arthur just shook his head.

It was true that Vernon wanted to help; he very much wanted to lessen his stepfather's money concerns. But in addition, of course, it would be fun to trade some of the Ryder Stud horses on the exchange. In the last twenty months, there had been a more compelling motive: Vernon wanted to get Arthur's mind off Nell, if only for a few moments at a time.

For he had never seen Arthur Ryder stopped dead in his tracks before. Not even the death of his son Danny had done this—turned him to stone, unable to act. Roger, too, despite the fact he dealt with death every day, and often in the most shocking way, could not work Nell's disappearance into the equation. The two of them, Arthur and Roger, had stared too long into the same space. Perhaps, Vernon thought, sharing the same space might be some comfort to them.

Vernon had tried to handle things. "Things" included the bulk of police questioning, at the outset, Arthur and Roger having been unable to answer anything beyond yes, no and possibly. He also hired the best private investigator in London, a man named Leon Stone, known for his chameleonlike ability to melt into the background. Nineteen months before, they were sitting in Vernon's flat, as Vernon related the story. He told Stone, "It must not be money they want. It's been nearly a month now."

"Not necessarily," Leon Stone had said. "Ransom might have been the reason originally, and then something happened to change their minds."

Vernon leaned forward, toward Stone, who was occupying the deep leather chair on the other side of the glass-and-mahogany coffee table. He said, "So we have to factor into this search all of the circumstances that might have surrounded their change of plans. Bloody hell. That's impossible."

Stone held up his hand. "I should have added that it's unlikely they changed their minds. If they haven't asked for money, they probably don't want money, as you said." He asked Vernon if there was any reason to believe the little girl's father or grandfather might be responsible for this.

Vernon was appalled, possibly because he had thought about it. "You mean could they have staged it? Of course not!"

"It does happen." Stone shrugged.

Over the last year and a half, Leon Stone had been thorough, no question of that. He'd earned his hefty fee. He'd visited every stud farm in Cambridgeshire and others elsewhere. Cambridgeshire, though, was the heart and soul of racing and breeding.

"Why do you think this villain might have a stud farm?"

"Proximity, for one reason. Knowledge of Arthur Ryder's household for another. And for another, it's possible there might be some bad feeling between Ryder and other owners. Mr. Rice, let's look at the picture: one or more villains go to Ryder Stud in the night—no, let me change that—they might have been there during the day or sometime in the recent past to take in the situation before acting. Or the person might already have been there in the capacity of an employee—stable lads, exercise boys, trainers. There's the vet, too. I have a list of those people.

"Next: let's go back to the incident. Someone comes to the stables, for what reason we don't actually know—"

"You mean the object might not have been Nellie?"

"It's possible. The thing is, if the target *was* the girl, the person must have known Nell's habit of sleeping in stables if a horse was sick. That would certainly limit the suspects to family, friends and employees, wouldn't it?

"That's one possibility," Stone continued. "The other is that the villains were there for another reason altogether and Nell got in their way. Because she saw something, and they had to take her with them because she presented a threat."

"You think they came for the horse?"

Leon Stone shrugged again. "That's also possible. And not necessarily to take the horse, but to do something to the horse or horses. There are extremely valuable stallions there."

"Besides Samarkand there's Beautiful Dreamer, Criminal Type, Aqueduct and Fool's Money." (The last having been named in honor of Vernon, according to Arthur.) "No car or trailer seen, but I guess they had transport."

"I'm thinking one person, and he didn't need a car or van."

"He had to have something."

"He had Aqueduct." Stone smiled thinly. "Obviously."

SEVEN

He was given to anxiety attacks that overtook him
when he was outside, standing on ground no longer
firm or familiar. When this happened, Maurice
would take out a horse, any horse that seemed eager for a
gallop or just a walk up and down the cinder paths that
wound around for miles through the farm.

After Samarkand, Maurice's choice was Beautiful
Dreamer, an elegant stallion who would shake out his mane
and raise his head as if divesting himself of Maurice or
anyone except Nell. The horses loved Nell.

*Beautiful Dreamer had always felt doomed to race around
some mile-and-a-half course as if this were all he was good
for, and only tolerated the winner's circle in which he often
found himself. Though he rather liked the flowers, armfuls
of roses thrown about his neck, and smiles and gold glinting
about him. No more than he deserved. It had happened so
often he wondered if there was anything left worth winning.*

*Now, it was this boy again, who was better than some
who rode him. He actually liked the boy. But he knew what
would happen, and it did after they'd walked the paths for
fifteen minutes. Yes, he felt a shift in the boy's position, body
stretched out, head on Dreamer's neck, arms dangling. At
least his feet were still in the stirrups, which would hold him
in place a little.*

*Asleep again. Dreamer would have to be careful not to
walk under any overhanging branches. Better get off the path
and onto the road, which is what he'd wanted to do anyway.*

Why was it that whenever the boy got up on Dreamer, he

fell asleep, yet didn't seem to know it? If he did know it, he wouldn't try to ride Dreamer. Or maybe he would; yes, maybe he would, if he wanted to escape once in a while. The boy was just lucky he was up on Dreamer and not Criminal Type, who'd do anything.

The old road. Beautiful Dreamer walked a while careful to move out of the way of branches, to where the path went parallel to a road that nobody used anymore. It was scarcely more than a single lane, two if the cars were small. No cars, not even one of the Ryder Stud farm's cars drove along it anymore. Once the hedgerows had been so tall you couldn't see over them, so straight they could have taken a plumb line, and so tidy a yardstick would have fit neatly against the bottom. But now large parts of dried-up hedge crumbled like brick too long stressed.

Beautiful Dreamer walked on, careful and quiet. Walked, but yearned to break into a trot, then a canter, then a gallop. He saw a winter landscape, small clumps of snow bearding roots of hazels and oaks, ice gloving their high branches, dripping water, but he passed through spring—clouds of daisies, mists of cowslip, wild rose, pennyroyal, violets. Beautiful Dreamer did not so much have memories as he did comings and goings, entrances and exits, other places becoming these places. The past was like the path he had left, which wound around and sometimes turned back on itself, crossing the present.

He heard the lads at stables calling out time: time for feeding, time for grooming, for morning stables and evening stables, time for this, time for that, time after time. It meant nothing, yet they needed it. Memory was time. He still heard the raised voices under the vaulted sky; he still stormed around that rough three-quarter-mile turn; he still won or still lost; he still smelled the collar of roses.

Beautiful Dreamer loved to walk down this road but only when the boy was riding him, sleeping. When one of the exercise lads or anyone else came on it by accident, he reared up and refused to go.

"What's this? I never knew ya t'go skittish on me. You afraid a sumppin, then?" And the lad would squint, peer through the shadows of the road and its banks and point out that not only was there nothing to fear, "But there ain't

*hardly nuffin there. Just that old barn and shed and over-
grown ring."*

Say what he would, Beautiful Dreamer refused to budge.

He came within sight of the barn and thought perhaps he
should shake the boy awake, then thought, no too painful
or at least the boy might think so. No, the boy would have
to wake up himself and confront it.

Beautiful Dreamer had seen her the day he was born. It
was her hands, besides the vet's, that caught him and helped
him out. He could see her now. He could hear her now,
singing a breathy song, half words, half humming "Beautiful Dreamer."

That song was why he'd been given his name. That song,
and her singing. That was why. Beautiful Dreamer listened
for a while and then headed home.

EIGHT

Vernon lay in bed in the moonless dark, hands clasped behind his head as usual when he was reviewing his day before going to sleep.

He had acquired that very afternoon a tiny religious publishing house that was turning over a small but steady revenue. He added this to the other two companies he'd bought named WeightLess and QuestCo, all showing income which he could list as SayWhen's assets. In the next month or two he'd offer stock on the open market, SayWhen's initial IPO selling at twenty-five pounds per share. The fact that SayWhen hadn't yet brought in any money of its own didn't bother Vernon at all, though it might bother the Securities and Investment Board.

The companies loved him for he had insisted they remain autonomous. QuestCo was a company specializing in acquiring companies. It had not come up with anything especially brilliant thus far, though it was engaged in investigating a company called NuBru, an old wine refinery, whose chief chemist had come up with a drink made out of grapes that tasted like the real thing, and—more important—had the effect of the real thing. QuestCo was having a problem finding the site and the company for although the NuBru talked about people it employed, it didn't have an actual address.

"Located somewhere in California," QuestCo's CEO had told Vernon.

"It's wine—sort of—so where else?" Vernon said.

He had considered having SayWhen actually work for its

twenty-five pounds per share. He had of course put the twelve-step program on the home page, with snappy little drawings illustrating the steps—and their lack thereof. All sorts of falling-down drunk men and women, white, black, Asian, young and old, plus tipsy cats and tanked dogs, even a mouse with its stiff little legs up in the air and a minuscule bottle by its side, and a general air of flagrant abuse (although a couple of the dogs looked pretty happy). There were also links to other Web sites remotely connected with alcoholism and its curse.

Don't tell SayWhen there's no cure for alcoholism! Who'd want to take the high road to sobriety on club soda and San Pellegrino if he thought he'd never be cured?

Get real, Big Book.

The thing was this: the idea would have to hit the ground running because it wouldn't be long before some wet-behind-the-ears dotcomer would refine Vernon's original idea and improve upon it. Company start-ups were dicey things, not for the weak at heart, or (possibly) the sound of mind.

"Vernon, has it occurred to you this NuBru company is actually producing *wine*? I mean, if you can't tell the difference, then how do you know?"

"Of course, it's occurred to me. Anyway, I didn't particularly like the name, NuBru—sounds like beer, doesn't it?" He was sitting on a hay bale, watching Arthur, who was inspecting Fool's Money's ankles, which Arthur said were hot. "So I got them to change it to WineDesign."

Arthur just looked at him and shook his head.

"What? What?"

"Nothing."

"Their product could perfectly well be what they say it is. They've done tests to show its lack of toxicity. An inconsequential effect on the liver and other organs—"

Arthur gave him another look. "That's meaningless. What's 'inconsequential'? What, indeed, is 'effect' here?"

Vernon didn't answer directly because he didn't know the answer. "Someone's going to work it out sometime, Art, how to produce a nonalcoholic drink you can get high on."

"Well, just tell your SayWhen clickers to have themselves frozen when they die."

"Come on, Art, we're at a point in history where we can do practically anything."

"That's scary, if you're in on it."

"How droll."

Arthur tried not to smile. "Felicity always said you were like this even as a kid. You'd try anything if you saw profit in it. You used to break pencils in half, sharpen them and sell each part for a penny more than a regular pencil, except for the half with the eraser. That, you charged two pence for."

"I was that cynical when I was a kid?"

"Pretty much. You could never convince Nell of it, though."

Vernon suddenly leaned back. Anytime she was brought into a conversation abruptly, like that, out of the clear blue, as just now, he always felt he'd been punched suddenly in the chest. In the stall, perhaps everywhere, came a sudden stillness as if everything were holding its breath.

Vernon certainly was.

Nell.

Even at fifteen she'd been brilliant. When he'd first seen her, she was in Samarkand's stall, rubbing him down after a ride. She was bent over. Her remarkably fair hair was long and covered her face, almost reaching the ground when she was bent over that way. She was quietly singing. It was a song he couldn't make out but thought he knew.

"Hey," he'd said, "what's up?"

She straightened, surprised. Then she drew her hair back from a face that had seemed to him translucent. Nothing was hiding; everything was in it—how she cared for the horse and expected a lot more from it than she did from Vernon.

The "Hey, what's up?" sounded more like the banal introduction of a kid, not a thirty-four-year-old adult, which he had been. "I'm Vernon Rice."

"Hello." She wiped her hand down the leg of her jeans and held it out.

He clasped it and thought whimsically of an iron butterfly, soft but very strong. It seemed to curl within his own hand. He was not given to metaphors usually.

"This," she said, "is Samarkand. Sam, for short."

He had lumps of sugar in his pocket that he'd picked up from the restaurant he'd stopped at for coffee. He was going, after all, to a stud farm. He liked to be prepared. Prepared? Was he going to offer a hedge fund to a horse? Now he pulled two of the cubes out of his pocket and held them out (rather timidly) toward the horse.

Samarkand looked at him, turned around in the stall (making Nell press against the wall) and presented his backside to Vernon.

"He's not that easy," Nellie said. She couldn't help laughing.

He was ashamed of himself for blushing. My God. "That was pretty stupid of me, with the sugar, I mean."

"Not at all. The important thing is you thought ahead, you came prepared. You know how many people manage to do that?" She made a circle with her thumb and forefinger. "Zilch."

Now, he was as stupidly glad he'd brought the sugar as a moment ago he'd been stupidly ashamed.

Nimbly, she changed the subject, as if she'd had a lot of practice putting people at their ease, saying, "You're down from London, aren't you?"

"That's right. I know I should have come before to meet the family. I was living in Europe for a little while, now—" He shrugged. "It was rude of me not to come the minute I got back." He felt chastised without her saying anything; he realized he was chastising himself.

She had turned Samarkand back around without seeming to have touched him. She said, "It certainly wasn't as rude as their going off to a registry office and not inviting us." That she was not really annoyed by this "elopement" of his mother and her grandfather was clear. She had said it to let him know they were both on the same side. "I like Felicity; she's really nice."

"Excuse me for getting personal, but are you really fifteen?"

His expression made her laugh. "That's all, sorry to say."

"You seem so much older."

She stopped the curry comb and looked off somewhere. "It's from being around horses all my life, I think. I think it gives a person poise." She had finished with the brushing and returned the brush to a shelf and picked up a bucket.

He was afraid she was going, and he wanted to keep her there. "What was that song you were singing?"

Color rose slowly up her neck and across her face. He'd seen sunrises that couldn't hold a candle. " 'Love Walked In.' "

He remembered the song. " 'And drove the shadows away.' " He smiled.

So did she. "One of my favorites. Do you know all the words?"

"No. Some, but not all. Your voice is very pretty."

She shrugged that away.

"You don't want anyone to hear you."

"It's embarrassing to be caught singing to horses. You know."

She said this, to Vernon's intense surprise, as if he must. Yet he did know, didn't he? He remembered being fifteen and how hard it was, falling in love with girls you couldn't have.

"What's wrong? Did I spook you?" She swung the bucket a little.

His look now was quite serious. "You could say that."

She smiled and walked off, the bucket swinging from her gloved hand, trim and neat, hair nearly lost in the sun's dazzle. Vernon watched her out of sight, thinking she was the most together person he'd ever known.

The day she went missing was the worst day of Vernon Rice's life.

NINE

"Who was she?" asked Jury.

Melrose Plant had the latest fruit basket on his lap, checking its contents. He looked up. "She? Your questions more and more seem to be coming out of some continuing conversation with yourself."

"The woman in the pub."

Melrose cocked his head, trying to tune in on Jury's wavelength. The penny dropped. "Oh! In the Grave Maurice."

Jury nodded. "The one who seemed to know Dr. Ryder."

Melrose pried a banana out of the basket.

"Don't take that. Wiggins is Banana Man and has already spoken for it."

"I'm not taking anything. I hope I've better things to do than rummage through fruit baskets."

"You will in a while. This woman—"

"The entire hospital knew about that kidnapping. It wouldn't mean the woman I overheard was any more important than the others."

"I'm just casting about."

Silence while Jury looked out of the window upon the blank face of the sky, and Melrose tried to decide between a plum and a pear. Why not have both?

Melrose said, his tone not very hopeful, "You were kidding?"

Jury frowned. "About what?"

"That I should go to Ryder Stud to buy a horse."

"Yes."

Melrose exhaled pent-up breath. "That's a relief."

"What in hell would you do with a horse?"

"Exactly!"

"You can just negotiate."

Melrose sat up. "Negotiate?"

"For the horse. You don't actually buy it. Negotiating would allow you to go back, maybe more than once."

Melrose slumped down in the chair. "Richard, I don't want to know about horses; I'm still stuffed to the gills with hacheonela and Rumbrim grasses. With box parterres and . . . stuff." He flapped his hand in Jury's direction.

"You didn't want to be a gardener, either, but you did a bang-up job. As always." Jury smiled brightly, the smile quick to fade when Nurse Bell entered the room.

Seeing Melrose, she braced her legs, dug her fists into plump hips and said, "It isn't visiting hours!"

"I'm not visiting; I live here."

She waggled a finger in the air. "I've spoken to you before about this, Mr. Plant. You cannot take these liberties—"

Melrose stood up, digging one of his old cards from his tweed pocket. "It's Lord Ardry, actually, Earl of Caverness, Baron of Ross and Cromarty, et cetera." He handed her the shabby card.

She looked at it. "Well . . ." She smiled at him coyly, displaying teeth that could use a dentist or a crane. "Still, we've got to be careful about maintaining proper hours." Her finger wagged again, but in a more friendly fashion. "We've got to see our patients get their rest." She had drawn out a thermometer, shaken it and now shoved it into Jury's mouth. She talked all the while she took his pulse. "Things could so easily turn against them, I mean the patients. Just last week there was an elderly gentleman who'd come in with a bad heart. Fit as a fiddle, he looked"—she checked her watch and chuckled—"and then wouldn't you know it, he slumped over in his wheelchair when the attendant was wheeling him toward the visitors' room. His daughter and grandchildren were waiting for him and just as he raised his hand to wave—that's enough," said the nurse to Jury as she yanked the thermometer from his mouth (as if it were a lollipop he'd been licking) "—and as the little grandson was rushing toward the old man, he went down like this!" She snapped two fingers. "Never got to say good-bye, he didn't. Then there was the poor little girl that came in with her appendix—"

Said Melrose, "I always travel with mine, too."

Nurse Bell paid him no mind. "—and died on the operating table. Heart, can you believe it? Poor little Dory. Had a heart arrhythmia and nobody knew it. Doctor"—here she looked at Jury just to let him know not *all* of Dr. Ryder's patients walked out under their own steam—"blamed himself. Then there was old Willie, that was getting on perfectly well until he choked to death on coffee from the dispensing machine."

God! But the woman was a ghoul. "How could a patient choke to death surrounded by nurses?"

She didn't answer, only looked at the thermometer ruefully. "Oh, I don't like this, Mr. Jury. Temperature's up. I'll have to tell doctor, won't I?"

Melrose hated it when "doctor" was used almost like a first name. Like God, for instance.

Nurse Bell turned to go and then turned back. "And you"—here came a frenzy of finger waggling—"five more minutes and then out. Five minutes!" She left, her heavy rump swaying and her uniform bristling with starch.

"What in hell was it? Your temperature, I mean."

"Who knows—517, probably. Let's get back to the horse-trading plan."

"Let's not." Melrose threw himself into a fit of mock weeping.

"Oh, don't be so childish. Look—"

Melrose raised his untearstained face to see Jury holding *The Daughter of Time.* "I've got several more days in this place, being ministered to by—" He nodded meaningfully toward the door. "I need something to think about, something to chew on, and I find this girl's disappearance very interesting."

"You've got her father right here. Chew on him."

"Come on, he's hardly objective."

Melrose sighed. He knew he'd do it and Jury knew he

knew it. "So I tell this Ryder chap I'm interested in buying some horseflesh."

"For God's sake, don't call it 'horseflesh.'"

"Gary Cooper always did." The actor was one of Melrose's all-time favorites. That badge he threw down in the dust at the end of *High Noon*!

"No, he didn't. What are you doing?"

"Nothing."

"It looked as if you threw something. Anyway, pay attention. What would be even more convincing"—here Jury sat forward, pushing the tray table out of his way—"would be to go after a particular horse, or find out what horses he had there and read up on them. Do what Diane Demorney does: learn a lot about one horse instead of a little about all of them." Jury thought for a moment. "Red Rum, that's a good horse. He won the Grand National, and more than once, I think."

"I'd have to know general things; I can't see me going back and back, knowing only Red Rum."

"The one Wiggins was talking about—"

"Seabiscuit?"

"Of *course* not Seabiscuit. Seabiscuit's an American horse. He's also dead. You've really got your work cut out for you, don't you? No—Samarkand, his name is. He's a famous horse."

"Then he wouldn't be for sale."

"No, but now it occurs to me that you'd have to know something about him; I mean if you're knowledgeable about horses and racing. You could easily get information about the stud farm from, you know, sources . . ." Jury shrugged.

Melrose got up and leaned over the bed to shake Jury's hand. "Thanks! Sources! That's really helpful." He stood there. "I expect I should get started right away." Melrose checked his watch. "Good God! I've been here more than the five minutes!"

Jury leaned back, looking rather smug. "You going back to Northants? You really should start this investigation as soon as possible."

Melrose just stared at him. "Talk about nerve! Not only

isn't this an investigation—one of your cases—I'm not an investigator."

"Sure you are. Stop complaining and I'll tell you something about Nurse Bell."

"What? She works nights outside a club in Soho? She's pregnant by the hospital's CEO? What?"

"Her first name is—ready?—Hannah."

It took a moment for the penny to drop.

Then they both smiled meanly.

TEN

"That book," said Agatha, craning her neck to see what Melrose was reading, "has horses on the cover." She righted herself on the drawing-room sofa and inspected the cake plate.

"That's because it's about horses." Melrose took another sip of his tea and wondered if the buffeting about of the morning light—rhomboids along the Oriental carpet, spandrel along an archway—was making up for Agatha's unilluminating presence, the light in sympathy with him. A pathetic fallacy, but Melrose would take his pathos where he found it.

Agatha continued: "Why on earth would you be reading about horses? You don't have one; you don't even ride." Having pinched another muffin—they were smallish—from the plate, she eyed it with suspicion. "What is this?"

"A muffin?"

"You know what I mean! It's green. What did Martha do to it?"

"It's a creme de menthe muffin." This had been Melrose's idea. He had told his cook Martha to add a bit of food coloring to the muffins, which he now had christened with the names of various liqueurs. He had also directed Martha to keep back the scones and tea bread. Ruthven (Melrose's butler and Martha's husband) had tittered.

"Oh, but won't she make a fuss, sir?" said Martha, smiling broadly.

"That's the idea," Melrose had answered, matching the smile.

Unfortunately, not liking did not mean not eating and not staying. If nothing else was available for her tea, she would start in on the fruits of the Della Robbia jug he had brought back from Florence to give to someone, anyone, perhaps even Agatha. He was not fond of it.

Returning the green muffin to the riotous muffin plate, she took the most muffinish-looking muffin there. This was the color of the latté served in Latté at the Library.

"Creme de cacao, that one is."

Gingerly unwrapping its furled little skirt, Agatha said, "I honestly think Martha's getting senile, serving up this sort of rubbish."

"I'll tell her from now on to serve the rubbish you're used to." Melrose turned back to his book. He was reading about Red Rum, the horse Jury had mentioned, a three-time Derby winner of old who had the distinction, when he died, of being buried in the winner's circle at Aintree. This was a fellow he'd have to remember. On the marquetry table beside his chair lay a small black leather notebook in which he set down this information.

Half of her light-brown muffin gone, Agatha said, "You've been writing in that thingamajig"—here she discounted the little notebook's usefulness with a gesture, waving it to its thingamajiggish grave—"ever since I came. It's quite rude of you, also, Melrose, but then you never were one to observe the social niceties."

"I didn't know that's what we were doing." He smiled down at Red Rum, making another note. He was really drawing Red Rum's tail, since his doing anything in the notebook irritated her so much. The recording of things to which she was not privy bothered her. Melrose had an actual insight there. He blinked. Perhaps Agatha deserved some sympathy if she was one of those people who were afraid that life would come crashing down if they didn't know everything that was going on around them. It was as if all sorts of rascally things might be taking place. (Just look at those muffins!)

"You're not, I hope, thinking of buying one?"

"Yes, as a matter of fact. Indeed, I think I'll have that

old stable brushed up and put in a riding ring and perhaps a racing course—"

"Good God!" The muffin half fell from her hand. "Surely you can't be seriously thinking of ruining these beautiful grounds!"

"They're not all that beautiful, as it happens. Momaday does nothing." Mr. Momaday had been taken on as a gardener, and he called himself a "groundskeeper." He did precious little of either, spending most of his time tramping around Ardry End's hundred acres, looking for something to shoot. Acres and acres of grass, weeds, wildflowers, deciduous trees, a few crumbling marble statues and a gone-to-ruin hermit's hut. Melrose could not imagine his father countenancing that. What he said was, "I'm also thinking of hiring a hermit for that hermitage out there—yonder." He loved this word.

"Are you talking about that old broken-down stone thing? Hire a hermit, indeed!"

"That's what people did in the nineteenth century. It was fashionable to have a hermit on one's grounds. I believe the Romantics went in for it."

"You're making it up, as usual." She poked a piece of muffin into her mouth.

"I swear it's true!" It was, too. He clamped a hand over his heart. "Hermits got to be collectors' items."

"I can tell you this: if a hermit comes, I go."

Melrose studied the ceiling.

She went on. "As to this horse business, I can just see you trotting around the village as if you were Master of Foxhounds."

Melrose tuned her out. Having squeezed whatever mileage he could out of horse and hermit, he went back to his book. It was one of several he had taken from the library. Ah! This was interesting. A Thoroughbred named Shergar had been kidnapped by the IRA and held for ransom. The ransom wasn't paid; the horse was never seen again, at least not in the UK. This was a strange little story, showing how much England valued its horses, or how little, depending on the way you looked at it.

Delighted to have found this entrée into horses and lost girls, Melrose snapped the book shut, gulped down his cold tea and stood. "I'm off, Agatha. Stay as long as you like."

"Off to where?"

"A number of places, including the library."

"Just an excuse to go to the Jack and Hammer."

Melrose raised his eyebrows in mock astonishment. "Since when did I need an excuse to go to the Jack and Hammer?"

His first stop really was the library, where he dropped off his books and went back to the shelves to look for fresh material. The horse books seemed geared largely to prepubescent girls, involving matters such as jumping and dressage. Nothing here on Thoroughbreds or racecourses.

On his way out, he stopped and said hello to Miss Twinny and asked her if she'd like to have a coffee with him, but she declined. "Oh, so nice of you, Mr. Plant, but I've got to get some books sorted before noon. Were these of any help?" She indicated the ones he'd left on the returns area of the front desk.

"Absolutely. I thought I might stop by the Wrenn's Nest and see if Mr. Browne has anything I could use." Melrose could have kicked himself when he saw the expression on Miss Twinny's face. Theo Wrenn Browne had tried to shut down the library, which would have cost Miss Twinny her job. It was Marshall Trueblood who had saved both library and librarian by talking her into setting up an espresso bar.

Melrose changed the subject by nodding toward that little café now. "Still going great guns, isn't it?"

She smiled. "It's quite wonderful, Mr. Plant. Do you know there are people coming over from Sidbury? Why, there are never enough tables to go around. I just might have to expand!" Delighted, she laughed.

"Horses? You want something on horses?" Theo Wrenn Browne looked as if he'd been broadsided.

Melrose was standing in the Wrenn's Nest Bookshop, stupefying its owner. Why did everyone find Melrose's interest in this animal so problematic?

"Yes" was all he answered.

"May I ask why?"

"You just have."

Silence while Theo Wrenn Browne tried to work this out.

Melrose started off. "Don't discommode yourself, Mr. Browne. I'll just wander through the stacks."

Theo quickly came out from his station by the money drawer and followed on Melrose's heels. "Mr. Plant, I'd be only too happy to help you."

The trouble with Theo Wrenn Browne was his capacity for being a sycophant on the one hand and, on the other, for sneering superiority. He was disliked by all of Melrose's circle—except Agatha, who found in Theo Wrenn Browne a compatriot, a fellow-traveler in malice. They had collaborated on the Chamber Pot Caper a few years before, in an attempt to close poor Miss Ada Crisp's secondhand furniture shop next door to the Wrenn's Nest. Following this had been the attempt to drive the library out of business. Marshall Trueblood's solution of opening the lattè and espresso bar had turned the library absolutely trendy. It had become a hot spot. That was Theo Wrenn Browne, a snake at worst, a weasel at best, as today he was weaseling after Melrose.

To demonstrate his interest in the hunt, Melrose pulled down a volume, largely of photographs of self-congratulation, to judge from the rubicund faces of the hunt members. The dogs were quite handsome, as were the horses; it took only a few humans to ruin the overall effect. The one with hounds churning at his feet was the master of hounds. He and the whipper-in were all wearing pink coats; all the others were in black coats or tweeds. Melrose smiled because (again except for horses and hounds) they all looked remarkably silly. He handed this book to Browne and pulled out another titled *Thoroughbred Racing: From Churchill Downs to Saratoga Springs.* These places were in the United States, but wouldn't a horse be a horse most any old where? And it would be good, too, letting the Ryder person know that he wasn't a dunce when it came to American racing, either. The book fell open at a two-page spread of the wondrous Secretariat. Even Melrose had heard of Secretariat. No wonder people loved to watch it, but imagine what it must be like to *do* it! Looking at the photographs of Secretariat racing round the course, Melrose thought it must be, for the jockey, a *Eureka!* Like Manet putting the last touch of light to a field of flowers, or Keats

upon seeing that Grecian urn or Lou Reed attacking his
guitar.

"What are you doing, Mr. Plant?" Browne broke into
Melrose's fantasy life.

"What? Oh, just practicing the cello. I was thinking it's
easy to understand why everyone loves horse racing."

Browne, finding an opportunity to rain on Melrose's pa-
rade, said, "Well, now, not everyone, Mr. Plant, not by a
long chalk."

"Oh?"

"Indeed not. Not your animal activists, no. And they're
getting more and more prevalent. There's a group over in
Sidbury who've done most unpleasant things. If you're
planning on drawing any of your horsey friends from there,
best be advised. There's a hunt tomorrow; you can go and
see for yourself."

Melrose had no friends in Sidbury, horsey or otherwise.

"There's an even bigger group in Northampton. They're
really organized, they are. You'll be harassed—don't think
you won't. They'll hound you right into the ground." Theo
covered his mouth with his hand, snorting with laughter.
"Oh, that's rich, now isn't it?" When Melrose didn't respond, he said it again: "Hound you," and he laughed. "If
you organize a hunt, they'll be certain to picket; they'll
stand by the sidelines and jeer."

"Jeering isn't a particularly efficient way to put paid to
anything. At least it wouldn't be for me; with me they'd
have to get physical—pull me off my horse."

"I certainly wouldn't put it past them, me."

The rhythm of Theo's speech often wound up back in
North London if he didn't keep an eye on it.

"Then what I need is a Glock, not a book."

On their way from the shelves to the front of the store,
they passed a window embrasure where three little children
were sitting, unsmiling and silent. Two of them Melrose
recognized as the Finch children, Bub and Sally, and although they must be a year or two older than when Melrose had last seen them in the bookshop, they still looked
three and six. The third child he couldn't recall seeing
around the village, but he probably weighed in at some age
between Bub and his sister. This child had a face so

crowded with freckles it looked as though some of them had fallen on his faded T-shirt and made spots. The three smiled at Melrose, rather pathetically. It was clear they were all hugely unhappy tots and were perhaps thinking that Melrose (their hero), having delivered them once from the dreaded bookseller, might be counted on to do it again. Melrose returned their smiles and noticed that the three were holding hands, as if for a comfort none could sustain if the hands were separated.

"Hello, there. It's Sally and Bub, isn't it? And could this be Patrick the Painted Pig?" He said this to the third child, another fallen into the clutches of Mr. Browne.

Theo immediately took the floor. "These kiddies, Mr. Plant, were back there defacing my books. They've been directed to sit right there until the book police come!" Roundly, Theo gave him an exaggerated wink, as if his clever fabrication would charm Melrose, who might form part of this conspiracy against the children.

Was the man crazy? Melrose had bailed both Sally and later Bub out of trouble. "Well, now, Sally and Bub and Patrick—" Here the second little boy blushed, but still looked pleased.

Sally chimed in, "He ain't Patrick. His name's Regis."

"Regis? Now there's a kingly name. Now, tell me what this is all about."

All three spoke up at once. No, all four did. Theo was the first one in with a version of "events." "They were tearing, *tearing* that book apart! Just malicious is what they are. I've a call in to Mrs. Finch but she hasn't returned it."

"Ah, then is Mrs. Finch with the book police?"

Giggles all round.

Melrose asked, "What happened?"

Sally burst out: "Me and Regis found this book and we both wanted it, so he was pulling on it and so was I." This was delivered in one spurt of breath.

Regis frowned mightily. "No, that ain't right. Me, I wasn't doing nuffin'. I was only holding on to the book."

Sally stuck out her tongue at Regis and whined, "Bub, here, though, he wasn't even near the old book!"

Melrose liked this standing up for her brother. He thought it quite noble in the circumstances. "All right, it's clear enough. You should be banished from Mr. Browne's shop." He turned to Theo. "Banishment is the only answer."

Banishment obviously appealed to the kiddies; they stood and dropped hands, ready to be banished. The hero had spoken.

"What they will have to do after this, if they want a book, is to go to the library."

The kids looked as if they'd be willing to march into hell, if it meant escaping from Theo Wrenn Browne.

But Theo was not at all happy with this solution, which was a perfectly logical one. Melrose knew he wouldn't be, of course, since he derived too much pleasure from abusing children. "Well, that's all well and good, but what about my book? Cost sixteen quid, that did, and someone's—" He stopped when he saw Melrose smile.

"Of course someone has to pay for it." He removed his money clip from his pocket and peeled off a twenty. "You can make the four-pound deduction from my books here." He patted them. "Now, you three must remember to tell Miss Twinny you'll be perfectly quiet in the library and will bring books back on time." He peeled a five-pound note from the wad and handed it to Sally, who gaped at it. "Give this to the lady in the café and tell her you're being treated to a lemonade or hot chocolate or whatever they have. You might tell her to keep the change for the next time."

Now all three were gaping. Not only were they not being punished for their behavior, they were actually being rewarded!

"Now, run along, and no more fighting over books."

They were off and out the door before Melrose had come to the end of his edict.

The Jack and Hammer was directly opposite the Wrenn's Nest. Melrose crossed the street after bidding good morning to Ada Crisp, who sometimes sat outside her second-hand furniture shop, sometimes with her Jack Russell terrier, but more often not, as the terrier's travel agenda took him all over the village. Miss Crisp sat among her china bowls and chamber pots, in a revenant light left over from autumn, rocking and waving at Melrose.

January and February, Melrose had decided, were the two most luckless and lackluster months on the calendar. It was difficult to get inspired (if one's bent was inspiration) by the ragged hem of a blown climbing rose around the Jack and Hammer's windows, or the faded turquoise coat of the Jack up on the beam, simulating bangs with his mallet to count the hours.

The inside, however, still retained a bit of New Year's cheer, largely because Dick Scroggs hadn't as yet taken down the lines of colored lights around the door or from the big mirror behind the bar. Melrose got Scroggs's attention—difficult, if Dick was buried in the paper—made a sign that he wanted a drink and walked through to where his comrades were seated round their table in the window. It was Trueblood's turn to get the seat with cushions, and there he comfortably sat, to the left of Joanna Lewes.

Diane Demorney blew out a thin stream of smoke and said, "We saw you coming out of Theo's. You know we said we were banning the place because of that library business."

Melrose sat down. "Did we? I thought we were already banning it just on general principles."

"We were going to make up placards and stand in front of the shop, I thought."

"Speaking of banning," said Melrose, "did you know there was a hunt in Sidbury?"

"For what?" asked Diane.

"A fox," said Trueblood, firing up a match to light a small cigar. "They organized it a year or two ago. Probably to protest the protest. You know, all of these country folk are scared to death their privilege will be taken away."

"According to Theo, there are a lot of animal-rights activists in Sidbury."

"Oh," said Diane, "those people who spray-paint fur coats. They sprayed my sable once, in front of Selfridge's."

"You're kidding! What did you do?" asked Joanna.

"Bought another one."

"I doubt," said Melrose, "that's how these people would want to be identified."

Joanna looked thoughtful. "Or maybe they would." Joanna was the author of some two dozen romance novels, which she had advised them all to steer clear of. ("Such drivel.") She went on: "Maybe their need for publicity is what motivates them, not animal rights."

Diane stepped in here. "If my cat had any more rights I'd be the one watching the bung hole nights and she'd be inside with brandy and a book." She turned to Joanna. "Your latest is quite good, Joanna." Upon Joanna's telling them all they'd be wasting their time with her books, Diane had started reading them.

"Thank you. I just don't think those are the rights they're defending, or say they are."

"How cynical," said Trueblood.

Joanna turned to Diane. "You should do a bit of investigative reporting there, Diane. You work for the Sidbury paper."

Diane "working" was an oxymoron. She was languor's home, ennui's back garden, apathy's arbor. However, she did indeed pen the astrology column for that paper—the daily horoscope. Diane was impeded by only two things: she couldn't write and she knew nothing about the stars. People loved the horoscope, though, for they believed it to be a tongue-in-cheek parody. Diane didn't know any more about parody than she did about writing or the stars. "You mean go to one of those things and say what they're doing?"

Diane had always been, generally speaking, a master of vagueness. Melrose said, "It's the activists I think Joanna is talking about."

Instead of an answer, Diane held out a cigarette for someone to light—God, if no one else was available. Trueblood lit it. She blew a narrow veil of smoke toward them and reflected on this reporting. It was rather restful watching Diane's mind at work. One never had to venture far and there were a lot of lay-bys along the way. "I suppose I could do." But her nose wrinkled at the thought as though a displeasing odor had wafted through the room.

"Do what?" asked Trueblood.

Diane heaved a sigh. "Go to a hunt. Haven't you been listening at all? Where is it?" she asked Melrose. "When is it?"

Melrose looked at his book jacket bearing the image of

an American Thorougbred named Spectacular Bid. What a name! "According to Theo, there's one tomorrow. Why don't we all go?"

"Excellent!" said Trueblood. "It's one of my half days, so I'll just close the shop."

"One of? How many half days do you allow yourself? There's only supposed to be one a week," said Melrose.

"Depends. This week it'll be three. Well, I've got a life to live, haven't I?"

They all looked at him.

"Very funny, very funny. So why don't we all go?"

Joanna said, "I'd love to, but I've got fifteen pages to write because I didn't do today's ten. I only did half."

"Your self-discipline is awesome," said Melrose.

"My self-discipline is no more nor less than my Barclays account. That's awesome."

This statement was made without a hint of conceit; indeed her implication was that her royalties were so far from being deserved it was pathetic.

"Okay, when shall we meet? Where?" said Melrose.

Trueblood said, "As to the when, I'd say eightish—"

"Eight is not an hour, it's pirate's treasure," said Diane.

"They start fairly early in the morning," said Trueblood.

Diane's smile was humorless. "They do; I don't."

"Nine, then."

Given Diane's expression, nine was only marginally better, but she agreed.

"And where? We can't do it here because it's closed till eleven. We'll meet next door. How's that?"

"Fine. Only what about this half-day business. If you leave at nine, that's more like a full day," said Melrose.

"Then I'll make up for it by staying all day the next day, as the next day is only a half day, too."

"That makes sense."

ELEVEN

"We should have signs," said Melrose, casting his eye over the courtyard of the country hotel appropriately named the Horse and Hounds. There was quite a crowd, an eclectic-looking bunch, from hunters in their pink coats and black hats to a rather seedy-looking elderly man with a piece of white posterboard hanging from a string around his neck that announced BEWARE THE HOUR DRAWS NIGH! Melrose wondered what it had to do with the hunt, or, indeed, the antihunt. Probably nothing, or no more than it had to do with the price of a pint in the Horse and Hounds. The hunt participants were up on horses, the restless hounds milling about, snuffling the brick and pebble-dashed courtyard as if they were looking for heroin, and the master was sniffily regarding the cup being handed him by one of the hotel staff.

Watching the cup being handed around, Melrose said, "It's rather like communion, isn't it? Passing the goblet down the line of the faithful at the altar. In any event, it's certainly ritual, no doubt of it."

"Of course," said Trueblood. "That's mostly what it's all about. Ritual, tradition, class. Always class these things turn out to be. A class war. You don't honestly think these people with their signs and slogans are interested in the fox's welfare?"

"I imagine they think they are. You can't generalize that way." Melrose thought the women looked haggard with their rough clothes and flyaway hair; the men looked better, more convivial, owing, perhaps, to one more round in the Horse and Hounds.

"We stick out like a sore thumb," said Marshall Trueblood.

"We do?" Melrose observed two of the protesters wearing fox kit and masks that covered the upper half of their faces, thus leaving their mouths free to hector the riders. LET'S RIP THE HUNT TO PIECES THE WAY YOU DO US read one of the placards. He felt that could have been better put.

Taken all in all, hounds and horses were definitely the best-looking gathered there. Diane, who was rooting about in a big black leather bag, said, "That's a spiffy-looking Master of Foxhounds, I'd say."

Trueblood said, "MFHs are always spiffy. I'd be spiffy, too, in one of those pink coats and up on that bay he's riding. It's all sex, anyway, isn't it? Sex, class, politics."

"Marshall, it's almost as if you'd given the matter some thought," said Diane in a God-forbid tone.

Hounds, horses, hunters set off down the road for some faraway field and everyone else more or less followed. When Melrose and Trueblood started off, Diane said, "Good Lord, you two. We're not going to follow on foot. We'll take the car."

Melrose was puzzled. "But, Diane, we won't be able to follow in a car unless there's a road that runs beside their route all the way. We'll lose them."

"No, we won't. You drive, Marshall." She handed him the keys to her car. "You drive so I'll be free to do this." She patted the leather bag slung over her shoulder.

"Do what? What is that?"

"Camcorder." She eased herself into the passenger's seat of the BMW. "You said I should do some investigative reporting, didn't you? Well, I'll need pictures."

They shrugged and got in the car, Melrose in the backseat.

"Just go straight down to the bottom of this road and then turn left."

Trueblood turned the key in the ignition and the motor purred into that sort of latent life reserved for BMWs, Jaguars, Porsches and Bentleys. Trueblood accelerated and its purr was a trifle louder, but still a purr. "Nice car, Diane."

"You should get one." They drove down the road, turned left and Diane directed, "A little way on and bear to the right—here."

Melrose leaned on the back of the passenger seat, and said, "Diane, you seem to know where we're going."

"Of course. Do you think I'd be out here driving aimlessly if I could be inside the saloon bar at the Horse and Hounds? Here—" She handed Melrose a smallish roll of paper.

He unrolled it to find a nicely detailed map of the route the hunt was taking, showing the local roads that ran near it, the places that one could get out of the car and see it. "This is terrific, Diane. But wouldn't the hunt be all over the map? Can you predict where the fox will go? Where'd you get it?"

"From Eugenie St. Cyr-Jones. She seems to think the route is fairly predictable."

"St. Cyr-Jones? Do we know her?"

"No. She's the local organizer against FOX. That's Friends of Xavier."

"Who's that? A saint? A cult figure?"

"It's the fox."

"Xavier? No," said Melrose, "the fox is called Reynard."

"Well, you can't have FOR as your slogan. People wouldn't know what it referred to. We'll see Eugenie St. Cyr-Jones at"—Diane took back the map, ran a red fingernail over the route and stopped—"here, at the low stone wall."

It put Melrose more in mind of Cluedo than an actual place. *Go to the low stone wall.* "But why are we meeting this St. Cyr-Jones woman?"

"For the interview. I thought it would best be done in the field. That way you see the hunt run by behind her. Or something like that."

"You've a finely developed aesthetic sense, Diane."

"Thanks. But actually, I just wanted to get one of these maps out of her, so I had to tell her I'd interview her. Who knows? It might be amusing."

Diane's highest priority. "Diane, you surprise me. You're shifty. Devious."

"I've always been devious."

"*There they are!* View hal-looooo! Isn't that what they yell?" Trueblood pulled the car over and they got out.

Hounds, and behind them horses were pouring over a stone wall, almost as one. Melrose could understand how country people could come all over John Peel-ish at the sight. He had forgotten what a visceral thrill the sight of pink coats and sleek horses could give one.

Diane didn't get the camcorder going until they were a field away, whereupon they all got back in the car and followed the hunt for another quarter mile. Melrose yelled, "We just passed a group of people by a low stone wall."

"Back up, Marshall."

Trueblood reversed and stopped.

"That's Eugenie," said Diane, climbing out of the car. Then she turned back and dropped the leather bag from her shoulder and handed it to Trueblood.

"I've never worked one of these things."

"It's simple." She removed it from the bag and pointed to a couple of buttons. "You just press this, then this. It just keeps rolling until you stop it, here."

Trueblood shrugged, then put the camcorder on his shoulder and walked a little away. He began to feel quite the investigative photographer.

Eugenie St. Cyr-Jones was a large, stout woman in her early seventies. She was wearing a gray worsted suit of good cut, partially hidden by the white placard hanging around her neck, shouting its ambiguous message: HUNT IN, GOVERNMENT OUT! The woman beside her was introduced as Clarice St. John-Sims, and she was Eugenie St. Cyr-Jones's diminutive opposite. She seemed to be there to take up the slack. Of what, Melrose couldn't say. It must have been the names that provided the attraction between them, for he could see nothing else to explain it. Diane might have been the only person around who could have introduced the two of them ("Eugenie St. Cyr-Jones and Clarice St. John-Sims") without even blinking. Diane was good at things like that, bits of useless—but accurately reported—information.

Eugenie St. Cyr-Jones looked as if she spent most of her days in a state of high dudgeon, which probably made her a good candidate for protesting the protest. Diane had a tape recorder going and up to Eugenie's stormy face, a face that told the tale of many past protests.

While Trueblood moved the camcorder around to take in the scene, Diane suggested that Miss St. Cyr-Jones say a few words about her purpose in being here.

Eugenie St. Cyr-Jones had many more than a few words to say. "*Should* our government make the *criminal* error of trying to ban foxhunting they should be aware they'll have a real battle on their hands. To pass such a bill would be to threaten the very *livelihood* of the country. People fail to see beyond the spectacle itself to the repercussions of such government interference. The antihunting contingent—" Here she waved her arm around a group that was steadily forming, hoping no doubt (as were hounds) that blood would be let before the morning was over.

The antihunting contingent stepped in, in the person of a boisterous middle-aged woman. "Spectacle! That's all 'tis, just a bunch of country clowns huntin' a poor animal to its bloody end." Her hair looked fried in a pan, flat on top, frizzled on the sides.

Trueblood positioned his camera close up and then back to take in the entire group before his attention was caught by the promise of a melee out in the field. He moved in that direction.

The woman with the fried hair addressed Diane. "You ast'er this, ast'er 'ow she'd feel gettin' tore up by a pack o' them 'ounds! Ast'er!"

Diane smiled. "As you already have—" and looked at Eugenie St. Cyr-Jones.

Eugenie was clearly revolted by this person. "That's so *clearly* a loaded argument. Listen to me: in Sidbury there's a saddlery that employs a number of the local townspeople. It's the way they earn their living. Now, how long would that business last—and that's but one example—if the hunt was banned?"

Several of the onlookers exchanged words that Trueblood was hoping would turn into blows, but for the moment quieted down. He heard another commotion in the field, or the same one exacerbated. He turned to see that hounds were swarming. Had they homed in on the benighted Xavier? No, no, a horse must have caught its leg flying over the stone wall and gone down. Several black coats dismounted. Trueblood hoped the horse was all right; he didn't care much about the rider. The horse rose and shook itself and wandered away, unattended by the rider for the rider and another hunt member seemed to be shouting. Trueblood pointed the camera in that direction. Now the pink-coated MFH unhorsed himself and moved quickly to this little nucleus of persons, ostensibly to quell the fight.

Horses, the most sensible of the lot, left to their own devices moved about in search of some tasty grazing place.

Trueblood loved it! There were the hounds roving off, snuffling the ground, mixing in and out between legs of horses and hunters, all of them having a rave-up, hounds and hunters alike. The horses quite sensibly ignored them.

How often had this sort of thing happened during a hunt? Never, he bet. It was a scoop! Behind him—and now he turned the camcorder back to the protesters—a well-dressed, sensible-looking man interrupted the woman with the fried hair.

"Naturally, one doesn't enjoy the spectacle of a fox thrown to hounds, but what sticks in my throat is the sheer hypocrisy of some of your hunting-ban travelers. Some of them aren't even charities, though they want you to believe they are."

A theoretical argument. Who cares? Trueblood turned the camera off toward the right. Wonderful! Fists were flying! The master appeared now to be acting as referee. Oh, good! Someone in the group actually pushed him! Shouting! The rest of the hunt had dismounted now—their steeds making for the spot where their fellow horses were nibbling the frosty grass.

Hearing raised voices at his back, Trueblood turned around to get a look at the civilians, who appeared to be sheering off and scattering. Diane and Melrose were waving him toward the car.

"I got it all! Did you see it? The melee?"

"What melee in particular?" asked Melrose as he got in the car. "There seemed to be so many melees. But that bit was interesting, wasn't it, about some of these groups' advertising themselves as charities when they were really moneymaking concerns?"

"A documentary!" said Trueblood, starting the car. "I'm entering it for the BAFTA awards."

Diane stabbed a cigarette into her black holder. "They're so tiresome, aren't they, these do-gooders, these protesters?" She sighed and turned so that Melrose could light the cigarette. Then she said, "It's all a bit of a shambles, isn't it?"

"Causes," said Melrose. "There's something really off-putting about causes."

Trueblood nodded. "There's something absolutely *absurd* about this marching and meeting and arguing and brawling."

"If things start going wrong," said Diane, "I agree with that writer—what's his name? Raymond . . . Hammett? No, Dash something—"

"Dashiell Chandler?" offered Melrose. "Or it could be Raymond Chandler and Dashiell Hammett? Anyway, you agree with what one of the three said. What was that?"

"Bring in a man with a gun."

TWELVE

Maurice had thought about her disappearance until thought seemed to liquefy and then evaporate, as if his brain could take only so much. He was sitting at Arthur Ryder's big desk in the library, moving the leather swivel chair a half circle one way, a half circle the other. In his hand was the silver-framed photo of Nell, posed beside Samarkand. It was taken just before she disappeared. Fifteen years old. Was she as carefree as she looked in this picture? Was he?

He did not know his grandfather had entered the room until he spoke: "Maurice."

"Oh, hi, Granddad." Maurice set the silver frame back on his grandfather's desk.

"You never stop, do you, son?" Arthur's voice was as quiet as moths beating against a blind and his expression just as futile.

To Maurice, his grandfather sounded very tired. He said so. "You should slow down."

Arthur Ryder slumped into the big leather chair beside his desk and gave a short laugh. "Maurice, if I slowed down any more I'd be in a coma."

"Oh, sure. Right."

"It's all this whittling." Arthur smiled and put his pocket-knife on the desk along with the small piece of wood he'd been working on.

Maurice picked it up, turned it. "What is it?"

"Nothing. Absolutely nothing. That's what I aim for."

Maurice ran his thumb over the side. "But it's such a good nothing. The design is good."

Arthur laughed more heartily than he had before. "Maurice, I swear you're the only sixteen-year-old diplomat I know." Then Arthur thought, truly bloody kind, Maurice is. But kindness has a price; it makes a person thin skinned, empathy does.

"It's just nerves," said Arthur, inclining his head toward the bit of wood. "Just a nervous habit." Not quite true. It gave him something to look at other than the eyes of the person he was talking to. He found it difficult to look people in the eyes. Not Maurice, of course, and not Vernon. But others. It's like cats, isn't it? If they look you in the eyes and blink, doesn't it mean they trust you? Arthur did very little blinking; he just whittled away, blew the sawdust and tiny bits off the knife and the wood.

The phone rang and he picked it up, listened and said to Maurice, "Give me that stud book; it's on that first shelf. Thanks." Arthur flipped to the last page on which were written names and dates, and said, "If it's just the one time, you can have On Your Mark, . . . that's a hundred thousand, one-twenty-five if you want a guaranteed foal. . . . No. Samarkand? Of course not, Colin. He needs a rest." Arthur chuckled. "Maybe you and I don't, but then we didn't spend ten years of our lives in the winner's circle, did we? . . . No, I don't mean you'd get On Your Mark for just the one time; of course you can try two or three times. Like taking your coffee back for a refill. . . . Hell, Colin, of course it's a lot of money; you talk as if you'd never done this before. I know it's a lot of money, you also know On Your Mark won the 2000, the St. Leger, the Derby and a lot of other races here and in France." This was said without a trace of rancor. After a few more exchanges, Arthur rang off.

"Colin Biers would have all of the stallions in my stables lined up for a crack at his mare to make sure he got another Honorbound." He leaned his head against the back of the chair and studied the ceiling. "I wonder what it would take to make another one." Arthur thought of that wondrous horse who not only had won every high-stakes race he'd been entered in, but who also had one of the mildest temperaments imaginable. Everyone loved Honorbound. The horse stood at Cavalier Farm, whose trainer, Keegan, would complain loudly to Charlie Davison that Truitt (who owned Cavalier) was making money hand over fist from Honorbound's seasons. "Works the horse to bloody death, the bastard" is what Keegan had said to Arthur many times. He was getting two hundred thousand per season and selling seasons to more than eighty or ninety applicants. The man was raking in millions. "The greedy bastard," said Keegan. "One of the greatest Thoroughbreds to run the course and that bastard has him mating with eighty mares a season. That horse," said Keegan, "could tell me anything I wanted to know about handling him right. Maybe he was training me, instead of my training him. He was a regular horse whisperer. All I had to do was keep my ears open." Keegan had kept asking Arthur Ryder to talk to Truitt, get him to see reason, to cut back on Honorbound's seasons.

"You did," said Maurice. "How?"

"It wasn't hard; it was simple, really. I told him he'd be flooding the market with Honorbound foals. We'd already seen some of the best, like Lillywhite, and all winners of stakes races, two of them won the Derby. Honorbound's worth his weight in gold. I expect he's smart to have that stall fitted out with a smoke detector, a fire detector and that thing that measures a rise in heat. To say nothing of the sprinkler system. Most elaborate I've ever seen. The stud fee went up to a quarter million. Vernon has talked about it enough, the money in selling seasons and shares. Reason tells you that the fewer foals, the more valuable each is; the more, the less valuable. It's supply and demand, that's all. Money's the only language Truitt understands." Arthur smiled. "Vern wanted to do it himself; he loves talking about money."

"You don't think Vernon's like that, do you?"

Arthur laughed. "Oh, God, no."

"Did Dad ever ride Honorbound?" He knew the answer; he just liked to talk about his father.

"Rode him at Ainslee. Truitt always tried to get Danny away from me, the twerp. Even though Danny was my own son. Truitt and Anderson, two of a kind."

"What was Dad's favorite ride?"

Arthur thought for a moment. "I think it depended on the race. Beautiful Dreamer, when he rode him in the 2000. Then Aqueduct in the Grand National. I'll never forget that race. There's never been a horse more relentless than Aqueduct. Watching him over those hurdles was like watching lava pour over rocks."

Maurice had propped his chin in his hands, listening. Ordinarily, his grandfather was a taciturn man, but that was because of Danny's death and Nell's disappearance.

Out of the blue, Arthur said, "Did you know Vernon hired a private investigator to look for Nell?"

"No." Maurice frowned.

Arthur nodded. "Vern's kept him at it for a year and a half. As far as I know, he's still at it. The man talked to people at every horse farm in Cambridgeshire, I think. Didn't get a hell of a lot of cooperation, but he tried. At Anderson's he had to palm himself off as an insurance investigator so he could get a look at the stables."

Maurice was thoughtful for a while, then said, "I'm going to London to see Vernon." He stood up.

"You mean *now*?"

"Yes, I think I will."

"It's been nearly two years, Maurice—don't forget."

"How could I forget, Granddad?"

It took only an hour from Cambridge to Paddington and another three quarters of an hour on the Circle Line to the City. He could have driven one of the farm's cars. His granddad never gave him a hard time about that and, consequently, Maurice didn't feel he had to prove he was capable of driving in London. He wasn't. A lot of people felt incapable of driving in London.

Vernon Rice worked in the City. Vernon probably wouldn't call it work, not what he did. "I sit around making things up. Daydreaming, you could call it."

"What sorts of things?"

"New companies. I look around and see what isn't and then bring it into being."

"Sounds like God."

They both laughed. This made Maurice feel exceptionally

good—that he could make Vernon laugh so hard—because he thought Vernon was really cool, and he liked the idea he could provoke such laughter.

He liked the office. It had a clean, uncluttered look, a lot of chrome, a lot of glass, Eames chairs and tables, an unburdened place.

Maurice liked the receptionist, too. Or secretary, he wasn't sure which. She was good-looking and sleek like the office. He had little experience of designer clothes, but he bet the dark-gray suit didn't come from Debenhams. She had smooth dark hair, an ivory complexion and didn't bother with costume jewelry; the only piece she wore was her watch, a thin curve that seemed to float on her wrist. He did not mind sitting here and looking at her and at this anteroom until Vernon was off the telephone. He sighed. It looked like a glamorous life he led. Maurice would have envied him like hell if there had been horses in it. But as there weren't, Maurice didn't think Vernon all that fortunate. Glamorous, maybe, but, in this one way, unfortunate. Maurice couldn't imagine life without Samarkand and Criminal Type and Beautiful Dreamer. He supposed that was what some people meant by something's being in your blood.

"He's off the phone," said Samantha, smiling.

But before she could get up to show Maurice in, Vernon had opened the door to his office. "Maurice! For God's sake, what are you doing in this horseless city? Come on in."

Maurice blushed a little. He usually did in the first few moments of meeting Vernon. It was probably because he felt somewhat clumsy and awkward.

"When was the last time you were ever in London? You don't like the place—go on, sit down." Vernon indicated one of the chrome and leather chairs. "Can you stay for dinner? My favorite restaurant's in South Ken. Ever been to Aubergine?"

Maurice smiled and shook his head. It was like Vernon to treat him as a crony, not as some kid of sixteen. As if he, Maurice, were a fellow traveler in the seeking out of three-star restaurants. "The only one I've been to is the Angus Steakhouse. Don't go."

"Glad you dropped me the tip. Speaking of tips, I can put you into a great fund that's paying eighteen and a half percent and is going public anytime now." Vernon checked his watch in case that time might be passing before his eyes and out the door. "Better still, and more up your alley, you can buy five or ten percent of a syndicate for a great horse—"

Maurice held up his hands, palms out as if backing away. "You're kidding, aren't you, Vern? You know I don't have any money."

Vernon gave him a disbelieving look. "Money? Who said money? You buy short and wait—"

He was interrupted by Bobby, who came in, said hello to Maurice, dropped a paper onto Vernon's desk, said good-bye and walked out.

Vernon said, "Bobby's only twenty-two, he's been here since he was eighteen and he's already made himself a small fortune. If you ever need a break from the horses . . ."

"Can you imagine me doing this?" Then he was worried he might be insulting Vernon and his offer. "What I mean is—"

"Can you imagine him"—Vernon nodded toward the door through which Bobby had lately gone—"who ran into me when he was on a skateboard? He started talking about hedge funds and mergers. He talked about stock in a new company I hadn't even got reports on. I hired him."

Maurice was surprised at his own reaction to this talk about Bobby. He was jealous. He must see Vernon as an older brother, which he was—a stepbrother. But that didn't count as much as Vernon hadn't come on the scene until he was thirty-two or -three. Maybe Vernon had always thought of Maurice as a younger brother. Still, it was odd that Vernon, a relative stranger, coming in from the outside, and in so few years, could lay claim to family feeling. Maurice realized now how rich his life had been before his father's death, before Nell's disappearance.

"Why is it I get the impression you're not thinking about syndicating your horses?"

"Oh, sorry. I was just thinking about Dad. And—" Maurice looked at his shoes; they seemed to be falling apart.

"Nell," said Vernon.

Maurice looked up quickly. "How'd you know?"

"What else is there to think about?"

If Maurice hadn't known about Leon Stone, he would have been surprised by this statement and by Vernon's intensity. "You're really serious about finding her. Granddad told me about the private detective you had looking for her."

Vernon nodded. He seemed to have lost his earlier buoyancy; he looked older by several years.

"You really care about Nell."

Again, Vernon nodded. "I do." He smiled. "Come on, let's have dinner. You can stay the night at my place. I'll tell the girls to go."

"Not all of them, I hope." Maurice was back to feeling comfortable now. And he wondered why Vernon had never married.

Did he always tell the girls to go?

"She's not dead," said Vernon, after a considering silence, in answer to Maurice's question.

"Why are you so sure?"

Over a plate of his favorite duck in Aubergine, Vernon studied him, or seemed to; he could as well be studying the banquette behind Maurice or the air around him. "Because it doesn't feel like it. Does it to you?"

Maurice did not know how to answer this. He seemed at the moment to be out of touch with his feelings, as if they had retreated at Vernon's question. "Well . . . I can't believe it. I can't believe she's gone forever, if that's what you mean."

"Not exactly." Vernon speared a bite of roast potato. "Hard to explain."

Maurice smiled. "It just sounds kind of mystical, I mean, coming from you."

"Me, the chaser of the almighty pound, dollar, yen and deutsche mark?"

Maurice colored slightly. "No, no. Well . . . only in a way. You seem so grounded, so, ah, practical."

"Money's a by-product, Maury. Not that I'm indifferent to it, God, no. Without money I couldn't eat here every week. But it's not what keeps me going back to the table. What attracts me to the market is its craziness, its unpredictability. The whole thing's a game where you can win big or lose your shirt. All of these market analysts—if they were sure of their own predictions, why in hell would they be telling people? They'd be out there, buying and selling themselves. No, if I wasn't in this business, I'd be a compulsive gambler."

"As in poker? Remember those games we played? Nell always won."

"She's got a winning mind."

The waiter came to pour more wine. The service here was so perfect that the diner was only partly aware of the waiters' presence, as if they drifted in and out like dream images.

"This Leon Stone, Vernon, what does he think happened? I mean, didn't he come up with some kind of answer to how whoever did it knew Nell would be in the stable?"

"Not really." Vernon shrugged. "He did wonder if there'd be reason for someone in the family to stage this abduction. But what could possibly be the motive? Even assuming someone could be that cold-blooded, the motive wasn't money, obviously. No. Stone thinks that whoever came didn't know Nell would be there. Stone thinks he— for he's pretty certain there was only one person—came to take one or more of the horses: Samarkand, Beautiful Dreamer or Aqueduct. Nell woke up and heard him, then saw him. She was a danger to him, so he took her with him."

"He thinks the person came for the *horse*?"

Vernon nodded. He shoved back his empty plate and crossed his arms on the table. "Listen, Maury: in what I do, you have to be able to imagine very strange things. Take what I mentioned earlier: you think the stock of some given company is going down, down, down. You sell short, meaning you borrow shares from another account, believing you'll make money when the stock plummets and you'll be able to replace the borrowed shares with the ones you bought at a lower price. That's strange, isn't it? Hard to imagine? You're not even using your own money. It's all on paper."

"So what you're saying is you have to think of weird possibilities."

"I can suggest one: she wants to stay at this place."

Maurice's mouth dropped open. "Wants to stay? Wants to? How could she possibly—"

"Think something was more important than you?"

Maurice colored deeply. "I don't mean—"

"Why not? You're her best friend, after all. Anything that would keep Nellie away from the stud farm would have to be powerful."

Maurice poked his steak around, still smarting from Vernon's idea. "Next you're going to say she fell in love with her captors."

Vernon spread his arms. "The Stockholm syndrome. You're catching on."

Irritated, Maurice stabbed at his steak. "You mean kidnap victims have actually done that?"

Vernon nodded. "It's happened."

"Come on, Vernon. Why not go with the most logical, reasonable answer? She's dead." He looked across the table. Of course he didn't want Vernon to accept that answer. He wanted Vernon to convince him there was another answer. Any other answer. Any other.

"The thing is, Maury, people don't respond logically or reasonably most of the time. I mean it. Hell, look at what I do for a living—"

But Maurice was following his former train of thought. "Don't tell me that in a year and a half, she couldn't have escaped." He felt angry now, angry not so much at Vernon as at Nell.

"I'm not telling you. That's what I've been saying: maybe she didn't want to."

"But why?"

"I don't know. Only, remember, they had Aqueduct."

"You're not saying she'd stay on account of a horse?"

"I don't know, Maurice. Nellie had an incredibly strong bond with those horses."

There was a silence.

"The last time I saw her, she was fifteen," said Vernon. "She's seventeen now and, damn it, I want to see her again."

"We may never see her again."

Vernon shook his head. "No. She'll walk in someday. You'll turn around and she'll be there." He reached across the table and put his hand on Maurice's arm. "You'll see. She'll just walk in."

Night Rider

THIRTEEN

The girl adjusted the rifle across her back, held in a sling she had made from a leather belt. She needed to keep her hands free and the sling made it less tiring. She had taken the gun from the mudroom where they parked their guns like umbrellas. They were careless; they didn't always lock them up, which she knew was breaking the law. She'd taken the rifle over a month ago on the night she'd finally decided to get out.

No surveillance is constant; no one's guard is always up. They didn't seem to have learned this: that the brief moments in which one walks to the other end of the barn or path or court, the careless absence for a cigarette or a coffee and, of course, the overconfidence that lets you relax your vigil and leave the torch forgotten on a chair. Any of those things would result in failure, would permit the jewels to be snatched, the safe cracked, the horse gone. Those things, plus faulty reasoning; that after the first horse was stolen, the belief that the thieves wouldn't come again, at least not again so soon.

But they had come the very next night, before there was time for the owner in the big rambling house to draw breath, much less to get surveillance in place. Now there were two guards, one to watch over the Thoroughbreds, one to guard the barns where the mares were kept. It had taken the owner a while, taken the third theft to alert everyone to the possibility that the Thoroughbreds weren't the target. That wasn't as dumb as it sounded since these mares would be of no value to anyone.

From the deep shadows of an empty stall, she watched the guard, an overweight, cigarette-puffing man who paid less attention than he should have. She'd been watching for an hour, waiting for him to leave his post. He did. He rose from his stool outside the stall, yawned, scratched his lower back. She knew his habits by now. He was a smoker and, as there was a rule against smoking here in the barn, he had gone down to the end and stepped just outside. He took the torch with him in case the lights should fail; they'd had a way of doing that lately.

She was dressed in black—black jeans, black windbreaker, gloves, boots, everything. Around her head she wore a dark scarf to hide her pale hair, so pale it was almost the color of the moon and might glimmer if it wasn't covered. In this costume, she couldn't have found herself in the dark. That thought was rueful.

She had been coming here also on nights besides the ones in which she took the mares; she needed to study the effects of the surveillance, the habits of the two guards. It was almost easier with the two of them because they kept each other occupied. They liked to talk, to joke around. This was funny. Instead of increasing the watch over the horses, the owner had actually diminished it.

One guard for each barn, but not one for each end. The thinking would be that it wasn't a diamond necklace the thieves were after, but horses, and a horse moving about made noise.

That's why it had taken her ten months, working with them nearly every day, to get the mares used to her and her touch, and different touches sent different directions to them. The important thing was to get them to move silently. They were so unused to moving at all and even the small amount of freedom Nell had bartered for did little to make them active, for most of them couldn't recall what freedom was like. There was little recollection, though, as nearly all of them had been foals of mares held in the same captivity, and they had been among the few chosen to take the place of the mares that died. That was how it worked. That was probably the way hell worked, too. So for ten months, during the time she was allowed to unfasten the rubber cups and take them for exercise, she had tried to school them in backing out of their stalls in silence and to move in silence. They were given only three signs to learn: her hand on the muzzle meant silence when they moved around; a touch on the right shoulder meant a turn to the right; on the left shoulder, to the left. It did not take the horses long to get used to these signals; the hard thing was that there were sixty horses to teach it to. But she managed with most of them.

It didn't matter if the men—the stable lads, the groom, the trainer, Mr. Mackay—who worked there saw her with the mares because they'd have no idea there was a grim plan behind her quiet treatment. Mr. Mackay and Kenny, the head stable lad, thought her exercising these horses was ridiculous and liked to tell her so. Nell thought Mr. Mackay should never have been let within a hundred miles of a horse. If she saw him take that whip to Aqueduct, she'd kill him. Her horse was not mistreated, was treated fairly well, actually, because they used him for stud. But she wondered why, since Aqueduct's real name obviously couldn't be put down in the book.

What surprised Nell was that, apparently, no one employed here talked about the mares off the premises. At least Bosworth, the assistant trainer, had told her it was worth their jobs talking about it.

"How in hell," Bosworth said, "you talked that woman into letting you take care of those mares I can't imagine." He seemed to enjoy it, though.

"I bargained."

"*You* bargained?" Bosworth laughed. "Well, Val Hobbs is the one holding the cards. What in hell did you have to call her hand?"

"My freedom."

He looked astonished. "*Freedom?* Love, the last I saw you didn't have any more freedom than those benighted mares do."

"But I could get out of here without much effort. No matter how much all of you are supposed to be watching me. After a year and a half—well, you can't watch all the time. She knows that. I could run."

Bosworth thought this over. "Guess you could at that. Surprised you haven't."

"That's what I bargained with—not running."

"And she believed that?"

"Why not? It's true." At least it had been for nearly twenty months.

It had taken her weeks to make the stables habitable. How had the mares stood it? Horses were fastidious creatures, like cats. They had stood it because they had had no choice. The smell was almost overpowering, or would have been to anyone who had never mucked out a stable. This was much worse. And mucking out was done on a daily basis, often twice a day, even more. It was done for the comfort and health of the horses, not to make the environment more pleasant for the humans; it was done as part of their care. The floor was cement rather than earth, not a good standing for a horse, but easier to clean, and still they often stood in their own feces.

On that morning she had first found them, Nell walked up the line of narrow stalls. There was barely room for a person to squeeze in next to the horse, to shove in between the horse and the insubstantial wooden partitions on both sides, shoulder high to the horse. There were two rows, fifteen horses in a row in these constricting stalls, thirty altogether and thirty in the barn beside this one. A rope was attached to the rear leg of each mare and when she peered into the shadows of each stall, she saw another rope anchoring one of the front legs—opposite rear and front legs, which meant the horse couldn't move more than a few inches forward or backward. Each mare had a rubber cup attached to its hind quarters. Nell crouched, keeping to one side, and looked at the hose that led from the cup to a container. The cup and hose were there to gather urine. Urine, for God's sake.

The horses weren't important in themselves; they were important in foaling, or, rather, in staying pregnant. If a mare had a hard time doing this, she was taken away. Nell didn't ask what happened to these horses. The little that she knew was bad enough. So they were kept for the urine that collected under them in plastic bags. She didn't understand that, either.

"Why are they kept like this? Why don't they get any

exercise?'' she had asked Mr. Mackay. It was hard standing up to him; he took as blame any question you put to him. He was the meanest man she'd ever come across. He was in charge of the stable lads and was no nicer to them. The lads, though, had the huge advantage of knowing these people and knowing why they were here. And getting paid for it.

"You ask too many questions."

She had also asked her questions of Bosworth, the assistant trainer, who she'd discovered over a period of time did not like this place and did not like the people who ran it. Consequently, he was more likely to be sympathetic to any criticism of them or questioning of the rules.

"Exercise? They're only here to pee and stay pregnant, the sorry beasts."

It was known that Bosworth was father to two dreadful boys who were in and out of the nick and, therefore, did sympathize with anyone forced to bring another creature into the world and have to put up with him.

The only exercise the mares ever got was when they were led into the breeding arena. Led there and back. As far as she could tell, that was their life, as Bosworth had said it was. Some of them, such as Belle and Jenny, looked exhausted. They were the oldest, the ones who had foaled most, and she despaired that they were undoubtedly looking death in the eye.

On those mornings or afternoons Mackay was off out of sight of the house she led each one out, one at a time, to a bit of pasture that was hidden from view by a tall, boxy hedge. They stood, the mares did. They stood and watched her in perfect silence.

"You don't have to just stand there, Belle. You can walk around, you can even run around."

But Belle didn't move. Like the others, she was too wedded to her little space. And that, Nell realized, was how she herself had felt until they'd finally permitted her to go outside. Belle du Jour. Nell had named them all. So that she could remember the names, she'd drawn a diagram of the stalls and set down the name of the mare who occupied each of them. Marie had been the first she'd taken. Marie was one of the mares at the rear where the big doorway opened on to the stand of birches and was more secluded than the front. Anyway, the guards stood at the front. She had named the mares either with names or words she especially liked. She felt that these good names would make the mares feel good for something other than foaling. All of this was before she'd made her bargain with Mrs. Hobbs. Had she been caught letting them out, she'd get hell. Later on she got hell for giving them water. (*"No bloody water, you hear me? They're only allowed a certain amount, at certain times,"* Valerie Hobbs had said, tensely.)

Yet she was never caught letting the horses out for a few minutes. Since only she was interested in the mares, only she went to the stables, except of course when one of them foaled.

At first she thought the foals must be the object. She knew Aqueduct was being used to cover several mares, and that must be why they'd wanted him. But it wasn't the foals that were important, she discovered. Most of the time they were taken away, two, maybe three at a time, a big horsebox backed up to the barn and the foals loaded in. For the poor mares, the foals were the only particle of real life they experienced, the only hint that they were not machines. Once in a while, though, a foal was left with its mother, left until it could take her place and live the same life from foal to yearling to its first visit to the breeding arena, and the whole thing start all over again.

Yet the farm did have outstanding Thoroughbreds who'd won big purses. So why were they not the ones used for stud? Again, Bosworth had told her. "Because they're not worth it, these mares. They're not here for their bloodlines. I told you: it's the urine."

"Is it illegal, what they're doing?"

At that, he laughed. " 'Illegal' wouldn't stop her." He looked off to the house.

"She's not a bad woman," said Nell, who felt a reluctant kinship with Valerie Hobbs, or perhaps it was an odd empathy—the woman's scatterbrained and uneasy alliance with the business end of things. (*"If I didn't have an accountant, I'd never turn a profit."*) And perhaps because Nell detected in Valerie Hobbs a heart that had taken a terrible beating and a trustworthiness she simply couldn't explain. Why should Nell trust her?

Nell held out a colored folder. "What's this?"

Bosworth brought his glasses down from their station on top of his head and looked and turned the thing over, front to back, in his hands. He shrugged. "Probably has to do with those mares." He shrugged. "Where'd you get it?"

This time Nell shrugged. "I just found it." She could feel Bosworth looking at her.

"Sure," he said.

There was a room off the kitchen that Valerie kept locked. Nell had noticed the closed door a number of times and wondered what was in the room. This morning, the key had been left in the door. Valerie was absentminded; she was always looking for keys, wallets, even her Wellies. Nell turned it, went in and saw nothing spectacular, even particularly interesting. Indeed, it looked much like her granddad's office, only smaller. There were photos tacked on the wall (horses, mostly), a largish desk, breeder's books. Nell leafed through one, looked to see how Go for the Gold was performing (very well), returned that to its place and moved to the desk, awash in papers: bank accounts, articles downloaded from the PC on the desk, bills, stationery and printed literature—folders, brochures—such as the ones she'd picked up.

The one she had shown Bosworth dealt with a drug which would offset many of the problems and symptoms of menopause. It pictured a woman looking supremely happy, ostensibly because she didn't have to worry about hot flashes, not if she took this drug. The company was an American one: Wyeth-Ayerst Laboratories. The drug was Premarin. *Premarin.* Mare's urine. Pregnant mare's urine.

Nell ran her finger along a row of dark-green ledgers, yanked one out, not knowing whether it would be helpful. It wasn't—nothing but rows of expenditures on feed and equipment, money paid out to vets, farriers, trainers, stable lads. Routine accounts. She put it back, pulled out another. This one was a record of the mares—their dates of acquisition, many of them having been here for as long as four years. Four years of living like this. Recorded also were histories of pregnancies, foals born, foals removed for slaughter, rates of "production" of urine. Mares whose production was low or who were too difficult to impregnate also were sent to slaughter.

She forgot she shouldn't be in this room; she forgot the room itself as she stared at nothing, the room, its furnishings, photos, windows replaced by the memory of that big horse van pulled up to the farthest barn and as she watched three foals and one mare were loaded onto it. They were going to slaughter because the stud farm had no use for them. That's all. Was there someone here rotten enough to do all of this? Yes, and he had walked up those attic steps a dozen times.

It was then, right then that she knew she'd have to do something, but had no idea how to do it.

Her opportunity had come when this farm and two others some miles away received threats. The letters had directed them to pay fifty thousand pounds or horses would be harmed. She had waited until the third night after the letter had appeared. That night she had stolen one of the mares, Marie, whose heart had not been destroyed by her imprisonment and who was only too glad to gallop, when the terrain permitted, away to the new place.

Then she returned before dawn, "woke up" the following morning and expressed her own shock and puzzlement that the horse thieves would have taken one of the mares instead of the far more valuable Thoroughbreds. Go for the Gold, or Prime Time, for instance. They put it down to stupidity, almost relieved that the thieves knew nothing about racing or horses.

The next night she repeated her mare theft by taking Domino. In Domino's case, she stopped every twenty or thirty minutes to let the mare rest or drink from the little stream. It took her four hours to make the three-mile trek.

They questioned now the motive for taking the horses. She had listened to them the next morning trying to work it all out. Maybe it was animal activists who were behind this. Maybe asking for money was just a cover-up.

Whatever it was, thought Nell, no one ever followed up on the threats; no horses were harmed.

But tonight, after taking Stardust and Aqueduct, she could not go back; Aqueduct's absence would tell them it was Nell doing this, even if nothing else would. Until now, most of the blame had been put at the feet of animal-rights groups. It could only be animal activists they were sure. On six different nights over the past month, she had taken six mares, three like Jenny, who was having a hard time conceiving and whom she was certain would be put down because of it. They might think she simply took the opportunity to run away, but that she'd had nothing to do with the horses that had gone missing. She would still try to save the other mares, but knew she couldn't manage more than a very few this way. When she was out of here, she would find another way.

When she reckoned the guards were deep enough into their story or joke, she moved very slowly down the row of stalls to where the circuit breaker was located. She flipped a switch. The lights fluttered and died.

No one came. She had done this before on an erratic basis so that when she actually needed the dark no one would be suspicious of the lights going out and would conclude there was something wrong with the connections; faulty wiring is what they put it down to. The lights were supposed to be on at night to fool the mares into thinking it was spring as if conception was more likely in April.

No one would come to fix the lights, because they always came on by themselves (or so it seemed) in a matter of minutes. The two guards were embroiled in their stories and smokes and when the barn went dark, one guard got up and looked, swore and flashed his torch around, but in another ten seconds was back to talking and smoking.

Nell carefully pressed in between Stardust and the side of her stall, laid a hand on her muzzle. When the mare uttered a small sound, Nell did it again and Stardust went quiet. Then she took the small boning knife from her pocket and cut first through the front rope, then the one that held the right rear ankle. The horse remained perfectly still as if the imprint of Nell's hand on her muzzle remained.

To Nell, the stillness was no miracle, nor was it even strange. Stardust responded perfectly because that's what she'd been taught to do. Very slowly she backed Stardust out, put her hand on the mare's left shoulder to turn her, then slowly walked her out into the night.

FOURTEEN

It was the barn that had told Nell where she was and she could hardly believe it; it nearly paralyzed her to think that all of this time she had been only a few miles from home.

She and Stardust had to stop halfway there so that the mare could rest for an hour; the place was too far to travel in one go, too hard on the horse. From Hobbs's barn that afternoon she had taken hay and oats. She had slung the oats in a sack behind her over the blanket and tied up half a bale of hay, which she'd tied with a rope to the saddle. It was enough to keep the horses going for a couple of days and nights.

Two outlying barns, for years unused, stood nearly a half mile from the other Ryder Stud buildings, which was one reason why her granddad had stopped using it. Also, the barn was unnecessary when he started trimming back on stock and land.

Nell did not believe in luck, certainly not in the good kind, certainly not her own. But she did believe in fate. She did believe a person was led to something, although it was often hard to tell what finding it meant, or what was meant for you to do there. It was a necessary belief; it kept her going. When she'd come upon Ryder land and the empty barn on that first night, it had deepened her belief in fate—not in luck, not in guidance and not in God. Fate was different; fate was the thinking through and the working out of a pattern already laid down. You had to believe in something, she thought, even if it's a cold, impersonal and imperious something.

The Ryder stables would be a source of bulk food and maybe some bran or barley. Where she would get her own food, after the supplies she'd taken from the house, she wasn't sure, but she wasn't worried about it. There were other things to worry about.

She remembered hanging her head, as if this absence from home were her own fault. She had stood beside the tired mare whose neck was bent, cropping at black grass in the dark and wondered what heavy hand was stopping her. It wasn't as if she'd run away, and yet it felt like it, it really did. In the place she was taken to, it hadn't been mere physical boundaries that had kept her from running; she had become inured to those. No, it was more an irrational notion that she shouldn't be free; this had become entrenched in her mind, strong as her mind was. She had relearned the limits of freedom.

But she did know, didn't she, what kept her in this now self-imposed exile? Even though she wasn't responsible, except, perhaps, for having a pretty arse. She put it that way, crudely and sarcastically, hoping she could diminish the awfulness of the rape. The footsteps on the stairs, the opening door, the dark and then being pushed down, turned over and forced to lie flat on her stomach. Always, he came at her from behind. Every time. A dozen times. She had seen him once, but no more than a glance grazing his face. She believed she knew him. It was a belief unsustained by memory because her memory, her conscious awareness of him had been wiped out. But she also believed that the memory could be triggered by something and then she'd know. Until then she never wanted to speak of it; it was something she would have to settle for herself, probably, if at all.

And she'd learned the limits also the first time she'd seen the mares in those two barns. When she walked down the line, rubbing each of them on the rump or flank, she saw a number of them were pregnant. Yes, some of them were unmistakably in foal.

The stillness was eerie, unnatural. Fugitive sounds—a tiny rustle of hay, the soft movement of a tail flicking—

were all. Nell thought these horses projected a resignation unlike any she had ever witnessed.

She studied the stalls. The panels separating the mares were thin. Where the panels on each side came together with the dividing wall, they squared off a little platform that she might be able to sit on if there was any way to climb up there. Nell did not know why she wanted to do this; for some reason she felt it was important. Maybe once she got up there, she'd know.

She found an old crate against the wall that she pulled to the entrance of the stall and got up by standing on it and letting her arms power her the rest of the way. Then she sat down, legs dangling. "All right," she said. She could touch the heads of the two horses in front and if she turned around, the two horses behind her. Maybe that's why she'd wanted to get up here; up here she could reach them. From here she could see down the rows in both directions. She turned her head and saw they were looking at her. *I wonder if they think I'm something else to be drained of fluids.* On the ceiling, fluorescent lights stuttered and shimmered. It was day, but the lights were on and she wondered if this was to extend daylight or spring to confuse the mares into foaling in the dead of winter.

Nell looked toward the end of the barn and, seeing no one about, began to hum a few bars of her favorite song, and then to sing in a voice barely over a whisper. *"Love walked right in—"* She went on with what she could remember of it.

If she balanced carefully, she could lean back on the narrow ledge of the panel. She looked at the light, which threw a veil of sickly white over the horses. It might as well have been a layer of frost covering everything—the barn, the mares and her, even the stillness, even the singing.

FIFTEEN

She had this recurrent nightmare: a vast track of sand, an endless sweep of dunes, some ridged and shadowed like steps that a moment later would be swept away and another bit of geography would form in the sand. Along the horizon she saw a chain of what she took to be camels until her dream eye, coming closer, told her they were mares. There were no stalls, but still the mares were chained. But to what? There was only the sand. Yet they couldn't move. They stood exposed to sun and wind, a black line across the farthest dune.

And the awful silence, except for the wind, the subtle shifts in the sand, the wind rearranging the dunes.

Every time she had awakened from this dream, she recognized the peculiar amalgam of shame and remorse was caused not by what she had done, but by what she hadn't. She dropped her head on her raised knees. Sixty mares: there was no way in the world she could get all of them out, or even most of them. No matter who the people there thought was responsible, they would still have increased security. But she depended upon their thinking: if it was she who had taken the mares, why hadn't she taken her own horse, Aqueduct? That was why she'd left him for last: it might be the one thing that would throw them off the track.

Her head stayed down and she shook it back and forth against her knees when an image was too painful. Don't go there, don't go there. One thought struck her as incongruous: did they miss her? Despite wanting to blow the place to kingdom come and kill every last one of them—face-to-face, so that she could see the cold fear in their eyes—despite this she wondered, did they miss her? It was all too complicated, too hard to grasp, an emotional thicket, tangled and barbed.

In this dream tonight something had brushed against her face that wasn't the wind. There was nothing else there. She awoke in the deep dark rubbing her face, and saw Charlie, the little foal that she had brought along with its mother, looking around the open barn door. Charlie had been inspecting her and apparently hadn't decided whether she was trustworthy.

She fell back against her straw pillow, glad to have been awakened and thought about the dream again, for every time she had it she would go to sleep one person and wake up another, her sense of herself subtly changed, as was the surface of the desert in the dream. What clung to her nearly sunken consciousness was that there was something she had to do.

I've done enough.

No, you haven't. Somebody else? Perhaps. But you? No.

"Oh, who *says*?" she had yelled one night at the stars, scaring the horses, who started whinnying and snorting. She had gone into the barn and from one horse to another, offering each lumps of sugar, a stroke on the cheek and an apology.

Tonight a soft whinny came from the barn. The mother Daisy probably looking for Charlie. The foal trotted back to the stall.

They had grown so used to being tethered; it was difficult now for them to move around. They were anchored here by ghost chains, as the amputee still feels a ghost leg. A limb there and not there.

Again she thought of the dream and the chains in the sand. But you couldn't chain anything to sand. She wondered if she herself was that line of dark horses on the horizon, that she felt chained even though she had not been, literally. This had not come about merely as a result of her forced imprisonment in that gabled room under the eaves. "When can I go home?"

There was no answer.

She had felt herself to be a much younger self, more vulnerable, less aware, one who had regressed. Her passivity, while it had lasted, was a means of self-protection, a mildness that would appease these people and would convince them she wouldn't try anything.

From the window of her room she could see the courtyard and stables, three long lines of them. This had shown her it was a stud farm, like Ryder's, only slightly larger. But down below there was little activity, which she found strange. Only Aqueduct (and why had they wanted him?) and a few other horses were led from their stalls to the exercise ring. She would watch from her window for hours, interrupted only by a tray brought in by a girl who'd been told not to speak to her. But the girl, Fanny, having told her she was not to speak, continued speaking (feeling, apparently, that she had already broken the rule when she opened her mouth). Fanny was trying to earn enough money to go to America. This was the girl's single wish. She had an aunt who lived in Chicago.

"Do you take care of the horses ever?"

"Oh, no," Fanny answered. "It's got to be done just right."

"What has to be?"

Fanny shrugged.

A little while after she'd been here, Nell realized she would have to stop acting fifteen and be herself again, with every ounce of self-control and resourcefulness she could muster. She would never find a way out of this place if she couldn't convince them it was safe for them to give her a little freedom. The "When can I go home?" part of her would have to go and that other part of her, cool and in command, would have to reassert itself. It did not actually take a lot of effort; it had come over her quite naturally. Sometimes she wondered about this.

This composure and self-command might have been induced by the horses, the way she knew a person had to handle them. One had to be calm, consistent, efficient and dependable. You couldn't be a certain way one day and a different way the next.

Hadn't she said something like that a couple of years ago

to Vernon Rice? Being around horses, she had said, "gives a person poise."

Vernon Rice. She wondered what he was doing right now (except making money, of course). *He had just walked in when I was currying Samarkand. A total stranger, a stepbrother.*

Nell looked again at the white patches of stars and felt comforted.

He just walked in.

SIXTEEN

A queduct needed to run. She could feel his frustrated energy through her legs on his flanks and see it in the way he shook his mane and looked ahead as if the world were a row of hurdles he knew he could jump. She knew he wanted to jump that string of walls that zig-zagged across the fields for almost half a mile. They called them Hadrian's walls. It was the way she'd been taken that night, and the man who'd taken her had been a very good rider because some of those walls were dangerously high. She'd never been able to jump all of them. But Aqueduct could; Aqueduct loved the walls.

At two a.m., an hour when no one would be out, she rode the horse to the main buildings of her grandfather's farm. It took a half hour, so she wasn't surprised that the outlying barn in which she'd stabled the mares was no longer used.

They could have galloped along this road between the barn and the main Ryder property, but Nell wanted to save Aqueduct's energy for the training course. She wanted things to appear to be back to normal, or at least to have the illusion of normality, the comfort of the familiar, no matter how small.

It was lovely in this wood in winter; it always had been along this old road, no matter what the season or the hour. Iridescent with frost or thin coatings of ice, the small twigs broke and fell. But Aqueduct, never a skittish horse, did not start or stop. With the moon itself like ice, as hard and bright as she could remember, the scene was a landscape of dreams. *But we're always dreaming,* she thought, images floating upward when the mind is off guard. There's always a dream going on down there, some part of the mind that didn't care what was going on up here. She pushed a low-hanging branch out of the way, ducked under it, came out on the narrowing path to the stables and house. Her mares needed hay; she planned on hooking a bale of it onto the saddle if it would hold, maybe half on each side. She could walk beside the horse if the load seemed too heavy.

When they neared the barn, she hesitated, pulling back on the reins. They would remember Aqueduct—Samarkand and Beautiful Dreamer and Criminal Type. She thought they would remember.

"Come on, Duck," said Nell as she slipped down from the saddle. She walked the horse to the first row of stalls, afraid almost to look, afraid she would see unfamiliar faces in every stall, improbable, in the relatively short time she'd been gone, yet she felt that time to be fatal, to be her fault, as if her absence had been deliberate, as if she had forgotten them and, having forgotten, had nullified them. Such a fancy was arrogant, she supposed, as if her absence could make such a difference, as if it were a magic act, that she could throw up a veil that would make them disappear at will.

But the horses were here and if they weren't sure of her, they knew Aqueduct soon enough. It had always made her feel good to watch horses greeting one another. Aqueduct stopped at a stall and then went on to the next as if looking for someone. In the frozen stillness the only sounds were the soft nickerings. The horses were far enough from the house that no one would hear.

Yet it was like walking back into a past that no longer belonged to her, as if she'd mislaid it, left it deliberately behind and could no longer lay claim to it. She had forfeited it by not coming back. You wake up one morning and everything's changed. Or you go along thinking you can take a step back to find the ground is gone behind you. You get careless and profligate with your time and your feelings, and then find out it's too late.

Two years ago she would have said that she was happy; what she now knew was that happiness was irrelevant.

She stopped at each of the stalls, Samarkand's and Beautiful Dreamer's, and Criminal Type's and Fool's Money's (where she thought of Vern and smiled), stroking the neck of each, getting in return what she hoped were (but wasn't sure of) signs of recognition. Of course they must remember in some small way, some instinctive way. She could not be romantic or sentimental about it. She found the hay, small bundles of it.

In the tack room, she took her favorite saddle from the bench, thinking it wonderful the saddle was still there, as if everything connected to her then, her absence could have rendered nugatory. Then she took the too large one from Aqueduct's back, adjusted her own saddle on him, then secured the hay to it. She hoisted herself up once more and walked Aqueduct across the horse yard, away from the barn and along the bridle path past the house. The house was at some distance; she stopped and gazed at it.

It was not that she could not imagine her father's sadness, and her grandfather's, and Maurice's—somehow especially Maurice's—desolation. But she couldn't return yet, not quite yet.

They reached the training course and she leaned down and opened the gate. When they walked onto the track, a feeling of exhilaration washed over her, and she felt it in her horse, too. She wished that Maurice were here with his stopwatch, measuring time not by seconds but by halves of seconds. Split seconds, photo finishes. Faster than drawing breath. But he wasn't.

Aqueduct shook his head and lowered it; she could feel the tension bulk his shoulders. She had rarely done this; racing was more Maurice's job, not his job, but his pleasure. They had jockeys for this. She untied the hay and let it drop to the ground. She rose slightly in the saddle, leaned forward, hugged the horse's flanks with her legs, gathered the reins and in the dead dark whispered, *"Go, Duck!"*

The horse leaped forward so quickly she thought he'd leave her behind. Then she forgot everything but the horse, the reins and the rushing air; it blew over her like a cowel. Nothing she'd ever felt had been this fast, at least nothing she'd felt a part of. The track was a mile long. It was around the second turn that she saw something lying in their path but it was too late to stop. Three seconds after she'd seen it, Aqueduct jumped it as if it were a low hurdle.

SEVENTEEN

Black-haired and black-coated, the woman lying on her side looked as if she'd been thrown down, a rider thrown from her horse. Nell squatted down and took out the penlight she always carried. Its light accentuated the woman's porcelain skin, so perfect that it reminded Nell of pictures she'd seen of geisha—flawless faces covered with white powder. On her left hand was a gold wedding band; her hands were too soft, her nails too manicured to belong to a woman who spent much time around horses.

Nell could assimilate these details not because she was unmindful of the woman's death itself, but because noticing details had been much of what kept her alive for the past two years and eventually permitted her to escape. She had developed a lot of the objectivity and emotional insularity of a detective or reporter. She stood, heart thudding, wanting to get up on Aqueduct and gallop away.

She didn't know much about fixing the time of death, little about rigor mortis, but she did know it came and then passed. This woman seemed completely relaxed, so that could mean she was killed either very recently or some hours before. Killed how? Nell ran the small light over the form and saw nothing. Had she been stabbed? Shot? Strangled? And it had to have been in the last eight hours because there was invariably someone at the track at five or six o'clock, Maurice or an exercise boy, someone. Probably she had died in the early-morning darkness. Nell looked at apt Aqueduct. "I should tell them. I should do something." The horse's head appeared to nod. "I can't go to the farm, Duck." She looked away. Then she looked down. Expressionless, the face of the woman whom she didn't know was still beautiful.

Who was she?

In the time she'd been gone and after they had given up on her, anything could have happened. Her father might even have married again, needing someone, not to take her place, but to fill a lack. But that hardly explained this. Again she felt that urge to go to the house. . . . No. It would all be too difficult, too painful for them to understand. A tear rolled down her face as she went on looking at the woman lying at her feet. She brushed it off.

A call box. There was one a little down the road from there, and the road itself wasn't far. "Come on then, Duck."

She saw the call box and clicked her tongue, moving the horse along at a canter. No cars, no houses along here, and she was grateful for that. She pulled Aqueduct onto the grassy verge and jumped down. She opened the glass-paneled door and slipped in, wondering if one had to have coins even to call emergency. No, thank God. When she heard the voice of the policewoman, Nell told her in a rush about the dead woman and her location. Questions tumbled from the policewoman's lips, and in the midst of them, Nell apologized and hung up. Cambridgeshire police could certainly find the body.

Fifteen minutes later, as Aqueduct jumped the lowest of Hadrian's walls, she heard the sirens; looking over her shoulder, she thought she saw the turning blue lights, eerie through the predawn mist, turning on the top of the police car. Aqueduct's breath steamed in the cold damp air as Nell tossed the bag of feed over his back and tied the hay to the saddle again. She figured she'd have five minutes to get into the covering line of trees.

She could hear nothing now, not at this distance. None of it—the dead woman, the call box, the ghostly blue lights—none of it seemed to have any relation to her.

The police would be wondering who had made the call, but she had nothing to tell them, no idea of who the woman was. Yet the woman made her uncomfortable for some reason, tugged at her memory as if some deep spot in her mind had been disturbed. But by what? It had something to do with her family—her dad, her granddad, Maurice, Vernon.

This tug at memory made Nell wonder about the horses. Did they "remember" in the way of human remembrance? Or did they live only in the moment? But such thoughts only dragged her back to the mares she hadn't saved. Not that she ever really thought she could save them all. . . . Or had she? She tried to work out some other way of getting them away from the farm.

Despite her disappointment in herself, she applauded herself on one score: acting. She must really have been hellishly convincing to get them to let her help with the mares. She laid her forearm across her eyes, thinking of them lined up in those narrow stalls. *It's almost worse,* she thought, *than if I'd done nothing.* That thought made her feel like both a traitor and a coward. *Had* she thought she could save them all?

EIGHTEEN

Two unmarked police vehicles were angled in the courtyard when Melrose arrived in his Bentley the following morning. He assumed they were police from the light sitting atop one of the cars. He also thought the two men might be plainclothes detectives.

The civilian standing there talking to them clearly needed a coat (for it was beastly cold this morning). He was probably in his late sixties or early seventies, and Melrose supposed he was Arthur Ryder, with whom he had an appointment. Ryder stood with his arms crossed, hands in his armpits, warming them, and looking down at the ground.

Since police detectives don't usually turn up for no good reason, something dire had happened; Melrose then saw what the something dire was: men carrying a stretcher out of a wooded area, then around the corner of the barn and heading for an ambulance he hadn't noticed because it was parked on the other side of the house and had just now backed up a few feet.

Had Jury been strangely prescient about all of this? Melrose thought he should, in the circumstances, be politely unobtrusive and come back at a later date. *Ha! The hell with that idea . . .*

So he leaned against his car and lit a cigarette and waited. The detectives turned their heads and seemed to search his person with their eyes. It was then that Ryder looked up, a man sparing himself whatever lay before him as long as he possibly could. Finally, he shook the detectives' hands and nodded, then walked across the horse yard to Melrose.

"Mr. Plant? I'm Arthur Ryder." For such a big man his voice was surprisingly soft.

Melrose took the hand he offered and said, "Mr. Ryder."

"Look," said Ryder, "I should have called you to postpone our meeting. We've had a bit of trouble here."

When there was no hint of Arthur Ryder's elaborating on "a bit," Melrose said, "I'm sorry. I hope it's not too serious." Which it clearly was, given the stretcher being loaded into the ambulance.

"About as serious as things get, I think. There's this woman who was murdered."

Melrose had already concluded that. "Good Lord. I hope it wasn't a member of your own family."

"No. A stranger. Never saw her before in my life."

"Good Lord," Melrose said again. "Well, then, I expect you'd rather not talk business—?"

"No, that's all right. Wait here until I finish with these policemen. They're calling in police from the city. Cambridge, I mean. Apparently, it's better handled by them."

Looking toward the horse stalls, Melrose said, "Would it be all right if I had a look at your horses?"

"Go on. I'll meet you there in a minute."

The ambulance pulled away. Melrose watched it down the long white-fenced drive. *This* certainly put another spin on the whole Ryder Stud Farm question. Melrose looked toward the place from which he'd seen the men carrying the stretcher through the trees and made out, in the distance, what might have been yellow crime-scene tape lifted slightly in the wind. He was sorely tempted to walk there, but thought it would appear too intrusive. Instead, he went off to the stalls.

He approached the first horse box trying to recall if the book had said you should or should not look a horse directly in the eye. Here he was, some people's idea of a country squire, and he didn't know the first thing about the country.

A small bronze sign on the stall door read SAMARKAND. The horse was a handsome specimen, not precisely light gray, very pale. Dawn, that was it, or twilight. The horse was busy chewing. Not busy, perhaps, for he was chewing too slowly for that, but he seemed to be more interested in Melrose—

(Novice.)

—than he was in food. Melrose—

(Toff.)

—always seemed to excite no more than a soigné attitude in animals, a sort of "And you're here *because* . . . ?" response. He had often seen their shoulders (if they had any) move in what he would swear was a shrug. The next horse was glossy and as black as soot.

"Wonderful horse," said a voice behind Melrose.

Arthur Ryder had come up behind him and was running his hand down the black muzzle. "Criminal Type. He's twelve now, but he can still outrun most of them. Brilliant horse. One of my son's favorites. He was a jockey."

"Yes, I've seen him race." *Whoa!* That might lead him into troubled waters. It did.

"Where?"

Melrose appeared to be recollecting, his mind flowing with all the races over the years he'd seen with Dan Ryder on a horse. "Well, there was—"

"Cheltenham Gold Cup? That was a great race, wasn't it?"

"It was. Your son was a great jockey."

Arthur Ryder had pulled something from his back pocket and then stuffed it back into the pocket again. It was a bit of wood. He said, "Look, I'm feeling too disoriented to talk business at the moment. Come on into the house. What I need is a stiff drink."

Melrose hesitated. "I can come back, Mr. Ryder—"

But Arthur shook his head. "Not at all, not at all. Maybe a stranger's the best sort of person to have around at a time like this. There's no one here right now but me."

Melrose followed him into the rambling white house.

They sat in Arthur's office, a room overflowing with magazines, books, newspapers; a desk strewn with papers, ledgers bound in leather and other paraphernalia of record keeping. It was the sort of room one felt comfortable walking into, even more comfortable (despite the circumstances) having a drink in the morning with the person whose room it was.

Arthur Ryder was turning his glass back and forth in both hands. "Obviously, I'm glad it *isn't* anyone I know. Poor woman. But I'm completely mystified. My *training track*, for God's sake!"

"What did the police say?"

"The same thing. They think it must be someone who doesn't wish me well." His tone had an edge to it.

Melrose did not want to sound like the police. He was uncertain what pose to strike. "Is that feasible?"

"A bit far-fetched, but yes. You know the thing is it's not as if she were my own family yet . . . I feel a curious responsibility for her. That's strange, isn't it?"

Melrose nodded and sipped his whiskey and wondered. The question was rhetorical, anyway.

The telephone interrupted them.

"Excuse me." Arthur went to his desk, snatched up the phone. "Vernon! Have you heard about . . . yes. Yes."

As Arthur went about explaining to the caller what had happened, Melrose moved to a wall, its length divided by a wooden molding. Above the molding, covering the wall, were small and large photographs and snapshots, all of them of horses, some with jockeys on them. He had looked at a multitude of horses in various books. Matching up the remembered ones to these pictures was a great deal harder than matching up faces. But this one, Samarkand, he knew because of his unusual pale, moonlike shading. He stood perfectly posed in the winner's circle at some racecourse that Melrose didn't know. But then he didn't know any of them, did he? Melrose had had the sense to find a picture of Arthur Ryder's son from an old newspaper. All of these horses looked terribly famous: the way they stood, the way they looked only tolerably interested in the goings-on, the way they seemed above it all. For they were famous and fame knows only itself. This seemed particularly true in the look of the soot-black horse, Criminal Type.

"Sorry about that," said Arthur. "My stepson."

Melrose smiled and sat down. He wanted to get Ryder back to the thoughts he was having before the telephone call, but didn't know how to reintroduce the subject. Instead, he tapped the photograph of horse and jockey: "This is your son, isn't it?" In silks and that headgear, it was hard to tell one jockey from another.

Arthur looked and looked away, nodded briefly.

"I'm sorry."

"Ah—" Arthur waved the sentiment away, impatient with himself, not with Melrose. He picked up the whiskey decanter. "Have another." He splashed some more in both glasses.

Melrose said, "Your son was one of the great jockeys from what I've heard. He's been ranked up there with Piggot and that American, Shoemaker."

"He wasn't as good as either. Has any jockey ever been?" This time Arthur smiled, a brief flash, like light striking water, gone in an instant. He unpinned one of the larger photos and turned it so Melrose could see it. "Grand National, this was, twelve years ago. They broke the record by one and a half seconds. Odd, you never know how long a second can be until you see it in something like this. Danny was only in his thirties when he died. His son? Maurice?"—he said this as if Melrose had known Maurice and possibly forgotten the boy—"always wanted to be a jockey like his father. But then he shot up to five nine a couple of years ago and hasn't stopped yet. Now he's sixteen and nearly six feet tall."

For a moment Arthur was silent and Melrose did not want to disturb any fragile and ephemeral thought process, causing the images to fly apart like the colored bits in a kaleidoscope. He wanted to keep Ryder's train of thought intact and hoped the other man wouldn't suddenly recall why Melrose Plant was there and want to get down to business. Melrose thought probably the murder of this unknown woman had simply turned Ryder's world temporarily upside down so that practical matters would be for a little while in abeyance.

Arthur Ryder looked sadly down at his already-empty glass as if finding the contents had fled, along with his dead son, his lost grandchild—

—whom he had yet to mention.

Instead, he said, "You pay a heavy price for success,

don't you? Yet that's the reason you want success in the first place. So you can stop having to pay a heavy price. Ironic. You'd have enough capital, enough reputation that now things can be a bit of a lark. What I had here forty years ago was a small house, this room we're sitting in part of it, some livestock—cows and pigs—and three horses. I caught the racing bug—well, at least the horse bug—after I went with a friend to Newmarket auction. My God, but weren't they beautiful, those Thoroughbreds!" He picked another photo from the shelf behind him and handed it to Melrose. "This was the progeny of one of those first horses. Gold Rush was his name. And this was Golden Boy. I almost put him in a claims race, but thank God I didn't. Some trainer would have claimed him in an eye blink. So little by little I built the place. And that's the price, see. When Gold Rush won his first race I was beside myself with joy; it was the greatest thing that had ever happened to me since my boys were born. Yet the way I felt then has been less and less duplicated by wins worth far higher stakes and with far more fame. Winning becomes everything. You get a taste, you want every dish in the kitchen."

"But it has to be that way, doesn't it, if you want to get to the top or be the best? And to try to do it, that's admirable. You're right, of course, that you pay a price. But there's a price either way."

"Hm. Yes, that's true. Hm."

Melrose was going to ask him a direct question about the girl, when Arthur said, "I had a granddaughter—'have,' I mean—I catch myself using the past tense, which disturbs me." He reflected on this.

Melrose had to prompt him. "What happened to her?"

"She vanished."

Vanished. It was a word to chill the air between them. It was a word that so evoked light flying into darkness that Melrose felt the loss of this girl was, for Arthur Ryder, a total eclipse.

"She was taken."

That's how Arthur began his story.

"She was kidnapped, you could say, though there was never any contact with whoever did it and no ransom demand. Nothing. Ever. Which technically makes it an abduction, according to the police, and further puts it outside the scope of a long-lasting investigation. Of course, the police looked first at the people who work here, or did at that time. I've had to let several people go. It happened at night. Of course detectives checked out everybody who had some connection with the farm here. Whoever took Nell also took Aqueduct. He was one of my most valuable stallions. In terms of breeding, probably *the* most valuable."

The papers hadn't named the horse, to keep some piece of information out of public view so that the police could ignore false leads. "Then do you think the true object of this theft was the horse?"

Ryder nodded. "I can't think of why they'd take Nell if ransom wasn't a factor. But Aqueduct, there's an extremely valuable four-year-old, worth at least three million, even more when I sell seasons."

"Seasons?"

Arthur looked at him, a little puzzled. "You know, at stud. I could get as much as a hundred, a hundred and fifty thousand for one season, whoever owns the season brings his mare to breed. I don't like to go over fifty seasons; it's too hard on the stallion."

Melrose (who cursed himself for giving away the fact he didn't know the meaning of a common practice) totted up the "seasons" figure. Lord. In one year the horse could bring in six or seven million quid. Valuable, you bet.

"Without Aqueduct, I was in financial trouble. Big trouble. The breeders who were due to put their mares at stud and had paid for the privilege naturally wanted their money back. A few accepted other stallions, but wanted additional seasons to compensate." He shrugged, as if going on were too depressing. "In the two years' time, I haven't recouped."

"You've thought about the motive's being someone wanting to put you out of business?"

He nodded. "I have, yes. The police suggested that. But I honestly couldn't think who then and can't now. It's such a total mystery, the whole thing."

"But whoever did it couldn't himself enter your horse in a race. There are methods of identification—"

"Yes. But anyone intent on taking a horse would certainly have worked out some way of getting rid of particulars of identification."

"Still . . . well, if you ever saw the horse yourself, you'd know, wouldn't you?"

He smiled. "Not necessarily, I'm afraid." He picked a silver-framed photograph from his desk and handed it to Melrose. "But she would. You can bet she would. Nell."

Melrose looked at a face he could only describe as luminous. In this photo she could not have been more than fourteen, fifteen at most, if it was taken right before she disappeared. He found this remarkable, devastating. She was smiling or laughing at something the camera couldn't see. Strands of her sheer, pale hair blew across her face and shoulder. One hand was raised to pull the hair away. She was wearing a denim jacket over a white T-shirt, and on her it was haute couture. How had this child managed to get this way? Her father was handsome, certainly, but for Nell Ryder it was more than mere looks. He couldn't explain it. It was a kind of—poise, a sangfroid even. He felt a sense of loss of such immediacy, such a feeling of déjà vu, he was baffled. In all probability he would never see her, never hear her, never watch her ride a horse.

"She fit a horse like a kidskin glove," said Arthur, as if following the line of his visitor's thoughts. "She knew horses, she really did." He shook his head and replaced the photograph carefully.

Melrose cleared his throat. "She's beautiful."

Ryder looked at him. "To say the least."

The very least.

"I'll let George Davison show you the horse. I need to talk to my stepson again."

*   *   *

AQUEDUCT

The little sign was there, but the horse was not.

"We don't put any other horse in this stall. Superstitious, maybe, but there it is. Never knew a horse like him," said George Davison. "So high bred and low-down good-natured. That horse never had a mean bone in his body. Like Nell Ryder herself."

The horse, Melrose noted, came before the girl, at least

in the trainer's mind. "Do you think what happened will affect the stable, Mr. Davison?"

"Naturally." Any fool could see that, his look said. But apparently not this particular fool. "We lost enough income to—"

"No, Mr. Davison, I don't mean the horse being stolen. I mean last night. The murdered woman."

"Oh, her?" Davison shrugged. "Funny old business, that. But I don't see how it's anything to do with us." They were walking down the row of horse stalls.

"It seems so strange. What could this woman have been doing?"

"Someone just dumped her, maybe."

"Possibly. Very odd, though, if that's the case. You mentioned Nell Ryder. Her grandfather told me about her. It's one of the strangest things I've ever heard."

"He hasn't been the same since. This place hasn't, either. You think he'd be selling off stock otherwise?" He shook his head. "That little girl just disappearing into the night . . ." He shook his head again.

Melrose knew he shouldn't appear overly curious, yet wouldn't anyone, hearing such a story?

Davison was stopping the two of them at nearly every stall and giving Melrose a lowdown on each horse that Melrose could have done without. ("Stalwart, beautiful jumper, by Forward, out of Mr. Don; Gingerbread Man, progeny of Ginger Biscuit and Seaward—"

"What do you think happened?"

Davison said, "That girl, she was a gypsy, you ask me." He was looking in at a roan named Bobolink and rocking a bit on his heels.

"What do you mean?"

"Well, she pretty much did what she wanted. You know, independent."

Melrose smiled. " 'Gypsy' usually suggests someone unsettled or a traveler. Is that what you mean?"

Davison shrugged, not so much out of indifference as uncertainty about what he did mean. "Maybe. She was kind of a puzzle."

But the girl in the photograph had looked not at all like a puzzle but perfectly straightforward.

"I liked her, though; you had to like her. Here we are; here's Aggrieved."

They stopped in front of a stall at the far end.

Melrose smiled. "Aggrieved."

"Course you can change the name if you want—"

Not in a million years, thought Melrose.

"—only he's got a good track record and the name means something, you know."

"No, I won't change it."

The horse was the color of polished mahogany. He shone with good health and good breeding.

"Aggrieved was a great two-year-old. Won twelve of fourteen starts. Yeah, one of the most promising I've ever come across and lived up to the promise all around. The next year he won fourteen out of eighteen starts. But I don't expect you mean to race him. He's eleven now. Go on and look him over." Davison unlatched the stable door and the horse stepped back, shook out his mane.

"Oh, I don't need to do that. I'm sure any horse from this farm is as he's represented." The fear of discovery made him pompous.

Davison looked at Melrose as if he must be completely mad. But all he said, and said it mildly, was, "Best you look."

Hell, thought Melrose, trying to dredge up what he could from his reading about what to look for as Davison went into the stall and led the horse out.

Melrose walked around Aggrieved, sizing him up with a few *hms* and *humphs* and favorable nods trying to recall one thing—*ah!* The legs! He knelt down and ran a hand up and down the foreleg. But were the legs supposed to be hot or cold? He did this with the other foreleg, but steered clear of the hind legs. "Good bones," he said.

"Best check the teeth."

Oh, God. And the prayer paid off, for Davison did the honors of getting the mouth open with both hands.

Melrose looked, squinting. "They look fine," he said. "He appears to be absolutely fine to me."

That Melrose himself appeared that way to Aggrieved was a whole other thing. The horse had simply closed his eyes against whatever this person was doing. They knew,

Melrose was convinced, they *knew,* all right. They could ferret out lies.

"I'll just tack 'im up for you. Then you can put 'im through his paces."

Oh, great; oh, wonderful. You couldn't get me on that horse with a crane.

Davison started off for the tack room, turned and came back. "Damn it all! We can't use our course. That tape's up, that police tape."

Melrose tried not to laugh. How low had he sunk that he'd be grateful for a murder if it saved him from massive embarrassment. He blushed. "Oh, I'm sure the horse is all right. I'm not in my riding clothes, either." He did laugh then, in a silly way.

Davison scratched his head. "You think he'll suit, then?"

"Absolutely. I can leave him here, can't I, until I get a— something to move him in?" Horse box? Trailer?

"Trailer? Of course." Davison ran his hand down the horse's flank. "And that way"—he said to Melrose—"you'll be able to see how he performs when you come back!"

"Right." Between now and never, he could read fifteen books by Dick Francis and work out how you do it.

"You're a good ol' boy," said the trainer to the horse.

The good ol' boy opened his eyes, looked from Davison to Melrose and drew his top lip back over his fine teeth. He looked almost exactly like Humphrey Bogart in one of the actor's more considering moments, moments with a gun in his hand.

"That your car there, the Bentley?"

It was the only one parked in the turnaround, so who else's could it be? "Yes, it is."

"Mr. Plant!" called Arthur Ryder, coming toward them. "I'm really sorry, but so much has been going on. . . . George has taken care of things, though. Best trainer in the country. Do you like Aggrieved?" Arthur also ran his hand down the horse's flank. "I love this horse, always have." The horse seemed to lean into him, as if calmed by Arthur's company. "So he's all right, is he?"

"More than all right."

Arthur nodded. "Good. Would you want to leave him here until you get transport?" There was the distant ringing

of a phone. "Sorry, again. I'll be back straightaway. I've
been on the phone with the Cambridge police. That's them
ringing back probably. Maurice can help you if you need
something." This was called back over Ryder's shoulder.

Maurice was walking toward them. He had an intensity
that bordered on the savage. He was handsome, with looks
that apparently came from the jockey in the photographs
who Melrose had virtually committed to memory, so that
he'd recognize any pictures here of Dan Ryder. Again,
though, Melrose understood the nature of resemblance,
how it could be counterfeited in an expression of face and
voice, gesture and movement. Attributes the camera could
not always catch.

Melrose bet the boy's looks would be devastating to
girls—the nearly black hair, the pale skin, a romantic figure
one might meet up with in an Arthurian tale, knights or
chevaliers. A poet, a Rupert Brooke profile. Heroes. What
was that line Jury had quoted more than once from Virgil?
Agnosco . . . flammae? That would be Maurice's effect on
women. There was something in his looks that would remind them of something lost. Someone, somewhere, some
time. The face one couldn't quite place, but that shouldn't
have been let go.

Nell. Maurice. They were only a year apart. Together
they could probably cut a path through the romantic world
worthy of Dido and Aeneas. She looked as if she could
easily match the boy's intensity. He wondered what the
difference was between them. He did not know why he
wondered this.

Melrose thought all of this in the short time he watched
Maurice coming. He imagined Maurice thinking that here
was the stud farm in financial difficulty and here was this
rich, no doubt self-satisfied aristocrat come with all of his
money and knowing sod-all about horses to take away one
that Maurice had known all of Aggrieved's life, a horse
now to be used by the toff's family only to have all his
fleetness bred out of him.

Ah, if only the boy knew! Aggrieved would be living the
life of Reilly! Momaday finally had something useful to do
(from Melrose's point of view if not Momaday's), cleaning

out the old stable on the property. Melrose's father had been quite adept at the art of dressage, an interest Melrose had not inherited. For which he was grateful.

The boy looked if not exactly sad, then serious. It was the look of a mourner at a wake, where life was going on with laughter and song and which he couldn't understand.

"Mr. Plant? Granddad said you came to have a look at Aggrieved." He glanced from Melrose over to the stable. "You're buying him, then?"

"Yes. He's a beautiful horse."

Maurice looked at him as if that might be the expected and banal answer from one who knew nothing about Thoroughbred horses, or any other horses, probably.

Melrose cast about for a way to get on the subject of Nell Ryder. He didn't have to.

"Everybody loves this horse. Especially Nell. She's my cousin; you probably heard about her."

"Yes, your grandfather told me about her."

Maurice nodded. "Nell—"

The name broke off and drifted, like a spar from a wreckage. He still had a hand on Aggrieved's rump.

Melrose helped him out: "She was very good with horses, at coaxing them to do what she wanted, wasn't she?"

Maurice looked at him almost as if wondering why and from where Melrose had learned this. He seemed both to want to and not want to speak of her. "She was brilliant; even George said she'd make a first-rate trainer." Now Aggrieved was back in his stall and Maurice began to inspect the mixture of oats and bran in the hanging manger. "I hope you have other horses."

"Well, not exactly yet."

Maurice looked pained. "You know horses are very social animals. They've got to have others around them. Even if it's just a pig or a goat." He looked at Melrose for confirmation, suspicious of the munificence of the Ardry End barnyard.

Having not told the big lie, Melrose felt comfortable with a lot of little ones. "I have a lot of land and a lot of good pasture. I have a pig in a sty, a goat in the barn, a swan in the pond (an aunt in the drawing room) and ducks in the lake." He felt as if he were playing some variation of Cluedo. "Believe me, Maurice, this horse will get the best of care."

"Stable has to be mucked out every day. I expect you know that." Maurice didn't sound as if he believed it, though.

Indeed, Melrose found him far more suspicious than his grandfather Arthur had been or even George Davison. "Absolutely. I've got a really good stable lad." The thought of Momaday as a "lad" made him want to laugh. "Tell you what, Maurice; I'll take some Polaroid shots and send them to you straightaway (with Aggrieved holding up a copy of that day's newspaper). How's that?"

Maurice's face lightened up considerably. "I wish you would. See, that way I can have a picture in my mind of where he is and what he's doing and feel I'm watching him."

Melrose found this almost heartbreakingly sad. "I will. And I'll ring you or write to you or both. And you're always welcome to visit him."

The boy seemed far easier in his mind and now quite friendly. "It's really hard for me, selling off the horses."

"Oh, but surely only a few?"

"Yes, but still . . . Granddad really has to do it when he's low on funds. Some of the staff has been let go, a few of the lads and one trainer. We've got fewer entries in high-stakes races, too."

Arthur Ryder came out of the house and was walking toward them. "You're leaving him for now, right?" He looked off toward the stables; then he put a hand on Maurice's shoulder. "This boy knows more than I do about these horses."

As most kids will do when their elders get to extolling their many virtues, Maurice blushed and moved from under his granddad's grip. He said, "I've got to see to Dreamer; he's got a cold or something. Maybe we should call the vet. So long, Mr. Plant, and don't forget, will you?" He held out his hand.

The grip was firm. "I certainly won't." As Maurice trotted in the direction of the stables, Melrose said, "He's very capable, isn't he? He certainly is fond of these horses."

"Hm. I hope to God this business hasn't upset him too much. Did he say anything?" Before Melrose could answer, he went on, "It could have reminded him—" Then Arthur looked away and then back.

Melrose remembered that it was the second time some statement of remembrance had been interrupted. "No, he didn't."

"I keep looking over my shoulder."

Melrose raised his eyebrows in a question.

"Looking for the next thing."

"I expect it happened last night."

"No. That was the last thing. I mean the next thing."

NINETEEN

"A horse? You bought a horse? What in hell are you going to do with a horse?"

Jury had fanned *The Daughter of Time* face-down on his sheet when Melrose entered the hospital room.

Melrose said, "Well, that's hardly the attitude I would have hoped for, considering all the trouble and expense I went to."

Jury wrenched himself farther up in his bed, wincing. "I appreciate that. I'm sorry. It's just lying here all day listening to Hannibal's dire predictions that's making me testy."

"Oh? I was thinking how you were getting to look like Sergeant Wiggins more and more: sheet pulled up to your neck, Josephine Tey splayed on your chest."

"I thought the idea was you were going to pretend you were an interested buyer, not that you would actually buy one."

"Yes, well, I thought buying would put me in Ryder's good graces more than simply browsing. Arthur Ryder seemed so grateful—"

"How much?"

Melrose shrugged. "Not much considering this Thoroughbred's record."

"How much?"

"What does it matter? A lot. But see, he's trying to avoid syndicating his horses."

"What's that mean?"

"Selling off shares. You know, sort of like a time-sharing scheme. Anyway, I've never had a horse."

"I've never had a camel, either, but I'm not going out and buying one."

Melrose sighed.

"Tell me more about this incident."

"You detectives certainly don't suffer from a lack of hyperbole."

"Not if you can see it on a CAT scan. Go on."

"I've told you absolutely everything that happened."

Jury had closed his eyes and was shaking his head slowly. "As Proust would say, *'N'allez pas trop vite.'* "

Melrose stared. " 'As *Proust* would say'? Are you kidding? Since when did you become Proustian? Or even speak French?"

"I don't. It's just that one phrase and *bonjour* and *bon nuit* and phrases like that I know. I learned it because I think it should be engraved on my forehead. It means—"

"I know what it means. I've had my schoolroom French. You speak it quite well. 'Do not go by too quickly,' or 'Go slowly' or 'Be precise.' Something like that. I agree, it's excellent advice, considering all we miss if we go too quickly."

"So. There are a hundred details you've omitted. Exactly how was the body positioned?"

"I don't know. I certainly wouldn't have left that out if I did. We were not all ranged around the body sipping tea."

"All right. What was the reaction of these people?"

"Well, confusion, consternation—"

"Same for everyone?"

"No. The trainer, George Davison, seemed utterly indifferent. There was no fear on anyone's part."

"That's odd."

Melrose frowned. "Not if she was a stranger."

"She wasn't, was she?"

Melrose raised his eyebrows, waiting for more.

"Can you honestly believe that chummy shot a perfect stranger in the middle of the Ryder training track?"

"Then Arthur Ryder is lying? Or his grandson or George Davison?"

"Not necessarily. There are several explanations. One: this could be someone they might have known without knowing they knew her."

"Oh, well, that's clear enough."

Jury ignored him. "Someone met for a short time at a race meeting, say, someone important for some reason, but forgotten. The identity is still unknown or at least was this morning when you were there. It could've been someone they knew *of*, but wouldn't recognize."

Melrose thought for a moment. "Daniel Ryder's second wife. No one knows her because he never came back to England."

Jury nodded. "There's a possibility right there. I assume she wasn't shot out of the saddle."

"I doubt it; she wasn't dressed for riding."

"What caliber gun was it?"

"No one told me."

"Never mind. Ballistics will turn up the range and angle and a dozen other things about the bullet."

"Why would the shooter shoot her there?"

Jury said, "I expect she could have been dumped—well, there's no use speculating when we don't have any of the crime scene details. I'd like to know what happened to the person who made the call."

Melrose sat back and studied the white ceiling. "Well, I'm stumped. Maybe Vernon Rice will illuminate the scene. I'm going to see him"—Melrose looked at his watch— "now." Melrose got up.

"What about the girl, Nell? What did you find out?"

"Nothing new about her disappearance. I saw pictures of her. There's something about her. It's not often you run into a girl in her teens who makes you think you've been there before."

Jury frowned. "Been where?"

"Wherever *she's* been. She gives déjà vu a whole new meaning."

TWENTY

Vernon Rice had both the sort of charm that could sell you time shares in Pompeii and, at the same time, some inbred faith that Pompeii was still a going concern. In other words, he could get you to buy, but it was an honest sell.

He spoke to Melrose as if he'd known him all his life, ushering him in with a wave of his arm and telling him that Arthur—whom Vernon called "Art"—had called to tell him Melrose was coming.

The room that Melrose stepped into was glass and angles, and sloping chairs with graceful legs that looked uncomfortable yet were anything but. The wide gray rug leveling off to white softened the contours of the furniture. The room was a throwback to some earlier period, despite its high-end German designer look. It didn't surprise Melrose to hear Vernon Rice say he was "shaking up a bunch of Manhattans" in a silver-plated cocktail shaker. Melrose hadn't seen one of those since his parents' parties. The Ryders were no strangers to the midday drink, that was sure. He wondered if they were alcoholics. He wondered—more to the point—if he was.

Then he remembered that Vernon Rice was not a blood relation, although his looks suggested otherwise. He could have been Maurice's father or Dan Ryder's brother, for he looked as if he inherited the family's striking good looks.

"Manhattan," said Melrose. "That's an old thirties favorite, isn't it?" Melrose had seated himself in a burnt-orange chair with sloping arms and rounded back.

"Definitely is," said Vernon. He had the shaker doing a little mamba in his hands, a little added flourish before pouring the drink into two stemmed glasses. The glasses held maraschino cherries speared by plastic swizzle sticks, each topped with a grass-skirted hula dancer. It was the best-tempered drink Melrose had ever had, he thought, a combination of shaker, whiskey, hula-hula girl and Vernon Rice.

"Don't tell anyone," said Vernon, "because it sounds macabre, but I've always wanted to live in the States in the thirties."

"But that was the Depression. Did you also want to live in Spain during the Inquisition?"

Vernon laughed. "No. But imagine watching the market collapse like that."

"Oh, fun. Somehow I don't think the men poised on windowsills would share your enthusiasm."

"I don't mean to sound cold-blooded, and God only knows I'd've grabbed a few coattails before they'd flown out the window, but it just makes me wonder if I could have done something."

"I doubt it, though I think you'd deserve a medal for trying. But the forces at work at that time, they were inexorable. God couldn't have stopped it."

Unconvinced, Vernon brought the shaker around. "Don't be so sure. Is anything really 'inexorable'?"

Vernon went on to detail causes and cures, cures he might have implemented, spoken of in an argot of finance that Melrose didn't understand at all. He looked at his glass. Where had this second drink come from? Or third? While Vernon talked on, the detached part of Melrose's mind marveled. Vernon was not a vain person; he probably didn't have the time to admire himself and his dazzling notions. For Melrose realized they really were dazzling, even though he couldn't understand most of what he was saying.

Vernon plunked down his glass. "Let's have lunch. I know a terrific place."

"Sniper's? That's a restaurant? Strange name."

"I love the place. It's all done up in camouflaging. Good

time to go, too, because it's always so bloody crowded during the lunch hour."

Melrose had been astonished to find it was nearly three when they left the flat. The Depression stopped when Vernon realized he couldn't make Melrose understand what he meant by short falls and zero floors. But Vernon had managed to chug through this Depression tunnel and come out into clean sunlit air, leaving Melrose to think there was nothing that Vernon Rice wouldn't try.

They were walking on Thames Street, out in the cold, glassy air, when Melrose asked him, "Is there anything you wouldn't take a whack at?"

Vernon stopped on the pavement, looking thoughtful.

Melrose laughed. "If you really have to think about it, the answer's no. Given sufficient challenge, you'd try anything."

Vernon smiled and they walked on down Thames Street.

Sniper's would not be easy to find if you didn't know exactly where it was down a dozen steps in a terraced building that bore no sign, charged with a sort of secrecy that would hardly pay off for a restaurant. Yet it certainly wasn't hurting for business. The arrangement, if not the actual ambience, made him think of the Nine-One-Nine, the gig of Stan Keeler, Jury's guitarist friend.

Sniper's really was a bit like a jungle. Light was murky, the plant life enormous. On either side of the foyer was a big aquarium whose neon-bright and startled fish swam in quick jabs as if searching for a way out.

The hostess, not meant to be part of the decor as she was dressed in simple, businesslike black, smiled at Vernon in a way that suggested he was a welcome addition to the maneuvers. She led them along a path through the black-green equatorial room. The size of the plants and their position between tables gave the illusion of concealment. The webbed netting and vines on the ceiling contributed to this, and recessed lighting was so artfully placed among the plants it diffused light into a mellow glow around them. Yet something kept the decor from a cloying cuteness. It was relaxing despite its metaphorical implications.

"Great place for a murder, isn't it?"

Melrose dropped back into the real world, delighted that Vernon had brought the matter up. "I seem to have dropped in on your stepfather at just the wrong time."

"Or the right one." Vernon smiled.

Melrose fumbled his silver around and wondered if Vernon Rice could read his mind and retreated momentarily behind the menu, filled with exotic-sounding dishes scattered among the ones he'd heard described as "soul food" and "comfort food" and very American: meat loaf and mashed potatoes, hot roast beef sandwiches. There were, of course, filets and fish, such as Dover sole, grilled, broiled, cooked however you wanted it. So why was he homesick for food he had never had at home? Once more forgetting murder—which at the moment struck him as quaintly dull or else an anachronism—he asked this question of Vernon.

"I mean, we never had meat loaf. It's American food, anyway. Why would I be homesick for American food?"

"Maybe," said Vernon, eyes still on his menu, "it's not the food."

"Well . . . but what about the place?"

"Maybe it's not the place."

Melrose protested. "But if it's neither, why? I don't get it."

"Jung probably would. Collective unconscious or something."

"Meat loaf in the collective unconscious? Why doesn't that sound right?" Just then Melrose realized he was speaking in very personal terms. To how many people had he ever confessed homesickness?

Was this Rice's secret? Was he himself so honest and so engaging he made you want to come clean? In this way he reminded Melrose of Richard Jury. It was the gift. He thought about this and thought he'd like to see them together, outcharming each other. For it was charm, a whole vat of it. He smiled, thinking of James Joyce.

"Why are you smiling?"

"James Joyce and Samuel Beckett could sit in a room and say nothing to each other for endless periods. I've always thought that was as good as companionship gets."

"I agree." Vernon frowned, considering. "Want to try it?"

Melrose laughed out loud. "Do I want to *try* it? Sit here for a half an hour saying nothing? If I'd walked in with a guillotine, would you want to try that, too? And don't pretend to think about it."

Vernon laughed as the waiter, dressed in an olive drab T-shirt and black jeans, came to take their order. Grilled sea bass. Meat loaf and mashed potatoes.

"Tell me about your plans for Aggrieved. He's a wonderful horse, incidentally."

Sorry that the talk of the murder had made a detour back to the horse, Melrose said, "He was talking about the business end, syndicating one or two of his horses."

"Right. It's the best thing he could do, but he doesn't want to. He seems to look at that as filthy lucre, you know."

"Well, he also told me the idea of selling 'seasons,' which he apparently does."

Vernon nodded. "He does, but not enough. Says he doesn't want his stallions overtaxed."

"An interesting way of putting it. Anyway, I thought perhaps you could help me do this for Aggrieved. Sell seasons."

"Why? You don't strike me as in need of capital. Not with what you paid for that horse."

Melrose didn't comment on his need, rightly assessed by Rice. "Aggrieved has a very famous bloodline. I should think it would be easy."

Vernon shook his head. "Not really, not if you don't have a working stud farm. See, when an owner buys what we call seasons, in this instance for Aggrieved, and if something happens to the horse, he'd expect to be switched to another equally valuable horse or have his money back. I think you'd be better off waiting. If you did it now, not understanding what's involved, you'd just be buying yourself a headache. Believe me. Ryder's business is a tricky one. Worse than farming in its unpredictability. When you acquire other horses, it would be best to stable them with a reliable stud farm and a reliable trainer. That's what most owners do."

Melrose opened his mouth to argue, as if he really were serious about this horse business, realized he wasn't and closed his mouth. One could be convinced at times one's lies were the truth.

The waiter was setting down their plates and Melrose bathed his face in the fragrant steam rising from his meat loaf. "I'll give it some thought." Then, as if suddenly recalling it, he said, "I got there just as the woman's body was loaded into the ambulance. Murder has a way of making other subjects irrelevant."

"Well, this one's as peculiar as hell. Cambridge police want me up there this evening to have a look at the body, see if I know her. From Arthur's description, she doesn't sound familiar. I admit I'm curious as hell." He shrugged. "But my car's in the shop. I'll rent a car, I suppose."

Melrose could hardly believe his luck! "Cambridge isn't far. I could easily run you there."

Vernon laughed. "You kidding? That's damned nice of you."

"Not at all, not at all." Melrose refilled their glasses with a very good Brunello, saying, "And I confess, like you, I'm curious. I've never been on the spot when somebody's been murdered and that she was found lying in the middle of the racecourse was really, well, weird; it couldn't have been an accident."

"Hardly. When Arthur called to tell me, before the words 'body on the course' were spoken, I froze. I thought it might be Nellie." Vernon stopped eating and stared out over the tables and the plants, transfixed.

"The granddaughter?"

Vernon looked at Melrose absently, as if trying to place him, and said, "Nearly two years ago she was kidnapped or abducted, according to the police." He turned his eyes on his plate, but didn't raise his fork.

"My God, but your family is not the luckiest around. Mr. Ryder told me a little about that kidnapping; he said there was never a ransom demand."

"That's right."

"It's a very strange story."

Vernon nodded. "They also took one of Arthur's great Thoroughbreds, a horse named Aqueduct. We assume Nellie saw or heard them—she was in the stable herself, you see, looking after a sick horse—and they took her to keep her quiet."

"Why take this particular horse, Aqueduct?"

"Aqueduct's a valuable 'chaser. But they couldn't have raced him under some fictitious name, unless they'd gone to a lot of trouble to make sure he wasn't recognized. Even then, George Davison—the trainer—would have known. George could have told from the horse's performance. He's amazing that way. Aqueduct could have been stolen for breeding purposes. His progeny have certainly measured up, won a lot of top races. But this wouldn't explain it because they couldn't put down Aqueduct as the sire."

Vernon had given up all pretense of eating now and was sitting back with his wineglass in his hand. He kept raising it and replacing it on the table, untouched. He seemed to have given up the pretense of drinking, too. "So—?"

Melrose took his last bite of meat loaf, sorry to see it go, and pushed his clean-as-a-whistle plate away. "To do something to the whole stable? To all of the Thoroughbreds? Or to do something to your stepfather? The only person who saw what happened was the granddaughter. Everything else is speculation, an attempt at reconstruction. For all anyone knows they could have come for completely different reasons than you think."

"I suppose you're right. But you have to start somewhere, and we started with what went missing. Aqueduct. Nellie."

"That's reasonable."

For the first time that afternoon, Vernon looked defeated. "She's not dead."

"Even after twenty months?"

"Even so. She's not dead."

"You seem so sure."

"I am." He returned to his cold plate then and cut off a bit of his cold fish, chewed it, swallowed. "I hardly knew her."

That, thought Melrose, was the first indication of self-deception. He had known her, all right, just as Melrose felt he himself knew her after nothing but seeing her picture.

Vernon cut off another bite and chewed it. He looked as if he were eating ashes.

TWENTY-ONE

He had been sitting in the Bentley for twenty minutes parked on a double-yellow line, wondering how he could get a look at the body and how he could get past the policeman in reception. Not being a relative or a witness himself, it would be impossible. He had been there, though, in the aftermath, when the stretcher had come out of the woods. And he had been seen to be there by the detectives.

Melrose got out of the car and leaned against it, quietly smoking. He looked around for a call box and didn't see one. Jury might have some ideas about all of this if he could get him on the telephone. By now, Hannibal surely must have returned his telephone privileges. Why did Jury put up with it?

There was a pub down the street and of course they'd have a telephone. He searched his person and then his car for paper to write on. All he salvaged from the glove compartment was a theater program for *Cats*. *Cats*? When in God's name had he ever seen *Cats*? He wouldn't see *Cats* if someone threatened to swing him like one. Then why was he looking at this theater program as if he had? He frowned. What was he thinking?

Melrose slammed the car door, stood with his arms on top of the car and his head bent, hoping to come up with some clever approach to Cambridge police. When he stopped banging his head and looked over the top of the car, he saw two children standing on the pavement licking iced lollies and staring at him. What were they doing out after dark? They were apparently waiting for him to do his next number.

"Just look at yourselves. Are you auditioning for Cirque du Soleil?"

They neither spoke nor gave up their places on the pavement. They waited. The inherent pleasure of watching a grown-up being a total idiot seemingly had a stronger pull than running from that grown-up idiot. Melrose walked around to the pavement. "You haven't seen *Cats,* have you? And then planted the evidence in my car?" He produced the program.

But they just went on looking and licking. What was it about him that made children look at him as if their dog had suddenly started talking? Melrose threw up his hands, turned away and started toward the pub down the street. The need to look back was too strong and he did. Now they were leaning, backs against his car, licking their ices and staring at the park.

The Cricketer's Arms was the familiar world of smoke and beer. He told the bartender he'd have a pint of whatever was on tap and went to the telephone. He pinged coins into the slots, thinking he should probably get one of those cell phones, but he despised them. The whole earth had turned into a public call box.

Hannibal answered.

Melrose couldn't believe she was actually screening Jury's calls. He put on his best North London voice and said, "Is Mr. Joo-ry there, love?"

When she said the superintendent wasn't to be disturbed, Melrose raised his voice a disturbed notch. "It's his auntie Agatha; I'm ever so worried since I found out about that 'orrible business. Can't I just speak to 'im fer a moment?"

Melrose could hear Jury arguing with her in the background. Then finally his voice came over the line, "Aunt Agatha!"

"Has she gone?" Melrose asked on his end.

"No," Jury answered.

"Well, can't you get her out of your room?"

"You're kidding. Aunt Agatha," he quickly added.

Jury enjoyed this sort of thing, Melrose was sure; it must have been similar to the intractability of witnesses and to intractable circumstance. "Listen. I need you to do something. I'm in Cambridge. I've driven Vernon Rice here because the police wanted him to have a look at the body, see if he knows—or knew—her. I imagine they also wanted to ask him more questions since he's still there and it's been forty-five minutes. I want to see the body myself. Do you want me to?"

"Yes."

"So how can I? I'm not family or friend or anything that would get me a ticket in."

"Simple. I'll just tell them you might have recognized her. Okay, Hannibal's gone, so I can speak freely."

"Thank God. Only I didn't see the woman. How could I recognize her?"

"You said you were very near the stretcher as they brought it by, moving it toward the ambulance."

"Yes, I was, but—"

"That's good enough."

"How can it be?"

A huge sigh from Jury. "I'm not helping you out in a criminal act, for God's sake. All you want is to view a dead body. Where are you?"

"Pub down the street."

"Go back to the station. I'll call Cambridge right away. I've a good friend there. Greene's his name in case someone asks. Detective chief inspector, he is."

Melrose drank off most of the pint waiting for him at the bar, bought a packet of vinegar crisps and ate them while walking back down the road. He had nearly finished them when he realized a dead body might best be seen on an empty stomach.

Nothing of that nature occurred, however. As a young woman police constable led him on and off the elevator and down a corridor to the morgue, his stomach was perfectly fine. And it wasn't as if he'd never seen a body before. Last year in Cornwall, for instance. But that was a case of the very recently dead, when they looked exactly the same as they always had. Except for the blood and the bullet holes. But the blood had been hidden by the thick dark rug, and the bullet wounds were invisible, at least from where he stood.

In the long corridor, he hung back. This episode had turned suddenly serious on him. In his mind's eye he saw the face of Nell Ryder and marveled at Vernon Rice's conviction that she could not be dead. And he had this irrational fear that he would look down at this dead woman and he would see Nell Ryder. It was as if the others who had seen this woman—her grandfather, Maurice, even the trainer, Davison—had blinded themselves to the face they saw.

Why was he *doing* this? Why? The photograph had looked alive, as if it had captured Nell, and the old superstition was true about the camera's catching the soul of its subject.

He had been walking slowly, and now stopped dead. With a conviction to rival Rice's own, he was sure that she was dead. His throat felt constricted.

"Coming, sir?" The pleasant WPC turned toward him and smiled.

Melrose picked up his pace. "Sorry."

"That's all right. Most people walk more slowly here. Is it a family member you've come to—sorry, you don't know yet, do you?"

"No."

They had stopped for a moment. They started walking again.

"It's right here, sir. See, there's a panel they'll slide back, and you just look through that pane of glass."

Melrose did not respond; he merely waited. The panel slid back and he was looking at the woman lying on the gurney. His eyes widened in astonishment.

"Is it who you thought?"

"No."

"You don't recognize her, then?"

"Yes. I do."

Sitting in one of the interview rooms, he had told the detective inspector working the case as much as he could about the woman at the bar in the Grave Maurice.

Unfortunately (Melrose told the detective), he hadn't paid much attention to the other woman, so couldn't help them there.

"Did she appear to know Dr. Ryder personally?"

"It's hard to say. She certainly knew *about* him. She knew about his niece, Nell Ryder."

"You think, then, this woman knew the family, or at least one of them intimately."

"I rather doubt the intimacy since none of them even knows this woman." *Or say they don't,* Melrose didn't add.

"Or say they don't," the detective did add.

"They wanted to know if I owned a weapon. A .22, to be more precise. I told them no, but they wanted permission to search my flat, anyway." Vernon told Melrose this on the way back to London. "Who the hell *is* she?"

Melrose was watching the rain-slick road, now dark. "When did Dan Ryder die?"

"A little over two years ago."

"Before Nell disappeared."

Vernon turned in his seat to stare. "You think *that* comes into it?"

"Merely a thought. It's just that you've now had three terrible events occur in a short time. It's possible all three are connected, don't you think?"

Vernon shook his head. "Possible, but unlikely."

Up ahead Melrose spotted the carnival red of a Little Chef, the black-and-white-checked trousers of its familiar logo. An icon of childhood. He would devil his parents to stop at every one. Even as a child he realized this was completely unreasonable, to expect them to keep stopping. But it was merely a step in a plan: for then he was almost certain they'd stop at every *third* one, and that made at least two stops per longish trip, often three. Melrose thought himself pretty cagy, even as a child, really good at working a room.

"Great, I could use some food," Vernon said.

Without knowing it, Melrose had pulled off the road and into the Little Chef's car park. He laughed. He must have gone on autopilot. "Did you like these places when you were a kid?"

They were climbing out of the car and Vernon slammed his door with a flourish. "Hell, yes. Little Chefs and Happy Eaters, though they were clones of Little Chefs. Let's go."

They walked toward what Melrose thought were impossibly lighted-up windows.

The tables, counter, mirrors were so cleanly bright they might have been scrubbed between each load of customers. The waitresses and waiters were as clean as nurses and doctors who had just scrubbed in. It was like having the hygienic benefits of an OR without the mortal consequences.

Melrose slid across the cool plastic bench in the long booth and grabbed the menu.

"Beans on toast," Vernon said, barely glancing at the offerings.

Melrose ordered everything fried—eggs, sausages, bread, chips and a tomato.

Vernon said, "You wouldn't catch me eating beans on toast at home." The waitress set down their coffee, smiled her clean smile and left.

"Of course not. It's what you eat at Little Chef. I know a detective sergeant who likes Little Chef but doesn't appear to connect it to childhood. He's not nostalgic so he loves it for its own sake."

"A Little Chef purist."

"Right."

"Arthur likes to tell me I never grew up. I say, How would you know, you didn't even know me then? and he says I don't have to; I know you now." Vernon laughed.

Melrose smiled. "You two get on very well together."

"Oh, sure. He pays absolutely no attention to me when it comes to investing, though. He could be tripling his income if he'd listen to me."

They were silent for a few moments, fiddling with menus that hadn't been plucked immediately from their hands. Melrose asked, "Was there some trouble between the family and Dan Ryder?"

"Arthur was pretty much fed up. And I don't think Dan and Roger ever really got along, despite being brothers. Totally different sorts. Roger is cautious; Danny was reckless, *really* reckless. He was always raising the bar. You know, to see how high he could jump—I mean, literally as well as figuratively. He took too many chances. His first wife, Marybeth, left him because of that, though she wasn't much of a treat to begin with. Danny was an addicted gambler. He died owing a ton of money to the wrong people, and I wouldn't be surprised if that was the reason he left England. These are the kind of people who don't forgive debts for sentimental reasons like death. The kind who manage to get back at the family if that's the only way they can collect."

"So did these people move on Arthur?"

Vernon nodded. "I paid off a lot of it to keep Arthur from knowing how much it was."

"That was certainly decent of you."

"Not really. It was just sitting around."

Melrose smiled. "I doubt you'd leave money sitting around for very long."

"Well, I had some stocks that weren't earning their keep. I hated the picture of Arthur's discovering his son was selling the farm, metaphorically speaking."

"Did you know Dan?"

"Not very well. I met him once or twice when Ma and Arthur were, you know, getting together. I saw him at the races. He was brilliant, I'll say that. This was before they got married. I was pretty old—thirty-two—"

Melrose liked that definition of "pretty old."

"—and had my business in the City. So I didn't get up to Cambridge very often. Not that I was giving it a pass, not at all. I liked it there. I liked Arthur and—the others."

He didn't want to single out Nell, apparently. "But you seem to get up there quite a bit lately."

Vernon looked down at his beans on toast. "Well, I should, don't you think? Arthur's suffered some terrible losses. Danny, Ma, Nellie . . ." His voice trailed off.

"Your mother was not a younger woman, was she?" Melrose cut off a piece of fried bread.

Vernon laughed. "No. They were contemporaries. Arthur never had a midlife crisis. My mother was a great person—very outgoing and at the same time private. They were married for only two years when she died." His eyes still on the plate he added, "I really miss her, Mum." He fell quiet.

Nodding at the untouched plate, Melrose asked, "Aren't you going to eat?"

Vernon sighed. "I didn't really want to eat this; I just wanted to look at it. Do you ever do that?"

Melrose thought Vernon looked hopeful that he wasn't crazy all by himself. "Oh, yes. Well, I eat at least a token bite when I feel that way. He held up the triangle of bread he'd been working on. He wondered how much of childhood Vernon still inhabited and also wondered how much emptiness could be appeased just by looking. As Vernon took a token bite of beans, Melrose said, "You said in the restaurant you didn't know Nell Ryder very well. How old was she when you met her?"

"Fifteen. It was only a few months before she disappeared."

"She'd be seventeen now."

Vernon fooled with his fork and nodded.

"I saw pictures of Nell. She seemed—I don't know—airy, ethereal, not quite of this world. Which is hard to do in one of those Barbour coats and muddy boots." Melrose ate his sausage. "That's not a good description of her, though. She looked like someone with a purpose. Someone dedicated, but to what I don't know."

"Horses, for one thing." Vernon paused. "To tell the truth, I can't think of another thing." He cut off a wedge of toast. "What you might be seeing in her is poise, a person poised on the edge of something and who manages to keep her balance." Vernon's eyebrows inched upward as if asking Melrose to confirm this.

Melrose nodded.

Vernon went on. "When I met her I took her to be some years older. I told her this and she said it was from being around horses all her life; it gives you poise and confidence. If you don't have it, they may allow you to ride them, or feed them, or brush them down, but eventually they turn their backs. She wants to be a trainer. Davison thinks she's a natural."

"Is the investigation ongoing?"

"No. But I've got a private investigator. He's still looking."

"After nearly two years?" Melrose raised an eyebrow.

"After ten, if it's necessary."

Melrose felt slightly abashed. He thought for a minute and then asked, "Was there a set time in the evening for seeing to the horses?"

"Yes, of course. Evening stables and then Davison goes around again before he leaves at night."

"Which means that everyone knew when things were battened down for the night and no one around?"

"You're suggesting that the person would have been either one of us or someone else who knew the schedule?"

Melrose paused. "Not exactly." He paused again. "Just a thought." Vernon Rice didn't appear to question Melrose's extended interest in the Ryders' misfortunes, but, of course, the body lying in the Cambridge police station pretty much took care of Melrose's motive.

"This private investigator you've been paying for all this time—"

"Leon Stone?"

"What is he continuing to do?"

"He hasn't got a fresh lead, but at least he's looking; the police aren't. Not that I blame them. An abduction unsolved after nearly two years? The case isn't closed, but it's certainly resting. They think she's dead."

He said this so matter-of-factly, Melrose would have thought he was indifferent to the case. "Why are you so certain she's not?"

"It's something you know, that's all." Vernon shook his head.

Melrose said, "There've been no demands. There should be, if not money, for something. Surely."

"Unless she went to save someone else."

"But that would mean she herself was valuable to them."

Again, Vernon shook his head. He shoved his plate away.

For a few moments they sat in silence as Melrose ate and Vernon looked bereft. Melrose was thinking. "Tell me: are there any high-stakes races coming up?"

"Yes. There always are. Here, elsewhere. It's not the purse of these races—although they can pay a lot—it's the boost they do to the reputation of the stud farm. Any horse that wins the Prix de l'Arc de Triomphe or the American ones such as the Derby or, God willing, the Triple Crown—those races are pure gold when it comes to breeding. But such races are run every year."

"Would Aqueduct have qualified?"

"Yes, but as I said before, he couldn't be entered as Aqueduct himself."

"But he could win registered as Bozo the Clown." Melrose paused. "Have you considered that someone wanted Nell dead? That she had enemies?"

"Leon Stone considered it."

"An idea you jettisoned?"

Vernon nodded. "In that case stealing the horse was simply a smoke screen? Something like that?"

"Something like that, yes. What runs counter to that idea is that they've never found her body. The thoroughness of police when it comes to searches like that is legendary. The woods behind the house would literally have not a leaf unturned. Still, it's a theory in the running. Did someone gain from her death?"

"But no death has been reported. So what would be gained?"

"Something in the future? Anyway, if Ryder is having financial troubles, I expect he wouldn't be leaving a fortune to anyone."

"That's where you're wrong. In terms of liquid assets, he hasn't a great deal. In terms of assets, period, he's got a lot. He's just not using the potential. He could, of course, sell the farm and realize a big profit. Anderson's been wanting to buy him out for years. But it would be far more valuable to keep Ryder Stud and simply syndicate the horses. And increase the breeding shares. Samarkand has sired a number of foals who've gone on to win in the six figures. In other words, Arthur could be making enough to pay Danny's gambling debts several times over. What he's resisting most is syndication. With a horse, for instance, like Criminal Type, say he sold off twenty shares—keeping another dozen for himself—at, say, fifty thousand a share, which would be low for that horse. There's a cool million just for the shares sold on one horse. He's got several that good or better. And that's not counting the shares in breeding rights. I've been trying to talk him into this for years, but here's where profit loses out to sentiment." Vernon smiled.

"Somehow in his mind, he sees Criminal Type cut up into twenty pieces? Literally?"

Vernon was now eating his beans and toast, which must be stone-cold by now, with enthusiasm. "Exactly. Arthur can bring himself to selling breeding rights only by selling very few. Less than any other owner around. Can you imagine the profit from a horse like Criminal Type, whose progeny thus far have already won stakes races to the tune of eight or nine million? Ten colts, averaging, say, half a million apiece? And that's only up to *now*."

"A horse such as Aqueduct would be worth a fortune, then, theoretically?"

The waitress was hovering, pouring a small waterfall of hot coffee into their cups. Melrose noticed a paler circle of skin where a wedding band had once been and wondered why she'd taken it off.

Vernon shook his head. "As I said, no one else could run him or breed him under the Aqueduct name." Vernon drew a crumpled pack of cigarettes from an inner pocket, together with a lighter. It could easily have been traded for a share in Aqueduct. It was platinum. As Melrose took a cigarette and leaned over so Vernon could light it, he wondered just how much money the man had.

"Do Little Chefs have a no-smoking section?"

"It's not this one, wherever it is," Vernon said.

TWENTY-TWO

"Back to square one," said Melrose early the next morning as he sat in Jury's hospital room. "Abducted. Horse hijacked. Square one."

"Considering you actually witnessed this woman whom nobody knows talking to someone in the Grave Maurice, I'd hardly say we're back to square one. You might be the only person who has a line on her. You said she was talking about Nell Ryder?"

Melrose nodded. "Now, of course, I'm sorry I didn't listen more closely."

"Hindsight. Even so, we've learned a fair amount about how things were and are with members of the Ryder family, that the jockey didn't get along with them, especially with his father; that Arthur had borne with him to the limits of his ability, probably because his son's one virtue was that Dan Ryder could ride a horse into hell and both come back unsinged."

Melrose noticed again the sheet drawn up to Jury's neck and his look of supreme self-satisfaction. On his bedside table, occupying a position beneath *The Daughter of Time*, lay a report sent to him by Cambridgeshire police.

Jury reached for it. "Aqueduct's stall was down at the far end. The girl was with him. It was dark, the only illumination coming from dim lights at either end. She may or may not have seen whoever was there. But that doesn't make any difference if he thought she saw him. Arthur Ryder told you the stall was always locked, that Davison did that last thing before he left?"

"That's right."

"And the lock wasn't forced, so the person must have had a key. Either that or someone left the door unlocked."

"You mean someone in the family?"

"Or in the employ of the family."

Melrose didn't like to think this. "I think that's an assumption."

"Maybe, but I'm holed up here. I can only go by what I'm told."

There was that self-satisfied little smile again. Jury was now staring placidly at the ceiling. Wiggins, more and more. "How he got to the house is anybody's guess. Could have walked, could have been dropped off—which would mean more than one person was involved in all this . . ."

"If he got there that way, he could have retraced his steps with the girl, probably a gun at her head—"

"He was either prevented from doing that or he took the course of action he'd planned all along: get the girl, get the horse. And don't forget, Nell Ryder was—is—supposed to be an excellent horsewoman."

"But none of this explains her twenty-month absence."

Jury was looking at the police report. "It would if she's dead, and she probably is."

Melrose's heart gave a lurch. He didn't want to hear that from Jury; Jury was too often right. But then he hadn't actually talked to these people, except for Dr. Ryder.

"The one I haven't heard anything much about is Maurice." As if awakening to the question, he asked, "Why is that?"

"You're right; there's been little if anything said of him. I don't know why. The boy's name rarely comes up. I think his grandfather is very fond of him. I spoke to him—Maurice—the night the woman was found on the track."

"His mother left him cold and his father's dead—that strikes me as warranting a mention. And where is the mother?"

"I don't know."

"Why did she walk out on him—the boy, not the husband? Dan Ryder was a gambler, a womanizer, no kind of father and irresponsible—except when it came to racing and horses. Where's your horse, incidentally?"

"At Ryder's. I have to do another Cambridgeshire run. That'll be the third one in twenty-four hours."

"Good. This time take this boy Maurice aside and see what he has to say about all of this. See if you can get him talking about his father and mother. And does he know anything about his father's second wife?"

"That I doubt. No one seems to have a clue about her." Melrose was looking from bed to door. "Where's Hannibal? I've been here for nearly a half hour and haven't seen her."

"Ah! I've a new nurse, or at least part of one. Her name's Chrissie. Then there's another one who relieves her occasionally."

"A new nurse! Is she prettier than Hannibal?"

"Even you're prettier than Hannibal. But Chrissie, oh, yes, very pretty. It's rather nice, this. Having your food brought and your bed changed and all you have to do is sit and look, and give this a punch"—he held up the buzzer positioned beside him—"if you want anything. I could get quite used to it, living like you."

"Like me? And where do you get that idea?"

Jury laughed. "Food prepared, linens changed. And don't deny you have those bellpulls all over the house. Pull it and Ruthven comes on the double." He held up the buzzer by way of analogy.

"It's not the same at all."

Jury settled back against his pillows again. "It is, too. Except for the horse."

TWENTY-THREE

Maurice Ryder liked to talk about one thing—Thoroughbred horses—which made Melrose wonder what blew back in the wind of his riding. Melrose had declined the offer to race Aggrieved—now peacefully chomping some vegetation unearthed beneath a springy layer of frost and ice (grass? acorns? truffles?)—after Maurice had ridden him around the track to give Melrose an idea of what the horse could do. Aggrieved could do considerably more than Melrose could do, that was certain. He had never seen Aggrieved on the racecourse, but he wouldn't want to see himself up on an animal that could even come close to Samarkand. How must he have raced as a two- or three-year-old, then? Racing past the stands he would have been a copper blur.

Maurice had taken Samarkand twice around the track and was going by again at full tilt, lifting the collar of Melrose's coat where he leaned against the post and rail fence. This horse was fast. Melrose was in charge of the stopwatch, which he thought was a lot of fun and promised himself he'd buy one as soon as he could. Samarkand had gone a mile at 1:44:36. ("Pretty good," said Maurice.) Melrose didn't know; he just like pressing the stopwatch button. It was more fun even than Jury's buzzer. Maurice had told him that he wouldn't take Aggrieved to the top of his form because he hadn't been really put through his paces for a while.

Melrose raised his binoculars once again looking to the far side and thought how wedded, how *welded*, really, horse and rider appeared. The boy was meant for this, thought Melrose. The racing gene must have come down from his father; what a misfortune the height gene hadn't followed suit. At sixteen Maurice was but a shade under six feet and was possibly looking at even another growth spurt. It was Dan Ryder who had this rogue gene for the rest of the Ryders were tall.

"It's not the height so much as the weight," Maurice had told him. "Jockeys eat what would be a starvation diet for me; I wouldn't even be able to get up on a horse, much less ride one. You'd be surprised the energy it takes."

"If not a jockey, what? Do you want to be a trainer?"

"I don't know."

"You'll inherit this place, won't you? You can do whatever you like. You and your cousin, Nell—"

Couldn't he have been a little more skillful? It was clear that this topic wasn't merely sore; it was bleeding. He wished Jury was here. He handled such questions with a deftness Melrose couldn't duplicate.

For a minute Maurice hadn't answered, just flaked the thin ice from the root of the tree where they stood. "If she ever comes back."

The boy hadn't commented further. But it would certainly not be intrusive or suspicious to bring up the woman who'd been shot. Melrose had, after all, been a virtual witness to murder. Naturally, he'd be curious.

After Maurice dismounted and tossed a blanket over Samarkand, who strolled over to where Aggrieved was still bent on his hapless quest for food, Maurice leaned against the fence beside Melrose.

"That was a bizarre business the other night. No one knows yet who she is." Since Vernon Rice would undoubtedly tell Arthur Ryder about the trip to Cambridge police headquarters, Melrose filled Maurice in on what had happened there.

"*You* knew her?"

"No, I didn't know her. I'd merely seen her once in the pub near the hospital. A friend of mine is—well, never mind." He'd better not bring that friendship up for the moment. "I just happened to be sitting near her when she was talking to someone."

Maurice looked away, frowning. Melrose wondered if he'd been a total chump bringing this up. He'd better have left it to come out in another way. "Didn't your father send you a photo? A snapshot of his new wife?"

"No, nothing." His look at Melrose now, although not outright antagonistic, was still not outright friendly. "Are you saying that's who she *was*?"

"I have no idea who the woman was. It struck me that it's a possibility. If you think about it, you'd wonder how anyone without any connection to the Ryder farm would end up shot dead on your track."

Maurice was silent, gathering twigs as if he meant to break the place up inch by inch. "Say it was her—Dad's wife—why would she come back here now?"

"Money. That's generally a safe bet."

Maurice frowned. "From Ryder Stud? From Granddad? Why would she expect any?"

"I don't know. There might be some unfinished legal business. His will, perhaps; something like that."

"But Dad died over two years ago. Why wouldn't she have come then?"

"That's a good question. Perhaps it's something she only recently found out about." Melrose paused. "Your mother. Where is she now?"

A pall seemed to settle over them, Maurice lifting his face toward the blank white sky. "I don't know."

"You don't keep in touch?"

"No."

Maurice executed in the single syllable an intensely complicated move, something such as his father must have done in threading his horse through the thicket of competing horses, taking it to the finish line. "Your father got custody?"

Maurice's voice was strangely lacking in expression when he said, "I don't think there was a big battle between them over it."

It was a sad pronouncement. "But I imagine you'd much rather be here than anywhere else."

The boy nodded and snapped a twig as if it were an icicle. "Things change."

With that rather inscrutable comment, they got up and went to their horses.

They got Aggrieved—a patient animal, considering what it did for a living—into the trailer, and Melrose said goodbye to Arthur Ryder and Maurice, saying he would surely see them again shortly.

Of that, he was certain.

TWENTY-FOUR

Mr. Momaday would keep Aggrieved's stall mucked out, and the rest of the small barn which he had managed to lather into excellent condition, making minor repairs to doors and posts. He had done as Melrose had instructed—he had gone to a saddlery in Sidbury for supplies. The hay net was up, the salt lick affixed to the wall, maize and bran and roots and fruits sitting about in tubs.

Melrose told Momaday that he would do morning stables and he, Melrose, would do evening. He wasn't absolutely clear as to what that involved; he just liked the sound of "evening stables." He pictured it as a Stubbs painting, or else one of the Romantics' featuring a thatched-roof cottage and a lot of heavily leafed trees.

Momaday instructed Melrose that it was only the one horse, so "stables"—plural—wasn't it.

"You want to call it 'evening stable'? Think about that. Does it sound quite right? I prefer the plural and it's my stables, so don't argue. Furthermore, Momaday, you cannot go around here with your gun shooting at anything that moves."

Momaday's insubordinate mumbles were somewhat mitigated by the fact he'd never killed anything.

Ruthven and Martha were by turns hugely impressed and hugely perplexed by the horse's presence, the presence being quite imposing. Aggrieved was a handsome horse, with his glowing reddish-brown coat and black mane. Martha made tiny clucks and cooing sounds as she would have done had Melrose brought round a bird or a baby. Ruthven went on about the color, Momaday saying the horse was chestnut, Ruthven saying he knew a bay when he saw one, Melrose not knowing the difference. Ruthven went on to inform the little group, stiff as the starched collar he wore, that Melrose had been an excellent horseman in his younger days.

"Younger days?"

"When you were five or six, m'lord."

"My God, Ruthven, I wouldn't even have fit on this horse then."

"I'm thinking of your old pony."

"Ruthven, somehow I don't think 'excellent horseman' is an accurate description of a kid on a pony."

Momaday thought this was rich and juggled laughter around, largely through indrawn snorts and said, "Prob'ly fell off that, too." Snort, snort.

"What? *Too?* Where do you get 'too'?"

"Ah, ya remember that big gray over to your friend's house? Climbed up one side and fell right over t'other." A succession of snorty breaths accompanied this nugget.

Melrose had, at the time when this happened, thought it a good joke; Momaday thought it a better one and told everyone who crossed his path about it. No matter how self-deprecating Melrose could be, Momaday could deprecate him even more. Momaday intuited that his boss would never fire him, and he was right. Melrose had never fired anyone. He had wanted to, he had tried to. But an image of the ex-servant and present wretch filled his field of vision, calling up a picture of this poor devil fighting his way through snowdrifts with nothing but a dry loaf to nibble on before complete snow blindness felled him where he stood. This person would have a faithful dog struggling beside him and when the old ex-retainer froze the dog would sit atop the snowy grave until it, too, froze. It was like that.

Melrose thanked his staff (for what, he wasn't sure) and told Momaday to lead Aggrieved (whose patience was monumental) to his stall. As they walked away, he heard the undertones of man talking to horse, with a lot of snorty laughter, possibly on both sides.

He waited for Momaday to leave the barn and go about

whatever his business was. Melrose was eager to saddle up his horse and walk it around. He realized he was giving Aggrieved short shrift, a horse that the trainer Davison had said could beat "anything on any track—slow or fast, turf, muddy, dry." "Determined" is what Davison had called Aggrieved. "Determined."

The horse was chomping away, his nose near the hay net. Melrose wondered about all the other stuff, the succulents and barley and so forth. He wondered how they were to be fed. He picked a nice apple from a bucket and tentatively held it. He was still trying to remember about looking at a horse straight on. He moved to the horse's side and held the apple out, nearly under Aggrieved's nose. The horse muzzled it up and chomped. Really, he was so easygoing in the benign setting of this stable that it was hard to picture him in the competitive world of racing.

Melrose looked about to see if Momaday was lurking, then took out his book *Riding for Beginners*. The "beginner" didn't bother him; it was the cartoon figure of a very young girl, in jodhpurs and riding jacket, with her sappy smile, who was to put him through his paces. My Lord, were there no *adult* beginners? Did all beginning occur around age seven? By the time this child got to be his age she'd have won the Olympic Gold for dressage twice over. Her name was Cindy Lou. She was from Kentucky (naturally). But he supposed riding was the same, here or in the States.

Cindy Lou showed him how to get the bit in a horse's mouth, and having done that successfully, Melrose led Aggrieved out of his stall so that he could saddle up. Ah, he liked the ring of it! "Saddle up." It put him in mind of old American Westerns, which he had, actually, never seen. But one still knew the drill and the climate and the tone. Of course, he *had* seen *High Noon*, but that was much more than just a Western. As he was fastening the strap beneath the horse to secure the saddle, he replaced the image of Cindy Lou with Gary Cooper. He would like to adopt Gary Cooper's elegant insouciance, his shy forbearance, to wit, his persona. That, of course, could only come with practice.

Melrose looked outside again to make certain no one

was about, that Ruthven, for instance, wouldn't come rushing up with a pot of tea and a carrot. Then he positioned a large wooden box by the horse's side. Left foot in stirrup; hoist and swing right leg over. Those were the instructions from wall-eyed Cindy Lou, who, he was sure, could get to be a pain. Okay, he was ready: one two three *hoist* and there he was sitting in the saddle! Actually up on one of the country's premier racehorses and *sitting*! Oh why hadn't they all been here to see this smooth-as-silk move?

Melrose shook the reins a little and they were out of the barn and walking through the grounds, which were extensive. Next, through the woods, by way of the public footpath. Aggrieved walked and Melrose swayed. The horse, he thought, was taking in the sun-dappled scenery, for his head moved up, down and around.

A narrow road ran between Ardry End and Watermeadows, a vast Italianate estate, gorgeously decayed, where lived the charming Flora Fludd. He would have a good reason to wind up over there at Watermeadows, now he could ride. Melrose gently pulled back on the reins, amazed again that the horse responded to his fingers. He considered a canter along this narrow road. He thumbed the book to see what the annoying Cindy Lou had to say. She warned against such a move, her palm held flat out like a white mollusk. It would be undertaking too much too soon. She advised at most a short trot and reminded him that one must fix one's seat in the saddle and rise, fall, rise, fall to the rhythm of the horse.

Melrose tried to do all of this as Aggrieved trotted along, sure he was going up when he should be going down. Finally, he thought he had the hang of it. They trotted on for some twenty minutes and came to the main Northampton Road, which he had no intention of riding on, then turned back toward the house and the stable, outside of which he meant to slide off the horse's back smooth as silk, but in pulling his left foot from the stirrup, caught it and fell to the ground.

Hell's bells! There they all were, watching, especially Momaday. Ruthven walked toward him.

"You're all right, m'lord?" he asked as Melrose righted himself.

"Oh, yes, just not one of my best moves."

"Lady Ardry is here, in a state of high dudgeon, it appears. She insists on seeing you immediately."

"Ruthven, why is it different from any other time? She always insists. Oh, very well." He handed the horse over to Momaday.

Ruthven always enjoyed Agatha being in a "state," not only because he liked seeing her upset but because it kept her from carping about the offerings on the tea table, one of which she was stuffing in just as Melrose walked into the drawing room.

Around a mouthful of scone, she accused him of something or other, but what it was, Melrose couldn't make out except the tag end:

". . . to have done it!"

"Done what, Agatha?" He was engaged in thanking whatever gods that happened to be hanging about Ardry End that she hadn't witnessed his fall from the horse.

She was glaring as if from every corner of the room as she buttered up another scone. He poured himself a lovely cup of Darjeeling, plunked in a sugar cube and a dollop of milk, selected a moist-looking piece of cake and sat down, wishing that Aggrieved was here, hay and all, to be taking tea with him instead of Agatha. Perhaps the Sidbury Feed Store could construct a scone net, which could be hung from the Georgian ceiling molding.

He asked her again. "Done what?"

"Oh, you needn't play the innocent with me, Plant. It's all over the paper!"

Melrose frowned. How on earth could the Sidbury paper have gotten news of his acquisition of a racehorse? More important, why would the paper think it news at all? This rag Diane Demorney wrote for would now, in January, just be catching up with the flower show. But here was Agatha opening it, turning it for Melrose to see and tapping the offending piece with her finger.

Melrose left his chair to lean over and see it. Of course, it had nothing to do with Cambridge, how could it? The newspaper was interested only in what went on in its own backyard. He plucked it from Agatha's hands and read:

HUNT SUPPORTERS FOIL ANIMAL-RIGHTS GROUP

There on the front page was a picture of himself, Diane and Trueblood, in one of their careless moments (he would have said), but then all of their moments were pretty careless. They gave the impression they were attacking (or counterattacking) some of the animal protesters, when the three were about as aware of animal-welfare issues as the annual rainfall in Papua New Guinea. True, Melrose would never kick a cat (though he wouldn't answer for Diane if it got between her and the martini pitcher), but insofar as the whole movement was concerned they were totally uninformed. Yet here they were, in that moment when Melrose had quickly put out his arm to support a young woman with a sign who just then had caught her foot and was falling toward him; and Diane, raising her stiletto heel to shake out a stone; and Trueblood holding his camera above his head to keep it out of harm's way.

What a wonderful photo op! He must send a crate of succulents round to the Sidbury photographer. What an image for misconstruction!

"It makes me out to look the proper fool, Plant! You're aware of that, aren't you?"

Oh, indeed, he was aware. He kept a straight face as he sat down and sipped his cooling tea. Here was a moment to relish! Should he try to work out *how* this made Agatha out to be a fool—not that *that* was ever too difficult—or just play it?

Play it. "The point is, Agatha, if you must take up a cause, you also must be aware that there'll be a backlash from the anti-cause (was that a word?)."

"Oh, don't be ridiculous, Melrose."

"Okay." Melrose was eyeing the ruins of the tiered plate, looking for a pastry that had escaped Agatha's ravaging. She had a way of biting off and putting back when she was especially irritated, taking it all out on the scones and seedcake. He did find an Eccles cake without tooth marks.

"I've always thought it shameful, *shameful*, the way you neglect Mindy, here!"

Mindy-here was flopped on the hearth in her usual position, soaking up heat.

"How do you work that out, Agatha?"

"She gets *no exercise*! Do I ever see you out with that dog on a lead?"

"No, but that's only because you're over here having tea during dog-leading time."

Agatha, he saw, was actually waving that half-buttered scone around instead of eating it. She must really be on the boil! He said, "I can't help but think we strayed from the subject, since I really don't believe the animal-liberation people are trying to get us to walk Siberian tigers."

"You know nothing about it!" Realizing she had a scone in her hand that could as easily be in her mouth, she put it in and munched. Then having resurrected her weak argument, she said, "You surely must see the idiocy if not the inhumanity of a pack of hounds running down a poor little fox!"

"Yes, it *is* idiotic. Oscar Wilde said so and I agree. But that particular idiocy is a wholly different argument and not the one you're trying to make. As far as I'm concerned the entire hunting issue is a smoke screen for a class war." He didn't know if he believed that or not, but it was as good an argument as any. "Why choose a thing that is *least* abusive—certainly 'least' in terms of numbers—to make an issue of? If the welfare of animals was really at the heart of yesterday's masquerade, then why not spend one's time and energy on ridding the earth of far more brutal practices—slaughtering seals, mowing down wolves and deer from a helicopter, obliterating animal habitat, tracking and shooting the Siberian tiger in order to grind its bones for medicinal purposes"—which had for Melrose a terrible mythic ring to it—"so what it really comes down to isn't the welfare of the fox, but of the pink- and black- and tweed-coated citizens of the upper classes whom we would like to unseat."

Agatha's attention, hard to keep in the best of circumstances, had strayed and was riveted on the long window off to her left. "A *horse* just passed that window!"

"Momaday's walking it."

Hopeless.

TWENTY-FIVE

The Sidbury paper was open on the table in the Jack and Hammer, the table's four occupants having a good old laugh.

"How *droll,*" said Diane Demorney, in her Noël Coward mood, her cigarette dripping ash over the paper and coming dangerously close to the martini glass. Diane was dressed in conventional and nondroll black, one by that Asian designer she'd been favoring lately (Issy? Icky? Mickey?) "We three mistaken for animal activists. They've obviously never come up against my cat. All I was doing"—she tapped the picture with her cigarette holder—"was shaking a stone from my shoe."

"What'll we do for an encore?" said Trueblood.

"Wear mink and walk down Oxford Street," said Vivian. "I wish I'd been there."

"We did invite you, old girl," said Trueblood. "We should join the hunt. Must be someplace we could rent a horse."

"Look no farther than my back garden. I have a horse stabled there."

He might as well have said he had a 747 hangered there, for the looks he got. He smiled.

"What on earth for? You don't *ride,* do you?" said the scandalized Trueblood.

"How *amusing.*" Coming from Diane, this was high praise indeed.

"My riding isn't all that good, but I plan on racing it. It's a Thoroughbred." Melrose felt quite smug.

Diane said, "Remember Whirlaway? That is, remember reading about him, it being long before our time? Whirlaway was owned by Calumet Farm, that racing empire that was ruined by greed and mismanagement."

Another Diane nugget.

"I can sympathize with greed, but why anyone would want to engage in a thing that needs management, I can't imagine." She seemed to be brooding over her drink.

Vivian asked, "But where are you going to race him, Melrose?"

"Well . . ." He should have given this more thought. Newmarket? That was in Cambridgeshire. "Newmarket, possibly. I'm going to have to get advice from the Ryder trainer."

"You know, Melrose," Diane said, screwing another cigarette into her black holder, "you could have a nice little horse enterprise yourself with all of that land of yours."

"I could plant cotton, too, but I'm not going to."

"Don't be a stick. Imagine what fun it would be for all of us. You've enough land there for an honest-to-God racecourse."

"And put up stands and have a few turf accountants around and a full bar?"

"Certainly, a bar. The rest is optional."

"Diane," said Vivian, "if I didn't know you better, I'd think you were serious."

"Of course I'm serious." She returned her look to Melrose. *"Or—"*

" 'Or'?"

"Is—what'd you say your horse's name is?"

"Aggrieved."

"You can rename it. Thunderbolt—there's a good name."

"Why on earth would I do that? Aggrieved is a high-stakes winner."

She waggled her cigarette holder at him. "For heaven's sake, Melrose, you don't want people knowing that; you don't want to give the whole bloody thing away. The idea is to get odds of say fifty to one and make a packet of money."

"If the odds were like that, old fish," said Trueblood,

"hardly anyone would bet on him and who'd do the payout?"

"Whoever is used to doing it. I don't know; I've never been much of a gambler. I mean except in the London clubs, such as they are." She shrugged and sat back. "What you could do then is join the National Hunt."

"No, I could not. I don't ride—" Recalling what he felt had been a very encouraging canter, well, almost a canter that morning, he added, "I mean I don't ride that *well* . . ."

Trueblood leaned forward. "But it'd be a great follow-up to this!" Trueblood tapped his knuckles on the paper. "I mean, it'd drive Agatha mad and the other so-called animal-rights person, that snake, Theo Wrenn Browne."

"Him?" said Vivian, surprised. "Since when has he ever liked animals at all? He's always kicking at Ada Crisp's dog and if anyone in the village tries to go into that book-shop with his pet, Theo drives them out. He hates animals." Then to Melrose: "How's Richard? Is he better?"

"He is indeed."

"Ah! Richard Jury!" said Diane. "Is he recovered?"

"Recovered, at least enough to leave the hospital tomorrow. He's coming here to rest up."

Diane actually spilled a few drops of her drink, bringing the glass down on the table in martini applause. "Wonderful!"

"He said he might have to spend a night in Islington to give his two doting neighbors a chance to take care of him."

"Everybody wants a piece of him," said Trueblood, signaling to Dick Scroggs for refills.

"How true," said Diane.

"You'd devour him where he stands," said Trueblood.

"He's highly devourable," said Diane.

TWENTY-SIX

Even had she not taken an oath to succor her fellow-man, Chrissie King would have done it anyway, and she stood in the door to Jury's room wishing she could.

"Chrissie, would you mind pounding some life into these pillows?"

"Oh . . . of course! Sorry, I was . . . my mind was wandering . . ." She rushed to the bed as if he'd called for artificial respiration. (Didn't she just wish!) She pulled and padded and resettled the pillows.

"Thanks, Chrissie. You pulled duty tonight instead of Miss Brown?"

She nodded. Actually, she bought the duty for twenty pounds in addition to picking up Sara Brown's duty tomorrow afternoon with a churlish patient Nurse Brown especially disliked.

"Can't say I'm sorry. I expect it must be a waste of time for you to have to tend to someone like me who's really okay now."

Chrissie's words rushed out as if in advance of the voice to utter them. "Oh, but you're not all that okay. I mean it's not you're really sick or anything. But with what you've been through . . ." Her head tilted nearly to her own shoulder as she looked at him.

Jury hid a smile. Chrissie wanted him unrecovered, too, just as Hannibal did, for wholly different reasons. "Dr. Ryder seems to think I am; he needs the bed. God knows, he needs this private room. So he's tossing me out tomorrow afternoon. I hope I'm not spoiling an evening out for you. You must have boyfriends to spare."

What, Chrissie wondered, *were they? Boyfriends?*

She had a way of shaking and nodding her head at the same time that intrigued Jury. "No? Yes?" He tried to mimic the head shaking by way of keeping her company. He wasn't flirting with her; at least, he didn't mean to be. Rather, he was attuning himself to her. It was a way he had—born with it or developed it—from years of questioning suspects, in those cases to discomfit them, in Chrissie's case to comfort.

Jury was aware that he insinuated himself into the lives of witnesses and suspects, but that really was the only way of going about it. It was the only way to see the skull beneath the skin. He had to admit he encouraged the attachment people had to him. It might have been something like transference, that psychiatric tool. But the psychiatrist was trained to remain uninvolved, like a target transfixed to a spot while the rifle sought to pick him out of the shadows.

That image of gunplay brought the whole awful incident on the dock back to him. Poor Mickey.

"Is something wrong?" asked Chrissie. "Shall I get Dr. Ryder?"

"No, no. I'm just tired, a little."

"Then I'll leave," she said sadly.

"No, don't. It's me I'm tired of. All of this self-involvement. I'm not tired of you. Listen: pull up a chair, will you? Tell me about yourself."

Even had there been screams for her attention all up and down the corridor beyond the door, Chrissie King would have pulled up a chair.

TWENTY-SEVEN

The next day, Jury was dressed and packed and sitting with Wiggins waiting for his doctor.

"Hannibal," said Wiggins, "has given me this list of medications and instructions and what to do if certain things occur, you know, like falling off a cliff or running from stampeding elephants."

Jury laughed. Wiggins seldom made jokes in this way. Roger Ryder walked in with, unfortunately, Hannibal, who for some reason attached herself to Wiggins.

Dr. Ryder said, "Superintendent, you're good as new. How do you feel?"

"Better than as good as."

"All you need to do is watch that bandage—" He pointed to Jury's midsection. "And don't do any rowing, will you?"

"I'll make an effort to resist."

Ryder smiled. "Don't make an effort, either."

Laughter? They looked over to see Hannibal in a near fit of laughter. What was it, Jury wondered, about Sergeant Wiggins that had this effect on others? He was hardly a bon vivant. But he seemed to reverse a natural inclination in others—turn sour sweet, make water run backward, find some hidden spring. Jury smiled. Wiggins would have made a swell dowser.

Jury took Ryder's arm and led him out of earshot. "There's something I really would like to do. I'd like to look for your daughter."

Ryder looked at him, too stunned to speak.

"I've been thinking about her, her disappearance, ever since you told me about it. In hospital, you've little to do but think. I know it's been nearly two years and you might rather not have this wound reopened—" Jury hated the cliché, but it didn't bother Roger Ryder.

"It's never closed, Mr. Jury." He paused. "You think there's some hope Nell is still alive, then?"

Hope was certainly reborn in the father, to judge from his expression. "I think so. The facts here just don't make it sound like the kidnapping or abduction we're used to seeing. I'd need to talk to people—to your father, to the others at the stud farm. If you could let him know I'm coming . . ."

"Absolutely. When do you think you'd feel like it?"

"Right now."

Roger Ryder rocked back on his heels. "Oh, no, Superintendent, I couldn't let you. I couldn't agree to spending your first day out of hospital—"

"I'm fine, Doctor."

"But . . . this sort of thing, it's exhausting, you know."

Jury didn't know if he was talking about an inquiry or being in hospital. "It's no exertion, really. My sergeant could simply drive me and I'd ask a few questions."

"But—"

"Look, I could go back to my flat straightaway and spend the entire afternoon having to answer a lot of questions about the way I feel, and be visited every fifteen minutes to make sure I really *do* feel all right. Or I could go to your farm and ask a few questions. Now, which of those alternatives sounds more likely to promote a quick recovery?"

"But—"

But Roger was smiling.

"Waterloo Bridge," said Jury.

"Waterloo Bridge?"

"Wiggins, can't I say anything without you saying it back?"

Wiggins actually looked as if he were considering this. Jury shook his head, and again said, "Waterloo Bridge. It's right down there." He pointed in an indeterminate direction. "If we leave right now, we may be able to get away from the curb by dinnertime."

Clearly against his better judgment, Wiggins pulled away from the curb with a lot of engine noise and a jerk that pulled Jury forward in his seat. "Is it that lad you want to see?"

"Benny Keegan. Yes."

"Why's that, sir?" The car idled at a zebra crossing, waiting on several pensioners tottering across it with their string and plastic bags full of groceries. One in particular was finding it hard going. "It's that zimmer bar holding her back," complained Wiggins.

"I'd be happy to wait while you kick it out from under her."

Wiggins slid Jury a look.

"Why do I want to see Benny? Because he saved my life. Isn't that enough?"

"Strictly speaking," said Wiggins, bringing the car to rapid life again, "it was Mr. Plant that did that. He's the one that got the ambulance."

Jury was flabbergasted by this literalness. "Strictly *speaking,* it was Sparky who saved me. If the dog hadn't gone there, Benny could hardly have followed him, which would have meant that Mr. Plant wouldn't have followed Benny."

"Well, yes, if you look at it that way. The truth of it is"—Wiggins kept plowing the rescue theme—"it was just a colossal piece of luck and a big coincidence."

"Luck, maybe. But not coincidence. It was purposeful on their part; they didn't just happen to be strolling by that dock . . ." Why was he bothering?

They continued along the Embankment. Looking down the river, Jury could see the black prospect of Waterloo Bridge. In another three minutes, they were there.

Jury nodded his head toward the curb. "There's a spot. Pull over."

"It's a double-yellow line. It's a loading zone."

"What the hell difference does that make? You're the Filth. Pull over." Wiggins did, and Jury slammed out of the car and crossed the street.

"Well, would'ya look who's here?" said Mags, in a surprisingly friendly way, considering Jury was, as he'd just told Wiggins, the Filth. Possibly this cool attitude toward police might have been owing to the benevolent overlooking by police of Mags's and the others' bit of London real estate—the wide concrete slab beneath this end of the bridge. By night, the little group, dispersed during the day to various begging and other posts (they had their routines just as structured as any CEO's), called this place home. The police allowed them to sleep rough here as long as they vacated the place during the day.

Mags collected old magazines (which were stacked about her feet now) for no reason other than that they were there. "You lookin' for young Benny, then?"

"I am. Is he around or is he across the river?"

"He was back early, then went—there's Sparky comin' along now!"

Jury looked upward to the Embankment walk, where a yellow balloon appeared to be sailing of its own volition above the wall and saw the white terrier, Sparky, walking, stopping, starting, stopping, with Benny following in his wake. Sparky was the busiest dog Jury had ever seen, and Benny the busiest lad. Benny was twelve and made deliveries for five tradespeople across the river in Southwark.

They disappeared from view and then were making their way down the steps.

"Mr. Jury!" Benny called.

When Sparky saw Jury, he broke out in a rousing chorus of barks and began hurling himself at the air as if the only thing holding him back from his object—Jury? the yellow balloon? the sun?—was gravity.

"Sparky, sit!" Sparky, an extremely well-trained dog, sat, but it was clearly a stretch of his bonds that he did so. "You okay, are you, Mr. Jury?" asked Benny, looking concerned. "Mebbe a bit wore out, but still like your old self? Of course, you'd be used to that kind o' thing—you know, gettin' shot at. Gettin' beat up, knives coming at you out of the fog, dark alleyways—"

It was clear that Benny hoped Jury was used to it. "You're right, but a funny thing is, it never gets any easier to take."

"I expect not. Gemma and me and Sparky came to see you in hospital, but this slag of a nurse wouldn't let us in.

Well, I knew they'd not allow Sparky, but he coulda just sat under a chair. And listen: they nearly called the Social on us, seein' we was two kids out and about without a grown-up."

"I'm sorry. I didn't know, Benny. I'd've done something about it if I had." It was laughable to think that these two children couldn't take care of themselves. Extremely laughable, considering what they'd been lately put through. "And how are you keeping?"

"Oh, I'm still doing the rounds, still puttin' up with old Gyp. But, listen: Mr. Tynedale told me I could live at the Lodge if I wanted. That was quite nice of him, I thought."

"He's a nice man, Mr. Tynedale. And are you going to?"

"Nah. Anyway, Gemma was pretty prissy about it, tellin' me all the things I'd have to do, like be careful of my language and take a lot of baths and give Sparky baths all the time. And learn how to bow, and so forth."

This litany of rules and regulations sounded to Jury extremely Gemma orchestrated.

Benny went on. "Do you think maybe Gemma's jealous, Mr. Jury? I mean, in one way Gemma'd like me to live there, but in another way, she wouldn't. The way I see it"—Benny stuck his hands in his pockets and rocked back on his heels a few times—"is Gemma's been, you know, top dog for a time—"

Sparky, who'd been looking from Benny to Jury, barked.

Benny lowered his voice and said from behind his hand, "Sparky don't—doesn't—like dog comparisons, Mr. Jury." In his normal voice he said, "Gemma's been kind of *primo doggereno*," Benny winked, having put one over on Sparky, "and doesn't fancy any competition, anybody like me taking over. Like reading. She reads to old Mr. Tynedale and she knows I like books. I'm an excellent reader; also, I'm a lot older so I can read harder stuff, too. And I think Mr. Tyndale wants someone who'd look after Gemma, see."

"Well, Gemma seems to do pretty well on her own, Benny. She certainly did a great job that night."

Benny didn't like being reminded of "that night" when Gemma went missing because he hadn't been in on the action; Sparky had, but not Benny. Sparky, thought Jury, smiling, had most definitely been *primo doggereno*.

But what Benny said was, "That ain't—isn't—no way to live though, Mr. Jury, I mean being on your own."

Apparently, Benny didn't think he himself was. Jury said, "The thing is, you get used to a certain way of—being, and it's not always a good thing to change it. Take yourself, Benny. You don't want to change how you're living. It feels right to you."

For that, thought Jury, was really it. It was balance. Balance lay in not deliberately changing things around. There was so much change thrust upon us (he thought of the death of Benny's mother) that it helped to keep whatever we could unchanged, to keep unchanged whatever was in our power to do so.

"Benny, I've got to go. Let me know what you decide, will you?"

Benny nodded. "Sparky don't want all them baths, I can tell you."

Jury smiled. "I don't blame him."

Hearing either his name or "bath" or both, Sparky barked.

TWENTY-EIGHT

"Cambridgeshire!" said Wiggins, after Jury got back to the car. "But—"

Jury sighed. "Not you, too, Wiggins. Look, I'm not going there for lessons in dressage; all I want is to ask Arthur Ryder some questions."

"But, sir, I think your doctor should—"

"My doctor has." Jury thought for a moment. "We'll stop in at Victoria Street first—"

Wiggins stared at him as if Jury had spaced out in hospital. "*What?*" His palms shot out as if keeping Jury the lunatic back. "No. I'll drive you anywhere you want to go, but *not* to the Yard!"

"I only want to see Fiona and Cyril."

"Fiona," Wiggins began as he pulled away from the illegal parking spot, "Fiona is fully aware of the situation. 'Now you tell Mr. Jury to go straight home' is what she said. Cyril, well, he keeps himself to himself, but I'm sure he'd agree if he wasn't a cat." The car flowed into traffic heading north.

Jury sighed. "Okay, then I expect we'll just go on to Cambridgeshire."

"I'm glad you're seeing sense."

There were rewards, Wiggins saw, in driving to Cambridge on the A10. Every half hour or so a Little Chef turned up, and they were pulling off into one now.

As they got out of the car and crunched across some

tired gravel, Jury took comfort in the fact that Wiggins took comfort in a thing so common as a Little Chef.

"I'd sooner it was a Happy Eater, but Little Chefs will do."

Jury passed through the door his sergeant held open, saying, "Not much to choose between them, is there?" He made this judgment only because he knew Wiggins would have such a good time refuting it.

"Oh, my goodness, there's no comparison," Wiggins said as the waitress led them to a booth near the back. "You remember that one"—he went on as they sat down and the waitress put menus on the paper placemats— "just outside of Spalding, wasn't it? You remember, in Lincolnshire?"

Not wishing to take a stroll down Happy Eater memory lane, Jury said, "Hm" and picked up his menu. "What'll I have? Anything looks like haute cuisine after hospital meals."

"I'm having one of the specials."

"They're all specials. Maybe some eggs."

"You should watch your cholesterol, sir." Wiggins didn't simply scan the menu; he analyzed it. "I'll have the waffle with sausage."

"Did you know that the connection between cholesterol in food and in the body has never been proven? An egg cannot deposit *its* cholesterol into *your* body. That's the argument."

Wiggins frowned. "That must not be accurate. Look at all the studies that've been done on cholesterol."

"Yeah. But the scientific community, whatever that might be, has never demonstrated it as an actual fact. It's only probabilities. Wine, now, and the occasional snort of booze, that absolutely *has* been shown."

Wiggins just looked at him. "Dream on."

When the waitress appeared, materializing out of some Little Chef netherworld, Jury ordered fried eggs, fried bread, fried bacon, fried sausage—

"Well, those things are already fried." The waitress frowned.

"Fry them again, then. Skip the tomato."

"Tea?"

"Of course."

"Fried?"

Jury looked at her. "Funny."

She shoved her order pad back in her pocket and walked away.

Wiggins said, mournfully, "And you just out of hospital."

"Why do you think I'm having the cardiac arrest platter?" Jury snorted. "I've got connections." He watched the waitress go through to the kitchen. "They don't have this cabaret at the Happy Eaters, Wiggins." Realizing that this would initiate further comparisons between the two fast-food chains, Jury quickly followed with, "What's your feeling about this girl?"

"Nell Ryder? She must be dead, sir."

Jury looked out of the window by their booth at the darkening sky. "I'm not so sure."

"But I thought you said—"

"I changed my mind."

"Why? Why do you think she's still alive?"

Jury pulled a dessert menu from the aluminum holder, seemed to concentrate on it, then shoved it back.

"Sir?" Wiggins looked troubled.

"It looks as if whoever did this never planned on asking for a ransom because they never planned on kidnapping Nell. That wasn't the object. They had to take her."

"Why couldn't it be a kidnapping that just went south? The girl died somehow, maybe they threw her in a trunk and she ran out of air. Something like that. She was dead, so of course they didn't ask for ransom money."

"Why not?" asked Jury.

"Because Ryder would have demanded some proof she was alive."

"Maybe, maybe not. It was worth a shot. It's happened before."

"It just seems so unlikely, what you say, too dodgy."

"Life is dodgy."

Wiggins rolled his eyes. "And you a policeman, sir. You go on evidence."

Then the waitress was there, setting their plates before them along with two mugs of tea.

Looking at Jury's fry-up, Wiggins's thoughts of the vanished girl vanished. "Sir, that food looks lethal."

Jury grinned. "This coming from a man who's about to dig into a plate of waffles and sausage? In the nutrition arena, nobody here wins."

TWENTY-NINE

Even in January, its white fences glazed by the sun, Ryder Stud Farm looked rich and verdant. When it came into view round a curve, the house itself was a startling white. Off to the left was a wide pasture in which horses grazed the cold grass. Jury told Wiggins to stop. He got out and walked over to the fence. In another moment, Wiggins came to stand beside him and they both looked at the horses, two of which peeled away from the others, galloped across the meadow and then ran back again to the others.

It was so fluid, thought Jury, so joyful. He recalled a poem by Philip Larkin, describing exactly what Jury was seeing, retired racehorses running for what looked like pure joy. Jury liked that.

Then another horse, distant, had turned from the others. Jury shaded his eyes and said, "One of them's coming our way. Do we have any binoculars?"

"No. Have we ever had?"

Jury returned his eyes to the pasture. Distant as the horses were he could see their grace and Jury rested his face in his hands. "Have you ever known anyone who hated horses? I haven't. Dogs, yes; cats, yes; wolves, foxes, coyotes, cows—but horses?"

Wiggins said, "I remember a cousin, one of them in Manchester, who went to a riding school, but could never catch on to it. She was always losing control, always taking spills, always the horse would start trotting away. I remember her complaining and complaining, but the thing was, she never blamed the horse. She thought it was her that was the problem, which it was, yes, but you know how people always want to think it's something else, somebody else, never their own fault."

Jury nodded, his chin still propped in his hands. As they stood there, the horse, silvery in the sun, arrived at the fence and stood looking or waiting for them to do something interesting. "We should've picked up some sugar cubes in the Little Chef." He ran his hand down the horse's face. It seemed amazingly placid.

"Nice horse," said Wiggins. "Are they racehorses, then? Thoroughbreds?"

"Some of them, certainly. I imagine this one is. He looks it. He looks a champion."

As if the horse perfectly understood him, it nodded. "Better go," said Jury. "Ryder might be wondering where we are."

They left the fence and recommenced their drive toward the house. They were pulling up to the front door when Wiggins said, "Cows? I never knew anyone to hate cows. Where'd you get that?"

The man who opened the door of the big white house was not Arthur Ryder. Still, he invited them in. "You're Superintendent Jury? Arthur told me to be on the lookout." He smiled. "I'm just a neighbor of Arthur's. He's seeing to one of his mares."

"Superintendent Jury and Detective Sergeant Wiggins," said Wiggins, a trifle imperiously. "And you are?"

"Roy Diamond. I've a farm a mile away."

Roy Diamond was a tall man—as tall as Jury—in a blue blazer with dull gold buttons imprinted with a figure Jury took to be horse related. Natty dresser. Natty life. He looked like that sort of person—privileged and no doubt rich. He also had that look of almost sinful health, as if he spent most of each day in the open air and probably followed the sun, possibly around the world. Jury made this swift and pleasant journey with him in his mind—Nice, Portofino, Corfu, Aruba, Barbados—in the few seconds it took Diamond to shift his gin and tonic to his left hand and jut out the now-free right. His smile was pleasant and his eyes a blue that could only be called crisp. They snapped.

Jury shook his hand and hated him. He hated a lot of people these days, he found, except for those in his immediate circle. But he thought he could manage a special dislike of Roy Diamond. He glanced around the living room—at its dark wood, the chintz-covered chairs, a sofa covered in a sturdier material, low lamps softly diffusing light. Fire in the grate. The fallen petals of roses littered a low table behind the sofa. It was one of those rooms you step into and feel at home. No, more than that: feel it must have been, in a forgotten life, your home. Something like that feeling of déjà vu that Plant had mentioned, that flash of recognition.

"Arthur tells me you're with New Scotland Yard."

"That's correct," said Wiggins, who decided to sit down, even if neither of the others would. He took out his notebook. "You're a neighbor, you say?"

Roy Diamond smiled. "Well, out here, 'neighbor' can be miles away. But, yes, I own Highlander Stud. It's that way." He hooked his thumb over his shoulder. He didn't appear to mind Wiggins's taking down information about him. "Arthur tells me you're interested in Nell Ryder. It was a terrible thing that happened to Nell."

Jury said, " 'Interested in' isn't exactly the way I'd put it." He smiled a chilly smile. "I want to know what happened to her. What do you think?"

The question, asked of him, seemed to surprise Diamond. "I?"

"You must have asked yourself that question."

"Of course I did." Diamond moved to a drinks cabinet and sloshed another finger of gin into his drink. "Oh, I'm sorry—would you like—?" He waved a hand over the collection of bottles.

Jury shook his head. "Medication."

"Hm. Yes, I did ask myself. I imagine I thought pretty much the same as everyone else." He stopped.

"What did everyone else think?"

Diamond gave Jury a look arrested somewhere between a half smile and a frown. "I get the feeling you're baiting me, Superintendent."

Wiggins glanced up at Jury to find his expression, as often happened, completely unreadable.

"I wouldn't bait you. But what did you think about the girl's disappearance?"

"That she was being held for ransom."

"Yet I believe Mr. Ryder doesn't have all that much available cash, no matter how wealthy he might be in terms of his holdings."

"That's right. He's got some of the best horses in the country. I bring some of my own mares here to be bred to his." Roy Diamond studied his drink. "By now, I guess she's dead, though I'd never say that to Arthur."

"You think he still holds out hope, then?"

"Wouldn't you?"

It made Jury vaguely uncomfortable, as if he appeared to be hard-hearted. "I expect so." Then it struck Jury that Roger, who wasn't getting a mention, was seen as having the lesser interest in Nell's fate. Perhaps it was simply because she had lived here with her grandfather.

"Have you any children, Mr. Diamond?"

"I did once. She's dead." Roy Diamond's confidence seemed to be draining away, as age might drain the briskness from one's step. *"Oz,"* he said, more to himself than the other two. He looked up. "It was Dorothy's favorite book, *The Wizard of Oz*—you know, because of her name."

Somewhat ashamed of his tone thus far, Jury said, "I'm really sorry, Mr. Diamond."

Diamond shrugged, put his drink on the table. "I've got to be getting back to the farm. Would you tell Arthur I'll see him soon?"

Jury nodded, shook his hand. Roy Diamond turned to Wiggins, who was still seated, and shook his hand also. "Good-bye." He turned by the door. "And good luck."

Arthur Ryder, who entered a moment later, was a man who, like Roy Diamond, obviously spent most of his time in the open air. The difference was Ryder did it with his sleeves rolled up. He seemed a little uncomfortable bound by his own four walls. The discomfort didn't stem from a police presence in his living room; he was genuinely pleased Jury and Wiggins had come. After they were all seated, he said, "This is really kind of you, Superintendent."

"Not at all. When you're in hospital you look for things

to engage you. Your missing granddaughter engaged me. I'd like to help. Since I'm not on duty, I've plenty of time.''

Ryder opened his mouth to respond when another man came into the room holding a pot of coffee. "This is Vernon Rice, my stepson. When my son called me, I called Vernon and asked him to come. Vern has his own investment firm in the City.'' Arthur Ryder seemed rather proud of this.

Vernon Rice was an extremely good-looking man with hair just about the burnished brown of the bay in the pasture. His eyes, although gray, were so bright they looked startled. They gave gray a whole new meaning. He held the pot aloft and looked a question at Jury and Wiggins. Jury declined; Wiggins accepted. Wishing it were tea instead, thought Jury.

As he poured the coffee into cups already sitting on a tray, Rice said, "I've still got a private investigator looking. I know it's been over a year and a half, but you never can tell.'' He handed Wiggins a cup and set the cream and sugar by him.

Jury smiled. He bet Vernon Rice could pin down the very day the girl had gone missing. He also had the impression that Rice was a "never-can-tell" person. Meaning he operated on faith. Strange for a man in his line of work.

"There was also a horse taken?''

"Aqueduct.''

"Could he carry two people and still jump stone walls and fences?''

"He's a 'chaser. He's won the Grand National twice.''

Vernon smiled. "He could jump rooftops if he had to.''

"Nell could ride him?''

"On a flat course, like the wind.'' As if the image was fixed permanently in his mind, Vernon looked toward the window.

But Jury's image of this agile girl was blank; he couldn't put a face to it. Wiggins had distilled what coverage there had been in the papers, but hadn't produced a picture. "Have you a picture, Mr. Ryder? I'd like to see her.''

Arthur Ryder rose, saying, "I've got a wall full. Come and see.''

"Could Sergeant Wiggins have a word with your staff? The trainer? Anyone else around?"

"Absolutely. But let him finish his coffee."

The look that Wiggins now trained on Jury made Jury wish to God he had a camera. It was almost clubby—Wiggins and his horsey friends.

Arthur Ryder said, "Vernon can show you the photos; I'll take Sergeant Wiggins along to talk to George Davison. He's my trainer." Wiggins, having drained his cup (to the lees), went off with Ryder.

Vernon led Jury into the large office, where an entire wall of photographs and snapshots dominated the rest of the room—photos of horses and, almost as adjuncts or afterthoughts, humans.

Except for one human who could never be an afterthought—a girl with flaxen hair, strands of it blowing across her face as she leaned her head against her horse's neck. It wasn't that she was beautiful; it was that she seemed so present, so here among them. She was always with a horse in these pictures. If a horse was not directly involved, one or more were present as a backdrop. The largest picture was a real stunner. This horse was the one Jury and Wiggins had met down the drive by the fence. Here, Nell Ryder stood a little in the forefront, the reins tangled in her fingers, and looking at the camera dead on. Jury felt it. No wonder Plant couldn't describe her. She was essence, all residue left back in the bottom of the bottle, a girl decanted.

His expression must have betrayed something for he caught Vernon Rice watching him. When Jury looked his way, Vernon smiled.

"Nellie has a lot of presence, hasn't she? I saw it the first time I looked at her."

It was almost, Jury thought, as if Vernon were coming to his rescue, letting Jury know that Nell Ryder had that effect on everyone.

Arthur Ryder had come in the back office door to stand beside Jury. He sighed. "Ah, yes, Nell. She was really— I miss her." His thought, unfinished, stumbled up against loss.

Still slightly mesmerized by the face, Jury said, "Describe her." Yet he thought one of the qualities that made Nell Ryder arresting was that she was indescribable, that anyone would stumble trying to do it, as had her grandfather. "What's she like, I mean, beyond the photographs? How long ago was this one taken?" Jury inclined his head toward the one he'd just been looking at.

"Two years ago. Just before—" Arthur Ryder stopped to clear his throat. "She was fifteen."

Jury found it hard to believe she was anywhere in her teens; the eyes that looked out from the photograph had too much wisdom in them. He knew he was projecting, reading something much too complicated into Nell's eyes; she was a young girl, really. Just a girl.

"Fifteen," Arthur said. "Seventeen, now. Her birthday was—is—just this week."

"Next week, Granddad." They all turned. Jury thought this had to be Maurice Ryder who'd come in from the outside through the office door. "Her birthday's next week." And who, his look said, are these gate crashers at the party?

His grandfather said, "Maurice, come on in."

He was already in, his expression said.

Arthur Ryder introduced them.

If any more gravitas was needed, Maurice Ryder supplied it. He looked, Jury thought, oddly sunk. It was as if the worst that could happen had happened: the coup de grace, the final blow: his cousin's disappearance.

Jury looked from him to the picture. They were close to the same age, but she looked so much older, as if the adult awareness that had grown in Nell by leaps and bounds had been arrested in Maurice, a dark-haired, handsome boy with a pale face and a starved look fed by misfortune. They did look alike, a family-resemblance sort of likeness. But it wasn't the resemblance Jury was interested in; it was the difference. Maurice looked from the picture to Jury, almost as if he were jealous of Jury's looking. But where Maurice (he bet) was obsessed, Nell looked focused. There was a world of difference between the two. Yet he didn't really know what Nell's qualities were.

"When did you last see her, Maurice?"

As if he really had to think about it, Maurice was slow to answer. "Evening stables."

Meaning, probably, that Maurice had seen her last. Jury thought Maurice would always want to be last: the last person to see her would leave his face imprinted on her mind.

"Where did you see her?"

Maurice inclined his head backward a little. "In the stables. She'd carried out her sleeping bag."

"Could you show me?"

"Okay." He turned to the door.

The stall Nell Ryder had been sleeping in was empty, as if it had been kept that way in case she should return with Aqueduct in the middle of the night and need it. It was as large as a small room. Several others down the line were occupied; Jury recognized a couple of the horses sticking their heads out as the ones in the field where he and Wiggins had stopped. Gingerly, Jury put out his hand, and the horse with the silvery mane nudged it.

"Looking for treats," said Maurice, smiling for the first time.

"What a gorgeous horse."

"Samarkand. He is, yes; knows it, too."

Jury would have been willing to ascribe certain human traits to animals, but vanity wasn't one of them. Anyway, it was just a way of talking for Maurice.

"Sam's my favorite. Nell, she'd never say who hers was; I think she didn't want to hurt the other horses' feelings."

That made Jury smile. "She sounds like a sensitive person."

"Oh, she was—is, I mean."

It must have gotten harder and harder to rescue the present from the past, Jury thought. "This is a wonderful place to grow up. Or did you?"

"More or less. I came with my dad a lot and spent summers here and holidays, so yes, I guess I did grow up here."

"You and Nell."

Maurice didn't answer beyond a nod of his head. Then he said, "After my aunt, Nell's mum, died, Uncle Roger tried to keep her with him in London. But his schedule got so fierce he just couldn't do it. Middle of the night emergencies, that sort of thing."

"What about your parents?"

For some reason, Maurice felt his father should be defended; he did not feel that way about his mother. "They got divorced. You know what mum said to me? She didn't want to put me through a long custody battle, so it would be better all around if I came to live with Granddad." He gave Jury a wry little smile.

"What about your father?"

"He got custody by default. Not that he didn't want it"—Maurice added quickly—"my dad's a champion, or was, I mean. A great jockey. Finally, he took off for Paris and got married again. Then there was the accident that killed him. It was on a racecourse near Paris, when his horse slammed into a fence."

"And his wife?"

"We never met her, his new wife."

"Did you ever want to be a jockey, then, like your father?"

"I always wanted to be a jockey. He was one of the greatest, you know. He's in the jockeys' hall of fame. But after I grew four inches like all at once, I gave up on that. I'll tell you who'd make a good jockey."

"Who?"

"Nell. She'd be awesome."

"That good on a horse, is she?"

"Yes. Nell had—has—"

(The present rescued again.)

"—an instinct. She just *knows* what's going on with them. And she always says anyone could if they'd just take the trouble. But that's not true. Not even George has that way about him. He knows it, too. He likes to say that Nell is really a horse, zipped up in girl costume."

Jury laughed. "Some costume, Maurice, if that's what it is."

Maurice looked at him and smiled for the second time. "You can say that again."

On their way back to the house, he saw Wiggins with two men, a wiry young man and a short stocky one. The older man Jury presumed to be Davison.

Wiggins introduced them as Neil Epp, head groom, and George Davison.

"You're the trainer, Mr. Davison."

"That's it." George Davison was one of those men who appeared to be all business. No time for messing about when there was work to be done. This police business might or might not be messing about.

The horse whose bridle Neil Epp was hanging on to was as black as the bottom of a mine. Black and sleek. Jury nodded to him. "And who's this?" he asked, looking at the horse.

Looking as proud as if he'd invented him on the spot, Davison said, "Criminal Type."

Jury smiled, liking the name. He ran his hand down the horse's neck. "Beautiful. I bet he's won a few for you."

"Indeed he has, despite the extra weight he always has to carry."

"Why's that?"

"To even the chances. Only time I ever lost me temper with the Jockey Club it was over that weight allowance in the Derby year before last, when Dan was up on him. Would've been, I mean. They said Criminal Type'd have to carry another fifteen pounds. Bloody unfair. So I scratched 'im."

Jury knew George Davison could talk all day about his horses to anyone who served as a listening post. It was almost by way of talking to himself.

"Your people going to get anywhere with regards to young Nell?" said Neil Epp. "Been two years, it has," he said, as if none of them knew it.

This earned him a sweltering look from Davison, who was no doubt a proponent of the less-said department.

"I certainly hope so, Mr. Epp. We'll try. Wiggins?"

"I've got it all, sir." Wiggins flapped his notebook.

They set off for the house. Jury felt he had to see those pictures again.

"I want to fix her in my mind," he said to Arthur Ryder and Vernon Rice.

The four of them took up positions again in front of the wall of photographs. Jury was almost convinced of the truth of that old superstition about the camera's catching the soul of its subject, which then resided in the photograph. Melrose Plant had said, "She gives déjà vu a whole new meaning." Jury said, "It's strange. I get the feeling I've seen her before."

"That's a common reaction, you know, from just about anyone who sees these photos," Vernon Rice said. "It's that she looks familiar, that a person already knows her. You do get what I mean?"

Jury got it.

Brand-new clothes. Same old dream.

THIRTY

He shouldn't have gone, that's what Dr. Ryder kept telling him, his first day out of bed, but he wouldn't listen, though I tried to reason with him, just out of hospital and insisting on going to Cambridgeshire, of course he'd fall asleep in the car, didn't surprise me, tired as he was.

Wiggins went on in this way for a good while after delivering Jury to Ardry End and the ministrations of everyone there, barely awake enough to receive enthusiastic greetings not only from Melrose Plant but also from Ruthven and his wife, Martha, who had cooked what she mistakenly thought to be Jury's favorite meal—roast beef and potatoes—when actually the meal that won the gold was one of Carole-anne's fry-ups in its greasy symmetry of egg, bacon, sausage and fried bread (the Little Chef version was merely a shadow on the wall of Plato's cave) and during which Momaday had presented his sorry self to go on and on about Aggrieved and how he'd be "whipping that horse into shape, never you mind, good as won the 2000 right now," and Martha (of all people!) telling Momaday the horse was too old for the 2000, and (following a brief argument on that score), Ruthven at last leading Jury up to his favorite room and watching him fall across the bed as if he'd been bludgeoned—all of this leaving Melrose feeling the evening hadn't so much as ended as collapsed around him, compressing and elongating like a bellows or in a wind tunnel with some Proustian crazy.

*   *   *

When Jury walked into the dining room the following morning, time had been restored to its familiar sequential meanderings. Melrose Plant was reading at the table, munching toast. "Have I held things up?" Jury asked.

Melrose merely looked at him and chewed. "The others have gone on ahead. They're hoping to reach the summit before dark."

Jury rubbed his hands, looking at the silver domes, smelling the sausage-drenched air. "I take it that's a no. I haven't held things up?"

"Suit yourself. As long as it isn't after eleven a.m. Nothing around here we can do to hold anything up—"

"Why do I have the feeling"—said Jury, setting a silver dome to one side and sniffing syrupy pancakes—"that my question will keep you going for some time, whereas another person might simply have answered, 'Not at all, not at all'?"

"Well, that's simple enough. This hypothetical person isn't busy scaling Everest. So of course he or she'd say 'Not at all, not at all.' "

Jury spooned eggs and a small pile of mushrooms onto his plate, then forked up sausages (a largish number), speared a tomato and sat down. "I told you."

"Told me what? Did you know that Forego girthed seventy-seven inches?"

"That question makes me feel like I'm having breakfast with Wiggins, who asks things like, 'Do you know that kava-kava, if made up into a poultice, is good for boils?' " Jury ate his sausage.

"And your answer was—?"

"Very funny. Is that a word? 'Girthed'?"

"It's a horse word. You've got to know something about them, of course."

"I do. Pass the salt."

"Are we a trifle *testy* this morning?"

"I am. I don't know about you."

Melrose took a look in the teapot and rang for Ruthven. "There's just too damned much to learn about horse racing. So I'm taking a page from Diane's book."

"There's only one page in Diane's book." Jury nibbled another sausage. He hated to see the sausage go so soon. "Take it, and there won't be any book."

"Anyway, I'm doing what she does and concentrating on just a few horses and a couple of races. I love their names. Spectacular Bid—isn't that wonderful?" He paused and thought about the name and was surprised when Ruthven suddenly appeared at his side.

"Sir?" he said, inquiringly, and to Jury, "Superintendent, and how are you this morning?"

"Fine, Ruthven. Tell Martha this is a great breakfast."

"We could use some more tea," said Melrose. "Hot water's gone, too." Ruthven returned to the kitchen. "They like you more than they like me."

"Everyone wants to stay on the good side of the Bill."

"So, using Diane's method, I think I can manage to learn enough. She makes you think she knows a lot more than she does."

"No, Diane makes me think she knows a lot less than she does."

"I don't mean us. I mean other people, strangers, who don't know her methods. There's no question she helped me out on that gardening business."

Jury had risen and returned to the buffet, looking under domes. "Where're the mushrooms? They were right here—"

"That's right. They were right there until you scraped the sauté pan clean with your little spoon."

"Could you just ask Martha—?"

"For you Martha would slaughter a hog."

And here she came with the teapot and a steaming silver dish, replacement for the one Jury was hanging around right now. "Mushrooms! I knew you'd be wanting more o' my mushrooms!"

"You're a lifesaver, Martha. That's just what I was asking for."

Pleased as punch, Martha walked out leaving Jury to spoon up the mushrooms.

"You've said nothing about the Ryders yet."

"I know." Jury brought his plate back to the table. "It's not for lack of thinking about them." He fell silent, turning his fork over and back and over again.

"Yes? Well? Think about them out loud then."

Jury sat back. "Vernon Rice was there, too."

"Ah! So you got them all at once."

"I got them all at once, yes." He picked up his teacup and held it out for a refill. "Also a chap who owns Highlander Stud named Roy Diamond."

"I didn't meet him." Melrose felt irrationally cheated. "And? What did you think of them? There seems to be an undercurrent here that I can't plumb." Melrose poured the tea and, when Jury didn't answer, said, "What?"

"Vernon Rice—" Jury heard an acerbity in his tone that he had wanted to keep out of it.

"It already sounds as if you don't much like him. I do."

"I know you do. But you spent a long time with him and by himself. I mean, out from under the Ryder Stud influence."

" 'Influence'?" Melrose gave a short bark of laughter. "Rice doesn't strike me as the type to be influenced by anyone." Melrose thought for a moment. "Unless you mean Nell Ryder?"

"Of course."

"But that isn't exactly 'under the influence of.' That's more that he simply cares about her."

"Try 'loves.' "

"Yes, I suppose—"

"As 'in' with."

"Are you saying—? But look here, she was only fifteen."

"Poe's cousin was only fourteen."

Melrose gave that laugh again. "Ye gods, that's *Poe*."

"His behavior was aberrant, you mean?"

Melrose scratched his neck, confused with feeling. "No, I expect not. I mean, back in Poe's time it wasn't all that unusual to marry a young girl. Virginia, her name was." It came back to Melrose in a little flood of what he supposed was Proustian involuntary memory. Baltimore—Poe's house, the little rooms, and the passion of the curator in defending Poe against his detractors, the plagiarized manuscript, the vulgarity of its perpetrator.

"You look unhappy."

"The curator of the Poe house recited the end of a poem, something about a cloud that took the form *'of a demon in my view.'* Melrose gave a self-conscious shrug. "I was just remembering . . ."

"No wonder," said Jury.

"You were in Ryder's office, weren't you? You saw the photos. Weren't you struck?"

"I was definitely struck." Jury drank his tea.

Melrose nodded. Then he said, "Aren't you finished? I want you to see my horse."

"That sounds a treat," said Jury, shoveling in some more mushrooms.

"There's nothing to it," Melrose said suavely.

"Of course, there's something to it," said Jury, "and I haven't got it."

"But he likes you. I can tell."

"Now just how do you make that out?"

"Look, he's trying to nudge you."

"To get another apple, that's why."

"Maybe we shouldn't give him any more. He might get sick."

Just then Momaday lurched up behind them. He was wearing the long cowboy coat Melrose had given him for Christmas, thereby feeding Momaday's image of himself as hunter, rancher, rustler, sheriff and a lot of other things that fit the myth of the Old West that Momaday wasn't. But it had him slapping that rifle into play, aiming and shooting and if he hit anything it was by sheer accident— that same Momaday had come up behind the two and barked an order: "Don't you be feedin' that horse apples!"

Both Melrose and Jury jumped as if they'd been found out by Aunt Polly and exchanged a look.

"Just one."

"One, that's right."

They had taken turns and fed him four.

Melrose changed the subject. "I was just telling Superintendent Jury here that he should get up on Aggrieved and go for a ride."

Momaday made a lengthy snuffling noise, his version of a laugh, and within and around this said to Jury, "Oh, you shoulda been here t'other day to see Mr. Plant, here (none of that 'Lord Ardry' and 'm' lord' nonsense from Momaday, never fear!) up on Aggrieved and trying to dismount"—snuffle, snuffle—"and t' fall clear off t' other side!" Laughing fit to kill, Momaday walked off, gun broken over his arm.

Jury looked at Melrose. "Nothing to it, right?"

THIRTY-ONE

"Y̶ou ate seven sausages. I counted. You ate more sausages than Aggrieved ate apples."

They were strolling through the village. Jury stopped in front of Betty Ball's bakery, where he expressed an interest in the pumpkin muffins on display in the bakery's window.

"Seven sausages. You couldn't possibly eat a muffin. They're left over from Halloween, anyway."

Jury reached in his coat pocket and drew out an amber vile containing some white pills. "Dimerin and sausages, the doctor's orders."

"Well, you don't need a muffin." He pulled on Jury's coat.

They crossed the narrow bridge that spanned the equally small and narrow river and Jury stopped and regarded the small green and its pond. It was as if the scene were miniaturized, like the miniature Bourton-on-the-Water where a Lilliputian copy of the village itself was kept on display. He looked off to the left at the largest house in the village. Vivian Rivington's. If he took his emotional temperature, his Vivian temperature right now, he wondered what it would read. But you can't do that, can you? For the real indicator is that surprise appearance, that sudden turning and seeing a woman walk through a door, or seeing her sitting on that bench. It's the only thing that makes the mercury spike, the only gauge. He could still see her as he'd done the first time when she'd appeared before him, recall her embarrassed look, her fingers fussing with the hem of a brown jumper. What in God's name was he up to, always falling in love at first sight?

There was only a ruff of snow round the pond like a collar of icing on a cake. It would soon melt away. Back then the entire green had been carpeted in snow.

"What are you doing?" said Melrose. "By the time we get to the Jack and Hammer it'll be closed again. We don't keep London hours here. Well, maybe we could, but Dick Scroggs won't keep them."

They started walking again. "I was just thinking about the first time I came here."

"Few things are more dangerous than that."

They were walking along Long Piddleton's main street now. "What do you mean, dangerous?" asked Jury.

"We make these minute revisions, look at it from a slightly different angle: that pond, that bench there or not, whatever it was that made it more desirable, its loss more bitter. Memory's plague causes unnecessary suffering."

Jury stopped short. "What in hell are you talking about? When did you start finding memory so finely nuanced?"

Melrose pursed his lips. "Since I saw it might get us from the green to the Jack and Hammer without your stopping and gawking every two minutes. And"—he spread his arms—"here we are!"

And here *they* were, too, still having misgivings about Jury's survival, so that to see him walk in was a real thrill.

"I quite liked that other case," said Diane to Jury, "except, of course, for that shooting at the end of it. Anyway, I'm not one to talk. I hit Melrose's vodka. His last bottle, I might add."

Melrose asked Jury, "Can I tell them about the vanished girl?"

"Go ahead. It's not a Scotland Yard matter. It isn't really a case."

"Okay." He turned to an audience already turned to him as if he had brought a lifesaving draft. "This all happened when I was in the Grave Maurice—"

"Where's that?" asked Trueblood.

"A pub across the street from the Royal London Hospital."

"Ah, that's where Superintendent Jury was," said Diane. "I remember sending a wreath of roses."

"Are you going to keep interrupting?"

No one spoke.

Melrose told them about the vanished girl.

At the end of this brief account, Vivian Rivington, with Agatha behind her, appeared in the sun-splashed doorway of the Jack and Hammer like a ray of hope, a thing Jury had given up on, lying on that dock in the dark. He could still see the stars in that implacable night sky. He smiled. It was hard to give up on Vivian. He wondered if her Italian count was gone for good.

"Richard!"

Her look was a mixture of wonder and relief. Perhaps she wouldn't believe he was alive until she saw him. "Hello, Vivian." He went to meet her and gave her a kiss on the cheek that she didn't seem to know what to do with. Then, suddenly, she threw her arms around him. He returned this heartfelt hug.

Diana, seeing her glass was empty, handed it off to Dick for another.

Trueblood then raised his. "To your long and happy life, Superintendent."

Diane said, "I could have warned you that night was fraught with danger."

"Oh, it was fraught all right. So why didn't you? Warn me, I mean?"

"You didn't ask me, did you?"

Jury laughed. "I guess I didn't."

"The stars! The stars!" proclaimed Agatha, as if she were finished with their wastrel ways.

"How are you, Lady Ardry?" Jury reached his hand across the table to clasp hers.

Put out by Melrose's adamant direction that she was not to turn up at Ardry End this morning, she waggled her finger at Jury. "You cheated me out of my morning coffee, Superintendent."

"So here you are having your morning whiskey," said Melrose.

She tried to numb him with a look and, as usual, failed.

Eagerly, Joanna said to Jury, "Tell us, tell us! This boy and his dog—"

Jury smiled. "It should be the dog and his boy. That's one damned smart dog. I was lying there for what was probably only a few minutes, but felt a lifetime—"

Agatha butted in to stall the story, annoyed she hadn't heard this account before the others over morning coffee. "And did your whole life pass before you?"

"No," he lied, not wanting to talk about it.

Joanna leaned toward Jury. "What was it like, nearly dying?"

Jury wanted to say terrifying; he had wanted to be terrified. Instead, what he had felt was the lure of the dark. He wondered how it was that inconsequential things came back to one at such moments. Because, he reasoned, they weren't inconsequential. He looked up to see five pairs of eyes, expectant.

"Terrified," he said.

"This case you're working on," said Diane.

"It's not a case. It's not my case, certainly."

"Never mind. I've got a theory."

"Oh, good," said Melrose. "Scotland Yard can go back to bed."

Diane plowed on. "This girl that's gone missing probably went off with her boyfriend, who'd told her they'd get married and when he just up and left her, she was too ashamed to go back home. It's not the leaving that's significant. It's the not coming back."

They all looked at her. Trueblood said, "Diane, that's one of the most Victorian scenarios I've ever heard."

"It sounds," said Joanna, "like one of mine."

"At this point," said Jury, "it's as good as any other." He smiled at her.

"Then what's your theory?" asked Diane. "White slavery?"

Trueblood said, "Aren't we ignoring the most obvious explanation? She's dead. It's the only thing that makes sense. There was no ransom demand because she's dead, maybe an accident, something the abductors didn't intend—" He shrugged away the rest of the scene.

"She's not dead." Jury said it before he could stop himself.

Several pairs of eyes regarded him.

"How is it," asked Melrose, "you're so sure of that?"

Jury picked up his beer. He didn't answer.

"I like your idea of recuperating," said Melrose.

"I'm not doing the driving. I'm just sitting here, enjoying the scenery."

"We're on the M1. There isn't any scenery."

Jury slid a few inches down in his seat. "I love this car."

"You can't have it."

"While I'm talking to Vernon Rice, where are you going to be?"

"Oh, I'll 'hang' as they say in the Grave Maurice. Unless you want me to come with you?" His tone was hopeful.

"No. You've already talked to him. Both of us would be intimidating. Anyway, he doesn't know you know me."

"Of course he does. He's Roger Ryder's stepbrother."

"Yes, but he doesn't know we have any working relationship. As far as Rice is concerned, you're just some aristocratic oddball."

"Thanks. Just remember, I had lunch with him. I mean we had quite a good conversation going." He shook his head. "I just don't get it that you don't like him."

"I didn't say that. Did I say that?"

"Oh, don't be as thick as two posts. You know you don't like him. But there's one thing you have in common."

"What?"

"You don't believe Nell Ryder's dead."

THIRTY-TWO

Jury sat on Vernon Rice's sofa and understood what Melrose had meant. It was slimmed-down, pared-down luxury. The furniture was Italian or German or both, the colors muted, the lines clean. The chair he sat in, although its angles had looked forbidding, was superbly comfortable. He decided he preferred his own ramshackle flat with its Early Oxfam appointments, which was just as well, since he wasn't getting this one.

Of course it overlooked the Thames, one of those breathtaking views estate agents were always advertising that usually turned out to be a small slice of the river if you held your head in a certain way. But this view answered all of the demands of "breathtaking." Right now the descending sun turned the pocked surface of the Thames to hammered gold.

Jury's dislike (he had lied to Melrose) of Vernon Rice only increased in these sumptuous surroundings (childish, but he didn't care; he let it increase), these proofs of the man's success. "Thank you," he murmured as Rice handed him an espresso.

"You sure you wouldn't like a drink? I've got some really good whiskey."

Jury thought, I'll bet. I'll bet it's a million years old. "Oh, no thanks. Coffee's fine."

"Something wrong, Superintendent? You look a little, uh, disgruntled." Vernon smiled.

So did Jury, trying to beat him to it, not succeeding.

"Sorry, but I guess it's just spillover from the hospital. Too much nursing."

"Too much shooting, maybe."

Jury looked at him and could detect nothing but empathy. "That's nearer the mark, yes."

"It sounds as if it were more than just a close call."

"How do you—?"

"The dailies, Mr. Jury. The newspapers were full of it. Don't tell me they weren't all over you in hospital the moment you woke up."

"They weren't. That must have been Dr. Ryder's doing."

Jury could remember very little of the first day—and possibly of the second or third. All he wanted was sleep, from which he awoke at one point to see Carole-anne framed in the window lighted by the sun, her red-gold hair on fire, and thought he was in heaven.

Insofar as police, hospital personnel and visitors went he had shut down his mind. It was as simple as that. He wanted no more than the sketchiest outline, the bare bones of what had happened. He wanted none of that *pas trop vite* Proustian precision. Leave out as much as possible, otherwise, he was afraid he'd tank.

"But of course they didn't know the rest of the story—"

(Was Vernon Rice a mind reader now?)

"—the papers never do; they make up what they want."

For the first time, more so even than in hospital, Jury felt like an invalid. His hand had shaken slightly returning his empty cup to the table. But not slight enough to prevent Rice from seeing it.

Jury said, "I want to talk to you about Nell Ryder's disappearance. I couldn't make out when I was at the farm whether you said you believed she was still alive because of her grandfather's feelings, or if you really—"

"Believe it? I believe it, yes."

Jury could sense Rice's desperation. He wanted everyone who'd known Nell Ryder to believe it; he wanted someone else's confirmation.

"What do you think of her father?"

"Roger's a good father, I know, even though he does have to spend most of his time in London. He goes to the farm almost every weekend, Arthur says."

"And his brother?"

"Danny was much different. He was a great jockey, but in other ways—" Vernon shrugged. "He had his addictions—gambling, women—not drink or drugs, though, which was probably because he had to keep his weight in line and his mind clear. But women—*lots* of women. I know a couple of husbands who weren't too happy with him. I think he broke up a marriage here and there. It's strange, you know, because you can't tell that just looking at his picture. But I'll tell you, one blink, a woman would be all over him."

"Did you know any of these women?"

"No—yes. I forgot the one I did some investing for. Sara . . . Sara—Hunt. Actually, she's some distant relation of the Ryders. I drove her out to Arthur's one Sunday. Wait a minute and I can give you her address. I don't know that she was actually involved with Dan." He shrugged. "Still, I always got the impression that for a woman, to see Danny race was to be involved."

Jury sat forward. "I'd like the telephone number if you have it."

While Vernon was fiddling with an address book, Jury said, "What about his niece, Nell? She's certainly beautiful. Would he have tried something on there?"

Vernon's eyes hardened, changing from a foggy gray to granite. "No. Someone would have killed him. And one thing I can credit Danny with is that he wouldn't have hurt any member of his family."

"And Nell? How did she feel about him?"

"Danny was great with horses, had a special relationship with them. I heard that he never used a whip, not even as a directional signal. Times I thought he could ride a horse through hell and not get burned. Well"—Vernon spread his hands—"that's all Nell needed to know. She liked him." Vernon paused. "He was one hell of a jockey; some said he was up there with Lester Piggot." Vernon shook his head, studied the mantel where a few framed pictures were lined up. "I really feel for Maurice; Maurice idolized Danny, poor lad. He'd have done anything for Danny."

"I talked to Maurice when I was at the farm. He seems

to be—as the Irish love of euphemism has it—destroyed by Nell Ryder's disappearance.''

"He'll never get used to it. Maurice tends to blame himself when things go wrong.''

"He thinks what happened to Nell is partly his responsibility?''

"Believe it. He's never said so in so many words, but I bet he does. Maurice has taken on his shoulders the sins of the father. I never know whether to hit him or weep. Not only that, he wanted to be another Danny—omitting, of course, the X-rated bits.''

"But he's too big. What a disappointment for him.''

"Yes. Add to that, though, that Nellie isn't. She's the right size. And it wouldn't surprise me if she wanted to be one, too, but never said so because of Maurice. She's like that.''

Vernon retrieved Jury's empty cup and his own and went to stand by the window as if he'd forgotten already why he was there. Then he came out of his trance and went to the espresso machine.

"She appears to evoke very strong feelings in people, and in some cases, just from her photos.'' Jury knew she had in him, also in Melrose Plant.

Vernon rubbed the side of his head. "That's because she's so intense, so—I don't know, focused, maybe—that when she looks at you, it's about you; she hasn't a dozen other scenarios crowding her mind. Only you. I doubt there's a man or woman or child who wouldn't respond to that.''

"Certainly you have.''

"Oh, yes. The first time I saw Nellie was only a few months before she disappeared. She was fifteen. She was in one of the horse stalls, filling the feed basket and singing under her breath in case—she told me later—anyone was around; she didn't want them to hear her. She was always singing in that whispery way so no one would hear. No one but the horses. She turned and smiled a little. Anyone else would've said, 'Oh! Who are you!' She just said 'Hello.' ''

"For a young girl, she sounds pretty composed.''

"That's just what I said to her. I said she had a lot of poise. She said it was probably because of the horses.''

Jury smiled. "She was good with horses, wasn't she?"

Vernon nodded. "Davison—the trainer?—has always been impressed with her. Thinks she'd make a great trainer."

"She was in the stall with Aqueduct because he was sick, is that right?"

Vernon nodded. "It was around dinnertime that Maurice told her he thought the horse might be suffering from stable cough."

"Did she often stay with horses like that?"

"As often as a horse gets sick. Arthur has a couple of vets on call, so anything that looks like trouble they can nip in the bud."

"Hm." Jury sat thinking. "I get the impression Nell was very self-disciplined."

"Extremely."

"All right. How then might she react to being kidnapped?"

The question took Vernon by surprise. "You mean, would the discipline kick in?"

"That's what I mean. Would she be cool?"

"Cool. I think she'd be up for that. She'd be able to bring that off, yes."

Jury smiled. " 'Fear wearing black.' Definition of cool. Maybe it's also the definition of courage. Would she be courageous?"

"Yes. Depending on what was at stake."

"If something wasn't at stake, you wouldn't need courage."

Light had been steadily lessening while Jury was talking to Vernon Rice, as if a door were closing on it. He looked at the line of pictures over the fireplace. He could see from where he sat that they were all of the Ryder family. "You've never been married?"

"No. Should I be?"

Jury laughed. "No, it just surprises me."

"Why?"

"Women like a man who'd go to a lot of trouble for them. Obviously, you would. It's romantic, among other things. I'm just surprised you haven't been snagged."

Vernon smiled. "I'm not all that easily snagged, Superintendent."

"I can see that."

"I was engaged once, a few years ago. I decided it wouldn't work."

"Why? I'm interested."

"I just didn't love her enough." Vernon rinsed out his and Jury's cups, saying, "I don't know about you, but I'm switching to whiskey. Want some?"

"Thanks. Just soda it up a lot."

"Worried about your drinking? You can always visit Say-When." Vernon told him about it.

Jury laughed. "Great idea. But that's not my reason. It's because I'm taking some sort of medication."

Vernon was at the drinks table uncapping what looked to Jury like a fifth of Glenfiddich. "What kind of medication?"

"Dimerin, I think it is."

"Oh, that stuff. It won't hurt. You could mix it with engine oil and it wouldn't do a thing to you."

"How do you know?"

"Because I own thirty-three percent of the company. I got in on their IPO. I don't do that sort of thing blindfolded. I really find out about their product. This particular corporation's stock is going to split soon—"

Jury smiled. "Save me the details of corporate finance. It's all lost on me." That sounded properly stuffy. Or superior. Why was Rice bringing out the worst in him? Or perhaps it was himself, bringing out the worst.

"Poor you. It's really very entertaining."

"Entertaining? That's what you do it for?"

"No. I do it for the money."

Jury laughed and took a sip of the whiskey. It was very mellow. "Let's get back to love. You said you didn't love her enough. How did you know in the end that you didn't?"

For a moment Vernon merely stared at his glass. Then he slid down on the sofa and looked up at the ceiling. "Because when she went away I didn't miss her. Because I could stand having her out of my sight; because I didn't want to touch her every time I saw her; because I didn't

have the urge to buy her flowers every time I passed a
flower stall; because I didn't look for her around every
corner; because she wasn't in my head every time I looked
up from a market report; because she didn't make me feel
stoned—and didn't make me feel glad I wasn't; she didn't
fire up my imagination; she didn't make me forget the
gloom of the past, as the song goes. Because she didn't
make me almost wish she'd disappear so I could find her."

That hung in the air while Vernon studied the diamond
facets of the glass he seemed to have been committing to
memory as one would a woman's face, which, in all likeli-
hood, one would never see again. "It was like that."

Jury hardly knew what to say. "It was?"

"Yeah. Really adolescent. Not what you'd call real love,
I guess."

Jury looked at him. "If it isn't, maybe it ought to be."
Jury drained his glass. "I appreciate your time. I've got to
go." He rose.

Vernon went to the door with him. "You'll find her."

It wasn't a question.

Jury never made promises about the outcome of a case,
and this one surely would end badly, if it ended at all.
That's what worried him, that it never would. "I'll try."

It wasn't an answer.

"I'm going to Wales," Jury said, taking a stool beside
Melrose in the Grave Maurice.

"*Wales?* Why on earth?"

"There's a woman there who knew Dan Ryder. I want
to talk to her." When the turbaned barkeeper stopped in
front of him, Jury ordered whatever was on tap. Then he
said to Melrose, "I see what you mean about him."

"What do I mean?"

"About Vernon Rice. He's one of the most likable men
I've ever met."

"Told you."

Jury turned and smiled at Plant. "That only makes me
that much more suspicious."

THIRTY-THREE

It was a gloomy day, even by January's standards. Vernon matched it well. He had just returned the receiver to its cradle and was standing before the big office window with its view of St. Paul's, or at least of its spire. Too many buildings were crowding into the City and ruining some of London's views. He couldn't turn his thoughts to that for very long or to much else. He hadn't liked the conversation with Leon Stone.

"With nothing new by way of either evidence or information, I've run up against a blank wall." Pause. "Vernon, I know it's hard for you to hear, but I honestly think Nell Ryder's dead."

"No, she isn't."

"That's wishful thinking on your part."

"No, it isn't. Wishful thinking is thinking you can sell ten thousand shares of British Telecom short and make a killing. *That's* wishful thinking."

Leon Stone sighed. "I hate to keep taking your money."

"First time I ever heard anyone say that." Vernon had laughed, not joyfully. Then he'd hung up.

He wanted Leon Stone to believe at least in part that Nell was still alive. Arthur didn't, not anymore, Vernon was sure. He stood at the window and went back over her disappearance again. The trouble with this was it was the same old track; he wished his mind would derail, shake itself up a bit.

That police superintendent, Jury, was the only new thing that had entered the picture. Seemed pretty smart, maybe he'd come up with something. Vernon swiveled his chair around and sat down in it, back on track, going over it all again. *Do not sit here brooding, for God's sake. Do not brood.*

"Want a ploughman's?" Samantha put her head around the door.

The door was always open, but she seemed to like this sort of hugger-mugger approach.

He looked around. "No thanks."

"I'm bringing something back for Daph and Bobby. You sure?"

"I'm sure. You know it's raining like hell."

"It's always raining like hell. See you later."

He supposed she was leaving; he couldn't hear her; the carpet was so thick in the outer office you could deploy an elephant herd and not hear it.

"Bye," he said to something as he looked at his TV screens, market reports on CNN and the BBC. He muted the sound and spent a few minutes watching the ticker tape. Then he got up, reached for his laptop, looked at what was there, from the laptop to the desktop, not much happening.

"Vernon."

Vernon looked over his shoulder and froze. He dropped the laptop and felt the pain only as some vague reminder you couldn't drop heavy objects on your foot and not feel it.

"Vernon," said Nell, "I need your help."

Love Walked In

THIRTY-FOUR

They stood staring at each other for some moments. Vernon was afraid to move in case the image shattered. But no lightning spiked, no thunder boomed, and he moved so quickly toward her he could not remember crossing the room. The cold rain saturating her clothes became his cold rain.

"Nellie." Arms around her, Vernon said it again.

As if in getting him wet, she realized she herself was soaking wet, she asked Vernon if there was anything around that she could wear. Her wet clothes had been discarded and she had wrapped herself up in Vernon's bathrobe; Samantha, having returned with the food Vernon didn't eat, had then been dispatched to buy Nell new clothes—jeans, shirt and wool jacket. And boots. Hers would never dry in time. "In time for what?" Nell asked.

"Dinner."

In between the wet clothes and the dry ones, Nell told Vernon the story.

He listened for half an hour, interrupting the flow of her talk only once to get her a blanket because she had shivered. He kept clothes and blankets in his office because he sometimes slept there.

With the blanket tucked about her, she went on. "I should have run away after Valerie finally let me out of my room."

"This is the Hobbs woman?"

Nell nodded. "I should have left them; I should have run."

"Nell"—he put a hand on her arm—"forget 'should.' You did what you thought was right. That's enough. Go on."

She told him about the imprisoned mares. "It's—I can't think of any words to describe it. But I suppose just stating the facts describes it, doesn't it?"

Vernon asked, "This guy who grabbed you in the barn that night—why did he? Do you know?"

Nell looked toward the window, thinking. She did not want to turn his attention to the man and the pitch-black room. She knew it would overwhelm the rest. "I don't know, I honestly don't. The first thing he did was to spray something in my eyes. I couldn't see."

"You couldn't identify him, then?"

She shook her head. "I know he was short and wiry from having to sit in front of him. He could've been a jockey, for that matter. He was certainly a good rider. As far as I know, I didn't see him again. I don't think he was one of the men who worked for Valerie Hobbs."

Vernon looked at her. "It was you," said Vernon. "The anonymous tip to the police."

"Yes. Who was that woman? I never saw her before."

"Neither had anyone else. She was Dan Ryder's wife. Widow, I mean. Police traced her back to Paris."

"That's—" She shook her head. "I don't understand."

"Neither do we. Arthur'd never seen her. Have you called him? Does he know you're back? Does your father?"

"No. Not yet. Please don't tell anyone."

Her look was so beseeching he wouldn't have told whatever she didn't want told to whomever she didn't want it told.

"Do you have any idea how much they . . . sorry." He realized he'd be laying a guilt trip on her. "Of course you have."

"It'll only be another few days. We can get the mares out, can't we?"

"One way or another. Yes, I can certainly try. Valerie Hobbs. That's the owner, as far as you could tell?"

"I'm not sure; I think she was. There were a number of

others, men. I didn't get to talk much to them. I mean, they weren't supposed to talk to me. One of them did; he was pretty nice. Bosworth."

Vernon was up and pacing from sofa to window. The rain had stopped: the dome of St. Paul's seemed to shine, rain washed or light washed.

Nell went on. "I don't think this Valerie Hobbs was the—what do you call it?—instigator."

He turned and smiled. "The perp? Perpetrator?"

"Yes. I think she was in someone else's pay."

"The bastard who grabbed you?"

She shook her head. The one who'd abducted her was not the one who'd paid repeated visits to her room in the night. "I never saw him again."

Vernon sat down beside her. "Nell, can you think of any reason someone would think you're a danger to them?"

"Not beyond his assuming I saw him—"

Samantha walked in with several Fortnum's boxes. She set them beside Nell, saying, "It's the only dependable place to shop."

Nell thanked Samantha, thanked both of them, for going to all this trouble.

"Trouble?" said Vernon. "Is there a woman alive who'd rather type than shop? She enjoyed doing it."

Samantha stuck out her tongue. She enjoyed doing that, too.

The boxes open, Nell pulled out a white silk shirt, Calvin Klein jeans, a blue and brown Harris tweed jacket and a black velvet skirt. Nell pronounced them all beautiful. "I'll get dressed."

"Good. We'll go to dinner."

Samantha asked, "Where, Aubergine? Did you make a reservation?"

"No, but I've got the maître d' in a hedge fund that's making him enough money he can retire. He's thirty-one, so he's pleased." To Nell he said, "Had you planned on overnight digs? You can stay with me. I've got three bedrooms and I'm your stepbrother." He smiled.

"Oh, my," said Samantha. "I can see a clever defense attorney mounting that as an argument against the possibility of sexual misconduct." She said to Nell, "Listen, don't worry on that score. He's about as romantic as a rise in interest rates."

"You'd know, would you?"

Samantha laughed, said good night and headed for the door. Vernon watched her go, smiling. She really was worth her weight in gold securities.

THIRTY-FIVE

Vernon poured himself a finger of whiskey and went over to the mirror, waiting for Nell. In the time she'd been here, a gloomy afternoon had changed to an iridescent evening. The lights of streets and buildings and houses glittered; St. Paul's dome was bathed in moonlight, and he wondered, How could a day that started as woefully as this one end up the way it had?

"Everything fits," said Nell behind him, adjusting items that needed none, buttoning a button on the Harris tweed jacket and then unbuttoning it, the same with the white silk blouse. "Even the shoes." She held up a foot. She smiled. Actually, she beamed.

To Vernon she looked not only happy but also gorgeous. "Perfect" was all he said.

"I'll bet this is a good restaurant."

"Would I take you anywhere else?"

"No. But there's probably a dress code." She looked unsophisticated and uncertain.

"They always hand me a tie at the door. Listen, if the cut of that coat can't get you in, we don't want to go. Come on."

The maître d' at Aubergine raised no question of coat or tie. He wouldn't consider questioning Vernon Rice; Vernon was too good a customer and too big a tipper. They were sitting in a quiet corner while Nell read the menu.

"Oh, God, I just realized I haven't had a decent meal in weeks!" She put her hands to her face as if ashamed to admit it.

"Then you're in luck. The food here is unbelievably decent. I expect you're a vegetarian?"

"Well, yes, I guess I am."

"They do something with mushrooms here that's just short of psychedelic."

"Order for me, will you?"

He ordered for both of them, looked at the wine list, asked for a wine which made the sommelier extremely happy. Then Vernon shoved his silverware around and leaned on the table. "Okay, now, continue talking."

Nell did, through a first course of a vegetable pâté, a second course of green salad and a third course of the heavenly mushroom dish. She talked little about herself, a lot about the mares. "She had this literature—pamphlets, folders, estrogen studies. I read about all of this. An American firm has had the patent on a drug called Premarin forever. It takes hundreds of thousands of horses to meet its quota." Her fork, like a tiny silver plane, appeared to be writing in air. "The way these mares are roped means they can't move more than a couple of inches any way. They can't lie down. Nine and ten months pregnant and they can't lie down. *Imagine* that kind of imprisonment for a horse, tied so they can't move. Horses are meant to run free. They only got the little bit of exercise I talked Valerie Hobbs into letting me give them."

"But what's this Hobbs woman expect to get out of urine collected from only sixty mares? And I'm also curious about how she could have kept this going for several years with no one—I mean the animal-rights people—finding out about it? What about the people who work at that stud? They don't talk about it? I mean on the outside?"

Nell shook her head. "They must not. One reason is they're not really interested; they don't care. Another could be they want to keep their jobs."

Vernon listened, taking her in all over again, like a climate once visited and never forgotten.

He pushed his plate aside and leaned toward her. "You want to rescue these mares more, I imagine, than you want to see this Hobbs woman behind bars."

"I hadn't thought of it that way, but, yes, I do. She didn't treat me badly. Why?"

"Because you've got a bargaining chip. Sixty horses in return for keeping Ms. Hobbs out of the nick."

She thought about that. "But that wouldn't be up to us, would it? My abduction's a police matter."

Vernon liked that "us." "Not entirely, but what you have to say about her will go a long way. She'll put up the ignorance defense: 'I never did know who this girl was or that she was kidnapped—' You know."

"Is it possible she really didn't? That it's the truth?"

"I suppose it's possible she wasn't the one who'd orchestrated the kidnapping, but she had to have known something. I can imagine the hell they caught for letting you get away. Although she seemed to have relaxed the rules on that to the point of—" He paused. "I could talk to Hobbs. She, and, possibly, the others who work there, they're easily bought, is my guess. I could buy the horses out of the stables."

"There are fifty-four there now, Vern."

He ignored that. "Could Arthur keep them?"

"I think so. I've had the ones I took in an empty barn and I know there's at least one more empty barn. It might mean building another. But the land—well, it's certainly big enough. I could personally watch over them."

Vernon had put his fork down a while ago. The duck, which he had shoved to one side, was, as always, perfect; he just wasn't hungry.

She looked at his abandoned plate. "Aren't you going to eat that?"

"You're a vegetarian." He smiled.

THIRTY-SIX

They stayed up most of the night, talking and not talking, their silences comfortable. Vernon had tried once again to get her to tell Arthur and her father that she was here and all right and would be home soon. Vernon pictured their response: joy, pure and unalloyed with the anger they certainly could have felt because she hadn't told them before, hadn't said she had been living on Ryder property for three weeks. For that was three weeks of grief they could have been spared. Vernon said as much.

Nell protested: "I can't. I want to get those mares out of there first. Do you really think Dad or Granddad would be concerned over the fate of a bunch of horses they had no connection to? I mean, in all of their relief to get me back?"

"Probably not, no." Vernon wondered if there wasn't something else preventing her, some completely irrational shame over being taken in the first place and then not immediately trying to escape. He couldn't pin it down. He swirled the brandy in his snifter, watching it lap the glass. "Okay. I understand that, Nell, but how would telling your father or grandfather jeopardize that, if you could convince them those mares are important to you?"

"For one thing, they wouldn't be thinking up ways to get them out, which is what is needed and is what you're doing. Dad wouldn't do that; he and Granddad would have Cambridge police at Hobbs's doorstep before you could turn around."

"Yet . . . isn't it police we *want*?"

"In the time it took to get a warrant, Valerie Hobbs could kill the horses. If she hasn't done it already. I don't think she has, though; it was just a threat."

"What was?"

"Killing the horses. I made a bargain: I wouldn't run if she'd let me take care of the mares."

"My God." Vernon turned away, angry with such recklessness, or was it such devotion to something he didn't understand. "You could have gotten away long before you did."

She sat back and looked at him. "Believe me, I've given myself more hell than you or anyone else could on that score. Look, I know it was awful of me not to go home. But, in a sense, I *was* home. I *have been* home for three weeks."

It wasn't as if she were denying her family for her own sake. Even as obsessive as she was about these mares, it wasn't her own welfare she was concerned with. "Okay," he said. "Okay, I won't keep pushing it."

"Thank you. And there's something else I'd like to do. I'd like to put them out of business."

"The Hobbs woman will *be* out of business."

"It's not illegal, the operation she's running."

"No, but it *is* illegal to conspire with kidnappers. Put who out of business?"

"The pharmaceutical company that produces this hormone drug." She reached into a pocket of the coat tossed over the back of the leather sofa and pulled out several folders, which she then tossed on the table between them. "At least, I'd like to do them some damage."

Vernon looked at her. He would have laughed had she not looked so implacably serious. He picked up the folder picturing a sweetly posed mare and her foal. "You want to put it out of business—that's what you're saying? Nellie, Wyeth-Ayerst is a major pharmaceutical company in the States. It's huge."

"All the more reason, isn't it? You're a shareholder. You tried to get Dad and Granddad to invest. You said they should do 'before the stock split.' "

Vernon was openmouthed. "How in hell can you remember *that?*"

"Because—" *Because I always listened to what you said, because you were important to me, because I was always glad when you came to the farm.*

There was a shift in her expression, a look not at all implacable, that Vernon could not read and wished he could, as if, like a horse, she had slipped her reins and could now run free, as if whatever drove her had stopped driving her for two seconds, and in that brief time, he felt he had her; had her worked out, clocked her pace, seen her colors. In the next second, the look was gone. It was amazing what could wash over a person in the blink of an eye. "Nellie, I'm a shareholder, but even if I dumped all of my stock tomorrow, it wouldn't hurt Wyeth that much."

"Oh, I know that. But you're what they call a player; you have influence—"

Vernon tried out a self-deprecating laugh, but she didn't break stride.

"—in the market."

"Wait a minute, wait a minute." Vernon held up one protesting hand. "You mean you want me to manipulate this company's financial picture—"

She nodded. "They're the only ones who produce this stuff."

"Oh. Do you want me to put British Telecom out of business at the same time?"

She just gave him a look.

Vernon sat back. "Even if I *could* do this, which I certainly doubt"—(but the prospect of such a trick excited him, that is, would, if such a manipulation was not illegal, which it was; he was doing this in a vacuum, or doing it theoretically. But it wasn't theoretical, that was the trouble—"even if I could, you do realize that the drug wouldn't be the only thing that you could say good-bye to. We'd be saying good-bye to God knows how many jobs."

Nell looked away from him and out the window to the lightening sky. Not light but its adumbration in the faint lines of buildings showing through the darkness. "I know."

"But you don't care?"

She turned back to look at him. "No." She held up the folder. "Listen to me, Vern. Listen: the foals are slaughtered since there's no use for them, to keep women more comfortable during menopause. To help avoid *hot flashes,* Vernon. What in the bloody hell is the matter with us?"

She was relentless. He frowned. She could even be ruthless.

Nell smiled. "This is something you could do; you're reckless, Vernon."

Actually, he wasn't; he only appeared to be because he would undertake tasks that would find most people running for cover.

"I'm sorry to lay all this at your doorstep. You haven't been living with it for nearly two years like I have. If you had done, if you had had all that time to think about it . . ." Her tone was rueful. "I'm sorry."

"Not on my account." He looked at the window, at the frosty light and the spire of St. Paul's spiking the early-morning mist that shrouded it. "I'll give this some thought. In the meantime—" He drank off his whiskey and made a face. "Why doesn't this stuff taste as good at six a.m. as if does at six p.m.? Come on, your room's at the end of the hall."

She got up. He put his hands on her shoulders; they felt fragile, despite her being a girl toughened by sun and wind and hard work. It was that look of hers, a look at once solid and ethereal. He was for a moment afraid. You couldn't keep jumping through hoops of fire without getting burned. But the fear subsided when she yawned like any ordinary up-all-night child.

Only Nell wasn't ordinary, despite these glimpses of that other girl, the one he had seen before in that swift two seconds.

And who was she?

THIRTY-SEVEN

The house looked marble cold and cavernous, more the crumbling remains of a house of banished royalty than a home. She lived alone, or that was the impression Jury had gotten when he talked to her on the telephone.

The raised voice Jury heard on the other side of a partly open window appeared to be remonstrating with something not human—a dog or cat. If it was a cat, the cat would remain unregenerate. Used to the cat Cyril in DCS Racer's office, Jury knew as much as anyone about the persistence of cats. He rang and heard footsteps.

Sara Hunt blushed, whether from having to deal with a stranger and a policeman or because she'd been caught red-handed lecturing a cat, Jury didn't know. Over her shoulder he could see the big ginger-colored cat who paused in his blameless paw washing long enough to fix his eyes on Jury. The cat had exceptionally green eyes (rather the color of Melrose Plant's) and a precarious seat on the newel post at the bottom of the stairs. One could tell the cat was hopelessly its own master and would get through any talking down with no other feeling than boredom.

Sara Hunt said immediately after she opened the door, as if in defense of her remonstrating with her cat, "He's just made a mess of my papers. He's shoved them on the floor and they weren't all that organized to begin with." Vexed, she looked at Jury. "I'm sorry. You're Superintendent Jury?"

"New Scotland Yard." He held out his ID.

Apparently she thought she was supposed to appropriate it for she didn't return it after taking a good look. She held the door wider and said, "They've come for you, Henry! Hear that, Henry?" She flung this over her shoulder. The cat went on washing. She turned back to Jury. "Hopeless. Oh, do come in." He followed her through the large entrance hall. The cat jumped off the newel post and made its way, haughtily, toward the rear of the house.

Sara Hunt stood aside as Jury entered a living room, which would also have been cold had it not been for the fire burning in the grate. Above the fireplace were framed etchings, probably of the area, if not of these actual grounds, a great many moss- and ivy-clad crumbling walls, romantic and fantastic. Out of an enormous Gothic window, its view partly obscured by a huge oak, he could see just such a wall.

"Here," she said, "let me take your coat."

"I will if you give it back." He nodded at the ID still clutched in her hand.

"What?"

"I'll need that. How else will I know who I am?" He smiled.

So did she and her smile was broad. "I'm sorry." She handed it back. "Do you really need to prove it? Wouldn't anybody let you in? Any woman, anyway?"

"Thanks." He did not respond to this flirty attempt to ingratiate herself to the police. He sat down in the armchair she indicated, covered like the sofa and other chairs in an Oriental print—birds, green stems, bamboo—much faded. He felt the need to restore, or right, the balance between them.

She seemed extremely composed and was probably one of those witnesses who could take over an interrogation and wind up doing most of it. Yet she didn't really seem to see herself in that role as she sat with her hands neatly folded on her knees, smiling slightly, waiting. He was, after all, trained to take over; unfortunately, she seemed just as well trained to derail any conversation she did not like. He intuited this.

"You'd make," he said, "a hell of a good double agent."

Her eyes widened and he saw they were a soft, ambiguous brown. Why "ambiguous"? He didn't know.

"I would?"

"Oh, definitely."

Her hair was a sort of toffee color, a tarnished gold, as if it were waiting for the light now streaking the window behind her to provide the highlights.

"I'm taking that as a compliment."

Jury laughed. "Why? Agents are deceitful and slippery."

"Because that's the way you meant it. They're also very clever. That's something I'm not. I've always lacked that—cleverness."

"Why do I doubt that?"

"No, but it's true." She smiled again. "So you've come to recruit me for an undercover job." The smile broadened as if she really meant it.

Jury couldn't tell. He was almost relieved to see the upper two teeth just a shade crooked, but then he thought there was something of childhood in that crookedness and that, too, might be deceptive. "Actually, I've come to ask you some questions."

"About what?" She settled back in her chair.

"You knew Dan Ryder, the jockey?"

At that moment, a presence up to this point absent, something veiled and ghostlike, entered the room, and Jury sat forward and just resisted the impulse to reach out for it. Yet her expression hadn't changed. That was the problem, wasn't it? Something had entered to change it, and it hadn't changed at all.

"I didn't really know Dan Ryder; I met him a few times. It was at—" She looked at the mantel, Jury presumed at the silver-framed pictures sitting there between two old brass candleholders. She rose and crossed to it and picked one picture up, which she handed to Jury. "That was Newmarket races. He's up on Criminal Type—or at least that's what I thought—and that's Arthur Ryder holding the reins. And the trainer, I forget his name. I'm in the background, there." She tapped the glass.

"Who introduced you?"

"Arthur did. I'm a very distant relation. Then I saw

him—Dan Ryder, I mean—again when he won again. It was Cheltenham Racecourse, then again at Doncaster. The Derby at Epsom was brilliant. Lucky Me won carrying 129 pounds. Halfway round he slammed into the fence and I was sure Danny was going down. But he righted himself and won by three lengths in 1:11:36. Yes, he was quite something."

Danny? Jury waited, but she said nothing more and replaced the picture. "That was all, just those three times?"

She smiled. "Isn't it enough for you?"

Definitely a derailer. "For me, possibly. As for you, it depends."

"On what? I'm in the dark, Superintendent. Why are you asking about Dan Ryder? He's dead. He died somewhere else, not in the UK. France, it might have been. A racing accident."

"Auteuil racetrack, near Paris."

She turned her look to the room, and Jury had a most unnerving response to it. He could have sworn she was looking at somebody or something he couldn't see. The feeling passed, but left him disturbed.

She said, "This must have something to do with Arthur Ryder's granddaughter. Her disappearance."

Jury nodded. "It does. Did you know her?"

"No. Wales is a long way from Cambridgeshire. I'm one of the Ryders merely by dint of an aunt once removed. I'm some kind of stepcousin."

"Obviously, you like racing."

"Yes. I go whenever I get the chance. A friend invited me to the Cheltenham Gold Cup."

He thought for a moment. "Then you didn't have any interaction with Dan Ryder? That seems strange given you know these races so well."

She laughed. "That's the point: I went to see the Derby, not Dan Ryder. I recall it so well because it was so dramatic. I didn't know Dan, as I said before. Twice."

Jury smiled. "Sorry."

She made to rise. "Would you like some coffee, Superintendent?"

"I would. Thanks." It was less a desire for coffee than it was to have her leave the room so he could look around.

The room's emanations—oh, surely, that had been his imagination?—coupled perhaps with the size of the house and its empty lower rooms—disturbed him. Or perhaps she did. Well, he knew she did, that was the pathetic truth. But what had her eyes been trained on during that look over his shoulder? He crossed to the sofa and sat where she had sat. There was nothing behind his now-imaginary shoulder but the high Gothic window, out of which he could see a figure draped in cloth, the stone folds of which hid her almost entirely. He went to this window and looked out on a sadly neglected garden, which no amount of nurturing sun or rain would restore to what it had been.

Houses such as this troubled Jury. Not because of their being neglected, but because of the presence of the past. What must it be like to be the last member of a family who had once lived here? Why did she live here alone? Wales was always touted as a land of great natural beauty. Why, then, did the distant mountains, the rocky land, the deserted garden strike Jury as harrowed and precipitate? Whoever found beauty here must like her beauty dangerous. He was still looking out at the mountains beyond and the blank day when he heard her footsteps advancing, and, turning, almost expected to see not Sara, but someone else.

Over the tray with the coffee service, she gave him a fleeting smile, one fled in an instant along with his rational self. He felt enveloped by pure feeling. The sensation passed and he was sorry to see it go.

"Is something wrong?"

"No, no. Here, let me help you with that."

She had stopped with the heavy silver tray carrying a sadly tarnished silver coffeepot and china cups. But before he reached her, she set it down on a side table. "That's all right; it's lighter than it looks." She poured strong black coffee into a cup. "Cream? Sugar?" she asked.

"Neither."

"Black is the only way to drink coffee, I think."

"And strong," he said, taking the cup she held out. He sat down again as she reclaimed her seat on the sofa.

She said, "I read about the death of that woman on the Ryder course. That is so strange. Arthur Ryder's an unlucky man."

"I doubt luck has much to do with it. Did you have any idea at all about that shooting?"

"I? Why, no. I told you I barely know the Ryders."

Jury sat back with his cup. "But you know his stepson, Vernon Rice."

Surprisingly, she smiled. "Ah, yes. I do know him, yes. He handled some investments for me."

"You like him, to judge from your smile."

She laughed. "It's just that he was so utterly friendly. He was beguiling, really. And the investments paid off handsomely."

"You trust Vernon Rice?"

She looked bewildered. "Yes, of course."

Jury smiled. "That 'of course' implies that anyone would."

"What are you saying? Vernon is some sort of con man?"

"No, not at all."

They were silent for a moment, drinking their coffee, aware of each other's presence. Then Jury said, "Dan Ryder was, as I understand it, quite a ladies' man." He felt the phrase to be old-fashioned and a little silly now.

She looked up from her coffee. "I don't—" She stopped. "I don't know if he was."

"I understand he had a number of affairs and broke up more than one marriage." Jury rose and moved again to the fireplace, where he picked up the snapshot of the winner's circle at Newmarket races. "Very charismatic, from what I've heard. Do you think so?"

"I wouldn't know."

"But you found him attractive?"

"I suppose so."

"I'm just curious." He laughed a little. "As a man, I mean. I wonder what exactly a woman finds attractive." He looked at her, holding her glance, which he suspected wanted to run away. "I've seen photographs of him at the Ryder place and he doesn't strike me as all that, well, alluring, you could say. What exactly did you respond to? Or perhaps it wasn't his looks. His manner? His touch?"

She sat for a few moments, her face expressionless. Then she said, "But then, you're a man, aren't you?" Suddenly she rose, looking stricken and pale, as if she'd just received a report of a death. Picking up the silver cream pitcher, she said, "I think this cream has gone off. Excuse me."

Jury watched her leave. *But we don't use cream.*

He took his cup and returned to the window and its view of the distant mountains.

When she returned with the cream, she had clearly collected herself. "I was about to go for a walk when you came. Would you mind? I mean, we could talk while walking, couldn't we?"

As she stood there with the little cream jug that no one had needed, Jury felt her anxiety and would almost have taken back what he'd asked her. She was still in love with Danny Ryder and desperate to keep the attachment hidden.

They gathered up coats, he helping her on with hers, and left the house. A walk had not been her aim. Getting rid of him probably had been. If she'd lied about her involvement with Ryder, she might have lied about other things.

Still, he could feel her need not to drag him from whatever corner of her mind she'd banished him to. What surprised Jury was that she still harbored these feelings after several years. Then he thought, how banal. Feelings, he well knew, could last a lifetime. Anyone who thought time healed all wounds must have sustained only the most minor lacerations.

Their walk in the grounds led them around the dry pool, filled now with shriveled leaves. In the center was a stone figure, a woman pouring what perhaps in a warmer month would be water, a circle of fish with incongruous, open mouths below her.

"Like a lot of things here," she said, "the fountain doesn't work." Her glance canvassed the desolate gardens. "I'm not truly neglectful; I get some boys in from the village to care for it in the spring."

"I didn't think you were—neglectful, I mean."

She turned, her hand bunching the collar of her coat more closely around the neck. "Then what? What in the world do you think I am, for you obviously have reservations about me?"

"Amorous."

Her hand dropped away from her collar. She laughed. "Whatever makes you say that?"

"That's why you live here alone, isn't it? In exile, you could say. Better that than a broken heart. Too much feeling, that's what keeps you here."

It was as if she couldn't believe what she'd heard. Her mouth opened, closed again.

"Much safer," he added. "Much." He looked into her brown eyes and a thread of green outlining the iris. Then at her soft mouth. He started walking again.

But she just stood.

He turned round and smiled. "Come on; it's too cold for standing still." He held out his hand, which was warm. She walked a few paces and put her own, which was cold, in his.

"Is this peculiar talk about my amorousness—is it to trick me into something? Some admission of guilt?"

"Of what?" He stopped and looked at her.

She laughed. "Oh, I see, no trickery involved in this discussion."

"No."

"You must be very good at getting suspects to confide in you."

"Not particularly. How long have you lived here?"

She hesitated, wondering, probably, if the question was loaded. "Since my divorce four years ago."

"It must have been painful then to drive you here."

Again she stopped and looked up at him, slowly shaking her head. "You really are clever. You could just ask me why I divorced my husband. I found his temper impossible to take, eventually. The divorce was acrimonious, to say the least. He liked cars, to race fast cars. I always thought that was a little, I don't know, adolescent."

"That's too bad. It's too bad about the way things start out and the way they end up."

They were walking by the disconcerting statue of the woman draped in folds of granite cloth. One could see nothing of the figure but an arm extended.

"Why did the sculptor hide all of her body except for that arm? Why is she so totally draped?" Jury asked.

"I don't know. My parents—or grandparents—put her there."

"Why do we assume the figure is a woman?"

"Yes, you're right. But no one has ever thought that it wasn't."

"It could as easily be, oh, Judas, suffering from the remorse of betrayal."

For a minute she was silent, watching the statue as if she expected the figure to turn its face to her and explain. "Perhaps it's because it's hard to imagine a man in that state."

"Come on! Are you suggesting men don't suffer that much?"

"It's been my experience they don't."

They were walking again, this time to the rear of the house. "Your experience, then, must be limited to rather shallow men."

She nodded. "I think that might be the case."

"Was your husband?"

They were walking around the ruins of the old garden, now primula-sick and celandine-choked. The garden had once been meticulously laid out, paths crossing and bisecting the plants and trees. He could see the blueprint.

"It isn't," she said, "Sissinghurst, is it?"

"Oh, but that's such an institutional garden. In the spring when those 'boys from town' come, after that it will be much prettier because it's more private. I've never really been bowled over by those stately home gardens."

"My father tried to start a vineyard, if you can imagine. Like the marquess of Bute? It didn't work. Something about the soil's lacking lime, or loam. I don't know. But I have a hard time imagining Welsh wine, don't you?"

He laughed. "Yes. I wonder what he'd have called it."

They came round again in sight of the statue, which could be seen from their point on the path. "What would make you that unhappy?" said Sara.

He looked at the heavily draped figure. The burden of statuesque grief disturbed him and he looked away. He said, "Same thing that made her, I'd say."

High above them, from the bare branches of a hazelnut, a crow careened off, circled once, then again before it wheeled away through the darkening sky.

Jury asked, "Do you ever feel a presence—I don't know how else to say it—in this house?"

"Ghosts, you mean?"

"I don't know what I mean."

"Let me tell you something: my parents were very much interested in the spirit world. They called in a medium, a rather famous and well-respected one. When she fell into her trance, she remarked on a *presence*—yes, that was her word—and she described it as being full of longing, of yearning. As she was leaving, my mother and father asked about this presence or ghost. They said they'd never seen it or felt it. I was standing there as she drew on a black cape. She smiled ever so slightly and answered, 'You wouldn't.' "

"Ah! I like that story."

"You can imagine how much attention I paid to her."

Jury paused. "Maybe you should have."

Her look, when he said this, was not at him, but behind him. She smiled and said, "Because of the presence."

"And other things."

They were walking now down some stone steps to what looked like a sunken garden. "I've often wondered," Jury said, stopping to look directly at her, "about the roots of obsession."

"And *I* am supposed to tell you? You think I know?"

"Possibly, yes."

The strained smile did not leave her lips. "Why on earth do you think that? Tell me, for I'd really like to know."

"Say a hunch."

"A hunch. Is that the way you solve your cases, Superintendent?"

At this point Jury felt he knew her well enough to let her drift away onto another topic.

"I'm confused," she said. "Just what exactly are you investigating? The murder of the woman found at Ryder Stud?"

The question was merely a cover for anxiety or even panic. He didn't answer.

He cupped her elbow with his hand and said, "Let's walk."

"But you're not here officially. It's not your case, you said."

"That's right."

"Then why, good Lord, *are* you here?"

"Because it disturbs me. Greatly. Not knowing if the girl's dead or alive."

"I should think that of course she's dead. She's been missing for nearly two years."

She had pulled a cigarette out from a pack in her coat pocket and Jury stopped to light it. They were standing by a small formal garden and a square pool, dry, as was everything else. The garden backed up against a limestone retaining wall.

"This must have been beautiful once," Jury said. He looked off beyond the pool, where a dark wooden doorway stood at the end of a path lined with beeches. "What's behind the door?"

"I don't know."

"You've never tried it?"

"I tried it, but it's hopelessly stuck. That doesn't bother me, though. It adds a bit of mystery to the place." She looked at him. "Oh, go on and try it; it won't budge, but I can see you want to. It's your job, after all, to clear up mysteries."

He left her standing by the pool and walked down the path. The door was very heavy and black with age, the handle and hinges rusted nearly through. They didn't look as if they could hold anything together. Jury put his shoulder to the door, but there wasn't so much as a micro-inch moved. Nothing gave, nothing cracked. He tried again, twice.

She called to him, "Didn't I tell you?"

He made his way back to where she stood. She said, "It would take a battering ram to unhinge that door."

"It's already unhinged. It's not the hinges that are holding it."

"Then what?"

Jury shrugged. He watched her grind out her cigarette on one of the pond's abutments and put the stub in her pocket.

"You're determined to leave this place as it is, aren't you?"

"That sounds like an accusation. Why do you say that?"

"Well, aside from the general malaise of the grounds—grounds you won't tend or have tended only erratically—

there's the way you put out that cigarette. Practically anyone else would have dropped it on the ground and crushed it. But you even put the butt in your pocket."

Wide-eyed, she shook her head slowly. "Are you always finding big things inside small ones?"

They were rounding the other side of the house when she said, "I must say it's good of you to give over your time to a case that's not even yours."

"I'm on leave; it doesn't matter."

"I'm sure it matters a great deal to *them*." She paused. "But I can't really understand Vernon Rice mentioning *me*."

"He thought you might know more about Dan Ryder. I'm having the devil's own time pulling together a picture of him. Family members are often mistaken about one another."

"I see. Look, why don't you stay for dinner? It's lamb."

Jury smiled. "Thanks, but I'll need to be getting back to London. A drink would be nice, though."

She gave him a whiskey and excused herself to look into how the lamb was doing and to fix up some sort of drink food.

He sat with his whiskey, sipping it and looking round the room. The air stirred. To throw off (but should he?) the weight of this feeling, he rose and began a circuit of the room. He stopped to look again at the pictures on the mantel and touched the lusters on one of the candleholders, which started up a glassy tinkle. He moved past sideboard and chest to a kneehole desk in the corner. French, he thought, because of its delicacy. The lightness and airiness of French furniture always made him feel he could pick it up with two fingers. The sides and front were inlaid with a delicate design of birds and flowers; the writing surface was of green hide. Beside a pen holder sat a mirrored picture frame, the subject here a dark-haired man, squinting slightly against too-strong light. Around his neck was a striped scarf and what looked like goggles. And that was a clue to who he was: Sara Hunt's ex-husband.

Jury looked at the picture, wondering why she would keep a photograph prominently displayed of a husband she had divorced, certainly not on the best of terms. He slipped out the dark brown moiré backing and removed first a piece of flimsy cardboard needed to keep the picture in place, and then another photograph.

Dan Ryder. Hardly difficult to recognize from seeing the wall of photographs in his father's office. What occurred to Jury at that moment was not that Sara had been lying to him—he knew she'd been lying—but that the act of hiding the picture behind another picture was so adolescent it made him smile. A rather ill-concealed trick that anyone could sort out. Or was it? Was it instead a sign that she was determined to keep him, that she wouldn't be budged? He replaced both photos and the backing and set the frame, carefully, where it had been. There was a small key with a tassel inserted in the single desk drawer. He turned it, pulled the drawer out and found, among the pencils and papers, more snapshots. There were a few of Sara herself, a few more, no doubt taken at the same racecourses as the pictures on the mantel, showing Sara standing in the background of the winner's circle. Dan Ryder was up on Criminal Type in two of them. At the bottom was a four-by-six enlargement of Dan by himself. He took this one, one of Sara and one of the winner's circle and slipped them in his pocket when he heard her approaching footsteps and her voice, already apologizing.

"I'm sorry it took so long." She set down a large plate of raw vegetables and some sort of dip. The kind of food that Jury hated.

Smiling, he said, "Not at all," and picked up a celery stick.

"You're welcome to stay for dinner, you know."

Jury thanked her again and again said he'd have to get back to London.

She looked disappointed, and he wondered what ground, between them, they had struck. It was no longer, certainly, a slippery slope. He watched her face, its expressiveness. She'd never have made a good liar. Her face would give it all away.

"You're staring, Superintendent."

"Hm. Make that Richard. I'm not here in my official capacity."

"All right, Richard, and you're still staring." She smiled.

That smile, he reminded himself, could be trouble. "I'm still turning it over in my mind."

"Turning what over?"

"The nature of obsession."

She sighed and dipped a piece of cauliflower and sighed again. "You're tenacious."

Again he felt that stir of air. What was it? He looked behind him.

"Something wrong?"

"Nothing. So you think we're all capable of it?"

She frowned a question.

"Obsessive behavior."

"I know *you* are."

"Oh?"

"You're obsessive about obsession."

He laughed and picked up his drink. "What do you understand by 'obsessive'?"

She thought for a minute. "I suppose loving or wanting someone too much, I mean to the extent he or she, well, takes over." She shrugged.

"Are you familiar with the feeling?" He smiled, trying to defuse the question of any danger she might see in it.

Impatiently, she swept her hand through the air like a necromancer who wanted to be rid of the room. "No. At least . . . well, how would I know if you can't define it?" She shrugged. "Anyway, I thought I knew."

"What?"

"Obsession is love—we *are* talking about love, aren't we?—love carried to an extreme. Love *in extremis* if that's really a term."

"I don't think it is. It's more like love turned inside out."

She thought about this. "Well, then, loving someone too much."

"You can never love someone too much."

She sat back with a lurch. "My God, but you're romantic!"

"Perhaps, but that's irrelevant. It's the very nature of love that it can't be too much; it protects you even from yourself; it patrols its own ramparts, has its own spyglass."

"I suppose I mean the sort of feeling that has you always thinking about the other person, always wanting to be with him, wanting to know everything about him, where he is, what he's doing, where he's going . . ." She shrugged. Her list ended weakly.

Jury liked Vernon Rice's list much better than Sara Hunt's.

THIRTY-EIGHT

"Turn here and go down that old road," said Nell, pointing the way.

They hadn't passed the stud farm or at least not any part Vernon could see. "None of this looks familiar, Nellie."

"I know. It's the land behind our farm. I mean, it's our land but a distance from the main buildings. It's a good half mile from the farm proper. Granddad decided not to use this part a few years back. I'd nearly forgotten it was here. If I believed in luck or deliverance, I'd say luck led me to it. But I don't believe in luck. Not the good kind."

Vernon suppressed a smile. "What do you believe in?" His BMW smoothed over the deep ruts in this unused road.

She seemed to be giving this serious thought. "Not much," she said.

They came to a clearing, what looked to him like an exercise ring, now harboring dead leaves and hedges. From the barn on the other side of the old ring came muffled sounds that he thought must be Nell's horses. Standing in the main doorway was a chestnut foal. It turned back into the shadowy dark.

Vernon smiled. He had always found foals irresistible—well, at least when he could get his head out of market shares and start-ups long enough to look. "How old's the foal?"

"Three months. His name's Charlie. He's Daisy's foal. I had to get him out before they came again with the truck that takes them to be sold or slaughtered. Out of the country. He's a male, see. Of no use at all to them. Come on; they must be hungry."

Vernon was carrying two bags of seed and a bale of meadow hay, and Nell was carrying a sack of oats and another of bran. "It was really nice of you to stop so we could buy supplies. Mostly, I've been taking stuff from the farm. I expect that's stealing, but I don't think Granddad would mind."

"Not if he knew you were the one doing it, that's certain."

They were trudging across the rain-drenched land. "You always were nice. You have no idea how much Granddad likes you. More, I sometimes think, than he likes Dad. Certainly more than Uncle Danny, whom he thought a great jockey but not a nice person. It really hurt him to think that about his own son."

"I doubt he's as fond of me as you think. You should hear him talk to me."

"You don't get it. You're the only one he *does* talk to that way. I remember him saying once, 'You can always depend on that nut Vern.' "

"Oh, thanks." Vernon laughed.

They had reached the barn and gone in. Nell moved down the row of stalls, forking the hay into racks. She stumbled and nearly went down and Vernon took the pitchfork from her. "You're too tired to do this. You looked like you could have used a week's sleep when you showed up. Last night certainly didn't make up for it."

Nell thought: *But it did. It made up for a dozen things; it made up for being by myself for two years; it made up for being the only company these horses ever had; it made up for being in limbo for so long; it made up for things you'll never know and, because of that, never understand.* She said none of this; what she said was, "Last night didn't tire me out; it made me feel better."

"Glad of it," he said, pouring oats into one of the buckets. The horse, Daisy, didn't seem to mind his presence. Beyond a few shakes of her mane and a bit of stamping she seemed perfectly relaxed.

Nell stood back, rocking a little on her heels, enjoying watching him fork hay into the racks, getting more on the floor than in the rack, trying to keep a distance between himself and the mild-mannered mares.

When it was done, Vernon said, "Backbreaking. My Lord, Nellie, I hope this isn't what you were doing as Lady Hobbs's indentured servant." He waved her toward him. "Come on, let's eat. I'm starved."

He got the hamper out of the back, and the horse blanket, which he shook out on the ground. He set the hamper down and took out the provisions, one provision being a bottle of a very good burgundy. Bobby was a wine expert, not because he drank it, which he hardly ever did, but because he traded in it. Bobby was an authority on anything he traded in. So was Daphne.

"I can't believe you went to all this trouble," said Nell, unwrapping a chunk of Cheshire cheese and a slab of cheddar.

Vernon was uncorking the wine. "Me? No, it was Bobby who went to the trouble."

"Well, it wasn't Bobby who thought of it, and it's *so* nice. A picnic in January."

He drew the cork from the bottle, saying, "You deserve a lot more than a picnic in January."

Unbidden, the thought flew into her mind. *No, I don't.* She had not expunged the sight of that musty attic room from her thoughts. No matter how much it receded, as if it were an image in a rearview mirror, it still caught up with her whenever her guard was down—hot, sweaty, implacably vile. She had been little more than contraband in that house. And following fast on the heels of the image was the question: *Had it happened at all?* It was like looking through fog.

When she looked up, she saw Vernon watching her. His clear gray eyes were sharp, like diamonds.

"Nellie, what else? There's something else?"

She lowered her eyes to the cheese she still held and shrugged. "No?"

He laughed. "You tell me."

She felt herself slip away and was afraid, when that happened, as it had many times before, that she was losing her mind. Vernon wouldn't press her for an answer, she knew. She felt that tightness in her throat that was the advent of tears. *Don't cry,* she commanded herself. *If you do, it will all tumble out.* If that happens, you cannot go back; he will cut you loose. *Absurd!* She knew it was absurd.

When she looked up, she saw Vernon still watching her. He did not look away. Slowly, he chewed a sandwich.

Blushing, she said this much: "I just wonder sometimes if I'm crazy, if I'm round the bend, as they say."

"Why?" He poured wine and handed her a plastic glass.

Nell looked off into blankness, saw trees, hedges, barn as items arranged on a picture postcard. "I feel sometimes as if things weren't real. As if I were seeing pictures of things, as if the scene weren't really there."

Vernon drank some wine, said, "Maybe it's me."

"You?" She was astonished he'd think this. "Vernon, you're the only real thing here!" Grabbing back that sentiment, she added, "Along with the horses, of course."

He laughed. "That's a compliment, for sure, to be as real to you as the horses."

Nell relaxed. The danger had been circumvented, and they ate and drank in one of those blessed silences, broken only by the sounds coming from the barn.

He said, "Listen, I'll bargain with you. I'll take on Wyeth Labs if you'll tell your dad and Arthur you're back."

"But—"

Vernon shook his head, hard. "No. No 'buts,' Nellie. You'll do it, and the sooner, the better. Like today."

Adrenaline sluiced through her veins. She said nothing.

"You shouldn't mind now because we're going to get those mares away from Hobbs's place." But that, Vernon thought, wasn't the all of it; the horses were only part of it. She was ashamed; he could sense it. She was ashamed to go back and it wasn't because she could have done it sooner. No, the shame was something else, and it was probably accompanied by these periods of disorientation she was talking about because she wanted to get rid of it, to have the shame out of her head and her life. But he would get nowhere by questioning her, even if he had a mind to; it would simply drive that part of her back into hiding.

"All right, I'll go back. But not today, Vern, please not today. I need to get myself ready for it, you know, psyched up." She picked up a smoked salmon sandwich, looked at it as if it might hold a clue to something she'd forgotten and took a bite.

They went on with their picnic, Nell turning to listen to the mares, any little sounds of impatience or distress. "They need some exercise, some freedom. What I do is, I take turns riding them and the others look for graze, pretty hard to find in January, but they always find something. I don't ride Daisy because she needs to stay near Charlie. And of course, Aqueduct has to be ridden; he's used to hard riding. At least he was once."

Vernon asked, "Why did they take Aqueduct?"

Nell was inspecting another sandwich. "Aqueduct's a 'chaser. He can jump over almost anything. Hadrian's walls, you know. Then I'd guess they wanted a horse who'd been successful at stud. I don't know." She looked at Vernon as she finished off her mystery sandwich and smiled. "You can ride with me. You *can* ride, that I know. You used to chase me, remember?"

It was abysmally sad, the way she spoke of this, as if her childhood had been swallowed up by her experience and her adolescence shattered like glass. "Caught you, too," he said.

"Never." She grinned.

"Bet?" He held up a chocolate hazelnut tart.

"I can have the whole thing if I win?"

"Most of it."

She got up from the blanket. "You can ride Aqueduct and I'll ride one of the mares."

"Those poor horses are in pretty bad shape. And how could they beat Aqueduct?"

"Oh, I wonder."

"The sinister implication being not if I'm riding him?" They walked toward the barn. "You have enough tack?"

"Uh-huh."

"Bits? Bridles? Saddles?"

"Yes."

Inside the barn, Nell went into a stall that held a beautiful bay. "This one, I think, might be one of those French saddle horses. They're especially good jumpers. And she's had three weeks to build up some strength. Her name's Lili."

Vernon was leaning against the half door, arms crossed over the top of it. "Why would you want a jumper?"

"Only because Aqueduct is. It evens things out."

"Why? Are we doing any jumping?"

"No, but you never know."

"Then the answer's not no, it's 'maybe.' "

She laughed. "You really don't want to compete, do you?"

"No, but we won't let that stop us."

Nell was fitting a bit into the mare's mouth. Over her arm was a saddle.

"All of this gear has gone unused for God knows how long," said Vernon. "But it looks shiny new."

"I've been cleaning it, polishing it up."

She had led the mare out of the stable by now.

Aqueduct was already out, eating oats from the bucket Vernon had left there. He was chewing solemnly and looking at Vernon.

(God.)

Aqueduct snorted.

THIRTY-NINE

The kid with the purple hair (hadn't that punk style gone out of punk fashion yet?) and wearing outsized earphones on the other side of the aisle was entranced by whatever he was listening to, his eyes closed, his fingers rapping on the small table on which sat his CD player. Music—though strictly speaking, it was likely not even music—leaked out around the earphones, trying to escape itself probably.

The scene reminded Jury of a similar one in Stratford-upon-Avon a few years back, and similarly having to do with trains and platforms, in which another lad with dyed hair and a boom box was playing (incredibly enough) a song sung by a French chanteuse, in heartbreaking accents of a love gone wrong and to which she was bidding her painful *adieu*. It was the only word he recognized in addition to *amour* and *j'amais*. But love songs being universally translatable along lines of hello and good-bye, usually the latter, Jury understood her sentiments perfectly. Yes, that was exactly how it felt; God only knew he'd felt it often enough. That time had been a bad one for Jury. He had lost someone he felt he couldn't afford to. It had been January then, too. Or March? Did this music presage another loss? Was the lad some winter angel appointed to appear in Jury's life when things were coming undone?

What was it this time, though? Or perhaps it was simply a cumulative process of undoing, a little unraveling here, a little there. Life sometimes seemed so fragile and weightless; it would blow away if he breathed on it.

But what was blowing away? What was wrong? Aside from the fact he seemed destined to listen to another man's music.

The boy adjusted his earphones and the music spiked. Some group. Heavy thrumming. Jury would never be able to identify them; he couldn't even recognize the groups of his own youth, much less the current ones.

An attendant came through trundling a well-stocked trolley: sandwiches, tea, coffee, soft drinks, crisps. Everything about the trains now was shipshape and Bristol fashion, clean as a newborn babe. Hell, you could change a baby on the floor without fear of germs. He bought some tea and a cheese salad sandwich he didn't want.

He went back to his ruminations over this day spent in the company of the charming Sara Hunt and the almost-otherworldliness of the faded gardens, the crumbling stone, the unpolished silverplate, the rose pattern of the slipcovered chairs worn to liquidity—everything in need of tending.

Jury tried to reweave the unraveling tapestry. Living in that big house was, he thought, a rather Victorian notion, a woman mourning the death of her beloved. Wouldn't it have been easier merely to put the pictures away instead of hiding them behind others? But that was the point, he reminded himself. She was stubborn; she would not give in; she would chance it. He leaned his head against the cold glass and watched the frosty pastures and fences pass. The fields looked antediluvian, left over, dead, nothing growing, nothing grown. A strange image. Jury closed his eyes, went back to Dan Ryder and Sara. The thing was, why should she even hide the fact they'd been lovers? She must have been aware he was the consummate bed hopper. It was public knowledge—well, at least the public who lived with one foot in the racing world. Dan Ryder slept around; Dan Ryder was—to use a Victorian appellation—a bounder. It could be pride on her part, of course; that might make sense of the end of the affair, of being dumped, but did not explain its beginning. There would have been no reason to keep quiet over that.

Jury realized he was basing this on intuition rather than

hard evidence. No matter; intuition had eventually brought in the hard evidence.

The London train slowed and stopped at a station Jury could not pronounce, and the boy removed the headphones and darted out to a kiosk on the platform. Jury watched him buy a candy bar and a packet of cigarettes. The kiosk fellow carefully smoothed out the bill the lad had handed him, reached round to the cartons displayed in the back and handed over the cigarettes.

The boy had forgotten to turn off the CD player and the headset squawked with antimusic before segueing into the next piece, but still kept to its slightly tinny, raspy tone. He caught some of the words; it was a love song, surprisingly. Jury thought about Nell's singing to the horses. What had it been? "Love Walked In"?

Love at first sight: it was a concept Jury had no trouble believing in. He had never understood it, how one person (such as he) could react with such certainty to another (such as he had to several women he'd known).

One look—as the song said—was all it had taken to fall for Vivian Rivington. That was years back. Helen Minton, Nell Healy, Jane Holdsworth—same thing. He had never really understood why so much of psychology refuted such an immediate attachment as shallow, banal, sentimental, romantic and adolescent. (He also thought that adolescence came in for too much of a bad rap.) Jury believed that love could of course come about along those lines that most people approved—that of knowing a person for some time before discovering one was in love. It struck Jury as dreary, rather like buying a car and not having to make payments on it for a year or two.

The boy had jumped aboard just in time, just as the train was moving. He plunked down the cigarettes and adjusted his headphones. Jury could put up with the hair, the rap, the noise, but not with the smoke. The lad made no move to light up, he was happy to see. He felt oddly depressed, a depression that seemed against his better judgment, as if he had a choice in the matter. He decided it was probably a hangover from Mickey Haggerty's case—not that he needed any self-induced punishment from that quarter.

Jury closed his eyes and tried to put himself in Sara's place vis-à-vis Dan Ryder. If reports were true, Dan Ryder had as much charisma as the Thoroughbreds he rode: all the glamor of a Samarkand, all the cunning of a Criminal Type.

The needle stuck. The record replayed that thought: *Criminal Type.* The needle stayed in that mental groove for a moment and then let it go. He could not build upon it to flesh out the man.

Another little galvanic burst of music came from the headphones as the boy dropped them on the table and left his seat to hip-hop down the aisle, still hearing the music in his head. The music rattled in the headphones enough to move them, although that was probably a movement of the train's making the headset inch across the table.

And now the lad was back and clamping the headset on.

Oblivion. A kind of oblivion, thought Jury, and who was he to deny someone else his road to oblivion to transport him to a better world or connect him with this one? Yet this one Jury thought to be infinitely superior to the one we imagine, imagination being full of such flashiness that we mistake it for light and color. There was far more flash than genius in our imagined worlds.

When the train finally approached the edge of London and slowed on the outskirts, the boy rose, his trip apparently over.

"Hey, man," said Jury, not at all sure that this word was still in the teenage lexicon. When the boy turned toward him, surprised, Jury said, "I like your music."

The lad smiled, seeming pleased to get a compliment out of some middle-aged stiff, something he wasn't used to. "You like Door Jam?"

Jury nodded. "The best."

"Cool!" the boy said, slapping his hand against Jury's palm in that handshake that always looked like a prelude to arm wrestling.

"Way cool," said Jury.

FORTY

"**O**f course you can do it," Nell said, sitting atop her mare. "Of course you can. That's Aqueduct you're up on, remember?"

Vernon remembered. Aqueduct took no prisoners. He was mounted on the horse now, feeling less and less in command of the situation. "He's got my number. Look at the way he's turning his head and leering."

True, the horse was turning his head and trying to look at Vernon.

"I don't remember you being so diffident around horses."

" 'Diffident'—good word. Better than 'coward.' "

Aqueduct was shaking himself as if Vernon were a big, annoying fly. "He's trying to get me off, just wait . . ."

Nell laughed; her horse whinnied. The whinny sounded amazingly like laughter.

"Anyway, the weight's off. You should be giving me another ten or twelve pounds, at least." As if Aqueduct actually needed it.

"I don't have any weights. Don't be such a stickler."

She was moving back, positioning her horse to face the first wall, which was quite low. "Come on, starting gate."

"Hold it, hold it. You said we weren't jumping!"

"I lied. Vern, you're a very good rider. Remember when we used to chase anything that moved around the pasture? Rabbits, foxes?"

Remember? Could he have forgotten? There had come to him, over the last two years, a recurrent dream that Nell had been up on Samarkand, a talented horse, but no 'chaser, about to jump Hadrian's walls. She had taken the first three with perfect grace, but the horse had shied at the fourth. At that point, as if this were a flat race, the flag had dropped and when it was raised, the horse was cropping grass between the walls and Nell had disappeared.

Vernon—and it would have surprised anyone who knew him—was superstitious. He believed in portents and prophecies, although he hated to admit it. And this dream had come out of Nell's disappearance. Only, he had dreamed it again just last night. The flag was dropped and she was gone. What worried Vernon was that he was the person with the flag. It was absurd for him to think that her disappearance had been somehow his fault. But he had set in motion a thought that plagued him. It was clear what it stemmed from: he was thirty-six and she was seventeen. All the same—

"That horse is no jumper, Nellie."

She flicked Lili's reins and turned the mare aside, saying, "Well, I admit we've been practicing a little."

Aqueduct jerked the reins and turned in a circle.

"Cut it out!" said Vernon, who'd never ridden the horse before. "What in hell's he doing?"

Nell laughed. "He's a 'chaser, Vern. He wants to jump. With or without you, he's going over that wall."

"Hell. Okay, okay."

He positioned himself beside her, both horses about forty feet from the first low wall. They flicked their reins and galloped toward it. Vernon was paying more attention to Nell's horse than to his own, now sailing over the wall. Aqueduct didn't need him to do it.

Lili did need Nell, though. Nell's hands, legs, tongue. Vernon had never seen the horse she couldn't get something out of. The horse made a graceful slide over the wall, though not with many inches to spare.

"Keep going!" yelled Nell.

Aqueduct seemed to want to keep Nell in view and slowed a little, but his what-the-hell? instincts sped him up again. It certainly wasn't Vernon's guidance that had the horse leaping four feet above the ground and sailing over the second wall. Vernon reined him in, thinking it was obvious Aqueduct had only just gotten started and aimed like an arrow at the third, even higher wall.

"Come on, Vern. You can do it. You're on Aqueduct," she yelled, coming up on the third wall.

"*You* can do it, you mean. You've *done* it!"

"Of course I haven't. Where'd you get that—oh, you mean my vanishing act over Hadrian's walls? You don't think my kidnapper would trust *me* with the reins, do you?"

"I thought that might have been one reason he took you. Because you're such a good horsewoman."

She smiled. "Thanks very much, but I have a lot of trouble with a couple of those walls."

"Then *he* must have been good."

"I expect he was." Nell thought for a moment. "He might have been a jockey." She closed her eyes. "He felt like the right size for it. I think sometimes I could recognize everything by touch." Her eyes opened. "Don't you?"

Vernon glanced at her and bent to rub Aqueduct's neck. He thought for a moment, then asked, "Do you have a cell phone? I forgot mine." First time in his life, probably.

"Vern, do I look as if I had a cell phone?"

Still up on Aqueduct, Vernon craned his neck, looking around as if he expected to find a public call box on the land.

Nell asked, "Why? Who are you so eager to call?"

"Richard Jury." He ran his thumb across his bottom lip, abstracted.

"Who's Richard Jury?"

"Sorry, I meant to tell you about him. He's a detective, a superintendent, Scotland Yard."

"That's pretty high up, isn't it? For him to be taking an interest in where I am? I mean, especially after all this time?"

"It's not official; I mean, he's not doing it in any official capacity. He was in hospital and your dad's patient. Roger talked about you—well, seeing who he was, I can understand." He looked around again. "Look, I'd like to get back to London—"

Nell brought Lili's head around; the horse was looking at a particularly attractive patch of vegetation. "Seeing as there are no telephones anywhere else."

"You're coming with me."

Her eyebrows raised. "That's an order?"

"Uh-huh. Are you going to do anything else with the mares?"

"Just bring them out for a walk round."

While she went to tend to the horses, Vernon rode Aqueduct to the old horse ring. He was glad he'd come to the farm occasionally to ride. He began at a gentle gallop, went around once at a canter and then he got the horse up to speed.

They blitzed the hard-packed earth. It was utterly exhilarating. He thought of nothing but speed and wind. Nothing else, not even money, not even Nell.

FORTY-ONE

Melrose was standing by the horse stall, presently horseless, wondering what Momaday was doing with Aggrieved. He was doing something, certainly, uncaring of Melrose's explicit instruction that he was not to take the horse out. Momaday's very touch put a blight on a thing.

I'm going to fire him, Melrose thought. Then he thought, *No. I'll get Ruthven to fire him. He knows how to do these things.* Who was he kidding? No one ever got fired at Ardry End. His father, of course, left "all of that domestic nonsense" up to Melrose's mother, who couldn't even fire a mouse. Indeed, Melrose had come upon her one day, kneeling by a hole in the study baseboard, shoving something into the hole. Embarrassed she'd been caught out, she blushed and said, "It's just a bit of cheese. I don't think they eat properly."

As Melrose had been six at the time, and already thought his mother a glorious person, her glory was thus made even more manifest. He grabbed her hand and told her she was nice and he'd never tell. Momaday was her polar opposite.

Melrose tramped over sodden ground to the hermitage to see how his new employee was doing. He had hired Bramwell to occupy the hermitage because he thought it might be a way to thwart Agatha, who had taken to spending some time tramping to the horse stall and participating in close colloquy with Momaday (who, heretofore, she wouldn't give the time of day to) about the care and feeding of the horse. If he couldn't bar her from the house, he at least wanted her off the land. God knows what the two of them would think up with regard to the fate of Aggrieved.

The hermitage was left over probably from the last couple of centuries and as it was a distance from the house and pretty much hidden by trees, he had forgotten its existence. How he could have forgotten it for two minutes running, he couldn't imagine, not with a skull and MEMENTO MORI carved on the lintel. He could hardly wait to show Richard Jury! A great place to stuff a body and he was close to stuffing Mr. Bramwell's into it.

Right now, Mr. Bramwell, hermit-in-residence, was out of his den—a substantial grotto, made of stones, tree limbs and moss, surprisingly warm and snug in winter, though Bramwell was constantly complaining about the lack of heat and light and had been since his arrival several days ago.

All of this hermit business had come about when he'd been talking about the eighteenth-century notion of hermits living on one's property. Landowners, wanting to be thought both richer and more worldly-wise than they actually were, and certainly more fashionable, often were on the lookout for a hermit. There were, of course, rules to be followed: never set foot off the property, never shave or cut the beard.

"You should get one—an ornamental hermit," Diane had said. "That's a marvelous idea. I daresay one would put Agatha off her feed." She waved her empty martini glass toward the bar and Dick Scroggs. He took his time.

"Withersby!" said Trueblood. "A perfect candidate."

"She's a woman: hermits were men," said Melrose. "Hired by the landed gentry to give the impression of bucolic idleness, or whatever."

Scroggs came with his small and ice-cold jug of vodka and an eye blink of vermouth and poured this into Diane's glass, popping in an olive on a toothpick. "You know, I could find you one," said Diane. "Put an ad in my paper." "Her" paper because she wrote the astrology column, to everyone's great amusement "That's what they did back then. Advertised."

"Why do I find this proposal hard to believe?" said Vivian.

Diane shrugged. "Lack of imagination?"

Trueblood said, "It's a great idea. Diane and I can interview the applicants." He nodded from Melrose to Diane. "I think it would be great fun."

"Oh, really?" said Vivian, swirling her sherry round in her glass. "Perhaps so. Considering what you two think fun." Vivian was still smarting over the Franco Giappino incident, when their combined cunning (a force to reckon with) had got him out of Long Piddleton. No one had ever told Vivian what ruse had accomplished this.

So that's what they had done. They'd come up with Bramwell. People willing to hire out as ornamental hermits were not too thick on the ground. Mr. Bramwell had turned up with two suitcases and a chip on his shoulder as if his last stint as a hermit had left him with a bad taste in his mouth.

Today, Melrose gave him a cheery "Hullo, there, Mr. Bramwell. How are you keeping?"

"How'd you be keepin' if it was *you* sleepin' on moss?" Short and stocky, Mr. Bramwell was somewhat more aggressive a person than Melrose would have preferred in a hermit, but Diane had insisted beggars can't be choosers when it came to hermits and she and Trueblood had had a hard enough time convincing the applicants that this was indeed a serious offer and their employer would indeed pay the king's ransom stipulated.

Artificially, Melrose laughed. "Now, that's a bit of an exaggeration, isn't it? We've put in a very nice cot for you and plenty of warm blankets."

Bramwell gave him one of those *hmph*-y gestures of his square jaw, narrowed his eyes and took out his stubby pipe (tobacco also having been supplied) and generally did little to project hermitlike subservience. "Not much o' a job, is it, mate? And when do them cameras start rollin'? I ain't seen hide nor hair o' Russell Crowe."

Well, it had been rather an outlandish lie that a major production company was making Ardry End the scene of a blockbuster film, but Bramwell was driving him nuts with his constant demands to know just what he was doing here, and he bet it was something to do with drugs, and there was no entertainment. He had quite a list of complaints.

"The production company's been held up by, oh, the star. Crowe is finishing another picture."

"Them film people's too coddled all their lives. Not like me, no, I've 'ad it plenty rough, me."

Bramwell appeared to be roping him in to hear the story of the hermit's life. He was tamping down tobacco preliminary to setting things afire.

"Mr. Bramwell, I've got things to do."

Bramwell made a dismissive, blubbery sound with his lips: "*You?* You're one of them titled that's been waited on hand and foot all yer life, like Russell-bloody-Crowe, on'y ya ain't as good-lookin'." He scratched behind his ear. "Now what's the name of that foxy blond-headed woman he goes wiff—?"

"Why don't I get you a subscription to *Entertainment Weekly*? Only now—"

Bramwell, guided by voices Melrose was not privy to, was off on another avenue of conversation, this about a childhood on the dole, and some female whom Bramwell referred to as "My Doris"—wife? sister? cousin?—who had wretchedly died during some routine operation, which explained his detestation of doctors and hospitals. "Now, my Doris had nuffin' wrong wiff 'er—"

Melrose, who had always been too much the gentleman to shut up anyone, was relieved to see Ruthven coming along the path with the cordless telephone.

"It's a Mr. Rice, sir."

"So, how's things, mate?" Bramwell said to Ruthven, whose face seemed to crinkle in the disturbance of a dozen responses he, too, was too much of a gentleman's gentleman to make.

Phone in hand, Melrose started to walk back to the house. "Vernon! How are you?" Then he stood stock-still at the news. "She came *back*? She just—*walked in*?" Melrose started walking again as he listened to the story of the previous night and the trip to Cambridge. He entered the study by way of the French window, sat down in the nearest chair. Vernon said he had tried the superintendent's number a couple of times, but he didn't appear to be in.

"His idea of 'recuperation' isn't most people's. I left him in London. He said he was going to Wales. You told him about some woman in Dan Ryder's life?"

"I did, yes."

"What about Nell's family?"

"She wants to wait until tomorrow to go there."

"But—"

"I know. But she's got her reasons, even if I don't know what they are. She's—remarkable. She's—prodigious."

Melrose smiled at that. "You always knew that."

"I always did, yes."

Melrose thought for a moment. "You know, there's something particularly interesting about all this."

"What's that?"

"Well, could she feel, I don't know, guilty for some reason? Ashamed? Something she apparently doesn't feel around you?"

"I thought of that. I expect because I'm not really family; I'm not as important to her, so my judgment wouldn't mean as much—?"

Melrose heard the question in those words. "Just the other way round, I'd say. And as for judgment, she knew you wouldn't judge her."

The silence hummed.

FORTY-TWO

"I don't see why," said Carole-anne Palutski, seated on Jury's sofa that evening, "you want to do your recuperating *there* and not *here*. Why'd you want to go to Northants, anyway? Not even to mention *Wales*."

Jury dropped his shoe on the floor and rested his foot on the dog Stone's back. Stone woofed. "Because I needed to see somebody."

"In *Wales*?" As if nobody ever saw anybody in Wales. "Don't be daft. We don't know anyone there."

We don't? Jury shook his head. "I've been many, many places in my long and illustrious career as a detective; you'd be amazed at the people I've run into that you don't know anything about. For instance, there's the family Cripps: White Ellie, Ash the Flash . . ." Jury went on in mind-numbing detail about the Crippses and a number of other witnesses, suspects, people helping with inquiries, all over the British Isles.

Carole-anne sat coiling a strand of copper blond hair round her finger all through this peroration, watching him. "What's she look like?"

"Who?"

"This woman in Wales."

After she'd taken the description of the woman in Wales up to her flat to brood about, Jury sat for a while, more tired, he knew, than he cared to admit. He let his eyes trail round the room, making comparisons with Rice's penthouse flat and Plant's near-stately home. That his own flat was sadly diminished by such a comparison didn't bother him at all. In the course of this little trip round his room, he noticed a picture that he had all but forgotten hung beside the window, as one will forget what is always there to look at. It showed half a dozen horses at a white fence, in a representation eerily similar to the scene he and Wiggins had encountered on that first visit to Ryder Stud. Not for the first time, he thought how things all have a way of coming to bear.

He sighed and then looked at the short list of calls Carole-anne had plucked from his answering machine, since the damned thing never worked properly for him. These were probably not all of the messages; they were the ones selected by Carole-anne, those of which she approved and out of which she fashioned her short list, as if the messages were competing for the Booker Prize. The other messages were still there for Jury to unspool if he could work out the machinations of the machine, a devil's device, as far as he was concerned.

In Carole-anne's often indecipherable writing were listed calls from Vernon Rice, Wiggins, DCS Racer, Rice again, Melrose Plant, Wiggins again. He started with Vernon Rice.

"It's Richard Jury—"

He was out of his chair like a shot, narrowly missing crushing Stone when he heard about Nell Ryder. He sat down again. "You mean she simply turned up in your office?" Jury levered on his shoe. "I'll be there inside of a half hour, depending how fast I can get a cab."

He wedged his foot into his other shoe, telling the dog, Stone, "He did tell me that, Stone. 'She'll just walk in,' that's what he said. And damned if she didn't just walk in."

FORTY-THREE

Jury looked at her for a long time, longer than was necessary for a simple introduction. The pictures on the wall of her grandfather's study had not lied. He found it hard to wrench his eyes away, and "wrench" was just what he felt he was doing. This introduction took place in the course of seconds, but it felt like as many minutes, in which he had taken and dropped her hand and felt as if he were stuck in an afterglow the cause of which he had missed.

She was wearing dark designer jeans and a white silk blouse. For a girl of seventeen, she wore elegance well. But what she looked like—that she was extremely pretty—was almost beside the point. That wasn't what held Jury, although he imagined many men would mistake this more mysterious quality for physical beauty. Rarely had Jury been unable to pin down a witness or suspect, to tease out what made the other person tick. But here he was, and would be, at sea.

Light from a low-glowing lamp behind her fretted her hair, the way light striking the surface of water filters down and diffuses. He had the eerie feeling he was looking at a scene underwater.

It surprised him when she apologized. "I'm sorry. I've put you to a lot of trouble."

"It was no trouble."

"I think it was. You've been in hospital. Vern told me."

Vernon was pouring whiskey into a cut glass tumbler, looking ruefully at the empty bottle. He handed Jury the glass and said, "I'll go down to Oddbins for some more. Nell," he said, "go ahead and tell all. The superintendent needs to hear it."

"But I've already told you every—"

Vernon shook his head, eyes closed. "He doesn't want it from me, he wants it from you. It's not just what's said; it's the way it's said. Right?" He was shrugging into an anorak.

"He's right," said Jury. "Except I don't want to put you through—"

Vernon said with a smile and a wave of his hand, "It seems to me it's what Nell's put *us* through, even though she wasn't responsible. Nell."

Vernon Rice seemed to have a lot of influence. But that didn't surprise Jury, given it was to him she chose to come. She nodded. He said he'd be back in a few minutes.

Jury asked her about what had taken her out to the stables the night she was abducted. "I've been told," he said, "but I'd like to hear it from you."

"Aqueduct. Maurice told me he seemed sick. Stable cough, he said. It's not unusual for a horse to get it. So I took my sleeping bag and went out to stay with him. I sometimes did that with a sick horse, though I didn't really see any signs of stable cough. Still, better safe than sorry." She smiled.

"Tell me what happened, Nell."

She told the story unemotionally. It was as if emotion, at least in this instance, had been burned out of her. At the end of it, Jury sat silent for a few moments, then asked, "Were you treated well—or, at least, decently?"

There was a hesitation so brief that no one, not even Vernon, would have picked up on it except for a person trained to notice brief hesitations. Jury looked at Nell; she looked away. There was a silence she was not going to fill. He didn't probe, at least for now. Instead, he said, "And you couldn't leave because of the horses. The mares."

She nodded; she shrugged.

"You didn't think your grandfather would do something to get the horses out of there?"

"They aren't, you see, doing anything illegal, so the authorities wouldn't be able to shut them down. What they'd have done—Dad and Granddad, I mean—would have been to take their guns and find this place and shoot the lot of them."

Her voice was near strident, almost to the point of desperation. *That was it,* he thought. That was what the child in her had wanted, what every child in danger prays for, no, *expects:* the protector to show up and "shoot the lot of them." Only, the protector doesn't turn up. So you find yourself in a position where there's nothing to fall back on. Her mother had died; her father lived in London, too busy for her a lot of the time; that left her grandfather.

"You seem to feel—"

The look she turned on him seemed to implore him to explain herself to her.

"To feel guilty. Why?"

"If I was able to get away, I should have gone home. And I was able to."

"They failed you; why should you go home?"

That startled her; it startled her, but at the same time made her utter a small, relieved sigh. She was sitting on the edge of the sofa, balanced there, as if the suspense of this line of thought were a high-wire act. Then she laughed, but the sound was tight. "There was nothing any of them could do, though."

"That might be literally true, but that's not how you felt. They should have been looking for you—"

"They *were.*"

"But they stopped."

For a moment she said nothing, then, "It was only reasonable to stop."

"Vernon Rice didn't stop."

She dropped her head and seemed to be studying, as he had, the wavelike pattern in the carpet, a stormy gray growing fainter in color but the wave growing wider. "And you think that's why I stayed away. That I was so spiteful—"

The notion of spite here was ludicrous. "*Spiteful?* That's the last thing I'd think. No, I'm only looking for connections, for reasons."

"Reasons. You think I'm lying to myself. You think the real reason I stayed there for all that time was for some sort of revenge. That my family couldn't keep me safe. You don't believe it was the horses."

There was in what she said some deep truth that connected her with the mares. But Jury blamed himself for stating it so clumsily that she'd misunderstood. "On the contrary, I think the horses were absolutely the reason. By 'connections' and 'reasons,' I mean, how is it that you feel such compassion that you stayed when you could have left, and why were you willing to put yourself at risk again and again by going back, when you could simply have stopped? That first time, you could have taken Aqueduct and just ridden off. But you went back. Every time you went back it was more dangerous. You even went back to your room, your bed."

"After the fourth mare I waited. So I needed to stay with the mares I had and take care of them. It was nearly three weeks between stealing the fourth one and the fifth, then the sixth. And after that, I just stayed in the barn. It was on Granddad's property and we once used it, but not anymore."

"You couldn't have been far from there all along. How far was it?"

"I'm not sure; driving, I think it would be less than two miles."

"And you didn't know this Hobbs woman? I mean, before."

She shook her head. "The farms are so far apart that unless you do business with one—" She shrugged and studied the rug again; it seemed to be the repository for their unspoken, perhaps unbidden, thoughts. "Being that close, all of this time . . ."

"But you still feel guilty."

"Yes." She looked up. "For the ones I left behind."

Jury looked at her across this small sea of gray rug, at the pattern of barely distinguishable waves, by some illusion washing toward her, lapping at her feet. He felt a cold knot in his stomach, as if he had waded out into freezing water to reach her, but couldn't. "The ones you left," he said. For some people there was always something more to do, something more to save. "Did you think you could get all of those mares out?"

She nodded. "Maybe, at first. If I was clever enough. Brave enough." Her smile was weak, as if she should never have expected to be either.

Astonished, Jury just looked at her. What she had already done was not enough to show her that she was both brave and clever. He hardly knew what to say in the face of such self-abnegation. He reverted to practical questions.

"This fellow who abducted you—would you know him if you saw him again?"

"I don't think so, not to see him. Maybe if I felt him—"

She stopped so suddenly, Jury was suspicious. He thought of her former hesitation. "Nell, what else happened?" He knew the moment she looked at him and then didn't look at him. Rather, she looked everywhere in the room, except at him. "This fellow, the one who abducted you, did he do anything else?"

She bent her head as if she couldn't get it down far enough, far enough away from him. "It wasn't him."

Jury waited.

"Another one. Another man, but I only saw his face once, and not well. That's because he came at night and made sure the room was always dark. He made me lie on my stomach and went at me that way. I never saw anything except his hands on either side of my face." As if her listener might need this demonstrated, she put her own hands by her face, palms flat and turned inward. "Just his hands." She seemed not to know what to do with them now.

Jury leaned over and took her hands in his. "This is part of the reason you feel you can't go back."

She was crying as she nodded. She said, "I didn't fight it after the second time. To fight him off meant only that it would last longer."

Jury moved to the sofa and put his arms around her. "None of this was your fault, Nell. None of it."

"But you won't tell anyone. Please don't tell anyone. Vernon would kill him if he ever saw him."

"No, I won't." He pulled a handkerchief from his pocket and gave it to her where she still had her face buried in his chest. She reached out a hand, took it. Interesting she'd chosen Vernon, and not her father or grandfather, to kill the bastard. Jury thought: *And if I ever see him. I'll kill him.*

She had apparently made herself presentable enough to sit back. "If Mum hadn't died—"

The *if* stayed unfinished. The *if* was always unfinished, wasn't it? And death was no excuse for abandonment. It never had been, never would be. Such is our complete unreason when it comes to loss.

Was it the shutout, Jury wondered, that had evoked in her this love of creatures that could communicate only through signs and gestures? Was it herself she saw in these helpless mares and because of that was determined to do what her mother never could? Nor, when it came to it, her father or even her grandfather, though they were far better than her mother. They had at least stuck.

Nell went on. "She was a terrific horsewoman, Mum. Maybe that's where I got the ability."

That and a few other things, thought Jury, looking at the rug again. Loneliness, and an abiding rootlessness, an incurable homesickness. When Mum went, she took home with her.

"Mr. Jury."

His head snapped up.

"What're you thinking? I mean, you look so sad."

"Oh. I was just remembering my own childhood. My own mum. I didn't have a horse."

"That's too bad. You should've."

He smiled. It was as if humankind were divided between the horse owners and the horseless, as if horses could take the place of missing parents.

Her expression was completely serious and concerned.

"You're going to Ryder Stud tomorrow?"

Her face clouded over a little. "Yes." Then she surprised him by saying, "You could go with us. Would you?"

"Well . . . yes, if you want. I'd be glad to."

They both turned at the sound of the door's opening. Vernon came in with a large carryall that clinked.

"Sorry it took so long."

"That Oddbins chap must have been giving you a detailed account of the slopes of Burgundy and Muligny."

"Nope. I just ran into a pal of mine and we had a drink." He set the bag on the floor beside the drinks cabinet.

Jury didn't believe Vernon had met a pal. He had stayed

away for this half hour to give Nell room to talk more
freely.

"You both look like you could use a drink." He held up
a bottle of whiskey and one of red wine. "Okay? Interested?" They nodded and Vernon set about fixing the
drinks.

"Tell me about the place," said Jury.

"It was ordinary enough. Not as much land as we have.
The mares were kept in stalls some distance from the main
building." She described the barns, the narrow stalls, the
way the urine was collected, the way the mares were tethered so they couldn't move more than a few inches. All of
this as if limning a picture he'd better not forget. But she
said little about the rest of the farm. Her room, the kitchen,
the locked office. "It was where I found out about this
operation."

Handing her a drink that looked to Jury as if it were
right down Wiggins's alley—a brightly colored club soda—
Vernon asked: "That's where you got the stuff you
showed me?"

"Yes. Once I had a chance to look through her books.
There were stud books. But what I was mainly interested
in was the mares. Wait a minute." She rose and went down
the hall to her bedroom.

Jury took the moments to tell Rice what she'd said about
going to the farm the next day. "What do you think? Is
it okay?"

"Absolutely. As a matter of fact, we could—"

Nell was back with one of the Premarin folders and the
snapshots and handed them to Jury. "That's Valerie
Hobbs, there."

Jury looked at the two snapshots of the woman holding
the reins of a horse and the third shot of what he presumed
were the mares. He picked up the folder.

"It seems so benign, doesn't it, when you read about it
in there?"

Jury read about the drug. "I notice they don't show you
any horse farms, do they? What would women do if they
knew about the way these mares are treated?"

Nell said, "Some would stop taking it—no, I imagine a

lot of women would stop. Some would just go on. Like they go on wearing fur. I don't blame them, really, even though it's selfish and inhumane. There are so many things that make a person's life hellish. I expect it's hard to let go of any sort of comfort."

"This is terrible," he said, putting the folder on the table. "But you found nothing else?"

"I didn't know what to look for, specifically. There was the book in which she kept an accounting of the mares and the amount of urine they produced, and breeding of each one."

Jury held up one of the snapshots of Valerie Hobbs. "Do you mind if I keep this for a while?"

Nell shook her head. "No, take it."

He pocketed the photo, then said, "About that night and those walls—"

"Hadrian's walls is what we call them." She seemed to like this and smiled in an almost sunny way.

Jury returned the smile. "What about the stable lads, the trainers? I'm just looking for whoever would be a good enough rider to jump those walls."

"A jumper, a steeplechase jockey, could do it. He was small enough, I think, to be a jockey. With the right horse, maybe even Maurice could do it."

"Maurice? I didn't know he excelled as a rider."

"That's because he never talks about it. He always wanted to follow in his dad's footsteps and of course he's not that good. He was well over five feet when I—left; maybe he's grown since I saw him. Anyway, for Maurice, if he can't be as good as his father, well, he doesn't want to be anything. I've always tried to get him over that but I never could."

Jury studied her for a while, then rose. "I should be getting back to my digs. What time are we leaving?"

Nell waited for Vernon. He said, "Ten o'clock all right for you?"

"Couldn't be better." He turned to Nell. "Thanks for talking to me." He turned to go and Vernon said, "I'll see you to the door."

Outside the flat, Vernon said, "You know what I think?

I think it'd go down much better for Arthur and Roger if they didn't know Nell had sought me out first. So couldn't we just say we found her?"

Jury thought for a moment. "Say *you* found her. I agree with you. Make something up, and tell her what you're going to say." Looking at Vernon, he smiled. "You know for someone who spends his time shoving money around, you're a sensitive chap. But why she wants me along, God only knows."

"Yeah. Sure." Vernon smiled.

As if God knew.

FORTY-FOUR

It was Arthur Ryder who opened the door, surprised to see the two of them there in tandem. "Vernon!" He kept his face straight. "Have you got a warrant?"

"Ask him," said Vernon. "He's the Filth, not me."

Arthur shook Jury's hand. "I expect you know already about the woman who was shot? Simone Ryder?"

Jury nodded. "I heard, yes."

Arthur Ryder shook his head. "I don't know if that makes the whole thing less or more mystifying." He looked from one to the other. "It makes me anxious just to ask, but—have you got news?" They were still standing by the open door and as he said this, he was looking past them at Vernon's silver BMW. "One of your people, Superintendent? Doesn't he get to come in from the cold?"

"No," said Vernon. "Look, Arthur, we do have news—"

"Christ!" The single syllable nearly broke in two, sounding both anxious and sorrowful. "She's dead, isn't she?"

This reaction interested Jury. Vernon Rice would never have thought that. He'd always believed Nell was alive. He'd always *known* it.

"No, Arthur. She's not dead. She's alive."

"You mean you've *seen* her? What—?" Then he was off the sofa and almost throwing himself across the room as if he meant to reach the door by the shortest way possible. He flung it open.

"Art!" called Vernon.

When Nell saw him, she sprang from the car and ran around it, ran toward him. When they met in the center of the courtyard she jumped up and tried to wind herself around him.

Vernon watched and sighed. "She bloody well didn't do that when she met up with me again."

Jury couldn't help himself; he cuffed him one up the side of the head, laughing.

"What? *What?*"

Arthur and Nell, both laughing, both crying, reached the door.

"I just can't believe it," he said, releasing her from the grip of his arm. "Where'd you find her? *How* did you find her?" This was directed at Jury, naturally assuming it was police work.

"Don't give me any credit for it. It was Vernon."

"Pure luck. I was coming back from Cambridge, Art, and some instinct took me down that old road that leads to the compound you don't use anymore. The horse barn, the exercise ring—"

"*That's* where you were?" he said to Nell.

"Not for the last two years, Granddad, no. Only a few—days."

Jury thought Vernon was right in not letting Arthur know Nell had sought him out in London. Vernon, being Vernon, didn't take this as Nell's *preference* for him, but just that he was the one who could be of the most help. And *why* he failed to conclude that the person who can help is the *preferred* person, Jury damned well couldn't work out.

Arthur still held her hand, as if reluctant to lose physical contact, as if she might disappear if he didn't hold on. "I've got to call Roger. Or have you?" he asked Vernon. "Have you seen Roger?"

Vernon shook his head. "This is the first place we came. Where's Maurice? We need to tell him, too."

"Don't know," said Arthur, absently. "Outside, probably the stable."

"I'll look for him," said Jury. He wanted to talk to Maurice alone.

Outside, Jury found one of the stable lads, who pointed him off in the direction of the training track. He found it on the other side of a stand of oaks and elms, the path running through the trees. When he got to the track he saw that the crime-scene tape was down, but whether removed by Cambridge police or Maurice himself, Jury didn't know.

Out there, blowing into the straight on the other side were Maurice and a horse Jury recognized as Samarkand. If that horse was running at this breakneck speed at his age Jury would love to have seen him as a three-year-old. He must not have touched the ground; he must have been wind.

And Maurice himself, bent in half over the horse's neck, would have made one hell of a jockey. Continuing to grow as he had must have been bitterly disappointing to him. Jury wondered if Maurice hated his body. He filed that question away for future consideration.

Maurice saw Jury as he came out of the second turn and pounded on past. He then stood up in his saddle and slowed Samarkand, rode the horse from the track and dismounted.

"Maurice." Jury held out his hand.

Maurice shook hands with him, tossing his head to get the dark hair off his forehead and out of his eyes. Jury thought it a gesture something like Samarkand's shaking out his mane. "You must have been frustrated watching yourself get taller and taller. It took you out of the race."

"I guess I was. Why are you here? Has something happened?" Anxiety raised his voice a notch.

Another five minutes of not knowing wouldn't hurt him. "You told me you weren't much of a rider. You were being modest." Jury smiled. "You know, I'm still wondering about Aqueduct—" Jury paused and looked at him.

"Wondering what?"

"That night. Just how sick the horse was. You recall telling your grandfather he—Aqueduct—had a bad cough—what you called, I think, stable cough?"

"That's right. It's like an allergy; it could be a reaction to hay or straw."

"And you told Nell this, too."

Maurice nodded.

"Knowing Nell would stay with the horse, as she often did."

Maurice said nothing. His normally pale complexion paled even more.

Jury waited, but Maurice wasn't going to say any more. "Nell said she didn't see any signs of it."

Maurice started to answer this charge, but then did a double take. His eyes widened. "She *said?* What're you talking about?"

"Nell's come back. She's up at the house." Jury started to say something else, but Maurice jumped up on Samarkand (to the horse's apparent dismay) and was off. Walking to the house from this spot would have taken three minutes, maybe four. But Maurice must have found even three or four minutes too long. That was going to be some reunion! Jury wanted to see it, yet he stayed here by the track.

Scene of the crime.

FORTY-FIVE

"Owning that horse"—said Agatha as she marmaladed a scone—"will permit you to join the hunt."
Melrose set aside his book, took a sip of tea and said, "Agatha, if there is one thing not on my short list, believe me, it's joining the hunt."

Having made quick work of the scone, she dusted her fingers. "You should; you should do more as befits your social standing here." She scanned the cake plate as she lifted her teacup.

"And why should I engage in something befitting my social standing when around here, there is no society?"

"Oh, stop being whimsical, Plant, it doesn't—"

Melrose saw her glance toward a window, openmouthed, and heard the scream: "Aaaa-rrrr-aaaaah."

"Good lord, Agatha! What's the matter?"

She was pointing at the long window on the south side of the living room. Melrose looked just in time to see the unkempt hair of Mr. Bramwell disappearing from view. Well, about time he earned his pike, or whatever hermits scratched around to get. Melrose could hardly contain himself, seeing Agatha's reaction, which was even more than he could have hoped for had there been rehearsals. Her face was chalk white; her eyes stared. Nor had she dropped her finger, for she was unable to move.

"Oh, come on, Agatha. It's only the hermit." He reclaimed his book as if nothing had happened.

"The *what*? What on *earth* are you talking about? Have you gone *mad*? Have you gone *zany*?"

That was a nice word, thought Melrose. "Don't you remember the book I was reading the other day? We were talking about ornamental hermits"—*this* was better than he'd expected for now she was gathering up her things (and his, if that little jade horse was any proof)—"ornamental hermits were a lot like ornamental shrubs—"

"That's it, Plant! I'm done! Finished! Finished with you and your crazy ways." Hefting her voluminous carryall, she rose. "Completely round the twist, that's where you've gone." She repointed her finger at the window. "That *creature* has apparently been permitted the freedom of your grounds. You surely don't think this place is *safe* with him running about. Probably a sexual deviant to boot."

"I don't know, but I'll ask."

"*Oh!* And to think all of the time I've given over to seeing that Ardry End runs smoothly. It's either your hermit or *me!*"

Melrose slipped down in his chair and stared at the ceiling, considering a dozen rejoinders and discarding each in turn as not quite worthy of the occasion. Life offers few such delicious moments, moments that taste like his father's hundred-year-old port, stashed in the cellar, must taste like. He decided no, nothing made of words was up to it. An answer to "either your hermit or me" should be fashioned out of jewellike words, words spilled across the table like a velvet sackful of rubies.

He settled for "We've a contract. And hermits have a union, you know, just like bus conductors. So—?" Melrose shrugged slightly, his eyes brilliant, at least he felt they must be brilliant for he certainly *felt* brilliant. He saw that in all of her consternation, she was still holding on to the jade horse.

"Very well. You shan't see me again anytime soon."

"No, but I hope I'll see that little jade horse."

Melrose stood drinks for Diane and Trueblood later in the Jack and Hammer, rewarding them for the trouble they'd gone to. "It couldn't have been fun, interviewing a lot of men like Bramwell."

"Oh, it wasn't bad at all, sport. Helped me sharpen my investigator's prowess, my detective's instincts." Trueblood lit up one of his sunset-colored cigarettes and said, "For instance, the one who wanted to know what newspaper he'd be getting was a definite no. I mean, I don't think a person who reads the *Times* is to be trusted as a hermit, do you? And the one who wanted to know what pubs were in the area, same thing. Got rid of that lot in a quick hurry. Then there were demands for days off, nights off, even half days and early closings. 'Well, you're not going to be running a hermit *shop*,' I told them. 'You're not going to be selling bloody hermit *souvenirs*.' 'Awright, mate, exactly wot *does* this 'ermit fella do, then?' I immediately stepped on anyone who asked what the duties were. Quite amazing some of them. You'd almost think"—Trueblood knocked off the ash that had been teetering on his coral cigarette—"that they'd never seen a hermit before."

"They never have," said Diane, running a finger above the rim of her glass as a signal to Dick Scroggs.

Melrose said, "The thing now is—how do I get rid of him?"

"Why, you just tell him his talents are no longer needed."

"*Fire* him, you mean."

"Yes, or just, you know, make him redundant. Tell him the war's over."

Diane arched an eyebrow. "Just tell him you're finished. You don't have to elaborate or explain yourself."

"Isn't it obvious I can't fire people? Momaday's living proof of that."

"Well, yes, but Momaday's ostensibly being useful. Or at least he's in a potentially useful line of work as grounds-keeper," said Diane.

"Wait! Wait!" Trueblood jumped up, nearly overturning everyone's drink. "I've got it!"

Diane clutched her martini with both hands to avert further disaster. "*Stronzo!*" Diane liked to trot out an Italian expression once in a while since Melrose had come back from Florence. She didn't speak Italian, but her accent was impeccable. It annoyed him to death.

"The answer to getting rid of Bramwell: Theo Wrenn Browne is the answer. His shop. You've seen that CURRENTLY HIRING sign he just hung in the window, as if he

were some corporate chain, like Waterstones? If we play
our cards right, Theo could be coaxed into hiring
Bramwell."

Melrose frowned, turned this over, then smiled. "Excellent! How?"

"There's only one way to do that, old trout." Trueblood
now lit up a jade-green cigarette. "Make Browne believe *I*
want to hire Bramwell. He'll be all over him then."

"This 'ere milk's gone off, mate," said Bramwell to Melrose, raising the jug from the breakfast tray Martha had
fixed for him.

This person was being waited on hand and foot. Melrose
ignored the milk and said, "Mr. Bramwell, you really aren't
suited to the hermit life."

"I coulda tol' you that from the beginnin'. But t'pay's
good."

"I've found you a far superior job. Of course, you'd have
to be interviewed for it."

"Wot's it pay? I gotta collect me dole money, don't
forget."

Melrose pushed a hanging vine out of his face. He wasn't
interested in discussing government fiddles. "I don't know
precisely what it pays, but at least as good as this job, I'd
think."

"I'll take it."

"You don't know what it is."

"Well, it's gotta be better'n sleepin' rough in this lot."
He waved his arm around the hermitage.

"If you live in Sidbury you could easily commute. There's
a bus between Sidbury and Little Blunt." Melrose had
never seen this bus (he'd never seen Little Blunt, either),
but he'd heard about it, as one might a distant star beyond
one's galaxy. He took out a small notebook (the one that
looked much like Jury's except Melrose's was all leather
and Jury's was all plastic), wrote the address of the Wrenn's
Nest, tore it off and handed it to Bramwell. "You can see
Mr. Browne tomorrow—and one suggestion: don't call him
'mate'; he's not as good-humored as I am."

Bramwell made a wheezy noise meant to sound like the
end of hysterical laughter.

"Never mind, just don't. Tomorrow afternoon. But first you'll want to stop in the antique shop and have a word with Mr. Trueblood." If Theo didn't see Bramwell go into Trueblood's shop, he would certainly see the both of them go into the Jack and Hammer together. Browne stood at his window half the day just to see what was going on.

Bramwell's face was contorted with confusion. "Why the bloody 'ell do I want t'see 'm for? Or 'is shop?"

"Because he has a position open, too, and you might want to compare the two."

"I don't know nuffin about bleedin' antiques."

No, and you don't know nuffin about hermits, either. "Just talk to him, will you? He's right across from the Wrenn's Nest. I'm sure he'd take you to the pub next door for a drink." *That,* thought Melrose, was a brilliant stroke!

Bramwell thought so, too, apparently, for his frown unpleated. "Yeah, well, I guess. Anyway, it's time for me lunch." He started to shove the tea tray at Melrose just as a cab drove up and stopped before the front door of Ardry End. It was too far to actually recognize the face of the man who got out, but he was tall.

Jury! About time, too. Melrose started off across the grass at a trot.

" 'Ey? Wot about me lunch, then?"

Melrose threw the answer back over his shoulder. "Have your people call my people."

"Who were you yelling at?" Jury was looking into the distance, his hand shading his eyes.

"Just the hermit. Come on inside!"

But Jury didn't move while he pondered this answer. "Were you intending to elaborate on that, or—?"

"What? The hermit?" Melrose recounted the Bramwell saga.

"You're crazy," said Jury, as they walked across the lawn toward the hermitage.

Melrose stopped. "Crazy? *Crazy?* Do you see any sign of Agatha?" He spread his arms to take in Ardry End, its tower and gardens, its trees and paths, its hermitage.

Jury laughed. "You're right there."

Ruthven was on the steps of the house calling to Melrose,

who stopped. Jury stopped, too. Melrose said, "Oh, no, you go on, hermit expert; I'll catch you up."

Jury walked on.

When Melrose did get to them, Bramwell was making a call on a cell phone.

"A cell phone, Mr. Bramwell?"

"Gotta call me turf accountant, don't I? Mr. Jury 'ere was just tellin' me what 'e liked in the fifth at Newmarket."

As Bramwell turned away, Melrose gave Jury a look. "Oh, this is rich, this is." He could hear Bramwell's mumbled request of his bookie.

Bramwell turned back and slapped the little phone shut. "There now. Thanks, mate." He had taken to Jury immediately.

"Come on!" Melrose veritably pulled Jury toward the house, filling him in on the plan for getting rid of Bramwell.

Jury just shook his head. "You couldn't do something simple, could you? Like firing him or telling him to get lost and handing over a pay packet for the weeks he'd miss? Hell, no. You and your cohorts invent a plan that could go wrong in a dozen different ways. Why don't I just go back and arrest him?" Jury turned.

Melrose grabbed his arm and dragged him back. "No! No, you can't get rid of a hermit in the conventional ways. A hermit has to be *schemed* away. Otherwise—"

"Yes?"

"—it's bad luck. But why are you acting so high and mighty about it? I seem to recall something about a *notebook* you absconded with. The memoirs of Franco Giappino? His adventures in Transylvania? His many brides?"

Jury waved this away as they walked up the front steps. "Oh, that."

Ruthven was waiting inside. Ruthven waited as impeccably as he did everything.

"Superintendent, I'm happy to see you've returned." He was helping Jury remove his coat.

"Tell me about Nell Ryder," said Melrose. "What *happened*?"

"If you'll just let me get this other sleeve off, ah, thank you, Ruthven."

Ruthven bowed slightly and asked, or started to, "Would you care for tea, Superintendent?"

"I would, yes." Jury claimed the sofa. "In case I want a bit of a lie-down." He sank back against the soft cushions. "First, though, I talked to Barry—Chief Inspector?— Greene. Seems the dead woman was Ryder's second wife."

Melrose raised his eyebrows. "What do you make of that?"

"I don't; I haven't, yet."

Melrose sat on the edge of his wing chair. "Well, go on, go *on* about Nell Ryder. You said she turned up at Rice's office. Out of the blue."

"Out of the blue indeed."

Then Jury began and went on telling Melrose, over the lighting of Melrose's cigarette, over the appearance of the tea, about Nell Ryder's reappearance.

Melrose didn't speak, but sat back and marveled at this story that should have begun, Melrose said, with "Once upon a time."

"Maurice?" Melrose said, aghast. "But why would he have—he's been, or seemed, so heartbroken by Nell's disappearance—"

"Even more reason to be utterly miserable, if he had anything at all to do with her abduction."

"But what?"

Jury shook his head.

Melrose grabbed a tiny sandwich from a plate that Agatha was not here to ravage. "For nearly two years he'd have kept it to himself?" Melrose shook his head and poured out more tea. "Uh-uh, I can't buy that."

"After a while, it would get even more difficult to tell anyone, more and more, because he'd have let everyone flounder for a week, month, then six months, then a year . . ." Jury shrugged, sipped his tea and took a bite of smoked salmon sandwich. He felt starved. "What's for dinner?"

"I don't know. A slab of cow or a dead duck?"

Jury smiled and they sat in silence for a moment. Then Jury asked, "Can you imagine the patience it took for Nell Ryder to do what she did? Not to mention courage."

" 'Patience' isn't exactly the word, is it? 'Determination,' I'd say. No, 'focus' might be even nearer the mark. Those mares. They were the only thing that came within her line of vision. Everything else disappeared; everything else she just hacked down to clear the path. If her mind was trained on a distant light, she'd swim through a river of crocodiles to get to it. Someone like that"—Melrose shook his head—"is stepping to the beat of her own drummer, that's certain."

Dinner was, forensically speaking, a dead duck, but more specifically, a duck sautéed in a fig and marsala vinegar. Sour and sweet played off each other in a delicious and syrupy essence, not to mention the alcohol-laden one. With it were French green beans in a walnut vinaigrette and bourbon mashed sweet potatoes.

"Aren't you interested in Wales?" asked Jury.

"Wales? No, should I be? Oh, yes, I forgot with so much else going on. What happened?"

Jury told him about Sara Hunt.

"You think she's obsessed with Dan Ryder? Or was?"

"Still is. No, that flame has not gone out."

They ate and drank in silence for a few minutes.

Then Melrose looked at Jury. "What are you sniggering about?"

"Wondering how an alcoholic would deal with these soused dishes. Vernon Rice has one of those dotcom things called SayWhen."

"What does it do?"

Jury speared a bite of marsala-soaked duck. "Nothing, really. It mostly commiserates."

"What does he sell, then?" asked Melrose.

" 'With-a-Twist.' "

"Pardon?"

"It's the newsletter that's sold," said Jury. "That's what it's called—'With-a-Twist.' It does some sort of riff on personal experiences. I'm not sure what. But the site is meant to give people incentive to stay off the booze."

"Wouldn't you think a grown man, a grown *broker,* a grown *venture capitalist* and day trader—wouldn't you think he'd have better things to do with his time?"

"Don't be so holier than thou." Jury sniggered again. "I

just wish he'd start up one on smoking. I could use some commiseration there."

"But you stopped smoking two years ago!"

Jury gave him a look and shook his head. "Is today your 'I'm a Simpleton' day? For God's sake, smoking is a complex matter. How many packs a day do you go through?"

"Only one. I limit myself to just the one so I won't get addicted."

Ruthven entered.

"Let's have some more incredibly soused potatoes and another bottle of whatever."

"The Hermitage?"

"That's the ticket."

Ruthven retreated.

Melrose asked, "Where was the place she was taken to?"

"About two miles from Ryder's, to the north. She was that close."

"Weren't they afraid she might be recognized?"

"Apparently not." Jury thought about the walls. "If you were a good horseman, it's more direct to jump those walls. And this person was apparently a very good horseman. Nell thinks he could easily have been a jockey."

Ruthven returned with the wine and the potatoes. "These damn things are making me drunk," said Melrose while Ruthven spooned up the potatoes for him.

"It wouldn't be the whole bottle of wine, right?"

Ruthven tittered as he served Jury.

"No, it wouldn't. That's what I usually have and I'm sober as a judge."

Ruthven said, "Will you be ready for dessert in fifteen minutes? The soufflé will be out of the oven then."

"Yes, thanks."

Ruthven made his exit with tray and server.

"Soufflé. What kind?"

"Chocolate. With fairy cakes."

"Do those things really exist?"

"Of course. Fairies exist, after all. It's a child's confection, a cupcake with wings."

They had cleaned their plates and Jury sat back with a sigh. "God, this is *so* nice. Waited on hand and foot, whiskey, wine, duck."

"Is it?"

"You don't think so?"

"I'm used to it. Mind if I smoke?"

"It's bad manners to smoke between courses."

Melrose plucked a cigarette from a porcelain box, lit it with his Zippo. "And nor do I know why the second Mrs. Ryder was done in on a training course."

Jury sat back. Then he said, "Possibly a joke."

"Oh, how *droll*. 'I saw the funniest thing the other day, a dead body on a racecourse.' "

"Not that kind of a joke. Or joke's the wrong word."

"Well, whoever did it is no doubt pleased to see all the trouble they've caused."

"Yes. That's the other part—"

Ruthven had returned with the soufflé, served with a raspberry confit in a delicate tracery of red.

"Delicious looking. Martha's really outdone herself."

They ate in silence for a while, savoring the mingling of chocolate and raspberry.

Jury looked up suddenly, holding his fork like a little spear. "Unless—"

"Yes? Unless what—"

Jury shook his head. "Nothing. It's a bit far-fetched—"

"At Ardry End, you're in the land of the far-fetched, believe me."

"I was going to say, it reminds me of the way *he* died. Dan Ryder. Thrown from his horse."

"Hm. Interesting. What *about* this woman, then? This second wife. Your Cambridge detective—did he fill you in on anything?"

"Simone Ryder. She was here, apparently, to talk to an insurance adjuster."

"But that accident occurred—when? Over two years ago, didn't it? She hasn't collected the insurance yet?"

"No. The thing is, there's a double indemnity clause in the policy."

"Ah-*ha!* Shades of Barbara Stanwyck and Fred MacMurray."

"What?"

"Surely you've seen that classic noir film. *Double Indemnity*. They murder her husband after taking out insurance with one of those clauses. If the death is caused by accident, pay up twice the face amount."

Jury looked up from the design he was making in the raspberry sauce with his fork. "Wouldn't it be a bit difficult for Mrs. Ryder and her boyfriend to kill her husband by means of a fall from a horse?"

"Oh, I don't know. I imagine you could plot a murder any old way."

"So, she makes sure the indemnity clause is intact and then Ryder's wife and her lover somehow orchestrate this riding accident. With the horse's cooperation. Hm."

"Then Edward G. Robinson starts smelling something fishy."

"Edward G. Robinson?"

"He was in charge of claims," said Melrose. "One of those terrier types who get their teeth into possible fraud and won't let go."

"How was Stanwyck's husband supposed to have died in this film?"

"Train. Fell off the back; that's when you could go out onto the platform for a smoke on American trains." Melrose looked at his own cigarette and considered. "Why was she in the Grave Maurice? It isn't exactly a pub one would seek out. Or a place where a woman like that would choose to meet someone. So I assume it was simply handy, and that would be because she'd been to the hospital, or was going to it. I don't see how she could have been going to meet Roger Ryder, as he was there when I came in. Left just a moment after."

"But she wouldn't have recognized him. I doubt she was carrying a snapshot of the good doctor around. Remember, the Ryders had never met this woman."

"So they say."

"So they say, yes."

They drank their coffee and were silent.

Jury asked, "What sort of racing do they have in Wales? Is there much of it?"

"Point to point. There's a lot of that. Are you thinking of Dan Ryder's going there because of this woman Sara Hunt? Point to point is mostly amateur stuff, but certainly professionals ride in it."

Jury nodded. "I'm thinking of them, yes. Wondering how easily they could have seen each other."

"You're convinced she was."

"Absolutely. You should have seen her reaction when I asked her about him. She had to leave the room." Jury thought about Sara alone in that magnificent, desolate house in its setting of ruined gardens and broken statuary and felt a kind of longing he could not attach to any particular place in his own experience. Whatever it was, he felt a pull to go back. What seduced him? The woman? The house? The past?

Melrose went on. "From what we know about him, any halfway decent-looking woman who'd admit to so much as an acquaintance with Dan Ryder might as well go whole hog and admit to an affair."

"That's what I think."

"Perhaps she didn't want to be thought of as one among many."

"Unless—"

"Unless what? There you go again."

Jury picked up his fork again and ran the tines through the slightly congealed raspberry confit. "There I go, yes." He put down the fork. "I think perhaps I need to make another trip to Cardiff tomorrow."

"Wales *again*?" Melrose sighed. "That means you'll have to go to London. I'll drive you."

"Thanks."

FORTY-SIX

Jury felt, when he'd sat down in the same seat he'd occupied on his return trip to London two days ago, that he might have found the answer to time travel, that he really was going back in time, but that to be able to do that was a sentimental fantasy; to want to do it was a failure of nerve, although he could not say expressly how or why. If he wasn't careful, he'd be getting into one of those dreary discussions with himself that usually ended with part of him irritated and part of him smug and all of him losing.

He wondered about the lad with the CD player and earphones and when the train pulled into the station where the boy had got off, Jury looked for him on the platform. He wanted to repeat the process without knowing why and wondered if it was no more (and no less, of course) than that desire to have the past back again, which plagued him generally.

Yet, in this case, the meeting was not past—or at least not yet—but in the future. But he felt far more ambivalent this time than he had in his previous encounter with Sara Hunt. And he felt the future could be a wrenching disappointment.

Jury lay his head back against the seat and wished for the return of the lad with the earphones and Door Jam.

When she opened the door this time, she seemed more at ease, thinking (Jury supposed) anything bad that might happen would have happened in their first meeting. He wondered why, since the police generally didn't have to come around twice unless there was a problem.

"I guess I feel flattered that you think I'm worth seeing again."

"Oh, I think you're worth seeing many agains."

"Many agains." She laughed. "I like that."

They were standing in the large, square black-and-white marble entryway. She looked, he thought, quite beautiful in her plain skirt and sweater, the skirt long and black, the sweater cropped and a little boxy, a dusty blue, cashmere, probably. Brown eyes, toffee-colored hair, a color you felt you had to touch as well as see to know for certain. He restrained himself.

"I hope I'm not being too intrusive."

"In seeing me? Lord, no, you can imagine the number of visitors I get out here."

He smiled. "Actually, I can't."

"My point exactly." She hung his coat on the coatrack. They walked into the living room, grown no warmer in its outer reaches than before. A pool of warmth collected around the chairs and sofa in front of the fireplace, some invisible boundary around them.

"You're timing's perfect. I've just made tea."

As he had on the train, he sat again in the chair he had sat in last time and she sat again on the sofa. While she poured the tea, his eye canvassed the room, took in its feeling of emptiness largely owing to the sparse furnishings and the huge cast-iron Gothic window, cheated again of light by the tree outside.

"It's so large and so isolated," he said, "you must get lonely at times." Yes, that was properly banal.

Perhaps because of the banality, her look was a little condescending. Probably, he deserved it. "I don't think loneliness has much to do with size and isolation, really."

"Then what?"

"Oh, please, Superintendent. Not again. You're baiting me."

This surprised him, for he hadn't been. He was saving his baiting for later. At the moment, he was perfectly serious. "Why would I do that?"

She set down her cup. "Because of something you'd seen or heard when you were here last. You want something; I don't know what. Information, I expect."

She sounded quite matter-of-fact and undisturbed by all of this; she sounded, in a word, innocent, unconnected to anything involving the Ryders. He heard a tiny sharp snap and looked up. She had bitten into a crisp biscuit and was smiling at him around its edge.

"Yes, I do want to tell you something. Two things. One is that the Ryder girl, Nell, is back."

Sara looked wide-eyed and said, "But that's wonderful! What happened? Did someone bring her back?"

Jury told her a pared-down version of Nell's return, an edited version, for he did not know what did or didn't apply to her, if anything.

"Her father must be ecstatic. I can't imagine, I really can't, having something like that happen to a child." She plunked another lump of sugar in her tea, as if the sweetness of the girl's return called for some additional sweetness on her part. "What's the second thing?"

"The woman found dead on that training track has turned out to be Dan Ryder's second wife."

She had raised her teacup, and it stopped and hovered at her mouth as her eyes widened. "But that's—well, it's damned *strange,* isn't it? What did they think she was doing there? I mean—" She replaced the cup in the saucer, carefully. "It was one of the Ryders, then?"

"I don't know."

They drank their tea and looked at the fire in silence. Jury's eye went to the silver-framed picture of the man who was probably her ex-husband. He rose, walked over to the kneehole desk and picked up the picture. "This your husband?"

"*Ex*-husband."

"Then you didn't part on such acrimonious terms after all. I mean—" He held it up.

She had turned her gaze to the big window and whatever she could see through the tree beyond it.

Nothing but a blank wall, thought Jury. "—to keep his photograph around?"

"I've always liked that picture." She said, rising suddenly, "Let's go for a walk in the dissolute gardens." She held out her hand to him. He took it.

There had been snow over the last two days, but not much of it had stuck, only enough to make this landscape ghostly. Knots of snow lay in the stone hair and on the inner side of the elbow of the girl pouring from a jug, and in the open mouths of the fish waiting to receive the water. There was ice on the steps down to the path between the maples and on the path, too. It crusted the surface of the fountain. Skeletal flowers, brown and black, were adorned with pockets of snow and ice blisters that gave them an ethereal look, spiky, white-webbed plants on the pocked surface of some star up there that he could see faintly now in the half-light of a late afternoon.

"I love it in winter," said Sara. "I shouldn't say it, I guess, but I think I like it more now than in the spring or summer. It seems closer to the way things are. The truth, perhaps."

"You think the truth is cold and colorless?"

"Well, I've usually found it to be not terribly warm and inviting." She looked up at him. "In your line of work, I expect you think so, too."

"Yes, but I have to begin with something cold and uninviting. Homicides generally are."

"Still, I'd think you'd be more jaded than I am."

But he wasn't. "No. Disappointed, angry, sad—those things, but not cynical, which I suppose is another term for jaded."

"But you must constantly be dealing with lies, bad faith and betrayal. You must see that all the time."

Jury thought about Mickey Haggerty. Then he thought about Gemma Trimm, about Benny and Sparky. He smiled. "Yes, but there are things that counteract that. The good guys are still winning."

She was astonished. "How? Why? Because there are more of them?"

"No. Because they're good."

Smiling, she shook her head. "I don't quite get that." She paused to shake snow from a skeletal bush. "You know, you haven't told me why you came back."

He watched her face. "To find out more about Danny Ryder."

"But I told you."

"No, I don't think you did."

She looked down at the empty pond. Without looking back at him, she said. "I don't know why you say that. It's as if you don't believe me."

"I don't."

She hadn't expected that. "Why?"

"When I asked you to tell me what it was about Ryder that attracted you, you left the room. You couldn't deal with it."

She waved an impatient hand at him. "That's ridiculous."

"We could do it again," he said, only half joking.

Sourly, she regarded him.

"You walked out because you couldn't bear thinking about him, his physical self. You had an affair with him, didn't you?"

She didn't answer.

"He must have been one hell of a charismatic guy because from the way I heard it in one blink a woman would be all over him. Since I've only seen pictures of him, I can't quite fathom this. He's good-looking all right, but not handsome enough it would compensate for his size. He was a fairly little guy, five five, and that's actually tall for a jockey."

Sara put her head in her hands. "My God! Such machismo! You, of course, *aren't* a 'little guy,' and I guess you set the standard."

Jury smiled. "Something like that."

Her head snapped round. "What conceit."

"Uh-huh. But back to Ryder—"

"You're so tenacious about this, about my knowing him. Why?" They were standing by a stone bench. She sat down.

"Because you had more to do with Dan Ryder than you're admitting to."

She sighed. "All right, damn it, but it won't help you; it isn't what you think. Call Dan Ryder a secret passion. It's completely adolescent." Ruefully, she smiled at Jury.

He said, "Everyone's had feelings like that."

"When we were thirteen or fourteen, maybe, but not thirty or forty."

"Do we ever stop being thirteen or fourteen? Or six or seven, for that matter? I think we carry all of that around with us; we just have more practice in hiding it."

"It was an—obsession. For two years, I'd be like one of those rock-star followers, what are they called, those girls?"

"You mean 'groupies'?"

"I'm a racing groupie. Or I was. Whenever I could, I went to Cheltenham or Newmarket or Epsom Downs— that's the last time I saw him, the Derby. After that he went to France. Wherever he was racing, I'd go. Of course, I couldn't really see him, not amongst a dozen flying horses and riders. But I knew the colors and the number and name on the blanket. Given the way jockeys ride, their faces are invisible. I had binoculars. And the race itself, I suppose that had something to do with it. There's something so romantic about it. I could sometimes see him on the telly in the winner's circle. But in person? I only met him in person twice: once at the farm, the Ryder farm. Vernon Rice took me because I said I was interested in horse syndication." She looked up at Jury. "Whatever that is; he talked about it at length, but I wasn't paying attention. But it was certainly a way to get to where Dan was."

"So this obsession was fed by nothing on his part?"

"Fed by nothing." She looked ashamed.

Jury thought, as she talked, that she was devolving into an ever-younger persona, versions of herself not at all arch, coy or evasive, and he thought of Carole-anne, who seemed to have kept her entire adolescent self intact. It bloomed and closed again, like the delicate petals of hibiscus furling and unfurling, night into morning. Perhaps he should ask Carole-anne about obsession.

It was dusk now, bluer and colder. Still talking, Sara rubbed one arm to stave off the chilly air. Jury removed his jacket and put it around her shoulders.

"Oh. Thank you." Her smile was utterly genuine, vulnerable.

"I didn't mean to stop you talking." He sat beside her.

"I'm glad you did. You're very good at this, you know."

He laughed. "At what?"

"This. Getting people to talk. For a while there I wasn't even aware of you; I was just talking to myself. I guess I wanted to talk about Danny."

"I guess you did."

"It's hard to put it in words." She looked at her feet, turning the ankles in and out in a way children had of doing. She sighed and shrugged. "That's the sum of my experience with Dan Ryder."

"But when you heard he died, it must have been awful for you."

"Oh, yes. Yes."

She brought her hand up to her forehead and he thought she might be going to cry, but she didn't. She just said it again, "Oh, yes."

It was nearly dark, that purple no-man's-land before nightfall. "Let's go in," said Jury.

As she had done before, she rose and held out her hand to him. He liked it; it was as if someone were wanting, for a change, to care for him, and he took advantage of it. With the hand she'd reached out, he pulled her toward him very quickly and kissed her quite hard. It happened in only a few seconds.

"Come on," she said, pulling at him. "Let's continue this discussion inside. And why are you laughing?"

Jury said, "I'm on sick leave; I'm supposed to relax."

"So? We'll relax."

Once inside, she led him into the kitchen, also large, also cold. She opened a cupboard and reached in and brought out a bottle of red wine with a label that looked as if it had been picked at over decades.

"Special occasion. Puligny-Montrachet. One of the absolute best years. Quite old, quite rare, and very relaxing."

"I'm depending on it."

With the wine held above her waist, she pressed up against him and kissed him lightly. "And if wine doesn't do it, there's always—" She laughed. "You know."

"Oh, I'm definitely depending on you know."

They climbed the back stairs leading from the kitchen to the first-floor bedrooms. She was holding his hand again.

The bedroom that she led him into, obviously hers, had high windows that gave onto that part of the garden in which they had been sitting. Jury looked down at the bench and felt he was looking at some distant self, the one he had brought here, the one that would not be going back with him. *You don't need this, mate,* he told himself. *You really don't. This woman is trapped in a dream and she's not going to wake up because you're so bloody wonderful. You know something's wrong—*

Fuck off, friend.

He tasted the wine. Delicious. But it could have been plonk and he'd still think it was delicious.

Sara rested her head against his chest, and he ran his hand over her hair and smiled. Yep. Definitely taffy colored. Pulling away, he set down his glass, and she pulled him back and started unbuttoning his shirt. He reached his arms around her waist and unzipped the skirt, which fell to the floor in a black puddle. There was so little effort required in undressing. It was as if the clothes were so lightweight, so transparent, they blew off.

In bed, with his mouth slightly opened, barely touching hers, he asked, "Is this better than a dream? What do you think?"

And back she murmured, "It *is* a dream."

He looked off at the cold windows. A dream within a dream. He did not think he liked that.

She said, "I just can't seem to help it."

Jury rolled over, grabbed her. "That's what they all say."

FORTY-SEVEN

She had wanted him to stay the night, but he had not, making the excuse that he really needed to return to London. He had promised Nell Ryder. She had argued, but not vehemently, that it wasn't after all his case.

"I think I made it mine."

"You're supposed to be taking things easy. That's what you said."

He laughed. "You call what we've been doing 'taking things easy'?"

So once again he was on the train, now its familiarity soothing. He wanted to sleep, not so much because he was tired but because he'd rather sleep than think. There were too many insensate moments in life not to be grateful for pure sensation and the last hours had certainly been that.

At the station's newsstand he had bought a *Telegraph* and *The Sporting Life*. Jury had read a racing form about as often as he'd read *Ulysses* and thought Joyce's density no match for the racing form.

It was something that Sara had said. It bothered him, but for the life of him he couldn't think what it was, except that it had to do with racing. Cheltenham, Newmarket, Doncaster were places she'd gone to following Dan Ryder around. He didn't doubt that she'd done this, for what man or woman would confess to such an obsession unless they were sociopaths? That kid who stalked Jodie Foster, the nutcase who shot John Lennon. Obsession was often not benign and harmless. But what was it, that detail that made him, right now, uncomfortable?

It looked like the same attendant who'd been on the train before, and who now came clattering through the car, shoving the food and drink trolley. As he'd done before, Jury bought a cheese salad sandwich and tea in a plastic cup. He hadn't eaten the other sandwich, and wouldn't eat this one; there were so few people in the car that he felt it must be discouraging not to sell your wares. He'd give the sandwich to Carole-anne; he now remembered that she loved cheese salad. He'd tossed the first one in the dustbin at the station.

Jury had called Plant to let him know he'd be spending the night in his Islington digs and would try to get to Ardry End tomorrow. The nice thing about Plant was that he didn't ask questions beyond "Are you all right?"

He took a few sips of the tea. He was getting to be as bad as Wiggins, who would have drunk the lot so as not to have the fellow think his tea wasn't any good. Wiggins watched flight attendants going through safety precautions, too. The tea was the same tea that he'd had on the other trips. Why did train tea always have that bit of whitish foam on top, as if its ingredients couldn't coalesce?

He returned to his meditation on Sara Hunt. He opened the print-condensed pages of *The Sporting Life* and ran his eye over the various kinds of races—claim, handicap, stakes—and the horses entered in them. Nothing jarred his memory for whatever it was, or perhaps it wasn't. It might have been something or someone else—

Davison. George Davison, Ryder's trainer. That afternoon they had been standing with Wiggins and Neil Epp in front of Criminal Type's stall. The Derby, at Epsom— that was what Sara had said. The last time she'd seen Dan Ryder race before his defection to France a few weeks later was in the Derby, up on Criminal Type. But Davison had made a point of that race. *"Only time I ever lost me temper at the board it was over that weight allowance. They said Criminal Type'd have to carry another twelve pounds. Bloody unfair. So I scratched 'im."*

Davison had scratched the horse almost at the last minute. Criminal Type was taken out of the field, and the horse and its jockey didn't race.

Why had Sara told him she'd seen the race? It seemed

such a pointless lie, as he wouldn't have thought one way or the other about that race, the only thing setting it apart being that George Davison had taken his horse out. It made no sense, what Sara had said. He slid down in his seat and closed his eyes.

She had been *with* Ryder that day? But in that case she would have known he wasn't racing at Epsom. She could fairly well assume that Jury wouldn't know that the Ryder horse was scratched. (Certainly, he'd pled ignorance of the racing world in general.) His head was hurting, probably in sympathetic response to his side, which throbbed. Dr. Ryder would thrash him if he knew Jury wasn't following instructions. So would Wiggins. So would Carole-anne. He'd be thrice thrashed, a pleasant little tongue-twister. He made sure the cheese salad sandwich was in his coat pocket. It might fend her off for a little while.

A very little while. Carole-anne, dressed in emerald green, had deposited the sandwich wrapper in the trash can and was now picking crumbs from her gorgeous green bosom.

"Are you saying you went *all* the way to Wales—?"

"And back. Twice, and lived to tell about it."

The eyes that leveled on him would have been cold had they not been so goddamned turquoise. Flashing turquoise, to boot. There she went now, hands on hips:

"Super! You know you promised that doctor that you wouldn't exert yourself in any way, that you wouldn't go out pub-crawling, that you'd stay in bed as much as possible—"

"I lied."

Well *that* flummoxed her. She was gathering up her argument, getting it into full gear, which of course demanded a fellow arguer, and Jury wasn't doing it. He smiled.

Carole-anne had to search around for another arguable topic.

Ah! The consideration card!

"It's just not very considerate, that's all, I mean to me and Mrs. W, as all we do is worry, wondering where you are and if you're okay. Not dead in a ditch somewhere. Like *Wales*."

"But you thought I was in Northamptonshire with Melrose Plant."

"Well, but you weren't! You were in Wales!"

That she saw no flaw in this argument was one of the things he loved about her. Jury rose, walked over and embraced her. "Sorry."

Her words were muffled by her head's burrowing against his chest.

Jury thought of the rain-swept, snow-swept garden, of its oddly aromatic winter scent. Carole-anne gave off that scent somehow. He released her. She went back to the sofa, argument momentarily suspended. "Then why'd you *go* to Wales, anyway? Nobody I know goes there." She uncapped her nail polish.

"Apparently nobody anybody knows goes there. Except me."

"What's she look like, this person?"

"You asked me that before."

"I know. I guess I just wasn't paying attention."

Not bloody likely. Jury thought he would doll up the description and ran the faces of several film stars by his mind's eye, discarding each of them in turn as perhaps not beautiful enough to fan the fires of jealousy. Would Judi Dench or Helen Mirren capture her imagination? (They captured his.) No. Right now she was tapping her foot, which didn't register very high on the impatience scale since she hadn't any shoes on.

"Well, if it takes you *this* long to describe what she looks like," she said, drawing her unpainted toenails back to rest on the edge of the table—"then she mustn't have made much of an impression."

"Juliette Binoche," he said, a woman so far from resembling Sara Hunt it began to worry even him.

"Oh, her." Unmoved, Carole-anne dipped the tiny brush in the neon-bright pink polish and let it hover over her foot as if sizing it up for the glass slipper.

"Am I to understand you do *not* think Ms. Binoche has the most alluring complexion in the whole world? No—the whole universe? Her skin is absolutely luminous." Though luminosity in another when he had Carole-anne right in front of him was definitely coals to Newcastle.

Carole-anne's chin was on her up-drawn knee, as she dabbed the nail polish on her little toe. "She's French."

Jury had always taken a secret delight in Carole-anne's non sequiturs, but this one puzzled him. "She's French. That removes her completely from our purview, does it?"

"I guess it removes *you*. She lives in France."

Ah! That was it. Juliette was inaccessible! And in Carole-anne's seamless accounting, Wales merely took off where Paris began. "Yes, she probably does live in France, but a man could easily have a lover there, what with the Chunnel making it so convenient."

"You're claustrophobic."

Was she splurging on non sequiturs tonight? "I am?"

She nodded. "You wouldn't last five minutes in the Chunnel." Down went that foot, up came the other.

"Oh, for God's sake, that's ridiculous. Whatever gave you that impression?"

"Suit yourself." Her entire self rejected his argument as the work of a fool. Even her toes shrugged.

"I get on elevators; I get on planes."

"I'm only talking about the Chunnel. You'd only be claustrophobic there. You don't have all-over claustrophobia."

"Then I'll fly!"

"You can't afford it. Between here and Paris it costs a fortune."

"So I have Chunnel claustrophobia. How interesting. All I can say is, either way, Juliette Binoche would be worth it."

"If you want to chance it."

By the time she was wriggling her toes to dry them, Jury was sure he was in love with Juliette Binoche.

Damn, but did she have to live in Paris?

FORTY-EIGHT

" Ardry End has seen the last of him!" exclaimed Melrose, in answer to Jury's question about Mr. Bramwell. "Let's drink to that!" Melrose raised his teacup.

"So you managed to fire him?" said Jury.

"Not exactly. It was more of a job transfer."

"What's that?"

"He's gone to the Wrenn's Nest."

"What?" Jury laughed. "How in hell did you foist him off on Theo Browne?"

"By making it known that Trueblood intended to hire Bramwell. You know that if Browne could take away anything Trueblood has—a basket of vipers, a dram of strychnine—he'd do it. Makes no difference that the result would be poisonous to Theo, at least it would be poison Trueblood couldn't have."

"Who thought this up?"

"Trueblood."

"That figures." Jury laughed again, and finished his tea.

"I thought we might drop in at the pub before dinner. Pots of fun, it'll be. Tell me what happened in Wales with that woman."

Omitting the end of it, Jury recounted his visit to Sara Hunt, ending with his doubts about her account of the Derby before Dan Ryder quit and went to France. "What I want to know is why she'd fabricate that."

Melrose thought about this. He said, "The race wasn't being offered as an alibi."

"No, probably not."

"I'd say definitely not. It was just part of the whole story of this obsession with Dan Ryder."

"You sound skeptical."

"I am, yes. The lie about the Derby wasn't meant to go anywhere. It sounds like one of those lies told for the pleasure of lying. That it gives her a sense of power or control to lie to a Scotland Yard superintendent. I'd say the question isn't why did she lie about the Derby, but why did she lie about everything else to boot?"

Jury leaned forward to pour more tea. "I don't get it."

"Oh, come on, Richard. Did she bewitch you—I see she did. Well. Have you told me everything, then?" Melrose smiled a little wickedly.

"Never mind. Why do you say the whole story's a lie?"

"I suppose to conceal a real obsession with a counterfeit one."

Jury looked at him.

"Ha! This woman must have you turned completely around. Look, it's not as if I don't believe in obsession—maybe it's the only emotional experience worth having, I don't know—but I don't believe in the one she foisted on you. If Dan Ryder had had such a grip on her mind and heart, and she knew Arthur Ryder and Vernon Rice, why wouldn't she have put herself in Ryder's way by playing the family card? In other words, Sara Hunt is a relation; she didn't need to keep her distance; she could have got herself invited to dinner, so to speak."

"But does obsession work along such rational lines?"

"I have no idea. The only thing I've ever been obsessed with is getting rid of Agatha."

"That sounds as if Sara Hunt thinks it's a game."

Melrose nodded. "Remember that suspect of yours who called herself Dana?"

Jury didn't answer. He didn't like this topic.

"Took you in completely."

"Thanks for reminding me," said Jury, glumly. "Are you saying this Derby story is the same thing?"

"Could be. It's not easy to throw you off the scent. You must have been getting close."

"Close to what, though? That she used to sleep with Dan

Ryder? So did a lot of women. But why the ruse? You say it's to cover up her real obsession. I still don't get it."

"Neither do I, even though I said it." Melrose drained his cup. "Come on, let's go to the pub."

Vivian jumped up and kissed him; Diane set down her martini with barely a sip; Trueblood rose and pummeled Jury's shoulder.

"I was here only two days ago," said Jury. "Not that I don't appreciate the boundless enthusiasm."

"You've been running around when you should be relaxing," said Vivian.

"When Uranus," said Diane, expelling a stream of smoke, "is running neck and neck with Saturn."

"But only half," said Jury, putting his hand on hers.

"An odd racing analogy," said Trueblood.

Melrose said to Vivian, "Jury wants to know the score on Giappino."

Vivian said, in mock wonder, "You haven't heard that Franco simply dumped me? Then you're the only one who hasn't." She favored all of them with a mirthless smile. Melrose and Trueblood found some other place to look.

Jury looked round the table. "So how did you lot manage to chase him off?"

Fiddling with a cigarette, Trueblood said, "Well, we might have given Count Dracula the wrong impression."

Vivian said, "You did indeed. I didn't tell you, but I got a letter from him. He said that with his brothers all being alcoholics, he just wasn't ready to take on this problem in a wife; that he was sorry he hadn't the funds to help with the foreclosure on my house—or whatever they call it in Italy, probably beating someone with sticks—and he was so sorry about my mother's dementia, but he couldn't take the chance of my inheriting it and thus passing it along to 'his' children. I loved the 'his.' I marveled at you"—her glance swept the table—"managing to get in all of those things. He found it, clearly, a heady experience."

Jury smiled, for he also knew what the others knew: it had been a huge relief to Vivian, who apparently was unable to call the wedding off herself; she needed all the help she could get. He said, "Vivian, if that sort of trivial stuff could set him off, be glad you found out in time."

"Here, here," cried Trueblood. "But next time, come clean, you know, tell the chap right up front about what he'd be taking on."

Vivian hit him with a pillow from the window seat.

Jury said, "Why don't you people stop messing about in other people's lives?"

Diane made a little moue of distaste. "I really don't think that showing up the real intentions of a prospective mate is 'messing about.' I'd certainly want to know. It's rather *amusing*, don't—Oh, good!" Diane, who had a clear view of the window, dropped the count like a hot potato and pointed. "Look! Theo's coming across." She said it as if the High Street were the Styx.

Theo Wrenn Browne, ever taken with the demands of fashion (yet never looking it), was wearing a green tweed suit that would have sent Hugo Boss back to sackcloth and ashes. Theo was also sporting a stubble of beard, deliberately unshaven. However, Theo, never quite able to meet the demands of masculinity, took two days to grow a day-old stubble. His suit jacket was buttoned only at the top button, his whole ensemble screaming *Last year! Last year!*

Diane, who would kill herself before putting a well-shod foot in last year's doorway, always enjoyed Theo's sartorial death throes, and said, as he stood by their table, "What a nice suit. It must be difficult to find just that shade of green. Aubergine, is it?"

Theo squinted and looked warily round at them much as the Cincinnati Kid might have scoured a table full of high rollers in some saloon. Unfortunately, he hadn't the Kid's savoir faire, and merely looked petulant, standing with his glass of beer, waiting for an invitation to sit down. Ordinarily, that got him nowhere, but today it did because they wanted to hear about Bramwell.

Trueblood pulled a chair round from another table and patted it. "Sit down, sit down and tell us about your new assistant."

Theo sat, gingerly. "Well, he's not that, is he? More a stock boy, I'd say. It takes training, doesn't it?" Browne turned his inborn irritation upon Trueblood. "*Too bad* you lost out there; I expect Freddie prefers books to antiques."

Freddie? Well, Melrose guessed he had to have a first name.

Theo went on: "Or the two of you just didn't hit it off."

His smile was vaguely vicious; Theo just didn't know who or what to train his anger on, so he kept it up in the air like a spinning plate.

"Or perhaps you're paying him more than I would."

It was plain Theo wondered if he was paying him *much* more.

"I will say that I admire your largesse—" said Trueblood.

Theo's smile was held in suspension as he couldn't be sure what was coming.

"—in not holding that time in the nick against him." Trueblood lit a cigarette and waved out the match.

"'In the nick'?"

Poor Theo could never run a bluff—too bad, seeing he was sitting across from the fellow who had invented bluffery.

"Oh? He didn't tell you?" Trueblood's eyebrows sought the headier heights of his slowly receding hairline. "I guess he thought it would tell against him. Yes, Freddie is what his gang called him."

"Gang? Are you really saying Freddie was with a criminal gang?"

Melrose gave Trueblood's shin a smart rap. If he carried on in this way, Melrose might have to put up with Freddie the Hermit again. Theo Wrenn Browne would fire him; Theo, he was sure, could fire people twenty-four hours a day. "Stop exaggerating. I didn't have a bit of trouble in that way."

"Of course you didn't. He never went *inside* the house; he was confined to his hermitage, wasn't he?" Trueblood shifted his attention to Theo again. "What did he tell you his last job was?"

"Book reviewer for the Sidbury paper."

Diane nearly choked and Vivian patted her back. Diane said, "There isn't any book reviewer on that paper. Nobody can read past fifth form, including me." Diane was always generous with her criticism.

"Freelance is what he said. Only the occasional review, which is why I didn't see it, he said."

Good God! thought Jury. This Bramwell ought to be working for M1.

"A stock boy," said Vivian, "is quite a demotion from book reviewer."

"Maybe, but I told him first he'd got to learn the ropes."

"And is he a hard worker?" asked Trueblood. "I passed by your shop earlier and saw him sitting in that easy chair by the window, reading."

This earned Trueblood another crack on the shin from Melrose.

It was clear Theo did not like this news, but had to defend Freddie—meaning, defend his own choice—and he said, "Well, when you're dealing in lit're'ture all day, it's awful hard not to keep from sampling it."

"Yes, except he was reading a racing form. Likes a flutter now and then, does he?"

Theo gripped his empty glass and went remarkably red. "I'm sure you're mistaken. Probably what he was reading was an inventory sheet."

"If your inventory lists Pieces of Eight in the sixth at Doncaster, yes, it could be." Trueblood deflected yet another attack under the table.

Theo, as he always did when he was losing (which was always), tried to go on the attack. Smarmily, he said, "Speaking of racing—just how's that horse of yours, Mr. Plant? 'That nag' as Freddie calls him."

"Aggrieved? Oh, he's doing well on his gallops. I'm considering the 2000 Guineas for him. Yes, I'm sure you'll see Aggrieved given short odds."

"He'll wire the field," said Diane, blowing smoke in more ways than one.

"What was that horse—Shergar? Is that his name?—kidnapped by the IRA and held for ransom? No one paid it. The horse disappeared."

Jury thought of Nell.

Diane dipped into what appeared to be a bottomless well of racing lore. "This horse in the States named Spectacular Bid was so outstanding, he was one of the very few horses ever to do a walkover." They all looked blank. "A 'walkover.' That's when there are no other entries in a race because no trainer thinks his horse can beat you. The horse gallops round an otherwise empty track."

Jury had to admit he liked that image. A horse galloping on an empty course and people in the stands cheering.

"Diane," said Melrose, "when did you turn into a bottomless well of racing arcana? I've never known you to hold forth at such length."

"One of my fans—if you can call them that, the gullible creatures—asked me—meaning the stars—who I liked in the seventh at Newmarket for the next day. He read off the list. I just picked the name I fancied most. Well, the damned horse won and this idiot is always pestering me for more tips. I did it again. Actually, I began to wonder if I had the gift. There are people who can do that sort of thing on a regular basis—"

"They're called bookies."

"—and it just got me interested in the whole thing. I read a book."

News that was met with the perturbation of a stock market crash.

"Anyway, going back to Spectacular Bid. There's a nice little story about him. His jockey was talking to a reporter who asked him if he was to die and come back, would he like to come back on Spectacular Bid? The jockey said, 'No, I'd like to come back *as* Spectacular Bid.' "

They laughed. Jury, too, and then he stopped laughing. His mind had been tripped by what she'd said. He sat, the drink in his hand undrunk, thinking. *But how could they be sure it would work?* Jury asked himself. Answer: *They couldn't.* He sat there in a slump, thinking, trying to work out what could have happened. He looked all around as if the vacuum might assist him in discovering what he wanted. He said, "Do you get *Le Monde* around here?"

They all stared at him with round eyes as if no one had ever made such a frivolous request.

Theo, obviously thinking he was one up in the culture department, said, "I've been considering getting some of the European papers in, you know, for those who wish to keep up on things."

"Such as who?" said Diane, who returned to the subject

of racing. "The one I *really* liked most was that other American horse, Go for Wand."

Trueblood raised a polished eyebrow. "Gopher what?"

"Not 'gopher,' 'Go *for*.' Two words. Go for Wand."

Trust Diane to rake over the course of American racing and come up with a name none of them had either heard of or could even sort a meaning from.

Melrose said, "That's an odd name. Are you making it up?"

Diane sighed. "Of course not. It's a name that was taken from an old Jamaican superstition that when one was accosted by a strange spirit who could cast spells, one had to go home for a wand to ward off the evil spirit."

Melrose sat back, brow furrowed in question.

"It's the truth. You know I don't have the imagination to make up something like that."

"No, I don't. You manage once a week to make up the solar system."

Diane ignored that. "She was good in mud—"

"So is Momaday, but I wouldn't give odds on him."

"—she nearly met Secretariat's record on the one course. She was only two-fifths of a second off Secretariat's time. Imagine, not just a second but a *split* second can mean the difference between winning and losing." Diane sighed. "How exhausting. Anyway, her last race was the Breeders' Cup. Right near the end she stumbled in the backstretch, threw her jockey and shattered her leg, went down, got up and kept on going. With a shattered leg, *she kept on going.* She collapsed in the home stretch. They had to put her down then and there. I've never been one to admire determination—it's so tiring—but can you imagine? To keep at the gallop with a broken leg? It's something to know that in this life of travail and tears—and, fortunately, vodka"— she raised her glass—"some things never give up."

Jury thought of Nell. "And some people." He raised his glass. "Here's to your mare."

"Go for Wand had that field wired," said Diane, sadly. "She had it wired."

FORTY-NINE

Vernon walked into his office at eight a.m. the next morning to find Bobby and Daphne already in theirs. He could hear them even before he passed by the door of their eerily dark room. They were fighting about something; they always were. They never agreed about stocks, bonds, IPOs, hedge funds, the Dow, NASDAQ—anything. It was almost like a deeply sworn feud that provided, together with a basic exchange of knowledge, their principal entertainment.

Divesting himself of coat and laptop, Vernon went back to the dark doorway. The only light came from five computer screens. Light pulsed, shadows moved. Vernon thought of Plato's cave. (It came as a surprise to people that Vernon had taken a first at Oxford in philosophy.) The cold bluish light of their separate screens washed over their faces, Bobby's and Daph's, as if submerging them. Three other computers tuned to different networks, different sources of financial information were lined up on a long table where they could view them when they needed to. It had long been a marvel to Vernon that they could share these cramped quarters and not go crazy. Perhaps the nature of the work was already so crazy that they could factor in their own without noticing.

"I want you to look into this bunch"—he tossed Nell's folder on Bobby's desk—"see what's going on with this drug. And with its stock offerings."

Bobby tore himself away from his screen. You could almost hear the rip. Even as he talked, he kept peeking at it. "Wyeth? That American pharmaceutical company? It's Wyeth-Ayerst Labs—yeah, that's the one that put out that diet drug called fen phen the FDA is pulling off the market. Bad, bad news that thing was."

"Anyway, I have a friend with a passion for horses and this company makes this drug"—Vernon nodded toward the folder. "They get it from the urine of pregnant mares. Premarin, it's called."

Daphne made a face. "Horse urine?"

"I'm sure the horses share your opinion. Unfortunately, they have nothing to say in the matter."

Daphne swiveled her chair around. "Wait a minute; I've heard of that. It's for menopausal women. Some sort of estrogen, a hormone-replacement drug?"

"Good for you," said Vernon. "Especially considering you're only twenty-five."

Bobby leaned forward, frowning. "But that must take a hell of a lot of horses."

"Oh, it does." Vernon described the way the urine was collected.

"God," said Daphne, "that *is* horrible."

"Wait. I haven't even told you the downside. Most of the foals are shipped off to slaughterhouses. A few are kept to replace the mares that die."

"*God,*" she said again. "Do the women taking this stuff know this?"

"I doubt it. If they knew, most would find some other drug. And there are perfectly good ones out there that do the job and without the questionable side effects."

Bobby cocked his head. "Sounds like you've been researching this."

"I have. So what I want you to look for is some way of making life less than pleasant for this pharmaceutical company. I'll be back in a few minutes."

Eyes on screens, they both waved him away in friendly fashion.

Vernon opened his laptop, leaned back in his chair and thought about Nell. He always thought about Nell.

He looked at his screen and thought about Nell. He was thinking about taking SayWhen public. No, he was thinking about Nell.

Samantha put her head round the door and tapped on the doorframe. "I'm going to the caff for breakfast take-out. What do you want?"

"Oh. Pork pie with a ploughman's." He thought about Nell.

"That's not breakfast, Vernon."

"What?" He looked at her.

She shook her head. "That's lunch, not breakfast."

"Oh." He rubbed his head. Then he ordered an egg sandwich, bacon and coffee. And thought about Nell. He looked at Samantha. "Is that breakfast?"

"That's breakfast." She tapped her knuckles against the door again, her silver ring rapping it.

"A blueprint," said Bobby, when Vernon later went back to the room, "for success." He turned his computer screen so that Vernon could see it. "This company's PR people must be first rate. You market Premarin, first by covertly selling menopause to American women as a disease, making them think they've just got to have hormone-replacement therapy; second, you assure everyone the horse farms are meeting 'guidelines' "—Bobby made squiggles in the air to indicate the quote marks—"not government guidelines but ones laid down by Wyeth itself and, of course, by employing its *own* inspectors to make sure the guidelines are met; third, you stomp all over any competition, especially any bunch that wants to make a generic. You've locked in your patent for half a century, of course. Now, by following this simple recipe you wind up as the *only* manufacturer of this drug, making a billion and a half a year. And think of this: it's not a drug taken intermittently because of illness; it's one the woman is taking for the long haul—in other words, forever."

Daphne was chewing gum and staring at her screen. "I don't believe this; I mean, how could this corporation get away with this? They took out the patent in '42 and have had no competition. These poor horses—" She turned her screen toward Vernon so that he could see the picture of the mares in their stalls. "They're tied so they can't move or lie down. Even calves in crates aren't much worse off. These mares are *pregnant* for God's sake. And they can't move. Are we back in the Dark Ages?"

Vernon looked at the screen, at the condition of the horses, at the narrow, narrow stalls. He shook his head. "Maybe we never left it."

"Where'd you get this literature?"

"From the girl who was in my office a few days ago; you met her. She got the folders from a stud farm in Cambridgeshire. It looks as if someone was apparently going to try to market this stuff in the UK."

"Never," said Daph, "they'd never get away with it. In the States, yes, you can get away with keeping seventy-five thousand horses in these deplorable conditions—"

Bobby sat back in his swivel chair. "You're saying Americans are more callous than we are?"

"No, Booby, I'm saying *America* is so much *bigger* than we are." She balled up paper and threw it at him, then turned back to her screen, punched in some commands and said, "The Premarin Web site." The page showed the face of a smiling woman. "Why's she smiling? Look at the side effects: possible nausea, increased risk of blood clots and uterine cancer . . ." She scrolled past a few pages. "Here it is—description: 'material derived from pregnant mares' urine.' You can't say they never told us. Except this writing is as tiny as fairy tracks. Who could read it without a magnifying glass?"

Bobby didn't appear to be hearing her, lost in one of his own stock-option meditations. "We could try selling short."

Daph looked at his screen. "Uh-uh. I don't like the downside potential." She pushed her glasses up on her nose. "It's unlimited. Bobby likes it; I don't."

"I wouldn't have expected anything less of both of you," said Vernon, leaning down to look over Bobby's shoulder.

Bobby loved all things chancy; he was staring at the display of the drug company's stock options.

Daph had the same readout on her screen. She shook her head and clucked her tongue like a prissy schoolmistress. "It's too strong, Bobby. You can't short it."

"Tell me something I *don't* know, for God's sake." He looked round at Vernon. "I could post something on the

Net. A rumor here, a rumor there." He turned his thumb down, pushed it toward the floor. The stock would make the same trip, his look said.

Vernon's return look was like a knuckle in the eye.

Bobby shrugged. "Just a thought."

"Corporate assassin," said Daphne. Then to Vernon, "He's going to land us all in the nick, Vernon, one of these days." Then to Bobby. "You can't short it, Bobby."

Daphne, Vernon knew, really liked this sort of fox chase. *"You'd sell your own gran for some dicey stock options,"* he'd told her once. Now, he looked at her screen. The stock was still climbing, fractionally, but definitely on an upswing. Then it held steady.

Bobby's fingers danced across his keyboard. He said, "Here's something interesting." *Business World*, a dependable money magazine, reported that another hormone-replacement drug was about to enter the market.

Daphne asked, "How can it if this pharmaceutical company holds the patent?"

Bobby shrugged. "What they're really worried about is a generic. Look at this." He scrolled down the page. "A synthetic alternative to estrogen is going on the market. Called Evista."

Daphne had pulled up another article. "Listen. 'One of its antidiabetics was causing almost universal dizziness, weakness, slurred speech and other symptoms and would almost certainly be up for review.' I'm quoting here. There's a report coming out on it."

"When?" said Vernon.

"Couple of days, it looks like."

"Get Hodges to go over it." Dr. Hodges was a retired physician and more or less on Vernon's payroll as a consultant for anything health related. "Then get Mike West to get hold of the report the minute it comes out." West was a lawyer in the States, also retained by Vernon's investment firm. "Also, see if you can turn up any studies on the other one—Evista?"

"Okay."

"Keep watch, baby," Vernon said, squeezing Bobby's shoulder. Daphne's mouth was hanging open, as it often was when she was watching the screen. "Babies, I mean," said Vernon.

FIFTY

"You could just have called Cambridge police, couldn't you? There's no real need for you to go there." Wiggins was driving.

"Watch the road, will you? We nearly cut that lorry off. Listen: ever since I got in the way of a bullet, you've been telling me what I need, what I should or shouldn't do, where I should or shouldn't go. I wish you'd stop it."

Wiggins spoke carefully, as if he were trying to calm a bad-tempered child. "I'm only concerned for your health, that's all."

He was negotiating a roundabout, and none too happily. In front of them was a Cortina that appeared to have no driver. No, Jury saw a blur of gray above the driver's seat.

"Why do they let people like that out on the roads? It's every bit as dangerous as speeding. Look—he can't be going more than twenty miles an hour." Wiggins leaned on his horn and the old car lurched, nearly stopped, then sputtered on. "He must be driving in sixth gear."

As this diatribe continued, Jury said, "It's Cambridge, Wiggins, not the tenth circle of hell."

"It's not much use," said DS Styles, "trying to question her. Her solicitor told her not to say a word without him being there."

"I didn't think she would, Sergeant, certainly not anything that has to do with the charges against her. She might not answer, but I can still ask."

"Suit yourself, but I say it's a waste of time."

Jury knew what he was really saying was that detectives from the Yard had no business being here. But since Jury was a personal friend of the DCI in charge of the case, then they'd probably do what he wanted. "I'm not really trying to interfere with your investigation; the case is yours; I know that." This suggestion of amelioration at least got Styles's hackles down. "I only want to talk to her for a few minutes."

"Suit yourself," DS Styles said again.

When Valerie Hobbs was led into the interview room, Jury was sitting at a table in one of the four institutional-looking gray metal chairs. Jury rose only a few inches from his chair and nodded at the WPC who brought her in and who then left. He judged Valerie Hobbs to be five two or three. He had not raised himself to his full height because he would have towered over her and he believed that might intimidate her.

He watched some response flicker in the light brown eyes. Her hair was not only bright, but silky, or rather the silkiness was what made it shine. She had a slightly cleft chin, a well-molded nose and a mouth that curved upward at the corners even when she wasn't smiling, which she certainly wasn't now. Still, some of the hardness left her face when she looked at Jury, who introduced himself.

She locked her arms across her chest. "What's Scotland Yard got to do with this? Is it because it's a kidnapping? Which I'm innocent of, incidentally. I'd like a cigarette, if you have some."

He did. Although he'd stopped smoking—oh, baleful day!—he'd stopped in a newsagent's and got a pack of Silk Cuts. He put the pack on the table. "You can have the lot." She inched one from the pack and he lit a match. As she inhaled and exhaled with closed eyes, he knew full well the rush one of those could give after you'd been deprived for any time at all.

She said it again: "I didn't abduct the girl." Her voice hit the scale at some point between raspy and sexy. For a woman who'd refused to talk, Valerie Hobbs was doing a pretty fair job of it.

"But you know who did."

She smoked in great long draws on her cigarette. "No, I don't."

"But someone had to bring her to your place. You say you didn't, then——?" With a questioning but good-natured frown, he dipped his head to see her face, which was turned down.

"I wasn't there."

This was such a weak rejoinder he wondered how she could offer it. Jury let that rest for a moment and said, "You came to know the girl, Nell, quite well."

"Not so very."

"She was at your farm for nearly two years."

"With someone like that, it could've been twenty and you still wouldn't know her." Her expression was one of self-satisfaction. It pleased her to frustrate his line of questioning.

But Jury wasn't bothered by the answer; he was only a little surprised she could have assessed Nell in this way. "Someone like that? How was she different?"

Valerie actually thought for a moment, as if it were important to get it right. "Determined, kind of aimed, I guess you'd say."

Jury sat back. That was interesting. " 'Aimed'? I'm not sure what you mean."

She took another long draw on the cigarette, slowly exhaled. "Like an arrow. Her attention would be on only one thing, say." She shrugged.

Jury waited a beat. "Why do you think she didn't try to run away long before she did? Apparently, she had a fair amount of freedom."

Valerie inspected a finger with chipped nail polish. "Those horses, I expect. I admit I did threaten to kill her own horse if she tried anything. Well, look at the bargain she drove after they brought me in: if I'd release the mares, then she'd testify on my behalf. I'll say this for her, she doesn't hold a grudge."

Jury could hardly keep from laughing at that way of putting it. Twenty months of captivity turned simply to a grudge. "No, I can see she doesn't. Either that or her forced imprisonment didn't mean all that much to her."

"That's kind of funny, right? She'd been abducted and

didn't care? Oh, she did at first, hammering on her door and yelling to be let out. But then she just stopped, as if she knew it wasn't smart. That girl was *very* smart. I could appreciate that, I'll tell you."

Jury's look was intense. "I'm surprised she was allowed to live, frankly. She was a constant threat to you, and as it happened, you were charged with conspiracy." He leaned closer to her across the table. "Valerie, you know what's going to happen to you if you don't cut a deal with the prosecution."

"No, I don't. She's not testifying against me. She said she wouldn't and I know that girl. You can't flip her."

In fresh astonishment, Jury sat back. That Nell Ryder had convinced this woman who'd held her captive for twenty months that she, Nell, would defend Valerie Hobbs was a feat of persuasion that even Vernon Rice would marvel at. It was all the more marvelous in that Valerie Hobbs read Nell correctly.

"Her testimony will probably reduce the sentence, but you're still looking at prison, Valerie."

She had fingered another cigarette from the pack and Jury cupped a match to light it. This time, as she leaned toward the flame, she touched his fingers, then looked at him through the smoke.

"The jury isn't going to look kindly on the treatment of those horses. The animal-rights people will have a field day. You won't be popular, to say the least."

She kept shaking her head as he was saying this. "That won't come into it; my solicitor says it'd bias the jury against me and it's nothing to do with the abduction. Anyway, there's nothing illegal about keeping those mares and even if that did come into it, we can just flood the courtroom with photographs of these huge horse farms in Manitoba that make mine look like nothing at all. Compared to what goes on in some of *them, mine* would be a stay at the Dorchester. Anyway, it's not down to me; I'm just paid to take care of them."

"Who is it down to, then?"

She looked away. "I'm not saying anything else without my solicitor being present."

Fine time to think of that, thought Jury, reaching into his coat pocket for the snapshots.

Jury sat back, looking her up and down, making a point of doing so. "You're about—what—five two?"

Surprised, she sat back. "What in God's name has that got to do with anything?"

"I think you're an extremely attractive woman."

This earned him a false smile and a cloying tone. "I wouldn't suit you; I'm only five three." She looked him over, as he had done her, at least as much as she could with a table cutting them in two. "You're *way* over six feet."

"Four inches over, yes."

"You're not half bad yourself."

"Thanks." Jury was fascinated. Valerie Hobbs could and probably would—despite Nell's testimony—go down for this crime all on her own, yet here she sat, confident enough to put moves on him. So what was it? How could she have been sold such a bill of goods? Assurance that she'd be all right, probably escape a prison term for this frightful crime? Someone with plenty of influence over her must have convinced her it would be a stroll in the park.

Jury took one of the snapshots he'd carried away from Sara's collection and said: "Here's another extremely attractive woman, also petite, like you. Ever seen her?" He pushed the picture across the table.

"No. Who is she?" She pushed it back toward him. "Should I know her?"

Jury sat looking at her.

She flicked ash from her cigarette onto the floor. She laughed briefly. "Are you trying to intimidate me?"

"No, not really. I think it would be difficult to do that. You really have nerves of steel, Valerie." Jury was leaning toward her again, his hands folded on the table, managing to make steely nerves sound erotic. "I wouldn't be surprised," he went on in the softest voice he could muster, "if you were a match for just about any man, even one who might be a match for any woman."

She looked uncertain, gave a half laugh and said, "You speaking of yourself, then?"

Jury laughed and sat back again. "Good Lord, no. Me? I'm quite easily taken in."

Valerie Hobbs uttered a soundless laugh. "That is *such* a lie."

"Perhaps, but—" He leaned forward again, fixing her with a look that one might say spoke volumes yet was being forever misread. "Has he really got such a hold over you that you refuse to give him up?"

Her cigarette stopped on its way to her mouth. "Has who?"

Jury shrugged. "There's somebody you're protecting."

Again, that mirthless little laugh. "You're bonkers, Superintendent."

Jury pulled out another snapshot, pushed that one toward her, too. "Same woman, only this time—"

Valerie Hobbs picked it up, looked from the snapshot to Jury and back again. And laughed. "The man she's with? Yes, I know him: Dan Ryder. Isn't that who this is? He's *dead,* for God's sake. D-E-A-D. You really haven't a clue, have you?"

It wasn't the reaction he'd expected.

Perhaps she was right; perhaps he hadn't a clue.

FIFTY-ONE

It was dark, the middle of the night, when Maurice took Aqueduct from his stall, saddled and cantered out to the far field and Hadrian's walls. Maurice knew Aqueduct could do it, whether with Maurice up on him was another matter.

The air was like crystal, clear and sharp. Aqueduct was the sort of horse you could feel glued to, as if horse and rider were one inseparable entity. That was a good feeling; it was also a dangerous one. You could stop paying attention because you thought the horse would do it for you.

Maurice had found it hard concentrating on anything since Nell's return. Like the crystal air, he felt he could be seen through; he felt he could break. What had been a massive relief when he'd first seen her was now a dead weight. Nell had almost vanished off the face of the earth. Maurice didn't want to think about it anymore.

The ground—hard, icy and wet—was soon churned to muddy slickness. The first three walls had been taken easily enough. Now they were approaching the fourth wall, which was higher than both the fifth and the sixth, so that if he could get over it, it would mean he could probably get over all of them.

It was this wall, the fourth, that had stopped Criminal Type (but he wasn't a jumper, anyway) and it seemed suddenly to rise up before him. He had lifted himself above the saddle, with his head nearly on the bridle, and then Aqueduct was flying, sailing through the sharp midnight air. That was, at least, the feeling as the horse surged over the top of the wall, but on the descent, Aqueduct's hind leg got caught in a stone outcrop and they came down like a thunderclap.

In a flash, Maurice knew, as he was thrown at lightning-bolt velocity against the wall, Maurice knew he would not have to feel it any longer: the betrayer betrayed.

FIFTY-TWO

When Jury got back from Cambridge, Carole-anne was glittering around his flat in midthigh black sequins, doing several nursey things, or at least what she imagined nurses must do—plumping pillows, lining up shoes, making tea, a steaming cup of which was sitting on the small table beside Jury's chair.

It did not disturb Jury that she was in his flat when he wasn't there; sometimes he wished she'd be in it more when he *was* there. He marveled that the three of them (with Stan Keeler making an often-absent fourth) were still here together. Mrs. Wasserman, of course, couldn't be pried free of her "garden" flat (basement, in other words) for love or money. But it did surprise him that Carole-anne had remained stationary for all of these years. He didn't wonder about her love life—well, not often—because it struck him as intrusive even to think about—

Put a sock in it, man.

—it, although he certainly watched whenever she was in Stan's presence.

"What?"

Carole-anne was in her hands-on-hips posture, a stance he really liked because it was very hippy and tonight had sequins on it. "Just wondering about the dress. Where're you going? To another rally of the public-footpath people?" Jury was taking off his shoes, feeling his tired feet had been to the rally themselves.

Doubtfully, she smoothed her hands down over the short black dress. "What's wrong with it, then? Stan likes it."

"I'm sure Stone likes it, too, but that doesn't mean you have to lead it around on a leash."

Puzzlement. "What's that mean?"

Jury had no idea. He just said it. "There's nothing wrong with it, nothing, believe me. *Oh-ho* and *mmmmmm* nothing. If you walked down a public footpath in that there'd be no argument from Lord Stickywicket about whether the footpath was his or yours."

Carole-anne gave him a look. "Super, why does it always take you forever to say something?"

Jury smiled. It was exactly what he'd said to Melrose Plant.

She merely flapped her hand at him, saying, "Oh, never mind." She began rearranging magazines on the cherry coffee table.

"Carole-anne, those magazines are ten years old; they don't care anymore."

"I'm going to the Nine-One-Nine." She sighed and shook her head. "Too bad you're recuperating or you could come, too."

In high-pitched mimicry, Jury repeated, " 'Too bad you're recuperating or you could come, too.' I'm perfectly capable of going to the Nine-One-Nine. It's only"—he checked his watch—"ten o'clock."

"You really are behaving peculiar. I don't know what's got into you lately."

He smiled. "Just three bullets." He lost no opportunity to play the bullet card. Shameful.

Carole-anne went properly remorseful, put her hand on his forehead to check his temperature (or possibly to feel for brains) and left. He then poured himself another cup of tea and reseated himself. It was not because he was tired or "recuperating" that he hadn't gone with her, but because he wanted only to think. He closed his eyes, leaned his head back. His thoughts were a blur.

Valerie Hobbs. She was a stubborn woman. Stubborn and seriously misled. He hadn't really hoped for more than he'd gotten. Valerie had her impulses under control, so that her laugh and her *"you haven't a clue"* response to the picture of Dan Ryder told him that he was wrong about

Valerie. But that didn't mean he was wrong about Sara Hunt.

Sara Hunt. Sara did not have as much to lose. Both of them would clearly go to the mat for a man they loved. Did women like danger? Did they find it romantic?

Suddenly, Jury thought of Maurice and sat up. Maurice needed to tell someone the truth about what he'd done.

With the receiver cradled between ear and shoulder, Jury hurriedly went through his address book, found the Ryder number and punched it in. The phone rang several times before someone got to it.

The voice, Jury was fairly certain, was Vernon Rice's.

"It's Richard Jury. Sorry, it's a little late, but it's important. I just wanted a word with Maurice, if he's around."

On Rice's end, dead silence.

"Vernon?"

"Yes, I'm here. Sorry." He cleared his throat as if that might get his voice working again. "I'm afraid this is . . ."

The voice just trailed off. Something must be seriously wrong. "Nell. Has something happened to her?"

"No. It's not Nell." Vernon tried again to clear his throat. "It's Maurice. There was an accident. Maurice is dead."

The words hit Jury one two three, as if he'd been clubbed. He got up, felt dizzy, sat down again. He could think of nothing to say as he shook and shook his head as if Vernon Rice could see he was reacting to this news. He couldn't find his voice to ask what had happened. He sat staring at the listing picture of the horses gathered at the white fence.

Vernon inferred that Jury was having trouble and told him briefly what had happened. "Maurice was out earlier jumping Aqueduct over those walls—you know, Hadrian's walls—and Aqueduct, well, who knows exactly what happened? Maurice was thrown, must have vaulted against the stone. Nell started looking for Aqueduct when she found the stall empty. She found the horse, unharmed. Then she found Maurice."

Nell had to be the one to find him. Jury shut his eyes.

"Do you want to talk to her?"

"No, not now. Maybe tomorrow. That poor lad."

"Yes. He went just the way his dad went. God."

Jury held the dead receiver for a long time before he put it back, got up and went over to the picture and set it straight. He didn't think he would ever be able to tell himself why. Where had he got it, this gentle scene? A hand on each side of the picture, as if either to imprison or protect it, he leaned against the wall and looked at the watercolor of the horses at the fence. As far back as he could remember, he'd had it. He leaned his head against a fisted hand and his face so close to the glass he could make out only an amorphous white, brown, black. He wondered why he'd never paid any attention to it until the other night, and felt as people will feel a sense of loss that comes from neglect—the call you didn't make, the book you didn't read, the woman you didn't kiss. Why did he feel that place, that pasture so infinitely desirable but inaccessible? Freedom, was that it?

Maurice, unless he'd known there at the end, would never know.

Jury turned and looked at the table near the window where sat his old turntable and records and felt himself spinning out of control. He could feel himself sobbing, but as if the sobs were those of another person, the arm another's arm that shot out and swept the magazines, the keys, the heavy ashtray off the table. He retrieved the ashtray and hurled it against the bookshelves, where it landed and bounced onto the rug.

The door flew open.

"Super!"

Carole-anne rushed in and up to him and threw her arms around him as if to contain the fury. Then she pushed him down on the sofa, keeping her arm around his shoulders as if afraid to take away this support, fearful he might erupt.

Stone sat at his feet and whimpered. For Stone, that was out of control. Jury put his hand on the Lab's head. "Sorry," he said.

"Oh, Stone don't mind. All the times he's put up with Stan raging around."

Stan Keeler raging?

"I should have gone with you. I could use a few lashings of his guitar."

"Well, right now what you need's a lashing of tea." But she hesitated, not wanting to take her arm away. She moved her face back, frowned in question.

"I'm okay."

She patted his shoulder and went toward the kitchen, stopping first at the record player and looking through the records. She took one from its sleeve, put it on and continued to the kitchen as the twangy voice of Willie Nelson sang of all the girls he loved before.

Pots and pans were rattling around and suggested more than tea was being prepared. Soon he heard the spit of something hitting grease.

Willie Nelson. Now he remembered where he'd gotten that recording. It was Carole-anne who'd walked in with it when Jury's old fiancée, Susan, had been in the flat. Carole-anne had put it on and told Susan it was "their" song. Carole-anne in a Chinese red silk dress with "their" song was a force to be reckoned with, and Susan lost the reckoning. He listened to the sounds coming from the kitchen and the voice singing along with Willie Nelson.

She came out of the kitchen holding a plate and a cup. "Why're you laughing?" A ton of relief was in her voice.

My God, he had been, hadn't he? "I was remembering my old fiancée, Susan."

"You don't want to go wasting your time on old girl-friends. Here drink this"—she handed him a mug of tea—"and eat this." She handed him a plate of fried eggs, sausages and a wedge of fried bread.

Carole-anne sat down across from him in his armchair and smiled.

Jury noticed that she had asked why he was laughing, but would not ask why he was crying. He knew she would love to hear why, but she would not ask.

Jury lifted his plate as if to toast her and said, "Shades of Little Chef."

FIFTY-THREE

"He died just like his dad," said Nell, seated limply in one of Vernon Rice's metal-spoked, punishing-looking chairs as if she needed some hard and abrasive punishment because she hadn't stopped Maurice from trying to jump those walls.

Vernon handed Nell a glass of mineral water and Jury a whiskey. He said to her, "Does that—" and he stopped.

Nell's look implored him to say the right thing. "What?"

As if there were any right thing, thought Jury.

They all looked down into their glasses. No one spoke. After a full minute of silence, Jury asked Nell what he supposed Vernon had meant to ask but drew back from because it sounded insensitive. "Does that bother you? The similarity? Maurice certainly knew he shouldn't have been jumping walls after dark. Not only putting himself in danger, but also the horse."

"Of course it bothers me. And Maurice knew better than to do what he did. He'd been really . . . morose, I guess you'd say. He wasn't that way two years ago. The jumping had to do with his dad. He needed him. I mean, with his mum gone, he had no one except Granddad and me."

"He was lucky there," said Jury.

Vernon had been walking round the room, stopping by the window to stare out over the gray City, looking at noon as if it were dusk, with its misty rain and blue-shadowed streets. He said, "I remember Maurice's unhappiness after Danny's death. But he got over that, or at least as 'over' as one can get when a parent dies. This was something more—I'm not putting this right."

Jury said, "Yes, you are. Isn't he, Nell?"

She set her glass on the rug and raised her eyes to give Jury a questioning look. "This was something more?" She rubbed her hands on her blue-jeaned knees. "We used to be really close; we were so much in the same position. Once, we could talk for hours. But in the little time I've been back, Maurice seemed to have changed so much."

"Did he ask you what had happened during those twenty months?"

She shook her head. "He didn't seem to want to know. I mean Dad and Granddad just pestered me for details. They wanted to know everything. But Maurice didn't want to know. I thought it must have been just too painful for him."

"I'm sure it was."

"I hadn't changed about Maurice."

"No, I'm sure you hadn't," said Jury.

"But you seem to think I was the cause."

"I think Maurice felt responsible for what happened."

"For *me?* That's ridiculous. He wasn't, not at all. Why would he feel that way?"

Jury leaned toward her. "Nell, how did this fellow who took you know you were out there in Aqueduct's stall?"

She looked from Jury to Vernon, as if she'd been set a puzzle to work out. "He didn't. It was just coincidence I was there."

Jury shook his head. "He came for you, Nell."

"*What*—? Why would anyone want me?"

Vernon nearly choked.

Someone had wanted her badly to go to her room a dozen times. But the sex, in and of itself, Jury intuited, wasn't the reason. "How did he know that you'd be there?" He paused. She said nothing. "Didn't you say that the horse didn't seem sick to you? Still, you stayed."

"Yes, well, but just in case. And Maurice is very good at reading signs of illness in the horses . . ." Her voice trailed off. She shook her head. "No. I know what you're saying. Absolutely no. Maurice could never have done such a thing. Never. Nothing, no one on earth could make Maurice do that. No one."

"I don't think Maurice knew what was actually going to happen. But I do think he did it. Wouldn't it explain his attitude toward you now?" Jury didn't add, *Wouldn't it further explain his accident?*

But Nell simply couldn't bring herself to believe that Maurice really had done what Jury said. She said again, "Nothing could have made him do it." She flashed Jury a challenging look. "What? Who?"

He turned away from that look, shaking his head. "I don't know," he said.

FIFTY-FOUR

But he did know.

Late the next morning, Jury was back in a taxi, driving from Cardiff to Sara Hunt's house. This time, he hadn't given her any warning.

When she opened the door and saw him, she froze. "I didn't know you were coming." She recovered quickly and smiled.

"No. I thought I'd surprise you. Nice little car, there." He looked at the red Aston-Martin parked in what he imagined could be called the backstretch of the circular driveway. "Yours?"

"My char's, if you can believe it. They live high on the hog these days. Come on in."

He tossed his coat over the banister and followed her into the living room.

"What can I get you? Coffee? A drink?"

"Not a thing. I'm not stopping here for long."

She sat down in the wing chair—perched in it, really, sitting nearly on the edge. She looked like a child. He wondered what he had seen in her that attracted him sexually, that had made him feel such a yearning, and wasn't happy with himself finding that longing abated.

"Is something wrong? You sound rather *official*—" Her smile was uncertain.

Jury merely watched her, looking directly at her for a few beats, and she did what he expected—looked away. And then back. He was still looking at her.

"For heaven's sake, Richard, why are you looking at me

that way?" Small movements of her hands—brushing hair back from her face, fingering the gold chain around her neck, turning a ring with her thumb—showed how nervous she was.

Jury sat with one ankle hooked over his knee. "You're pretty. Isn't that enough reason?"

She didn't know how to take this, smiled and stopped smiling.

There was the sound of something heavy falling in the rooms above them. "Oh, God! I'll have to see what she's doing up there. I could kill her sometimes."

Jury smiled. "I'll wait."

As she left, her laugh—not a laugh at all—cut off abruptly.

Jury leaned his head back against the chair, looking up as if above him were a glass ceiling and he could see as well as hear. The voices were indistinguishable, words melting in a pool. There wasn't, fortunately, any killing going on.

Then Sara came down the stairs. "Not too much damage—"

"Speaking of damage—of course you would only have seen him at the races, if you saw him at all, but Maurice Ryder—Dan Ryder's son?—is dead."

"Oh, my God." She clamped her hand over her mouth. Her eyes were barely visible above the hand and behind the tears. She rose uncertainly and walked to the window, clearly to get herself under control.

Jury said, "So you *did* know him? I'm surprised, given your fleeting association with the Ryders." She had turned as he said this and he gave her a disingenuous, puzzled frown. "You did?"

It took her a moment to clear her throat. "Not well, no."

Jury's faux frown grew even more puzzled. "That's quite a reaction you had for someone you didn't know well."

She still had not sat down, which was fine with Jury. He was quite comfortable. He rubbed the dark blue and gray diamond pattern of his silk sock, pulling it up a little, giving her a little room. But the brief hiatus wasn't going to do her much good.

He said, "There's something I'd like you to look at." He pulled from an inside pocket the snapshot Nell had taken from Valerie Hobbs's office, held it out, his arm extended toward her. Thus she had to come nearer, and she did.

"Do you know her?"

Sara let out a breath, relief, probably, for here was safe ground.

"No, I don't. Why?"

"You're sure?"

Her glance flicked from the picture to Jury. "Yes, I'm sure." Again she asked why.

"Only because"—he pulled out the enlarged snapshot of Dan Ryder—"both of you seem to know him."

She took a step back. "How—where—did you get that?"

"Dishonestly, but that's hardly the point—"

"It's *my* point." Quickly, she moved to the writing table and turned the tasseled key in the little drawer under the top. After her eyes and fingers did a brief search, she turned to him.

He could almost smell the fury mixed with fear. She seemed unable to frame whatever invective she was looking for and settled for the rather Victorian "How dare you?" She paused. "You have to have a search warrant, don't you, to do that?" She slapped the drawer shut.

"I'm not here in any official capacity. Just a nosy customer, a common sneak thief." Jury knew that wouldn't get him off the hook if she actually wanted to take it further, but she was going to have enough things on her mind to give her attention to a possible "investigative irregularity." "The thing is, you clearly knew Dan Ryder a bit better than you allowed. *Much* better, it appears. Why so secretive, Sara? So far, love isn't known to be a criminal offense. Why did you lie?" Now he watched her as she gave herself time to think of something plausible.

"Because I fancied you and didn't want you to think—"

"That you fancied someone else. Sara"—he couldn't help himself; he laughed—"I've got to credit you with originality. That's the first time, the very *first* I've ever heard that as a reason for lying—"

"I didn't lie—"

"—but I'm not really convinced I'm not a total mug and the love of your life. So why is there such a secret? Dan Ryder was hardly a Trappist monk. We know his reputation with women." Jury held up the snapshot of Valerie Hobbs. "For instance—"

"I told you I've never seen her." Suspicion incensed her. "What's your interest in her?"

"She doesn't know him, either. So she says. And then there's always this one—" He held up a morgue shot of Simone Ryder.

She looked at him so coldly Jury felt a chill in the air. "I've never seen her in my life."

Jury turned the picture and looked at it again himself. "You're sure of that?"

"Damn it. I don't have to listen to this."

"Yes, you do, so sit down."

"This is why you wound up in my bed."

Jury shook his head. "No. That's completely separate. Completely." Now he wondered if it was, and felt slightly ashamed. "Don't try to play the lover deceived; don't play the victim. I wasn't trying to get anything out of you. Sit down."

She had been pacing, fidgeting with objects she passed— the tasseled shade of a lamp, a glass paperweight—but at the tone of his voice, she reseated herself.

He arranged the three pictures on the coffee table like cards in a poker hand. "Interesting story. Just sit there and I'll tell it to you—"

"I expect I'd tell it better, mate."

The voice came from behind Jury. He turned.

"Hello, Danny." Almost ingratiatingly, Jury smiled.

"Christ, but you've been one busy little copper."

Jury liked the "little" copper. He bet Danny was always throwing that word and others like it around to describe other men.

He was a small man—height, girth, bones, hands, feet— yet still big for a jockey, which must have been a source of continuing pleasure for him. Jury didn't know what he planned to do with the gun, beyond pointing it at Jury, but he was perfectly set to let this film unreel.

"Danny!" said Sara. "What are you—?"

"Come on, girl. Sit."

Not a wise thing to do, perhaps, but Jury stuck his feet

up on the coffee table and leaned back, miming comfort. He only hoped his soigné attitude didn't make him fool-hardy, which was how he felt.

Danny Ryder laughed. "Christ, man, but you do take life and death neat, no chasers."

Jury waved his arm, inviting Danny to join them.

Absurdly, Danny did. He sat on the sofa next to Sara.

"First," said Jury, "I have no doubt you'd use that gun. It's a .22. Which is interesting." Danny was regarding it as if he'd never seen it before. "But it's a strange thing about almost dying, as I recently almost did—you use up a lot of your scare quotient. It takes a hell of a lot to scare me now."

Danny laughed.

"You ought to be able to relate to that. You're always putting your life on the line, Dan. I imagine it's part of the thrill, the rush you get when you're up on one of those great horses of your father's."

"Get us a beer, love," said Danny to Sara. "Us" meaning "me."

Sara, who looked taut as piano wire, rose and went toward the kitchen.

Danny leaned over the coffee table. "Now, here's an interesting photo collection."

"Yeah. Sara's dying to know who the brown-haired one is."

"And where'd you get her picture?"

"Valerie Hobbs's? From her photo collection."

"Yeah? So what else did she share?"

"Not a damned thing. I've got to hand it to you, Danny; you've got these women going in circles. Nothing could make them give you up. Nell Ryder got away, but I expect you know that."

Danny said nothing for a moment; he just regarded Jury. Then he said, "Hate to tell you this, but you've got this wrong if you think I'd anything to do with Nell's getting nobbled. I'm a right bastard in a lot of ways, but not a total villain."

"You weren't in this with Valerie Hobbs? That's what you're saying?"

Sara was back with the beer, no glass. Danny took it from her without comment. She sat—perched, rather—beside him.

"That's what I'm bloody saying, yes. As for Valerie Hobbs, I used to run into her at that flapping track outside of Newmarket. You know, Blaydon. Good sport, was old Val. Had a few drinks, a few laughs, but that's about it."

"Tell me about your wife, your so-called widow, Danny, now dead. You heard about that, I expect." Jury was sure he had not heard about his son, Maurice, nor did he want to be the bearer of that bad news. When Danny didn't respond right away, Jury said, "Sara *did* tell you about that? Or you read about her in the paper? You don't seem visibly upset by it."

The gun seemed to have become a prop that could be dispensed with. Danny set it down on the coffee table and said, "I hadn't seen Simone in over a year. All that held us together really was the money. The insurance money. She was here to collect."

"You shot her because she was in on the fraud."

"*I* shot her?" His laugh was almost buoyant. "Why'd I do that? It makes no sense. She wasn't the only one knew it wasn't me took the fall in that race." He hooked his thumb at Sara.

"By what sleight of hand did you manage that accident?"

"I can't take all the credit for that; it was fate slapped the cards down there. Black Jack. They got us down wrong, me and a jockey named Delacroix, they mixed us up in the lineup. That horse, Up All Night? That was *my* ride, not Delacroix's. He was supposed to be up on Bright Angel. It was dumb luck."

"Not for Delacroix, it wasn't. What about his own family—wife, Mum? Didn't anyone wonder what happened to him? And didn't anyone recognize you? In the UK your face was well known."

"Not in France, it wasn't. I never raced over there when I was working with Ryder Stud. All jockeys look the same in a race. You know the way they ride with their faces nearly mashed into their mount's neck." Danny gave a short, hard laugh. "It was bedlam, with Up All Night going down like he did. In all the aggravation, I couldn't have found me own arse, much less somebody else's. And who knows? Maybe there wasn't any wife. But I do remember there was a bit in the paper that Delacroix hadn't weighed in for the eighth race. But who was going to question who the body belonged to? My own *wife* identified me right on the spot. So if any of Delacroix's relations or friends were there, why would they be upset? Nothing happened to him, as far as anyone knew, until his next race, like I said. Poor sod disappeared. Wouldn't be the first time, right? What'd you think happened? You think I managed to engineer the whole thing? Listen, that horse's leg was shattered, a triple fracture. Had to be put down then and there. You think I'd do that to a *horse,* boy-o?"

He actually cocked the gun that had been lying impotently on the table. It was as if he didn't care sod-all if Jury landed him in the nick, but he certainly cared if Jury was saying he could do serious damage to a horse. It would be laughable except Jury knew he was perfectly serious.

"Sorry, Danny, if I have trouble believing in your equine devotion—not if you could stand by and watch those sixty mares tied up."

"What," asked Sara, "is he talking about?"

Danny looked utterly confused. "What in hell are you on about? That's nothing to do with me."

"Those mares were nothing to you? The jockey who could jump a horse over the moon without a whip? You're fabled for your uncanny way with horses, Danny. I'm astonished that you'd put up with what was going on in those barns."

"I don't know what the bloody hell you're talking about."

Jury knew then he'd got half of this whole thing wrong. Still, he was fascinated. "You mean those horses Valerie Hobbs kept—that wasn't your gig?" It was Dan Ryder's Achilles' heel, his feeling for horses. It was also the firing pin, apparently, the match to the fuse. Oddly, this might have been the key to Ryder's fatal charm: he did have one very real passion—horses. The women he was involved with must have mistaken this intense feeling as meant for them. Whereas, Jury bet Danny didn't give sod-all for any of them.

"Whatever Valerie Hobbs is up to, that's got nothing to do with me."

He wasn't denying it because of Sara Hunt, that was certain. He was denying it because what he said was true.

"So now you think," Danny said, "since I shot Simone, I'm going to knock off my girl Sara here because she also knows I'm alive?"

"Maybe not. But that wasn't the only reason you might want your wife dead. There was, after all, the money. Maybe you wanted it all. You waited until you got it, or Simone got it—I expect that they choked on that double indemnity clause. She had to collect it, of course. You waited until she did and then shot her." Jury paused. "Why the Ryder training track, though? Why'd you meet Simone there? Or had she perhaps decided to have a meeting with your father—?"

Danny was getting increasingly irritated. Not enough, though, to make him aim the gun. "Oh, sod off, mate. You haven't a *clue.*"

The second person who'd told him that in the last twenty-four hours. He couldn't help but smile. "Perhaps not, but if you didn't do it, who did?"

"It could have been the whole fucking Jockey Club, for all I know. Simone wasn't known for her discretion."

"That was it? You knew she'd give you away at some point?"

Danny flapped his hand at Jury, slammed the beer bottle on the table and said to Sara, "Get me a real drink, love, will you?"

Sara rose and went to the drinks cabinet, but kept her eye on them as she was pouring, as if one or the other might make a break for it while she was fixing drinks.

Jury realized how wrong he'd been. What was, after all, the point of Dan's killing Simone? The man was already risking identification with Sara Hunt. If Dan Ryder hadn't killed the woman, who had?

Dan was talking about Nell, now. "Always had a thing for that girl. Ashamed to admit it, but there it is. Always had a thing for her."

Sara put the drink on the table. She said, "Is there any female you don't have a 'thing' for?"

My God, thought Jury, the man's a liar, a swindler, possibly a killer, yet all she reacts to is mention of another woman. Ryder must be like a snake charmer: this one, at least, seemed to be mesmerized.

"She was only thirteen, fourteen last time I saw her—"

"Last time you saw her she was seventeen. She still is."

Danny stopped the whiskey in midair. Slowly, he put it down. "What the bloody hell are you on about now?"

"I'm talking about taking Nell Ryder, Danny."

"What? You think that's *me*." He laughed, sat back and reclaimed his glass. "Well, you been wrong twice now, so you might as well go for three times."

"Then who?"

"You ought to get me a job with the Yard, me. And you a detective superintendent."

"Maurice—" Jury stopped, looked sharply at Sara, who looked away. He didn't want to tell him Maurice was dead; he'd leave that for Sara to do. Yet Danny had given the boy up, hadn't he, with this charade? And it struck Jury that perhaps Danny had given *everything* up—especially his riding career, his horses.

"What about Maurice?"

"I'm sure it was Maurice who got Nell out to that stable by lying about Aqueduct. I can't see his doing this for anyone but you, Dan."

"Then he didn't do it. Because I didn't take her. Lord knows I never took Aqueduct."

Jury had to smile. Taking Aqueduct, clearly, was even more unbelievable to Danny.

"But it was Maurice. It's the thing that explains his behavior."

"What behavior?"

"The guilt. Imagine knowing he was responsible for Nell's abduction."

"You're dreaming, friend."

Jury didn't say the rest: why else would Maurice take such a chance as to jump those impossible walls at night? It would take someone with a hell of a lot of practice to make that trip after dark. The sort of person who abducted Nell. A jump jockey.

"You did go to Valerie Hobbs's place?"

"Yeah, I went there, but not more than a half dozen times in the months I've been here."

"You went to see her, then?"

Danny nodded.

Sara asked again, "Who is this woman?"

Jury held up the shot of Valerie Hobbs, but said nothing.

Sara left her seat on the sofa beside Danny and moved to the fireplace, her back turned. In a way, Jury felt sorry for her; here she was, thinking she had the man all to herself, at last. Danny, he noticed, at least had the grace to look a little concerned.

Jury watched Dan Ryder sitting there in silence—his relaxed posture, leaning back into the softness of the cushions, one foot braced against the edge of the coffee table, dressed in flannels and a black cashmere sweater. Jury bet the sweater was a gift from Sara. There were a lot of gifts from Sara: her house, her bed, her unswerving loyalty, threatened now only by the chance of another woman. Danny's charm was a gift from whatever god had a sense of humor. His manner was disarming. Even Jury felt a liking for him, or some sort of empathy, which had kept him from telling the news of his son's death. There was a backstage persona, something else going on in Danny Ryder that had nothing to do with hiding things; Jury was sure the man was hiding all sorts of things, but things not germane to the abduction of Nell Ryder or the murder of Simone.

"Then who took Nell, Danny? It would probably go a long way in reducing your sentence if I tell the police that you helped in this investigation."

"You're so sure I'll be tossed into the nick?"

"Yes."

Danny laughed as if this possibility concerned him not at all. "On whose say-so? You going to tell them you were around here for a deco and look who turned up? The jockey. The dead one."

"That's pretty much the way I'd say it, yes."

Danny reached out and picked up the gun, braced it in both hands and pointed.

Sara whirled around. "Danny!"

Jury said, "You won't shoot me, Danny. You're devious as hell, but you're not a killer. What you told me happened in Paris? I've no trouble believing it. You're emotionally lazy; not even the danger of being exposed would prompt you to kill anyone. You live by chance, Danny. Chance is almost a religion with you. The only thing you don't leave to chance is the course."

For some reason, this seemed to dig at Danny more than anything. "You think I don't take chances in a race?"

"Of course you do, you have to. But that's not what I mean. You know every hoofbeat pounding around that course; you know exactly what your horse is doing and can do and will do. Horses are what you don't take chances with. Your women are chance women, met by chance, bedded by chance and maybe even married by chance." He was looking straight at Danny, but Jury detected Sara stirring from her gloomy dream. Quickly she moved toward Jury and dashed the rest of her whiskey in his face.

Danny laughed as he put the gun back on the table.

Sara's face was splotchy with fury.

Jury pulled out his handkerchief and wiped his face. "Shame to waste it."

Danny laughed again. She looked daggers at him. "How can you let him go on that way? Maybe to you all this is bloody funny, but not to me!" In a second she'd put her hand on the gun, pulled it from the table and pointed it at Jury.

"No," said Jury, "I can see it's not funny to you at all."

Danny threw up his hands. "Easy, love. He's having you on; he's doing it on purpose; he wants to get you riled, girl; he might learn something."

Which he had.

"You," he said to Sara, "on the other hand, might just shoot me. You're more likely to do it than Danny, certainly. Because *you* are anything but emotionally lazy. Your emotions are incendiary."

The room fell quiet. "How did you get Simone to the Ryder stables?"

Danny looked at her, eyebrows raised in what Jury took to be genuine surprise. "Sara? What the hell—?"

Her expression didn't so much change as resettle into that look she had just turned on Danny, now leveled at Jury. "I don't know what you're talking about."

Jury didn't bother speaking to that denial. He said, "It could have been Valerie Hobbs who shot Simone—even more likely since she's so close to the Ryder farm—but I don't think Ms. Hobbs is murderously jealous. Just jealous. No one thought—no one would have—that the murder of his wife had to do with Danny himself because Danny was dead. But you traveled all the way from here to Cambridgeshire to kill her. I can't get that part of it right in my mind. You didn't know her; it's a puzzle as to how you might have done all of this."

Danny appeared more fascinated than anything else. He got up and took the gun from Sara's hand.

Jury went on talking. "Did you even know his wife was *here*? Did he even tell you it was Simone who was collecting the insurance money? Anyway, it would be a total waste of time to shoot me because I couldn't prove a thing." He looked from one to the other, then reached over and slid his photos together and took them from the table.

"Too bad about the insurance money, Danny, too bad Simone didn't live to collect it. But I wonder if not getting it is better than getting it, after all. You could never have reentered the only life that means anything to you. Is it so great a hurdle—the racing commission, the Jockey Club? You're clever; you could surely concoct some story about Simone's having the idea in the first place, that you were driven into exile . . . whatever. After all, she alone talked to the insurance adjusters. But I really can't imagine you never racing again. No, I can't imagine that."

At the sound of an approaching car, tires on gravel, they all looked toward the front window.

"Never mind about that," said Jury. "It isn't the police; that's just my cab. I told him to come back in an hour's time." Jury tucked the pictures into his pocket and rose. "Well, I'm off. I'll leave you two to sort it."

FIFTY-FIVE

"Wales?" said an astonished Melrose Plant before Jury had shed his coat and Ruthven had taken it.

"Actually, it *is* part of the UK, if I remember correctly." Melrose shrugged as if he would need more convincing than that.

Mindy preceded them into the drawing room, where she collapsed in front of the fire.

"Three times?" said Melrose.

Jury answered this indirectly. "Does it surprise you that Dan Ryder didn't die in that racecourse accident?"

Melrose's eyebrows shot up. "My Lord! You mean you *saw* him?"

"I did. I had an idea that Dan might still be alive."

"What made you think that?"

"A couple of things: one was that anecdote Diane told us at the pub. The one about the jockey saying he'd like to come back not *on* but *as* that great American horse—what was his name?"

"Spectacular Bid."

"It simply put a question into my mind, this 'resurrection' of a jockey, if it was possible that Ryder wasn't dead. You see, I simply couldn't imagine what would get Maurice to get Nell out to Aqueduct's stall. Who on earth could talk him into it but the one person he cared more about than even Nell?"

"His father. I see what you mean."

"But he wasn't the person who abducted her."

"If not Dan Ryder—? I don't get it; Maurice wouldn't have done it for anyone else, as you say."

Jury shook his head. "It beats me. The only thing I can come up with is that somebody convinced Maurice he was acting *for* his father."

Melrose leaned over and scratched Mindy's head. "I must say I'm curious as to how Ryder managed to fake his own death in a race."

"He didn't manage it. The jockey riding that horse wasn't Dan Ryder. He was supposed to be, but wasn't." Jury told him the rest. "It wouldn't have worked, of course, if Simone Ryder hadn't immediately identified the body as Dan's."

Melrose frowned. "That must have taken some extremely quick thinking."

"Yes, it would. Now, where Maurice fits into all of this, I'm not sure. According to Danny, he didn't ask Maurice for anything. He's had no contact with him."

"You didn't tell him?"

"That Maurice is dead? No. I left it to her to do that."

"You believe that he wasn't in contact with Maurice?"

"Yes. As I said, another person must have used his father to get Maurice to help."

"Hm." Melrose leaned back. He was about to speak when Ruthven entered the room.

"I beg your pardon, sir. I thought you should know that Mr. Bramwell is back."

"What?" Melrose was out of his chair like a shot. "Where?"

"Why, in the hermitage, sir. He's asked for some beef tea."

Was that, Jury wondered, a smirk playing around Ruthven's lips?

"Beef *tea*?"

"Yes, m'lord. He claims to have contracted a bad cold at Mr. Browne's establishment."

"Good Lord. Come on, Richard!" Melrose flung out an arm as if he'd yank Jury from his chair. "We'll beef tea *him*!"

The hermitage, as if welcoming the hunter home from the hills, had a nice little fire going in the cast-iron stove.

Mr. Bramwell was holding his hands out to it as if fire were his prime source of comfort. He did not wait for Melrose to open his mouth before he opened his own.

"That book place you sent me to weren't properly heated. I tol' him to build a fire, but yea know 'im, tight as a tic, that 'un. It's gone and got me all chesty." Here, Bramwell demonstrated by beating a fist against his chest and hacking away.

"Properly *heated*? My God, man, at least you were inside!"

"Felt like ruddy outside t'me. And would your Mr. Browne bring me so much as a cuppa? Ha!"

Melrose put his face as close to Bramwell's as he dared without catching a few things and said, "Mr. Bramwell, think: Theo Wrenn Browne wasn't in *your* employ; you were in *his*."

"Worse luck for me, then." He opened the little door of the stove with a sturdy stick, which he then used to poke at the coals, a comforting red. "If that's the way you treat those in yer employ, why I don't see how any of you keep staff round 'ere." *Thunk* went the little door as he slammed it shut.

"We seem to have had no trouble *thus* far." Melrose accidentally knocked his head against the lintel bearing the skull and MEMENTO MORI. A clump of moss fell in his hair.

Bramwell repeated his phlegmy cough. "I ought t'be in bed, me, 'stead o' sittin' 'ere."

"Well, perhaps we can find a nice hospital bed for you. Bedlam has a big turnover."

"None o'yer doctors, no thanks, not after what 'appened t' my Doris. Did I tell yea about—?"

"Your Doris? Yes—" Melrose would have banged his head on the skull again but he didn't want more moss in his hair.

Bramwell swiveled his gaze to Jury, for here was one who hadn't heard the story. "My Doris goes into 'ospital to get one o'them ovaries seen to, and what do they do but take out the whole womb. The whole bloody boiling, don't they? Well, I tells 'er, fer God's sake, lass, sue the bleedin' place. Absolutely disgustin' I calls it, doctor don't even know what bleedin' operation 'e's supposed t'be doing. My

God!" Turning again to Melrose, he said, "I'd sooner be right back 'ere sleepin' rough, me. That Theo Browne puts me in mind of a weasel." He settled himself back against his pillowcase of belongings.

Jury pulled at Melrose's sleeve. "A word?" He backed away from the hermitage entrance.

"What?" Melrose scowled.

"Are you missing the point here? The point *not* being to evaluate you and Theo as respective employers; the point being to *fire* this bloody fool before he seeps into every crack and crevice of Ardry End."

"He's certifiable." Melrose mumbled imprecations . . . um . . . mumm . . . ass . . .

"Fire him, for God's sake!" Jury pushed Melrose back to the entrance.

"Mr. Bramwell!"

Bramwell could look quite piteous and imploring when it suited him, as it did at the moment. (Oh, *he* knew what the two were up to!) He pulled his collar tight with a trembling hand.

Melrose opened his mouth, closed it, opened it again. He felt like a fish. Fortunately, he was saved from continuing by Ruthven, who, coated and scarved, approached over the acre or two between house and hermitage. This momentary reprieve turned Melrose hearty: "Well, here comes your beef tea."

Bramwell immediately dropped his orphan-in-the-storm persona and flexed his fingers, preparatory to picking up whatever was on the tray which Ruthven set down on the smooth stump that Bramwell used for his breakfast, lunch and dinner table, as well as for morning coffee and afternoon tea.

Melrose noted there was considerably more than beef tea on the tray. There was a substantial pile of sandwiches: cheese, chicken and prosciutto. This last really annoyed Melrose as he liked prosciutto with melon and there probably wasn't any left. "I see your dicey health isn't affecting your appetite, Mr. Bramwell."

"Got to keep me strength up. Thank you, Mr. Ruthven," he said as Ruthven shook out a big napkin, which the hermit spread carefully over his wide front. Selecting a sand-

wich of prosciutto, he said, "I'll say this fer yea, yea
don't stint."

He could have been saying this to Melrose, Jury, Ruthven or God.

No, thought Jury. *God stints.*

They were feeding carrots to Aggrieved, both of them
looking and listening for Momaday.

"I am completely cowed by staff," said Melrose.
"Cowed."

"By these two you seem to be."

"It's why I don't have more." It wasn't, really; he was
just enjoying feeling sorry for himself.

Aggrieved, seeing another carrot come out of Jury's
pocket, nudged his shoulder with some force. Jury shoved
him back. Melrose, unaware of this small fracas, kept talking about the staff he didn't have: "A chauffeur, a vegetable cook to help Martha—"

"Who wouldn't be able to stand it—" Jury bumped Aggrieved's elegant neck, payback for another muzzle in the
face.

"—more stable staff, a valet de chambre, a maid. No,
two maids, one a 'tweenie." Melrose liked that word. "A
'tweenie."

"Was there ever such a staff at Ardry End?"

"No. But it sounds good."

"I swear," said Jury, back inside the house, "I'm having
a nap."

"And I swear I'm having a drink."

Each having had what he'd sworn he'd have, they were
presently out driving along narrow country roads. Jury had
said he wasn't ready yet for the "vocal confusion" of the
Jack and Hammer.

"I've heard it called a lot of things, but never vocally
confused," said Melrose.

Early evening was shading off into night. It had been one
of those winter days when trees and houses had razor-sharp
outlines and the air was clear as a bell. Jury looked off to
his left and up a gentle-climbing hill. "Look up there."

"The pub, you mean? It's rather grand, isn't it, the way

it sits up there and *looms* over the village?" Melrose had already turned the car into the even narrower road sloping up the hillside. "Let's go inside."

Deserted. This was a word that conjured images of empty rooms, skewed curtains, of squares of deeper hue on walls where pictures have been taken down. The Man with a Load of Mischief did not seem so much deserted as sad. Had it not been for dust and leaves blown into corners, and wall sconces unresponsive to the push of a switch, it would not have surprised Jury to see the manager still behind the bar, or that arthritic old waiter passing by with a tray or customers spotted at tables and barstools around the room.

It was not dark but shortly would be, and filaments of what was left of mingy winter light managed to steal past the grime of the casement windows and suffuse the dead air with a bit of life. In the entrance hall, Melrose looked at those same framed prints of the hunt making its silly progress along the papered wall. Even the wallpaper had escaped the years' abuse, where one would expect it to be hanging in long flaps, it still clung fast. He followed the sound of Jury's voice into the saloon bar.

Jury said, "It's all here: the equipment"—he rested his hand on the china beer pulls—"the drink, the glassware." Bottles of whiskey, gin, vodka and dark syrupy liqueurs ranged across shelves, doubled by the mirror behind the bar. "I'm astonished the place hasn't been vandalized. My Lord, it's been—what? thirteen, fourteen years?"

Melrose brushed his hand over the barstool and sat down. "Do we have vandals around here? I mean, except for Agatha? And this place was vacated, if you remember, in rather a hurried way. I found Mindy up here, you know. Anyone who would leave his dog behind to fend for itself, well . . . I used to walk her up here in case she was homesick and so she could chase invisible stuff. She quite enjoyed that; I'll have to bring her here again." Melrose squinted at the row of bottles. "If those bottles of Johnny Walker and Bells are still here, what about the *wine* cellar?"

Down in the cellar they stood in more dead leaves and dust, but, of course, one expects, no, *wants* wine bottles to be dusty, for it proves something or other. Shelf after shelf, marching along the cold room, held the wines of Bordeaux, Tuscany, Spain; wines from the Médoc; Cabernet Franc and Merlot; *grand cru* from Puligny-Montrachet; Chardonnays from California; sherry from Spain; Sauternes—someone had known a lot about wine.

Jury said, "I never paid any attention to this."

Melrose was running his finger over the bottles. "Of course not. You were too busy with the body." He stopped, pulled out a bottle of white wine. "Grab a red."

Jury grabbed and they hastened up the cellar steps.

Again behind the bar, where he'd set out glasses for Melrose to wipe, Jury sank the corkscrew into a bottle and pulled, gently.

"Be careful with that. It's from Campania."

Jury started to tug. "That near Northampton?"

"No, Naples. You've heard of Pompeii?" He nodded toward the bottle. "That's a Falerno. Hard to find."

"Time has been careful. I expect I can be." The action of pulling made a pleasant little *op* and he poured the wine into the glasses.

They tasted. Jury held his up to the light. "Like the wine-dark sea."

"Um, um umm, *ummm*!" said Melrose, nodding and shaking his head simultaneously. "Wow, *wow!* When did I last taste wine this good?"

"It *is* good."

Melrose rapped the bar. "You know what we should do? We should buy this place. God knows why some family with a couple of Labs and disgusting children hasn't snapped it up for a country home."

"Because of its sinister past. People might like to *come* here for a drink, hoping the mystique rubs off, but I don't think they'd want to *live* here. What do you mean, buy it?"

"We should."

"Maybe you should; all I've got is the clothes I stand up in. Don't be daft; do you know even half the difficulties of running a restaurant?"

"Can't be all that hard." Melrose slid his glass toward the bottle for more.

Jury poured. "First, there's staff. Now, for someone who

can't fire a hermit, I'd say this alone would make the venture hopeless."

"You could do the firing. So that's one problem sorted."

Jury braced his hands against the bar, preparatory to delivering his feelings about all this. "You are hopelessly naïve, do you know that? A restaurateur takes on fixed expenses, rent, equipment, maintenance—the linen alone would sink most so-called entrepreneurs—and has to deal with a volatile, transient, undertrained or overtrained, temperamental staff; a perishable inventory—my Lord, the list goes on and on. And do you know what percentage of these establishments succeed? Maybe thirty percent."

"How is it you know so much about it?"

Jury took a drink of the rarefied wine. "Danny Wu."

"Who's he?"

"One of the restaurateurs of whom I speak. He owns a restaurant called Ruiyi in Soho. He also does other things as a sideline. At least Racer is convinced of that."

"Is his place successful?"

"Incredibly. You almost have to be a copper to get in."

"Well, there you are."

"No, there I'm *not* and neither are you. I know you see yourself swanning round the dining room recommending a wine to accompany braised llama and acorn sauté. You'd be out a fortune just after opening night."

"There's always another fortune."

"You know what your problem is? You've got too much money."

"I do?"

Jury shook his head.

"Anyway, you were just doing the food part. What about the room part? That shouldn't be difficult."

Jury clapped his hand to his forehead. "You have no idea how much work is involved in this venture."

"Work? Good God, I don't intend to *work*. That's what we'd be paying all of those volatile undertrained people for. *Work?*" Melrose made a *pffffffff*-ing sound, indicating his total abjuration of work. He pulled over one of the yellowing cocktail napkins, which Jury had slapped down on the bar, and took out his pen. "First, these napkins would probably have to be replaced, don't you think?"

Jury just drank his wine and shut his eyes. The wine was even better when he didn't have to look at Melrose. He wished he had Door Jam and a headset. Then he took the envelope from his inside pocket and found a pencil stub in a cup underneath the counter. "Let's say the food for a month would cost a hundred thou." Jury wrote it on the envelope. Underneath that he jotted in another hundred thou for pots and pans. As he turned the envelope for Melrose to see the absurdly fabricated sum, the snapshots fell out.

"What are these?"

"Our suspects."

"This is definitely Simone Ryder," said Melrose. "Or at least the dead woman I saw in the morgue. Who're the ones—?" Melrose stopped and pulled over the pictures of Valerie Hobbs and Sara Hunt. He looked at the one of Sara Hunt for some moments as he lit a cigarette. "You said you didn't have anything to connect this Sara Hunt to Simone Ryder?"

"Right. Not a shred of evidence."

Melrose smiled. "Well, now you have."

FIFTY-SIX

Melrose held up the snapshot. "The woman in the Grave Maurice. The other woman. The one Simone Ryder was talking to."

Jury took the picture out of Melrose's hand. "Sara Hunt. I'll be damned."

"I wasn't paying any attention to her. She was, for the most part, the listener. Simone Ryder was the one telling the story."

"And talking about her deceased husband?"

"I assume so. She was saying something about Roger's brother. Then 'insurance' and then—well, she must have been referring to herself going to a warmer climate, like South America. Ironic, isn't it? The very woman she's talking to knows Dan Ryder is still alive."

"But now," said Jury, "Sara was becoming more and more convinced she'd be seeing the last of Dan Ryder. He'd be in South America with this woman in the pub. I wonder what Ryder told her about his wife."

"But how in heaven's name did Sara Hunt and Simone wind up at Ryder Stud?"

"Simone might have been going there herself for some reason. Some unfinished business. But whatever it was, Simone and Arthur Ryder had never met, or that's what he said. But he *had* met Sara. Vernon drove her to the Ryder place. Beyond that I can't sort it."

"Could Sara have followed her?"

"Could have gone with her, for all we know. Sara is a

very determined woman, count on it." Jury plugged the cork back in the bottle.

"Sacrilege to waste this wine."

"Who's wasting? We're taking it with us. Come on; I need to call Cambridge."

They pulled their coats on, Melrose settling the bottle in his oversized pocket. He patted it like a baby.

As they went through the door of the pub, shoving the piece of wood back under the door to brace it, Jury said, "You'll be needed as a witness, you know, if she's indicted."

"I expect so. Only, is there evidence enough to make an arrest?"

"Maybe, maybe not. I'll let Barry Greene know—he's the DCI in Cambridge—and he can get in touch with the police in Cardiff. I honestly don't know. At least before we didn't have a blind chance of arresting Sara Hunt. Now we do."

After Jury had made his call and they'd toasted progress with another glass of wine, they decided to go out again, and Melrose told Martha to hold dinner. This time the Jack and Hammer was the destination of choice. "As long," said Melrose, "as you feel ready for vocal confusion."

"I'm ready. And it occurs to me there might be a way of handling the Bramwell crisis."

"No, he's not going with us."

"I'm thinking we might pop in to see Theo Wrenn Browne." Jury smiled thinly.

When it came to Richard Jury, Theo Wrenn Browne was, at best, ambivalent, at worst, wretchedly jealous. How he coveted the admiring glances slewed Jury's way! Yes, he was jealous of Jury in the same way he was jealous of Melrose Plant: both had everything Theo wanted. Although Jury didn't have a fortune to throw around (as did Plant), he easily made up for this in his job of detective superintendent at New Scotland Yard, and having all of that power over life and death. He could point a finger and nests of vipers would disappear. (This image sent a pleasant little shudder up and down his wiry body, the roots of which frisson Theo wasn't eager to investigate.)

"Mr. Jury, how nice to see you again! And is this visit business or pleasure?"

"Both. You have an employee here named Bramwell? Frederick Edward Bramwell?"

Theo was brought up short. "I did have such a person here, but no longer. He left. He hinted he was returning to Mr. Plant's place." Theo tittered.

Or at least it sounded like a titter to Melrose, who had posted himself by the tiers of magazines where he could listen and pretend not to hear.

Mustering just the right amount of gravitas, Jury said, "That's a rum go."

Rum go? Melrose looked round. Had he mistakenly walked into an H. E. Bates novel?

Now Theo didn't know whether to cheer or weep. Then realizing he could do better than "left," he said, "Well, I had to fire him, didn't I?"

"Damn! This would have been the perfect place."

"Pardon?" Theo danced his eyebrows around, puzzled.

"Oh, sorry." Jury sighed. "We've been trying to get the goods on Fast Eddie for years now."

Get the goods on? Had Jury been filling up on TV cop shows? And "Fast Eddie"—Melrose knew he'd heard that name. "Fast Eddie." It was from some American film, wasn't it? They called people those kinds of names over there.

"Fast Eddie? I'm not following you, Superintendent."

"We call him that. It's the initials, isn't it? Frederick Edward? His speciality is rare books, and I mean *very* rare. Like the Pleiades edition of *Ulysses*. Don't see many of those lying around, do you?"

Theo was overcome with ignorance. "The Pleiades edition? I don't think I'm familiar . . . I find all this hard to believe, Superintendent."

You're not the only one. Melrose turned a page of the Beano comic he was reading.

Theo went on. "You see, Mr. Bramwell didn't appear to know a *thing* about books."

Jury guffawed. "That's his game, Mr. Browne. He presents himself as being quite unlettered, to say the least."

The very, very, very least.

"But why on *earth*," Theo said, looking pained, "would such a person want with working in my bookshop?"

Jury leaned across the well-polished counter which separated Theo from the rest of humanity and said in a low voice, "Because he always makes his contacts through bookshops."

Theo drew in a breath, sharply.

"If Mr. Plant can persuade the man to come back here, you would be doing me a huge favor. And, of course, the Yard. This man's got right up my nose over the last couple of years."

Melrose sighed, wishing Jury would stop talking like a cop in a bad thriller.

Theo leaned closer to Jury so that now their noses were nearly touching. "Is he, well, *dangerous* at all?"

"Oh, I shouldn't think so, Mr. Browne. But of course"— Jury stepped back and put his palms up—"I certainly wouldn't ask you to do something you'd be uncomfortable with. After all, we can't *all* be heroes." Jury flashed him a heroic smile.

Well, that did it for Theo. Any appeal to his heroism completely unnerved him—not that there had ever been such an appeal up to now. Yes, he would have Mr. Bramwell back if it meant helping the police.

"So all we have to do is talk Bramwell into returning to the Wrenn's Nest."

Joanna Lewes, who was sitting next to Jury in the Jack and Hammer said, "Isn't that illegal or criminal or something to impersonate a police detective?"

"I *am* a police detective," said Jury.

"I know; but you were pretending this was a real case."

Jury laughed. "You're obviously unaware of all the 'pretending' the police do."

"Anyway," said Melrose, "how do I get him to agree to go back?"

Trueblood said, "Tell him Theo's a bookie."

"Oh, that's brilliant."

Trueblood lit a pink cigarette. "You have no imagination, you know that?"

Vivian said to Jury, "You're supposed to be resting and

yet you go gallivanting all over the country searching for"—she shrugged—"whatever. You'll land yourself right back in the hospital with that dreadful nurse."

"Hannibal." Jury smiled. "You could say Hannibal was really into death. Nothing gave her more pleasure it appeared than an unsuccessful attempt to resuscitate some poor sod flailing like a fish in the OR."

"Consider my Doris and be grateful they didn't remove all of your organs."

Jury laughed. "She was always—" He stopped, hearing Nurse Bell's whiny voice. *Dory. "Poor tike, poor little Dory . . . arrhythmia, and no one knew it . . ."*

"Something wrong, old bean?" asked Trueblood.

"What? No. I just have to—" Jury rose suddenly and went to the bar where Dick Scroggs was reading the paper. "I need your phone, Dick."

Dick fished it out from the shelf beneath the bar. "Here you are, sir."

Jury passed behind some member of the Withersby clan, sullenly nursing a beer. He got out his address book and thumbed to what he wanted. Then he punched in the number of the hospital, called and asked for the surgical ward. A crisp voice answered, and he asked for Dr. Ryder. He was, of course, put on hold. A long silence, bleak as the Withersby face down the bar. (Why did they all look so alike? That cropped look of the face, the squarish jaw, stopped too soon?)

He waited. It would be forever, if the nurse came back at all. He hung up, redialed the hospital and asked again for the surgical ward. Only this time he asked for Nurse King. Christine. Was she on duty? On duty and right there, said the voice.

Chrissie King came on the line. Jury could almost hear the devotion throbbing at the other end. He asked her if she could locate Dr. Ryder, or at least find out where he was and get a message to him.

"But I know where he is, I mean, I know where he said he was going—to Cambridgeshire. It was late yesterday he left. He said something about a funeral."

Dear God, Jury thought, taking the receiver from his ear

and resting it against his forehead as if to cut short the bad news. Maurice. How could he have forgotten?

The receiver back against his ear, he said, "Chrissie, you're a godsend, you are. Thanks."

"Oh, yes. Glad to . . ."

She said it as if he'd just asked her to go steady.

Jury hung up, found the Ryder number in Cambridgeshire and called. No answer. He put the receiver back and thought for a moment. Then he went back to the table and asked their pardon as he had to leave.

"So do you," he said to Melrose, pulling him out of his chair. "Come on."

The others were not so much curious as enthralled.

"Revenge. We didn't really explore that possibility."

Melrose, floating the Bentley from park into drive, said, "But we did explore it."

"Against Ryder Stud and Arthur himself, yes. How I could have overlooked Roger Ryder, God only knows."

"Because the focus was on the stud farm. That's where Nell lived, after all."

Hell, Jury thought. His side throbbed unsympathetically.

FIFTY-SEVEN

Nell walked into the office to get the breeding book where she would record the foal's birth and its forebears. She liked doing this; it seemed to give life an order that it otherwise didn't have. At least these books presented the illusion, the appearance of orderly progression, and that was worth something and should be respected. The horses themselves certainly should be, and if these bracketed markings did that, well, good.

She had passed Davison, who was muttering a blue streak of profanities, making for Fool's Money's stall with a man who looked familiar. A small man, no doubt a jockey from some stable around here. There were so many of them. She stopped Davison and asked what was wrong. Ah, you know, they're putting more weight on Fool's Money than he ought to carry. Nell had reminded him (utterly unnecessarily, for Davison knew it) that the greater the Thoroughbred, the heavier the weight. It was to even things out for lesser horses. The small man nodded. They walked on.

Halo, son of Lucky Me by Lockout out of Angel Eyes by Treasure. She repeated it like a mantra as she looked for and found the breeding record beneath a stack of folders on her grandfather's desk. Lying there, too, was his penknife and a bit of wood. She picked up the smooth wood, wondering what he was fashioning this time. She set it back down by the knife.

Halo, son of Lucky Me by . . . All of this should give the scrawny little Halo a promising start. The mare Angel

Eyes stood at the Anderson stables. She had been bred to Lucky Me as part of the season Anderson had bought, his mare to be bred to the Ryder stable's Lucky Me. *Halo, son of Lucky Me*—

It kept her, for a few moments, at least, from thinking about Maurice. She clasped the book in her arms and rested her chin on its scarred binding, and shut her eyes. *Maurice.* What disorder there had been in his poor life should have left the family unsurprised by his death, though of course she couldn't mouth that thought. She did not tell her grandfather that she'd been afraid for a long time of something, not this, certainly, but something. Everyone had to think of it as an accident, pure and simple. Thrown from a horse against a stone wall—what else could it reasonably be?

It could be a great deal else. It could be Maurice trying to show that he really was Danny Ryder's son. He'd been competing all of his life with the shadow of Dan Ryder. How could he not? Maurice was very smart: he knew the danger of jumping Hadrian's walls after dark, if one wasn't a good jumper.

She had liked her uncle, even despite his being such a deplorable father. She had liked him for his feeling for horses. It was strange to her how a man could be not much good in so many ways, ruinous to others, yet still retain a passion for one thing—in Dan Ryder's case, horses. In that respect, they were alike. It made her uncomfortable to think they were alike in this way for that might imply they were in other ways, too. At times she was afraid that her passion for horses had drained her of feelings for people. But she did love people—her father, grandfather and Vernon. She really loved Vernon in ways she knew were hopeless for a seventeen-year-old girl. Ruefully, she hoped she'd never have to choose between Vern and a horse. She laughed. *Don't be ridiculous. Of course you'd choose Vern.* And her other self said, *Doesn't that depend on the horse?*

Nell laughed again, straightened, wondered how she could laugh with Maurice dead. She felt cold; she felt the blood drain from her face. Maurice. But she hadn't cried. Tears sometimes came to her eyes, but didn't fall. She wondered again if she was, after all, a cold person. When was the last time she'd cried over anything but the mares or flown into a rage? She couldn't remember. Was it because of the last months at Valerie Hobbs's place, where she'd schooled herself in repressing her feelings so that she could stay clearheaded? Or simply keep from shattering to bits? *You're so dramatic!* But she had never really thought of herself as self-dramatizing.

In all of these ruminations her eyes traveled round the room—the books, the wall of photographs—Do I still look like my old self?—until her glance rested on the coatrack near the door. Silks.

She went nearly rigid. The green and silver silks were on a hanger. The stranger's, the jockey's, they must be. And then a shape came to her, burst into her consciousness like glass shards flying together, turned back to their recognizable shape. She felt as if she had in that moment turned into some other girl.

Nell whirled around and snatched the penknife from the desk. She flicked it open and moved to the rack and slashed the shirt, lacerating it again and again until it hung in rags. Then she dropped the knife on the floor and ran from the house to the stables.

In minutes she had Aqueduct saddled and was out of the stable yard and gone.

FIFTY-EIGHT

Diane had generously tossed Jury her cell phone, surprised that these weren't routinely issued to Scotland Yard detectives. Jury was using it as he and Melrose left the A45 for the A14, heading for Cambridge.

He snapped the cell phone closed. "I can't get through. There's something wrong with the damned thing."

"What's wrong," said Melrose, easing the Bentley around an articulated lorry, "is probably that Diane forgot to pay up for more time. Doesn't some voice tell you that?"

"I didn't get a voice."

Melrose entered a roundabout near Godmanchester. "Ryder will be there, not to worry." He meant Roger Ryder. "With Maurice's funeral coming up, he'd stay for Arthur's sake."

"Who is this creep ahead of us?" said Jury.

"Which creep? There are so many of them."

"The one in what looks like one of those ice cream vans. You know, jingle, jingle, jingle, and going five miles per."

It took them another hour to get to the turnoff that led to Cambridge, an hour filled with rather churlish observations from Jury about his fellow motorists; and okay okay okay from Melrose. Melrose tried to take Jury's mind off the incompetency of British drivers (all of whom appeared to be driving to Cambridge this afternoon) by getting him to talk about the case, but Jury proved uncharacteristically taciturn.

"You know, don't you?"

"Know what?"

"Oh, stop being *stupid*. You know why what's happened, happened."

"Pass him" was Jury's only comment, indicating the car ahead.

"I can't. A car's coming from the other direction. They do that, you know. This is a two-lane road and we've got hedgerows on either side and curves we can't see around."

Jury made a squiffy sound and stared out of the passenger window as if he'd happily roll up the hedgerow and toss it at the cows. There were several ruminating cows near the road.

"We're nearly there, for heaven's sake."

No comment from his passenger.

"You'd be a total disaster at an AA meeting, you know that?" Melrose knew this comment, unrelated to anything at all in the present conversation, would pry a response from Jury.

"AA? What's AA got to do with anything?"

"It doesn't, for you. The thing is you're supposed to share. 'Thank you for your share' is what they like to say."

"That is *so* a thing I would not be caught dead saying."

"Perhaps, but then you're not an alcoholic."

"A debatable point."

"Anyway, I think 'thank you for your share' is rather warm and friendly."

"Please don't say it again."

Melrose considered. "I'd say Long Piddleton is a really alcoholic place. I mean, there's so little to do."

The hedges gave way to dogwood and white birch trees and silver fern. The road widened.

"Does Vernon Rice have an alcoholics chat room on his Web site? I bet you'd always see 'thank you for your share' posted there."

"The only share I want is ten percent of Microsoft."

"Thank you for your share." Melrose turned off onto the Ryder drive.

In the distance beyond the white fence horses grazed, one or two turning their heads to inspect the Bentley and its contents. The car spat up gravel as it stopped by the front door, which at the same time was opened by a haggard-looking Arthur Ryder.

"Saw the car. I remembered it." He nodded toward Melrose and evinced no interest in his appearing here with Richard Jury. It was as if anything worth questioning had been nullified by the death of his grandson.

Jury apologized for intruding. "I wouldn't if it wasn't important."

"No. Yes. Come in."

Far from being annoyed by this unexpected visit from the two of them, Arthur Ryder seemed a little relieved to have something to focus on other than the upcoming funeral.

Standing by the large front window, Vernon Rice nodded to them and returned his gaze to the chilly scene outside.

Roger Ryder moved to shake Jury's hand and ask him how he felt. "Is there much pain still?"

"No, not much," Jury lied.

Roger knew it, too. He smiled. "You're tiring yourself out; you should be relaxing—"

(A word Jury would be happy to shoot where it stood, along with "share.")

"—but I think it very good of you to give so much time and effort to our family, Superintendent."

"I'm dreadfully sorry for your loss. Maurice will be missed."

"Awful, isn't it?" said Arthur Ryder. "Nell come back, Maurice gone, as if we had to pay a price for her return. I feel as if it's a kind of curse." They had been drinking tea, and Arthur told them he could get some hot.

Jury shook his head, saying, "I can understand your feeling it's a curse, but Maurice wasn't a payment for Nell. If you think that way, you'll find yourself wandering through mazes of pain and self-blame. Don't go there." He turned to Roger Ryder. "Dr. Ryder, it's you I wanted to talk to. Could I have a word with you?"

"Yes, of course." He looked around at the others. "Here?"

Jury nodded and they sat down on the sofa. Vernon turned from the window, his expression bleak. Jury looked at him. No one felt things more; he was as much of this family as any of them.

"When I was in hospital," began Jury, "tended by the excellent Nurse Bell—"

Roger laughed a little. "Not your favorite person, I believe."

"No, definitely not, but we might owe her a debt, or, rather, her mordant turn of mind. She was fond of bringing up unsuccessful cases. Wedged into her promenade of patients who hadn't made it—one of whom she seemed to think I was likely to become—"

Roger smiled.

"—was a girl, a young girl who'd died in the OR when you were operating. Dory I think was her name."

"Oh, Christ." Roger put his head against his fist. "That was more than two years ago." He leaned forward, forearms on knees, head bent as if in an act of contrition. "I blamed myself. The child had a heart condition—arrythmia, not dangerous in itself, it can be controlled with medication, but no one knew about it, including me, and I certainly should have; before operating, I should—"

Vernon Rice frowned. "What child?"

Arthur said, "That was not your fault, son."

Jury turned to Arthur. "You knew her, then?"

"Of course, we all did. She—"

"Bloody hell!"

This outburst came from the office and was repeated twice before the speaker, a small man with a big temper, stormed into the room. "What the bloody hell's goin' on, Arthur?" He was holding up the shredded silk. "I got four bleedin' races at Cheltenham tomorrow! I'll look good in this lot, I will."

"Billy, I don't know—" said Arthur.

The jockey jiggled the hanger; the pieces of silk fluttered in the air of Billy's shaking. Finally, they stilled into their green and silver diamond pattern.

Melrose stared. "You're one of Roy Diamond's jockeys?"

Billy nodded, muttering imprecations.

"He told me his daughter was dead," said Jury. "She was the little girl." It was only half a question.

Arthur said, "Dorothy, her name was. Dorothy Diamond."

"She was in—" Jury stopped before he said, *your* care. He looked at the shredded silk and asked, "Where's Nell?"

Vernon stared at him and bolted from the room.

Neil Epp, the groom, was still holding the tasty dish of carrots and fruits under Criminal Type's nose and wondered what the bloody hell was going on, for here came Vernon Rice heading (it looked like) for them, for Neil and Criminal Type, still bridled and chewing his evening treat. Vernon yelled at him to saddle the horse.

Neil was completely discombobulated by this second assault on his stables—the first being young Nell grabbing Aqueduct as if her life depended on him, and now here came Rice yelling to saddle up the horse. Owing to Neil's years of Dan Ryder's "Do-it-don't-ask" training he threw the saddle he'd been carrying over his arm onto Criminal Type's back and he'd barely done this before Vernon had thrown himself up on the horse in one of the most efficient mountings Neil had ever witnessed.

Rice turned the horse and was now heading for the meadow and the walls.

Neil Epp ran, yelling, "Hey, Vernon! Criminal Type don't go over the sticks!"

(Says who?)

Add to this the car that had just pulled onto the gravel lot and out of which got that Scotland Yard detective sergeant who'd been here before, and Neil thought it was the busiest day they'd seen since breeding rights to Samarkand had been initiated.

"Not fifteen minutes ago, Nell left," he said to the party of worried-looking men who'd just come out of the house. "She came running out, saddled up Aqueduct and took off like Criminal Type on a fast track. Now he's gone too, Criminal Type. With that Rice fellow up on him. Nell'd make a good 'chaser the way she takes those walls, or even a jockey. She's flat-out brilliant—"

Jury cut across Neil's career choices. "Where's the Diamond farm?"

As Neil directed him, Roger turned disbelieving eyes on Jury. "You don't think—?"

"Wiggins, you drive them"—he indicated Roger and Arthur—"and you drive me"—he turned to Melrose.

They ran toward the two cars.

Unfortunately, the quickest way to Roy Diamond's place was not by the road, but by Hadrian's walls, as the crow flies—or the horse.

Go for Wand

FIFTY-NINE

Roy Diamond was riding his favorite mount, Havoc, around his mile-and-a-quarter training course, trying to beat yesterday's record time.

Roy didn't know it but he had four very bad moments coming his way.

He didn't see the horse and rider streaking across his paddock where a few of his horses grazed, and he didn't see it had taken the last wall as if the wall were made of Devon cream. He didn't see this because he was galloping round the track and his peripheral vision lied: he took movement over that way to be the movements of his own horses.

Coming around the turn he realized this wasn't at all the case and when Aqueduct jumped the fence that enclosed the course, Roy felt fear, a thing he rarely felt because he always considered himself to be in command of any situation. Fear was a negligible, chaffy emotion wasted on Roy. Since the death of his daughter, most emotions were.

She was holding a whip up, clearly with the intention of bringing it down. Nell Ryder, as with her legendary uncle, Dan, never took a whip to a horse. He knew if she slowed she'd be on him with that whip, but what was much worse, with that horse. Nell talked to horses. Roy could see happening to him the same thing that had happened to Dan Ryder.

His jacket was lying over the fence and as he galloped round the track with her in pursuit he knew he had to get hold of the jacket. He saw that part of the fence coming up, reined in Havoc and reeled off the horse, snatched his coat and grabbed the gun from the pocket.

Roy was that popular: he always carried a gun.

Now the next bad moment happened: a cherry-red Aston-Martin was coming at full throttle toward the training track. Between the road and the track were two white fences. The Aston-Martin couldn't jump the fences, so it did the next best thing: went straight through them.

At the same moment Roy caught a glimpse of yet another horse racing across the field a hundred feet away, just as Aqueduct appeared about to fall on Roy like a wall of bricks.

Roy fired. In that split second between intent and execution, Nell vaulted from the horse, and like a kid playing leapfrog, slid over Aqueduct's head and down in front of him. The first shot caught her on the way down, the second as she hit the ground.

Then Roy got off two shots at the driver—was he seeing right?—of the Aston-Martin. Danny Ryder was out of the car and running toward them; Criminal Type jumped the wooden fence around the course and without even slowing, Vernon sprang from the saddle and fell on Roy Diamond, yelling.

Fear is no match for fury in a fight. Vernon wrenched the gun away and pushed it against Roy's temple. Whether he would have fired or not was a moot question as he didn't get the chance. Danny Ryder slid across the track, grabbed the gun-holding hand and knocked the gun from Vernon's grip. Then he tossed it—at the ground, the sky, the past— while Vernon was up and running to where Nell lay as if Aqueduct had thrown her. The horse stood with neck bent, its muzzle wandering over her.

Carefully, Vernon wedged his arm behind her and lifted her as if she were a bunch of broken lily stalks—that pale hair, that translucent face. His hand on her ribs felt the soaking wetness of blood. "Nellie!"

She gazed at him and managed two syllables: "Remem—?"

It was then that Roy Diamond's fourth bad moment arrived full force. Too late for Nell but in plenty of time to see Roy in hell, the four men piled out of the police car and the Bentley and made a rush toward the others. Seeing Dan Ryder, Arthur and Roger stopped dead. Danny looked and turned away in tears.

Jury and Wiggins ran to where Roy Diamond, who clearly saw the vanity of mounting his horse and trying to run, stood with his back to Nell. "Oh, no," whispered Wiggins.

Jury knelt by Vernon and put two useless fingers against what should have been the pulse in her neck. Then he rose and moved like a glacier to where Diamond was standing.

Roy said, broken-voiced but in fear, not sorrow: "I wasn't aiming at her!"

Jury grabbed one arm in a vise, scooped the gun from the dirt and pulled Roy away toward the house. Wiggins gripped the other arm, and between them, they pulled the man along. Roy wasn't helping the process.

"I was only trying to keep the damned horse from stomping me; I can't help it if she threw herself in front of the goddamned horse."

They were going through the back door of the house. Melrose and Danny Ryder were keeping up.

"Why'd she do that?" yelled Roy. "Why would she throw herself—my God, man, it was only a horse!"

That was simply too much for Wiggins, who kicked the door shut in Melrose's face, brought his raised knee around and shoved it into Roy Diamond's front, pushing out what sounded—*uph*—like the last breath of the man's life.

"Wiggins," said Jury.

Wiggins took the ballast of his knee away and Roy slid down the wall.

Jury grabbed Roy by his shirt collar and pulled him back to his feet. He slammed Roy against the wall.

"Sir—" said Wiggins.

"You had your turn," Jury said over his shoulder. Then he shoved his face into Roy's. They could have breathed with each other's breath. "Now, you listen to me, you hopeless piece of shit—"

"Sir—"

"—it would take me one second to crush you a lot harder than that horse." To demonstrate, Jury pulled Roy's head away from the wall and slammed it back hard enough to crack plaster. "I'm an off-duty cop and this is a personal dispute, see, and it would take no effort at all for me to drop you where you stand—"

Wiggins gripped Jury's arm. "*Sir!* You can't—"

Jury shook off Wiggins's hand and continued what he was saying in a sibilant whisper as he shoved the muzzle of Roy's gun against his temple. "My sergeant here is worried about police procedure, but me, I don't give a flying fuck for procedure." He pulled Roy away from the wall again and banged him back again. "Do you know what keeps me from blowing you away, *Roy*? I mean, right now, *Roy*? Your daughter. That's all. Your dead daughter." Then Jury pulled him away from the wall and nearly threw him at Wiggins. "Charge him and take him to the car."

"Which charge?" Wiggins called to Jury's retreating back.

"Resisting arrest."

As Jury walked out of the house, he heard the double note of a police vehicle in the distance. Someone had had the presence of mind, probably Melrose Plant, to call Cambridge.

The others seemed to have scattered to the winds, as if they crewed a little boat that was rudderless or no longer anchored. Melrose Plant leaned against a tree, smoking and looking at Jury. Danny Ryder leaned against his car. When Jury walked up to him, all Danny could do was shake his head and say, "Christ, but I'm sorry. Sara told me about Maurice this morning; I jumped in my car and drove without stopping. When I got to Dad's, Neil Epp told me what had happened, how all of you had raced over here. I knew it was bad news. I knew it had to be this fucker, Diamond, you were looking for." He ran the side of his hand over his eyes. "One minute, two—if I could've made it a minute sooner—"

"It's always a minute, Danny. There was nothing you could do. But you saved Vernon Rice from blowing that bastard's bloody head off."

Then he walked over to the course where Arthur and Roger Ryder were leaning against the fence, staring at the ground where a dozen feet away, Vernon was still holding Nell. The depth of their despair was so awful it paralyzed them; they seemed unable to go to where Nell was. Jury couldn't think of a thing to say. Not a word. He searched his mind for some words of consolation and couldn't find one. What bloody good was language when it failed you at every important juncture? Looking over at Aqueduct, who stood stock-still by the fence, he thought, *It's as hard for me as it is for you, boy.*

He walked over to where Nell lay and knelt down and put his hand on Vernon's shoulder. Vernon looked at him out of eyes that looked gutted by fire.

The sirens were close now, and there was more than one.

Vernon swallowed hard. "All she tried to say was, 'Remember.'"

That, thought Jury, was the word.

SIXTY

Still with his coat on, Jury stood against the wall in one of the interview rooms of the Cambridge station, looking at Roy Diamond. DCI Greene sat at the table across from Diamond.

"Six witnesses. We have you for both murder and attempted murder. You'll never talk your way out of this; it just won't happen."

Diamond had regained his cool manner, and said, "If that's the case, why are we talking?"

Greene tipped his chair back, looked at Jury. He had told Jury he was welcome to sit in on the questioning of Roy Diamond. Diamond's smooth manner grated on Jury's nerves, but he said nothing.

"I can tell you one thing, Inspector," said Diamond. "I'm putting in a complaint to the chief constable about being roughed up." He nodded his head toward Jury.

"Pity," said Greene, tonelessly.

"And the commissioner," Diamond added, "is a friend of mine."

Jury thought that if the bastard was playing the friends-in-high-places card, Diamond wasn't as sure of his "self-defense" defense as he wanted them to think. He came away from the wall and moved closer to the table. Diamond inadvertently tilted backward.

"Why are we talking? That was your question, wasn't it?" Jury put his hands on the table, leaned toward Diamond and said, in a voice he managed to keep soft, "We're talking because we want to know the rest of it."

Roy Diamond's eyes widened in mock surprise. "All I know is what I've already told you. All I know is what happened two hours ago: Nell Ryder jumped her horse over the fence at my training track and launched herself at me. That horse came toward me like an express train. *Then* the car comes at me, *then* the second horse. What choice did I have? I can only say I'm lucky to have had the hand-gun with me. It was clearly self-defense."

Jury's laugh was a bark. Of course, Diamond's solicitor would take that tack, unless he flew a kite of diminished responsibility.

Greene said, "We've got Billy Finn in another room, Roy. We'll have the motive sorted, no sweat."

Diamond said, "Well, you can ascribe any motive you want to what I've *allegedly* done; the trouble is that you don't have any evidence"—he leaned over the table—"because there isn't any."

"There will be," said Jury. "And another thing, what about this sideline of yours, the mares Valerie Hobbs kept on her farm? That *is* your operation, isn't it?"

"Yes. The operation is not illegal, as you very well know. Those mares belong to me, Superintendent. They're my property."

"Not any longer, they're not. You'll be compensated, not to worry. But I'd really like to know where you were going with this. Because it's my understanding an American phar-maceutical company named Wyeth has a patent on this mare's-urine estrogen drug."

"They won't have it forever. The patent is going to run out some time around the turn of the century, 2001 or 2. No, my operation is by way of being experimental. I want to see if a drug can be produced that doesn't have to go through a hundred steps to get that end product. Be cheaper to market it."

"How? How are you—or were you—going to see this?"

"I've several chemists working for me. I've a small plant in the Marquesas. It's temporary, of course. But I have three chemists, an accountant, an investment banker and a lawyer assigned exclusively to this operation. To actually grab some of the market we'd need thousands of horses, such as are on those farms in Canada. And I could hardly organize that in this country, could I? Not on my land, certainly. No place secluded enough."

"Accountant, banker, lawyer. Sounds like paradise, take away the island," said Barry Greene.

"What the hell are you holding over these people's heads, Roy? What do you know about Valerie Hobbs to have made her implicate herself?"

Roy expelled a narrow stream of smoke. "Enough."

Wiggins had been dispatched in the company of the crime-scene fingerprint expert to examine the room at the top of the stairs used by Nell Ryder.

"They covered all that pretty thoroughly," said Wiggins, "when they took Valerie Hobbs into custody. Certainly went over it for prints."

"I know," said Jury. "I've seen the results. But I'm especially interested in the bed. They lifted prints from the bed frame and the head. But since it's an old brass bed, it has metal bars. I don't think they lifted any from the bars. It's those I'm interested in, not just the single print, either; there should be an entire set"—Jury's fingers moved as if they were locking around a bar—"and I think you'll find them."

That had been an hour ago.

Jury wished he had a cigarette; all he had was a pack of gum. He was standing with his back against the wall again (and recognizing the aptness of that metaphor), listening to Roy Diamond smoothly answering the questions of Barry Greene. Where was the man's lawyer? Hadn't Diamond said he wouldn't answer any more questions without the solicitor's being present? The man was so sure he could sidestep any trap that the police might set that he kept right on going.

"Billy Finn doesn't know anything. He's my best jockey. What has he allegedly done?"

"Allegedly," said Greene, "abducted Nell Ryder twenty months ago and dropped her off at Hobbs stud."

Diamond snorted. "That's ridiculous."

Jury excused himself.

Roy Diamond said again he would answer no more questions.

*   *   *

Detective Sergeant Styles, marginally less frosty toward Jury given the events of that afternoon, in response to Jury's asking if he could speak to Billy Finn, turned up his hands and said, "If Greene says yes, be my guest. I'm getting sod-all from him. I'm going for a cuppa, me." He left.

Jury had watched Billy Finn when they brought him in on the heels of Roy Diamond. He'd heard Billy being questioned. He did not himself think Billy had been the one to take Nell from the stable that May night.

Since he had no cigarettes, Jury offered Billy Finn a stick of gum. Billy took it.

"Look, Billy, no one in bloody hell could remember where he was on a night in May twenty months ago. I'm not setting any store by an alibi. The reason for pulling you in is that shirt, the silks, the colors of Diamond's stables. Your silks being what Nell Ryder took a knife to."

Billy half rose in protest. Jury waved him down. "I know—there are a half dozen jockeys who might have worn those colors over the time they rode for Diamond. It's not necessarily the shirt itself. It's the pattern, Billy. The diamond pattern that sent Nell ballistic. That must be what she remembered, what suddenly came into her mind. Now, there were two things she was sure of: that the person who took her was small and that he took her by way of those walls. You're a flat racer, aren't you, Billy?"

Billy nodded, intrigued in spite of himself, Jury's manner having enough of a calming effect that he could forget why he was there long enough to be interested in the story.

"I think what we're looking for is a jump jockey. Those walls aren't easy; I don't think a rider would choose those walls to get himself over unless he knew he was a damned good jumper.

"Strictly speaking, of course, the fellow doesn't even have to be someone who rides for Diamond. It just seems more likely that it would be. To narrow it down even more, someone who is enough of a low-life to abduct a girl for pay, or someone who's into Roy Diamond for a lot. Someone who owes him. You know what I mean."

Billy nodded, chewing the gum furiously. "There's a guy, a jockey, Trevor—what's his last name? Trevor—bloody damn—he rode Dusty Answer in the Grand National last year. Trevor Gwyne, that's it, Trevor Gwyne. Never did like him. He's known for trying to unseat other riders; I think he was up before the Jockey Club a couple times and got suspended for a year. Anyway, I know Gwyne's a gambler and I know Roy's bailed him out a couple times. For big money. You may want to talk to him, right?"

Jury had been sitting on the table, close to Billy, and got up. "Absolutely. Thanks, Billy."

"Listen, do I get to leave? Tonight, I mean?"

"I wouldn't be at all surprised. I'll have a word."

At that, Billy almost relaxed.

Jury left the room and saw Wiggins coming down the hall. When he saw Jury, he waved whatever he was holding in his hand. "You were right."

"In here, Wiggins." They went into an empty room furnished like the others with table and folding chairs. Wiggins put down the fingerprint cards. "You were right; they hadn't tried to lift prints from the metal bars. Here, these are Roy Diamond's prints, *and* the configuration pretty obviously shows he grabbed on to the bar. Well, you can see here—" Wiggins pointed them out, though they needed no pointing, the prints of four fingers, the fourth, the pinky, slightly smudged. One under the other, clearly indicating the hand had been wrapped round the bar. The second shot was from a slightly different angle.

"They're his, all right."

There was no thumb print, but that was probably because the thumb would have overlapped the index finger when the hand wrapped the bar.

"This is good, Wiggins, very good."

Barry Greene was coming out of the room where Roy Diamond still sat, telling the constable to go in. He then walked to where Jury stood. "Right bastard, that one is."

Jury showed him the photos.

"Excellent. Of course you know what his solicitor will make of this lot."

"Well, he's not here yet and Diamond is so bloody sure of himself—it's worth a try."

They entered the room again and Greene told the PC he could leave. Then Greene spread the photos in front of

Diamond. "It would appear, Roy, that you'd been getting up to something in this bed. Nell Ryder's bed, I mean. But you remember, you must. In the throes of passion you grabbed on to the bars, apparently."

Roy Diamond looked at the fingerprint cards and his complexion changed to mottled red, which slowly leaked out, leaving his face almost sheet white.

Gotcha! thought Jury.

Roy opened his mouth to say something just as the door seemed to spring open in its hurry to indulge the hand that pushed it.

A voice behind Jury said, "That's all, folks. One more word and I'll do my Woody Woodpecker impersonation."

Roy Diamond's solicitor came through the door looking as accommodating as razor wire.

Jury knew that voice. He turned to its source. It was Charly Moss. *No!*

Yes. "Superintendent Richard Jury! See? I remember." The hand she held out to shake his was crisp and cold.

He took it in his warmer one. "Hello, Charly."

"It's been a long time. It's been since that trial in Lincolnshire. Remember?"

As if he could forget.

But she looked at him as if he must have. "So." Charly Moss slung her briefcase on the table, perhaps announcing her confidence in the knowledge that whatever she had was better than whatever they had. "Now." She literally rolled up the sleeves of her copper-brown sweater, the exact shade of her hair. "How much to-and-froing has been going on here since my client requested an attorney?"

Greene said, "Very little."

"That's good. That means there'll be very little which will be inadmissible as evidence, right?" She looked down. "Ah! Fingerprints! How unappreciated they will be."

"But they're—"

"Be quiet, Roy." She gestured toward the pictures, cocked her head with a "please explain" expression.

"Your client," said Barry Greene, "is being accused of kidnapping, rape and murder—just to name a few things." He tapped one of the photos. "These belong to the rape charge."

"I see." Charly, who was still standing, bent over the picture. "Hm. The fatal bed, is that it?"

Jury said, trying to control his anger, "She would have found it so." He shoved the photo of a dead Nell Ryder directly under her eyes and looked stonily at Charly Moss.

"This is terrible. The poor girl," Charly said, looking downcast.

Jury knew there was no reason to question her sincerity, but sincerity didn't mix with the evidence in the case.

"Only, it doesn't mean that Mr. Diamond here shared the bed. At least not with Nell Ryder. I can give you a couple of alternatives off the top of my head: he was in the bed at some point, perhaps by himself, perhaps with"— Charly pressed on the briefcase's silver catches and it opened like a trap sprung. She pulled out a notebook and ran her finger down one page—"with the attractive Valerie Hobbs—"

Charly Moss had not breezed in unprepared.

"—or he could have been looking for something that dropped behind the mattress or the bed, reaching down—" She held one arm up, hand grabbing at an imaginary bar. "I could go on . . ."

Please don't, thought Jury. A cold finger touched his spine.

Charly looked from Greene to Jury. "Is this your evidence, then?"

"Thus far, yes." Greene said coolly. "We're still gathering it. We have witnesses to this shooting, of course."

"Of course. Now, if you don't mind, I'd like to speak to my client." She smiled.

Jury had been a sucker for that smile the first time he'd met her. One of his favorite memories was of Charly and Melrose sitting on stools in that pub in Lincoln singing a drunken duet. He himself hadn't been in a good mood.

"I'll be talking to you, then," said Greene.

Jury said nothing.

Outside, Greene asked about her. He said, "She seemed to make you nervous, and I suspect that's hard to do. Have you seen her in action, then?"

"To tell the truth, Barry, it's not Charly Moss that worries me—not that she's not capable of blindsiding us. What worries me is who she's briefing."

Barry Greene frowned: "The barrister, you mean?"

Jury nodded.

Melrose was at first delighted. "Charly Moss! How—" The smile faded. "Oh, God. She's not briefing Pete Apted, is she?"

They were sitting in the Bentley; Jury slid down in the seat. "I was afraid to ask."

"It could be someone else, you know. It could be she's taking this on her own. More and more solicitors are doing that these days. She's certainly good enough."

Jury shook his head.

"But look at it another way: you don't know Apted would take the case. Indeed, you don't even know she'll recommend it. Lawyers aren't all without conscience."

"They aren't?"

Melrose laughed and aimed the Bentley into the night traffic.

SIXTY-ONE

They buried her next to Maurice in a small churchyard a mile from the stud farm. Very few people attended beyond the family—George Davison, Neil Epp and several stable lads.

The funeral took place five days after Maurice's and a week after Nell died, the delay caused by the autopsy required in the case of a violent death, or an unexplained death or a death by misadventure. Nell's had certainly been by misadventure. Jury couldn't abide the thought of the Ryder family having to wait longer than that, as if they would for days be staring down into an unfilled grave, existing in that limbo of grief that has no end in sight. The end of grief would always be out of sight, but at least the ritual would help to confine it.

The problem was that the police pathologist simply had too much on his plate to do the postmortem immediately. Jury asked Barry Greene if he could possibly allow him to bring in someone he knew from the MPD and Greene got that permission for him.

When Jury rang Dr. Nancy and explained the problem, he said, "Listen, I know it's what you hear once a day—it's too hard on the deceased's relations to have to wait . . ."

"You're right there, except I hear it twice a day." She paused. Then she said, "With good cause." She paused again. "I can be there tomorrow afternoon, say around four. Okay?"

"I can't thank you enough—"

"It's all right, Richard. I'm not all that busy."

Which he knew was a total lie.

"But you can buy me a drink after."

"Phyllis, I'll buy you the pub."

"Oh, good. I can quit my day job."

Dr. Nancy arrived exactly when she said she would—four p.m. the next day. Phyllis Nancy was legendary for (among other things, such as her fiery hair) her promptness, a quality hard to find in the Met, simply because time couldn't be dealt out the way it could in other walks of life. If Dr. Nancy said four, she was there by four. In the field of police work, understandably chaotic, she offered a sense of respite, even of sanctuary. She had once told Jury that years before she had shown up an hour late at a crime scene. The detective in charge had told her, when she was apologizing, "Hell, that's all right, Doc. The dead can wait." She had told him, "How would you know?"

They gathered—Jury, Barry Greene and Phyllis Nancy—in the cool room with its permanent smell of blood that couldn't be washed or mopped away, where a mortician stood over the plastic-sheeted body of Nell Ryder. Wearing a lab coat and a plastic apron, Dr. Nancy looked down and shook her head. "Poor child. What a dreadful waste." Then she turned on the recording device supplied her into which she would speak her findings.

DCI Greene stayed; Jury left. He had observed a number of postmortems before, but they couldn't have paid or promised him enough to stay and watch this one. He waited outside in the silent corridor. It was less than an hour later when Phyllis Nancy called him back. Barry Greene smiled ruefully and looked a bit bilious and left. Dr. Nancy told Jury she'd found nothing that would come as a surprise. One bullet had entered the abdomen, gone through the liver, ricocheted off the pelvic bone, gone through the stomach, hit a vertebra and lodged in an abdominal muscle. The course of the second bullet was less complicated; it had entered the chest wall, gone through the lung, nicked the esophagus and gone out the back.

"She would have died instantly," she said. "The bullet—.38 caliber, but you know that—messed up everything in its path."

Jury said nothing.

"I'm sorry, Richard." She seemed to think a greater show of concern was necessary and went on. "The trajectory was upward. The girl was on a horse, you said, and moving, which might account for the erratic path of the bullet. Was the horse running, or something?"

"No. Not at that point."

"But she was moving."

"Yes."

"Jumping off?"

"Yes."

Phyllis Nancy frowned. "I wouldn't think a movement to the side—you know, as happens when one dismounts—would account for the path of the shot."

"Nell didn't exactly dismount. She pretty much vaulted over the horse's head."

"But that would have put her directly in the path of the bullet and given the shooter a straight-on target."

"If she hadn't done, the bullet would have hit the horse, probably killed him."

Dr. Nancy just looked at him.

"His name is Aqueduct."

It sounded so much like an introduction, Phyllis smiled. "Aqueduct is one lucky horse."

"You don't know the half of it."

Taking off her apron, much like any woman who'd finished up in the kitchen, she said, "Where's this pub you're buying me? I'd like to hear the half of it."

They walked down the street to the Cricketer's Arms.

Jury told her the all of it.

They had watched the coffin lowered into the ground beneath a sky that should have looked like lead, heavy enough to fall and kill; instead it was a piercing, traitorous blue. When the short service was over, people dispersed, wandered off in different directions to their cars.

Wiggins said he'd wait in the car for him, then changed his mind and decided to go in for the cup of tea Arthur Ryder had insisted he have. Jury saw Vernon Rice head in the direction of the meadow, probably to oversee the mares.

Jury started to follow him, but stopped at the stables when he saw Danny Ryder.

Danny was standing by Beautiful Dreamer's stall. "I went to see Sara. She's not in a good way."

"I wouldn't be either, Danny, if I were looking at a twenty-year sentence."

There had been a plea bargain. *Crime passionale* had been put forth briefly by the defense and just as briefly considered. Second-degree murder had been found to be slightly more acceptable, and it had in this case carried a twenty-year price tag. It was a gift, considering the shooting of Simone Ryder had been a perfectly cold-blooded and planned—however briefly—murder.

"Remind me to get her lawyer if I ever go that route," Danny said, with an acidic laugh.

Jury smiled slightly. They had moved down the line to Criminal Type's stall. Jury wondered if the horses, in Danny's line of work, provided a comfort. "What route are you going to go, short of that?"

Since the insurance firm hadn't had to pay out the whopping sum, he hadn't been charged with fraud. *"What with me being alive, and all."* Danny's solicitor had come up with a partial amnesia (*"First time I ever heard that one"*) and the firm was perfectly happy to let it lie.

He said to Jury, "What in hell Simone was visiting Dad for, I can't imagine. But that's where she was going when she left the pub, to hire a car and go to Cambridgeshire, and she hoped she could find the stud farm. There were so many, weren't there? So Sara said she wouldn't mind seeing Arthur Ryder, too. It had been so long. And she knew where the place was."

Jury asked, "Was it the same gun, the same .22 you were making a display of?"

"Sorry about that, but yes." He looked sheepish. "There's an old road, just before you get to the main drive, and strangers sometimes think it *is,* then find it dead-ends on the field not far from the training track."

"Leaving out the question, Why would Sara kill her? Why would Sara kill her there?"

"Well, she couldn't do it in the Grave Maurice, could she? Anyway, I expect she shot her on the track out of pure malice. Malice, I mean, toward the Ryders. They snubbed her, she claimed. Sara is extremely sensitive to that sort of thing. In other words, she's completely paranoid. And she thought it was a message to me—you know, since I died at the Auteuil racetrack."

"Simone—could Simone have been going there to introduce herself? They'd never met."

"Could be. Except she wasn't known for her family feeling. There were times I thought she forgot I wasn't dead." Danny turned to Jury and looked him squarely, if sadly, in the eye. "Nell dies and I'm by way of being resurrected. Not much of a swap, is it?"

"You tried to save her life, Danny."

"Tried to just doesn't cut it, does it?"

It sounded, oddly, like something Nell herself might say. That one could never do enough.

"It does if that's as close as you can get."

Danny sighed. "I'll go in and see Dad and Rog. They've had their share of shocks in the last two weeks, I'd say." He paused. "You asked me what I planned to do next. Well, I mean to get back into racing if I can convince the Board and the Jockey Club I've just come out of a two-year-long coma. Maybe I can borrow the 'partial amnesia' defense. The last two years haven't been happy ones. Except for the time I was in the States." He smiled. "I couldn't hang around Paris very easily and didn't much care to go to Dubai. But I'd always wanted to go to Kentucky, Florida—the Derby, the Preakness—the Triple Crown. I love racing over there." The smile evaporated.

"I'm truly sorry about Maurice, Danny. I really am."

Danny looked off across the courtyard and up into the impossibly endless blue sky and shook his head. He brought two fingers to his forehead in a small salute. Then he left.

Maurice. That his death was completely accidental Jury believed less and less, especially after Barry Greene brought in Trevor Gwyne. Jury had thought the jockey would have had enough of a fright to go to ground after Roy Diamond had been gathered up by Cambridge police. But apparently, Greene found him in his London house sitting down to a meal.

When Greene had the tape running in the interrogation room, Jury was once again holding up the wall.

Trevor Gwyne, who had either more sense than most or none at all, decided that cooperation would get him further than proclaiming his innocence. This surprised Jury, as the only people who could testify to his guilt were Roy Diamond and Valerie Hobbs and it wasn't bloody likely they'd be saying anything soon. So it must have been owing to the persuasive powers of Barry Greene that Trevor saw the light. A deal could probably be struck ("Trev"), Barry had said, with the prosecution if Trev helped them out with Roy Diamond.

"Because what I think, Trev," said Greene, in the softest voice, "I think that the defense could show how Roy Diamond manipulated you because he was holding something over your head. He wasn't paying you to do this; he blackmailed you into abducting Nell Ryder."

Trevor said, "Well, but it wasn't even a proper kidnapping, was it?"

Jury loved that.

"I mean, Roy told me he wanted to talk to her. Nothing else. He said to spray this stuff in her eyes so she wouldn't see me. She was too surprised even to fight it. Well, she'd just woke up, hadn't she? I expect I gave her a bit of a fright."

To say the least. Jury pushed himself away from the wall. All *he* wanted to do was give this plonker a couple of whacks up the side of the head. But he didn't. He was here at Greene's pleasure. And Barry was good, very good.

Barry Greene gave Trevor a sour smile. "Do we have to abduct everyone we just 'want to talk to'?" No answer. "You're a jump jockey, aren't you, Trev?"

Trevor nodded. "You talking about those walls that went across the fields? For me, they weren't all that bad. I've seen worse at Cheltenham. But with that horse, that Aqueduct, those walls were nothing. It was that easy, it really was. He's one hell of a horse."

Greene went on. "Why did Valerie Hobbs agree to have Nell Ryder there? That puts the Hobbs woman squarely in the middle of a conspiracy."

Trevor shrugged. "Don't know, guv. But I'll tell you what

I think: it's that Roy Diamond had something on her, just like he had on me. That's how he works. I tol' you." Here Trevor's hand crept toward Greene's pack of Marlboros. Greene told him, sure, go ahead. Then he glanced over at Jury, raising his eyebrows in an invitation to ask questions.

Jury said, "Maurice, Trevor. Tell me what he had to do with all this."

"Poor kid. I swear I'd hate to think—"

Trevor flushed with something Jury imagined was shame—as well he might. But for all of the man's bad judgment, weakness, selfishness or whatever, that rush of blood to his face set him apart from Roy Diamond. Jury said to him, "Afraid you'll have to think it, Trevor, hate to or not. I'm almost certain Maurice's being the delivery boy, in a manner of speaking, had a lot to do with his death. It certainly had everything to do with his guilt. He loved Nell Ryder. He'd never have done anything to harm her. There's only one person he'd have done something like this for—his father."

Trevor nodded, took another deep drag of his cigarette. "You're right there. I told the lad it's his father that wanted to see Nell, but it couldn't be there, not at his own place."

"The thing is, no one knew Dan Ryder was still alive."

"Roy knew it."

Jury pulled out a chair and sat down, leaning forward, elbows on knees. "Go on."

Trevor said, "Let me correct that: it was either Dan or his twin."

"What was?"

"In the snapshot. An American friend of Roy's sent him a couple dozen snapshots taken at a racecourse in the States. Florida, Hialeah Park it was. Three of them showed Dan standing at the fence, watching."

Jury sat back. "A picture can be taken anytime."

"Yeah, right, except Danny'd never been to Florida. But that's not it; the picture's dated clear as a pane of glass."

"What do you mean?"

"It was the race itself, see. You know what a walkover is?"

"I've heard of it."

Trevor seemed by now to have forgotten the fix he was in and was enjoying educating these two cloth-eared coppers in the ways of the racing world. "A walkover is a one-horse race. It only happens when a horse is considered unbeatable by the trainers, so no other horses compete." Trevor smiled broadly. "Now, how often do you bug—I mean, you police detectives—"

(Jury preferred "buggers.")

"—think that happens? Not bloody often, I can tell you. But it did a little less than two years ago at Hialeah, with a horse called Affirmation. Probably wanted to make the punters think of Affirmed, and I guess it did. It must have been something to see." Trevor's eyes actually filmed over. "A real thrill, that would be. Better than a flying finish. To see a horse that good go round the track by itself with all of that crowd cheering. Anyway, that was the race. First walkover I heard of since Spectacular Bid, back in the eighties. That's what dated the snapshot; that race was run three months after Danny was supposed to have died."

"And Roy Diamond knew all of this, that's what you're saying? He knew about it for two years and did nothing?"

"What's to do that would work to Roy's benefit? Report it to you lot? Sooner tell it to me old gran. No, he had a bargaining point in those pictures."

"You showed one to Maurice."

"Two of them. Roy wouldn't let all three out of his hands. It was just a few days before I took the girl. Early morning, Maurice is at the training track; he always had a gallop after dawn, Roy said. I showed up, watched for a while through my binoculars. He was up on that great horse Samarkand. I wish I'd been around to ride *him* a decade ago. When Maurice stopped and dismounted and came over to the fence, I told him his father needed to see Nell. Of course, he didn't believe me, thought I was bonkers. He got pretty mad until I showed him the snapshots."

"He believed you?"

"Well, he would've done, wouldn't he? He *wanted* to believe me. There were the snapshots that showed the horse going round the Hialeah course and there was his dad, right by the fence."

Yes, Jury thought, standing now in the stable, Maurice would have wanted to believe Trevor Gwynne. And when

Nell disappeared that night, Maurice knew that something had gone horribly wrong and it could be down to him. The next few days must have been agonizing. For all he knew, Nell might be dead.

Jury remained standing by Criminal Type's stall, stroking the black face. Blacker than black. Probably the way Maurice had felt. Was Maurice one of those people who feed on guilt, like some mythological prince forced to eat his own heart?

For some reason, Jury thought then of the boy on the train from Cardiff. The winter angel. Maurice's polar opposite, who could wrap his music round his shoulders like a cloak.

Jury reached into his coat pocket where a few sugar cubes remained from the Little Chef raid. He unwrapped them and held them out to the horse. Criminal Type was not as polite as Aggrieved. He nearly got Jury's hand into the bargain. But that was the way when you were mobbed up: eat first, ask questions later. Jury smiled and left the stables.

Vernon had gathered thirty of the mares in the meadow and stood watching them, leaning against a post-and-rail fence, his foot hooked on the bottom rail.

He said, when Jury came up to him, "I thought I'd have to round them up, cowboy style, but they just seemed willing to follow one another out to the field." He pointed at one. "That's Daisy and Daisy's foal. Nellie said"—he stopped and cleared his throat—"Nell said that Daisy was a kind of leader. But look at them. They just stand there." He turned to look at Jury. "Do you think it's from being tethered in those narrow stalls for so long? But shouldn't they remember their lives before . . . ?"

His voice trailed off.

The mares were standing in a crescent, a head occasionally bent to look for graze, or a mother nudging at a foal—there were three foals now—but aside from that they stood quite still in that strange half-circle as if indeed they had been lined up there and tied.

"Probably they need a little time to get used to freedom," said Vernon.

He appeared to Jury to be almost desperate to explain

their eerie stillness. Jury said, "Freedom can be hard to get used to, you're right."

"And the sky," said Vernon, looking upward, "is so blue."

As if the day were a perfect setting for the horses to break away for a gallop, or perhaps as if nature had broken a bargain.

They stood side by side in silence for a long time, not speaking. Then Jury saw one of the foals leave the line and run for several yards, then another foal, and then one of the mares. And after that it was like an ice slide, ice calving, glaciers tumbling into the sea.

At least it seemed to Jury as extraordinary as that. As if someone had actually waved a wand and broken the spell and raised them from their sad and anxious sleep; first one, then another and another of the mares were running, manes and tails flying, running for what was surely joy, pushing the race to its limits.

There would always be a filly like Go for Wand, thought Jury; there would always be a girl to ride her.

Together, they would wire the field.

SIXTY-TWO

The door of Tynedale Lodge was opened by the pretty maid Sarah, whose eyes widened even more when she saw him standing there. His image reflected in her eyes; he could almost see himself shaping up as a hero, which only made him feel more of an idiot. What had he done, after all, for the Tynedales?

"Hello, Sarah. This isn't an official visit; I came to see how Gemma's doing. Is she about?"

Sarah's hand fell away from her hair. "Oh, why, yessir. I mean, I expect she is. I expect she's out in the garden."

"Thanks. I'll just have a look."

He made his way through the dining room to the study and the French doors that opened off Ian Tynedale's study. Outside to the left of the patio was a long colonnade, a walk flanked by white pillars. He saw her, as he had seen her before, on the same walk across the garden in which a marble figure stood in a marble pool, pouring water from a marble jug. The path she was on ran parallel to his. A line of tall cypresses bordered it. As they both walked, he felt as he had the first time, that they were somehow woven together. There was a poignant sense of belonging: everything that was there—man, child, statue, pillars, trees—was rightly there.

When they came to the end of their paths and she still didn't see him, he called, "Gemma!"

She didn't so much turn as swerve toward him, as a car might do, hoping to ward off a collision. She stood transfixed, as if she were the marble figure in the fountain.

"Gemma—" He walked toward her and then knelt down and kissed her cheek.

She held her doll in one hand and put her other hand on the spot. "You got shot."

"I did."

"You didn't die."

"No. Didn't anyone tell you?"

She shook her head.

"Did you think I had?"

Very slowly, still holding her hand against her face, she nodded.

"Come on, let's sit down."

Seated with her (the doll Richard between them), Jury thought it was hard to believe no one had told her he was all right. Was it because she hadn't asked? For Gemma wouldn't, one of those children who felt so dangerously deeply they could only survive by pretending indifference.

She was feigning it now, adjusting the doll's bonnet as if that, not Jury's life or death, was the issue.

He said, "What happened to Richard's black clothes? I thought he looked quite smart in that coat and hat."

"He's being punished!" Her voice went up a decibel, nervously loud.

"He is? But what did he do?"

"He kicked you and yelled at you. Don't you remember?"

"Yes."

It was Gemma herself who had used Richard as a club to give Jury several whacks because he'd left her in danger.

"Well, if he hadn't done that, you probably wouldn't've got shot."

Jury looked at her solemn, remorseful face, which now gave tremulous signs of dissolving into tears, as if a pebble had been tossed into a pool. No little girl, he thought, should have to exert so much effort in trying not to cry. But from Gemma's point of view, strong emotion can kill. She had displayed it once—she had cried and yelled—and look at the result: Jury had nearly died.

Jury thought for a moment, then picked up the doll and sighed deeply. "Poor Richard," he said. "No one understood, did they?"

Her face free of incipient tears, now completely fore-stalled by this surprising new development, Gemma put her hand on Jury's arm. "Understood what?"

"Well, Richard helped save me, didn't he?"

"*What? He wasn't even there.*" Remorse was fast giving way to testiness.

"Not the night I was, no. But he'd been there before, when he and Sparky saved you."

This wasn't going down a treat. "I did most of the work!"

"I know, but, see, Sparky went back the second time—"

"Christmas night."

"—because he had found you and Richard there once, he knew it was a place that needed watching. Richard understood that."

Her frown was deep: a dog and a doll. Jury could almost hear the words chasing around in her mind. Were a dog and a doll enough to keep a person from getting shot? If it was not so, if she had really saved herself, then why hadn't she saved Jury?

Nope: go with the dog and the doll. "Well, I guess he could have helped even if he wasn't there. He could've been sending messages to Sparky, too. It's not like us."

Isn't it? Jury smiled.

Gemma said to the doll Richard, "I'm sorry. I should've understood." Then she yanked the bonnet down over the doll's eyes, not altogether pleased with Jury's solution, as it put her at least a little in the wrong. But in another instant, her face cleared completely.

Jury asked, "Are you going to put his black clothes back on him?"

"Yes." She sighed. "He gets so bossy when he's wearing them, though." Rearranging the bonnet so the doll could see again, she hesitated. "Your name is Richard, too," wanting to clear this up about the two Richards. "You're not bossy at all. I wish he was more like you." She flicked a glance Jury's way to see if he liked hearing this.

"Thank you. I try not to be. But if I had a set of new black clothes to wear, I might be pretty bossy."

"No, you wouldn't. I'll bet you don't even boss around the criminals you catch. Probably, you didn't even boss *them.*"

He knew who she meant by "them" and tried to track emotion across her face, but it was free of fear, yet not so much she would name their names. "I don't remember if I did or not. Probably not. I was too upset by what happened to you and Benny."

"Benny? Nothing happened to Benny!" Not about to share the limelight with Benny, she got annoyed and stood the doll on his head. "Anyway, I'm sorry you got upset over me."

She said this in the most self-satisfied tone that Jury had ever heard, her mouth crimped like an old lady's, as she righted Richard and adjusted his gown.

A voice called her: "Gemma!"

Gemma slid off the seat and grabbed Richard. "It's time for me to read to Mr. Tynedale. You can come."

"I'd like to, but I've got to be getting back."

"To the Yard?"

"Yes, the Yard."

"I'm glad you came," she said before she scooted off. And then she turned and ran back. She put her hand on the cheek Jury had kissed, removed it and placed it against Jury's own cheek. It was, he guessed, about as close as she dared come to a kiss. "Bye!"

He stood up and watched her run and skip, skip and run, her black hair gleaming in the frosty winter light. Then he watched the space now empty of her.

Because she almost made me wish she'd disappear, so I could find her.

She was gone. In a moment, so was he.

DON'T MISS MARTHA GRIMES'S OTHER DAZZLING RICHARD JURY MYSTERIES . . .

The Man with a Load of Mischief

Introducing Scotland Yard's Richard Jury in Martha Grimes's intriguing first novel

At the Man with a Load of Mischief, a dead man is found with his head stuck in a beer keg. At the Jack and Hammer, another body was stuck out on the beam of the pub's sign, replacing the mechanical man who kept the time. Two pubs. Two murders. One Scotland Yard inspector called in to help. Detective Chief Inspector Richard Jury arrives in Long Piddleton and finds everyone in the postcard village looking outside of town for the killer. Except for Melrose Plant. A keen observer of human nature, he points Jury in the right direction: toward the darkest parts of his neighbors' hearts. . . .

"Grimes captures the flavor of British village life. . . . Long may she write Richard Jury mysteries."
—*Chicago Tribune*

The Old Fox Deceiv'd

Stacked against the cliffs on the shore of the North Sea and nearly hidden by fog, the town of Rackmoor seems a fitting place for murder. But the stabbing death of a costumed young woman has shocked the close-knit village. When Richard Jury arrives on the scene, he's pulled up short by the fact that no one is sure who the victim is, much less the killer. Her questionable ties to one of the most wealthy and influential families in town send Jury and Melrose Plant on a deadly hunt to track down a very wily murderer.

"A superior writer."
— *The New York Times Book Review*

"Warmth, humor, and great style . . . a thoroughly satisfying plot . . . one of the smoothest, richest traditional English mysteries ever to originate on this side of the Atlantic." — *Kirkus Reviews*

I Am the Only Running Footman

They were two women, strikingly similar in life . . . strikingly similar in death. Both were strangled with their own scarves—one in Devon, one outside a fashionable Mayfair pub called I Am the Only Running Footman. Richard Jury teams up with Devon's irascible local divisional commander, Brian Macalvie, to solve the murders. With nothing to tie the women together but the fatal scarves, Jury pursues his only suspect . . . and a trail of tragedy that just might lead to yet another victim—and her killer.

"Everything about Miss Grimes's new novel shows her at her best. . . . [She] gets our immediate attention. . . . She holds it, however, with something more than mere suspense." —*The New Yorker*

"Literate, witty, and stylishly crafted." —*The Washington Post*

The Five Bells and Bladebone

Richard Jury has yet to finish his first pint in the village of Long Piddleton when he finds a corpse inside a beautiful rosewood desk recently acquired by the local antiques dealer, Marshall Trueblood. The body belongs to Simon Lean, a notorious philanderer. An endless list of suspects leads Jury and his aristocratic sidekick, Melrose Plant, to the nearby country estate where Lean's long-suffering wife resides. But Jury's best clue comes in London at a pub called the Five Bells and Bladebone. There he learns about Lean's liaison with a disreputable woman named Sadie, who could have helped solve the case . . . if she wasn't already dead.

"Blends almost Dickensian sketches of character and social class with glimpses of a ferocious marriage."—*Time*

"[Grimes's] best . . . as moving as it is entertaining."
—*USA Today*

The Case Has Altered

Timeless, peaceful, and remote, the watery Lincolnshire fens seem an unlikely setting for murder. But two women—a notorious actress and a servant girl—have been killed there in the space of two weeks. The Lincolnshire police are sure the murders are connected—and they think a friend of Richard Jury is responsible. Jury is anxious to clear Jenny Kennington's name. But the secretive suspects and tight-lipped locals are leading him nowhere. And with the help of his colleague Melrose Plant, he must struggle to navigate a series of untruths in the hope of stopping a very determined killer.

"Masterful writing, skillful plotting, shrewd characterizations, subtle humor, and an illuminating look at what makes us humans tick . . . [an] outstanding story from one of today's most talented writers . . . brilliant."

—*Booklist*

"Dazzling. Deftly plotted . . . psychologically complex . . . delicious wit."   —*Publishers Weekly*

The Stargazey

After a luminous blonde leaves, reboards, then leaves the double-decker bus Richard Jury is on, he follows her up to the gates of Fulham Palace . . . and goes no farther. Days later, when he hears of the death in the palace's walled garden, Jury will wonder if he could have averted it. But is the victim the same woman Jury saw? As he and Melrose Plant follow the complex case from the Crippsian depths of London's East End to the headier heights of Mayfair's art scene, Jury will realize that in this captivating woman—dead or alive—he may have finally met his match. . . .

"A delightfully entertaining blend of irony, danger, and intrigue, liberally laced with wit and charm. . . . A must have from one of today's most gifted and intelligent writers."   —*Booklist* (starred review)

"The literary equivalent of a box of Godiva truffles . . . wonderful."   —*Los Angeles Times*

The Lamorna Wink

With his good friend Richard Jury on a fool's errand in
Northern Ireland, Melrose Plant tries—in vain—to escape his aunt and his Long Piddleton lethargy by fleeing
to Cornwall. There, high on a rocky promontory overlooking the sea, he rents a house—one furnished with
tragic memories. But his Cornwallian reveries are tem-
pered by the local waiter/cab driver/amateur magician.
The industrious Johnny Wells seems unflappable—until
his beloved aunt disappears. Now Plant is dragged into
the disturbing pasts of everyone involved—and a murder
mystery that only Richard Jury can solve. . . .

"Swift and satisfying . . . grafts the old-fashioned 'Golden
Age' amateur-detective story to the contemporary police
procedural . . . real charm."   —*The Wall Street Journal*

"Entrancing. Grimes makes her own mark on du Maur-
ier country."   —*The Orlando Sentinel*

The Blue Last

Mickey Haggerty, a DCI with the City police, has asked for Richard Jury's help. Two skeletons have been unearthed during the excavation of London's last bomb site, where once stood a pub called the Blue Last. The grandchild of brewery magnate Oliver Tynedale supposedly survived that December 1940 bombing . . . but did she? Then the son of the onetime owner of the Blue Last is found shot to death—the book he was writing about London during the German blitzkrieg . . . gone. A stolen life, a stolen book? Or is any of this what it seems? With Melrose Plant sent undercover, Jury calls into question identity, memory, and provenance in a case that resurrects his own hauntingly sad past. . . .

"Grimes's best . . .a cliffhanger ending." —*USA Today*

"Explosive . . . ranks among the best of its creator's distinguished work." —*Richmond Times-Dispatch*

New York Times
Bestselling Author
Martha Grimes

THE BLUE LAST

Mickey Haggerty, Jury's old friend and colleague, is
dying of cancer. So Jury can hardly refuse his request to
look into what Mickey suspects is a 50-year-old case of
switched identities.

0-451-41055-6

Available wherever books are sold, or
to order call: 1-800-788-6262

Martha Grimes
THE RICHARD JURY NOVELS

THE CASE HAS ALTERED	408683
I AM THE ONLY RUNNING FOOTMAN	410025
THE LAMORNA WINK	409361
THE MAN WITH A LOAD OF MISCHIEF	410815
THE STARGAZEY	408977
THE OLD FOX DECEIV'D	410688
FIVE BELLS AND BLADEBONE	410386

Available wherever books are sold, or
to order call: 1-800-788-6262

New York Times bestselling author

MARTHA GRIMES

THE SEQUEL TO *HOTEL PARADISE*

COLD FLAT JUNCTION

0-451-20523-5

"Grimes nimbly orchestrates the suspense, giving the
reader a sense of impending disaster."
—*New York Times*

In *Cold Flat Junction*, the irrepressible and
intuitive Emma Graham is obsessed with the
"accidental" drowning of an adolescent girl, forty
years ago. She seeks to unravel the story of the
drowning and the unsolved
murders that wind back to it.

**Available wherever books are sold, or
to order call: 1-800-788-6262**

Penguin Group (USA) Inc.
Online

Your Internet gateway to a virtual environment with hundreds of entertaining and enlightening books from Penguin Group (USA) Inc.

While you're there, get the latest buzz on the best authors and books around—

Tom Clancy, Patricia Cornwell, W.E.B. Griffin, Nora Roberts, William Gibson, Robin Cook, Brian Jacques, Catherine Coulter, Stephen King, Ken Follett, Terry McMillan, and many more!

Penguin Group (USA) Inc. Online is located at http://www.penguin.com

PENGUIN GROUP (USA)INC. NEWS

Every month you'll get an inside look at our upcoming books and new features on our site. This is an ongoing effort to provide you with the most up-to-date information about our books and authors.

Subscribe to Penguin Group (USA) Inc. News at http://www.penguin.com/newsletters